W9-DEM-582

Dodsworth

by
Sinclair Lewis

© 2011 Benediction Classics, Oxford.

Contents

CHAPTER 1

The aristocracy of Zenith were dancing at the Kennepoose Canoe Club. They two-stepped on the wide porch, with its pillars of pine trunks, its bobbing Japanese lanterns; and never were there dance-frocks with wider sleeves nor hair more sensuously piled on little smiling heads, never an August evening more moon-washed and spacious and proper for respectable romance.

Three guests had come in these new-fangled automobiles, for it was now 1903, the climax of civilization. A fourth automobile was approaching, driven by Samuel Dodsworth.

The scene was a sentimental chromo--crisping lake, lovers in canoes singing "Nelly Was a Lady," all very lugubrious and happy; and Sam Dodsworth enjoyed it. He was a large and formidable young man, with a healthy brown mustache and a chaos of brown hair on a massive head. He was, at twenty-eight, assistant superintendent of that most noisy and unsentimental institution, the Zenith Locomotive Works, and in Yale (class of 1896) he had played better than average football, but he thought well of the most sentimental sorts of moonlight.

Tonight he was particularly uplifted because he was driving his first car. And it was none of your old-fashioned "gasoline buggies," with the engine under the seat. The engine bulked in front, under a proud hood over two feet long, and the steering column was not straight but rakishly tilted. The car was sporting and rather dangerous, and the lights were powerful affairs fed by acetylene gas. Sam sped on, with a feeling of power, of dominating the universe, at twelve dizzy miles an hour.

At the Canoe Club he was greeted by Tub Pearson, admirable in white kid gloves. Tub--Thomas J. Pearson--round and short and jolly, class-jester and class-dandy at Yale, had been Sam Dodsworth's roommate and chief admirer throughout college, but now Tub had begun to take on an irritable dignity as teller and future president of his father's bank in zenith.

"It runs!" Tub marveled, as Sam stepped in triumph from the car. "I've got a horse all ready to tow you back!"

Tub had to be witty, whatever happened.

"Certainly it runs! I'll bet I was up to eighteen miles an hour!"

"Yeh! I'll bet that some day automobiles'll run forty!" Tub jeered. "Sure! Why, they'll just about drive the poor old horse right off the highway!"

"They will! And I'm thinking of tying up with this new Revelation Company to manufacture 'em."

"Not seriously, you poor chump?"

"Yes."

"Oh, my Lord!" Tub wailed affectionately. "Don't be crazy, Sambo! My dad says automobiles are nothing but a fad. Cost too much to run. In five years, he says, they'll disappear."

Sam's answer was not very logical:

"Who's the young angel on the porch?"

If she was an angel, the girl at whom Sam was pointing, she was an angel of ice; slim, shining, ash-blonde, her self-possessed voice very cool as she parried the complimentary teasing of half a dozen admirers; a crystal candle-stick of a girl among black-and-white lumps of males.

"You remember her--Frances Voelker--Fran Voelker--old Herman's kid. She's been abroad for a year, and she was East, in finishing- school, before that. Just a brat--isn't over nineteen or twenty, I guess. Golly, they say she speaks German and French and Italian and Woof-woof and all known languages."

Herman Voelker had brewed his way into millions and respectability. His house was almost the largest in Zenith--certainly it had the greatest amount of turrets, colored glass windows, and lace curtains--and he was leader among the German-Americans who were supplanting the New Englanders throughout the state as controllers of finance and merchandising. He entertained German professors when they came lecturing and looking, and it was asserted that one of the genuine hand-painted pictures which he had recently brought back from Nuremberg was worth nearly ten thousand dollars. A worthy citizen, Herman, and his tart beer was admirable, but that this beef-colored burgher should have fathered anything so poised and luminous as Fran was a miracle.

The sight of her made Sam Dodsworth feel clumsy as a St. Bernard looking at a white kitten. While he prophesied triumphs for the motor car, while he danced with other girls, he observed her airy dancing and her laughter. Normally, he was not particularly afraid of young women, but Fran Voelker seemed too fragile for his thick hands. Not till ten did he speak to her, when a partner left her, a flushed Corybant, in a chair near Sam's.

"Do you remember me--Dodsworth? Years since I've seen you."

"Remember! Heavens! I wondered if you were going to notice me. I used to steal the newspaper from Dad to get the news of your football heroisms. And when I was a nice young devil of eight, you once chased me out of your orchard for stealing apples."

"Did I? Wouldn't dare to now! Mavenex' dance?"

"Well--Let me see. Oh. The next is with Levering Mott, and he's already ruined three of my two slippers. Yes."

If he did not dance with any particular neatness, a girl knew where she was, with Sam Dodsworth. He had enough strength and de-cision to let a young woman understand who was doing the piloting. With Fran Voelker, he was inspired; he waltzed as though he was proud of his shining burden. He held her lightly enough and, after the chaste custom of the era, his hands were gloved. But his finger- tips felt a current from her body. He knew that she was the most exquisite child in the world; he knew that he was going to marry her and keep her forever in a shrine; he knew that after years of puzzled wonder about the purpose of life, he had found it.

"She's like a lily--no, she's too lively. She's like a humming bird--no, too kind of dignified. She's--oh, she's a flame!"

They sat talking by the lake at midnight. Out on the dappled water, seen through a cloud of willow leaves, the youngsters in canoes were now singing "My Old Kentucky Home." Zenith was still in the halcyon William Dean Howells days; not yet had it become the duty of young people to be hard and brisk, and knowing about radios, jazz, and gin.

Fran was a white shadow, in a lace shawl over her thin yellow dancing frock, as she drooped down on a newspaper which he had solemnly spread for her on the long grass. Sam trembled a little, and sounded very pompous, rather boyish:

"I suppose you went everywhere in Europe."

"More or less. France and Spain and Austria and Switzerland and-- Oh, I've seen the Matterhorn by moonlight, and Santa Maria della Salute at dawn. And I've been almost frozen to death in a mistral at Avignon!"

"I suppose you'll be bored in Zenith."

She laughed, in a small competent way. "I know SO much about Europe--I'm no Cook's tripper!--that I know I don't know anything! All I can do in French is to order breakfast. Six months from now, all I'll remember of Germany is the names of nineteen towns, and how the Potsdamer Platz looks when you're waiting for a droschke. But you've DONE things. What are you doing now, by the way?"

"Assistant supe at the Locomotive Works. But I'm going to take a big gamble and--Ever ride in an automobile?"

"Oh yes, several times, in Paris and New York."

"Well, I believe that in twenty years, say by 1923 or '4, they'll be as common as buggies are now! I'm going in on a new company here--Revelation Automobile Company. I'll get less salary, but it's a swell gamble. Wonderful future. I've been working on my mechanical drawing lately, and I've got the idea that they ought to get away from imitating carriages. Make a--it sounds highbrow, but I mean what you might call a new kind of beauty for autos. Kind of long straight lines. The Revelation boss thinks I'm crazy. What do you think?"

"Oh, splendid!"

"And I've bought me an automobile of my own."

"Oh, really?"

"Let me drive you home tonight!"

"No, sorry; Mama is coming for me."

"You've got to let me take you for a ride. Soon!"

"Perhaps next Sunday. . . . We must go back to the clubhouse, don't you think?"

He sprang up, meekly. As he lifted her to her feet, as he felt her slim hands, he murmured, "Certainly like to see Europe some day. When I graduated, I thought I'd be a civil engineer and see the Brazil jungle and China and all over. Reg'lar Richard Harding Davis stuff!

4

But--Certainly going to see Europe, anyway. Maybe I might run into you over there, and you might show me some of it."

"I'd love to!"

Ah, if she desired Europe, he would master it, and give it to her on a platter of polished gold!

There was the telephone call to her when he should have been installing machinery at the Revelation Automobile Company. There was the drive with her in his new car, very careful, though once he ventured on seventeen miles an hour. There was the dinner at the Voelkers', in the room with carved beams like a Hofbrauhaus, and Sam's fear that if Fran was kept on food like this, roast goose and stuffed cabbage and soup with Leberknodel, she would lose her race-horse slimness.

And there was even a moment when, recalling his vow made in Massachusetts Tech after graduating from Yale that he would cut loose from America and see the great world, he warned himself that between Fran and tying himself to the urgent new motor industry, he would be caught for life. The vision of himself as a Richard Harding Davis hero returned wistfully. . . . Riding a mountain trail, two thousand sheer feet above a steaming valley; sun-helmet and whipcord breeches; tropical rain on a tin-roofed shack; a shot in the darkness as he sat over a square-face of gin with a ragged tramp of Noble Ancestry. But his mind fled back to the excitement of Fran's image: her spun-glass hair, her tingling hands, her lips that were forever pursing in fantastic pouts, her chatter that fell suddenly into inexplicable silence, her cool sureness that made him feel foggy and lumbering.

In a slaty November drizzle, they were tramping the cliffs along the Chaloosa River. Fran's cheeks were alight and she was humming, but when they stopped to look at the wash of torn branches in the flooded river Sam felt that he must be protective. She was too slight and precious for such hardship as an autumnal rain. He drew the edge of his mackintosh over her woolly English topcoat.

"You must be soaked! I'm a brute to let you stay out!"

She smiled at him, very close. "I like it!"

It seemed to him that she had snuggled closer. He kissed her--for the first time, and very badly indeed.

"Oh, please don't!" she begged, a little shocked, her lively self-possession gone.

5

"Fran, you've got to marry me!"

She slipped from the shelter of his raincoat and, arms akimbo, said impishly, "Oh, really? Is that a new law?"

"It is!"

"The great Yale athlete speaks! The automobile magnate!"

Very gravely: "No, just a scared lump of meat that's telling you he worships you!"

Still she stared at him, among the autumn-bedraggled weeds on the river bank; she stared impudently, but quite suddenly she broke, covered her eyes with her hands, and while he clumsily dabbled at her cheeks with a huge handkerchief, she sobbed:

"Oh, Sam, my dear, but I'm so grasping! I want the whole world, not just Zenith! I DON'T want to be a good wife and mother and play cribbage prettily! I want splendor! Great horizons! Can we look for them together?"

"We will!" said Sam.

It was not till 1908, when he had been married for five years to Fran Voelker and they had had two babies, Emily and Brent, that Samuel Dodsworth came on his real struggle at the Revelation Automobile Company.

His superiors in the company had equally prized him for his steadiness and industry and fretted at him for being a dreamer. He was crazy as a poet, they said. Not only did he venture to blaspheme against the great Renault-Darracq dogmas of car-designing, not only did he keep on raving about long "stream-lines," but he insisted that the largest profits would lie in selling automobiles as cheaply as possible to as many customers as possible. He was only assistant manager of production in 1908, but he owned a little stock, and his father-in-law, portly old Herman Voelker, owned more. It was hard to discharge Sam, even when he growled at the president of the company, "If you keep the Rev looking like the one-horse-shay, we'll go bankrupt."

They tried to buy him out, and Sam, who had been absorbed in blue prints and steel castings, had to learn something about the tricks of financing: about bonds, transfer of stock, call loans, discounts to dealers. With Voelker's money behind him, he secured twenty-three per cent. of the stock, he was made vice president and manager of production, he brought out the first four-door model, and he saw the

Revelation become the sensation of America for a season and one of its best-selling cars for a score of years.

And never, these twenty years, did he come nearer to the Brazilian jungle than Wall Street, nearer to the tinkling pagodas than the Revelation agency in Kansas City.

But he was too busy to be discontented; and he managed to believe that Fran loved him.

CHAPTER 2

Samuel Dodsworth discovered that there was a snowstorm, nearly a blizzard, whirling about the house. He closed the windows with a bang and plumped back into bed till the room should be warm. He did not move so swiftly as he once had, and above the frogged silk pajamas which Fran insisted on buying for him, his hair was gray. He was healthy enough, and serene, but he was tired, and he seemed far older than his fifty years.

Fran was asleep in the farther of the twin beds, vast walnut structures with yellow silk draping. Sam looked about the bedroom. He had sometimes caught himself wondering if it wasn't too elaborate, but usually its floridness pleased him, not only as a sign of success but because it suited the luxurious Fran. Now he noted contentedly the chaise longue, with a green and silver robe across it; the desk, with monogrammed stationery very severe and near-English and snobbish; Fran's bedside table, with jeweled traveling-clock, cigarettes, and the new novels; the bathroom with its purple tiles.

Fran stirred, sighed and, while he chuckled at her resemblance to a child trying to slip back into dreams, she furiously burrowed her eyes into the little lacy pillow, which was crumpled with her determined sleeping.

"No use," he said. His rather heavy voice caressed her. "You know you're awake! Rise and shine! Face the problems of humanity and the grape fruit!"

She sat up, looking at him with the astonishment she had never quite lost at being married, breaking a yawn with a smile, tousling her bobbed hair that was still ash-blond, without gray. If Sam seemed older than his age, she was far younger. She was forty-one now, in 1925, but, rosy with sleeping, she seemed thirty-one.

"I'm going to have breakfast in bed you're smoking before breakfast again I haven't had breakfast in bed since yesterday," she yawned amiably, while he swung his thick legs over the edge of his lilac satin comforter and lighted a cigarette.

"Yes. Stay in bed. Like to, myself. Devil of a snowstorm," he said, paddling round to stroke her hair, to nuzzle his ruddy cheek against her soft fairness. "By the way, did I ever remember to tell you that I adore you?"

"Why--let me see--no, I don't believe so."

"Golly, I'm getting absent-minded! I'll have my secretary remind me to do it tomorrow." Seriously: "Realize that we finally wind up the old Revelation Company today? Sort of sorry."

"No! I'm not a bit sorry! I'm delighted. You'll be free for the first time in all these years. Let's run off some place. Oh, don't let yourself get tied up with anything new! So silly. We have enough money, and you go on stewing--'must change the design of the carburetor float--simply must sell more cars in the territory between Medicine Hat and Woolawoola.' So silly! What does it MATTER! Do ring for the maid, darling."

"Well, no, maybe it doesn't matter, but fellow likes to do his job. It's kind of a battle; fun to beat the other fellow and put over a thundering big sale. But I am rather tired. Wouldn't mind skipping off to Florida or some place."

"Let's!"

He had dutifully brought her heavy silver mirror, her brush and comb, her powder, her too-gorgeous lounging robe of Chinese brocade. When she had made herself a bit older by making herself youthful, she sat up in bed to read the Zenith Advocate-Times. If she looked fluffy and agreeably useless, there was nothing fluffy in her sharp comments on the news. She sounded like a woman of many affairs, many committees.

"Humph! That idiot-boy alderman, Klingenger, is going to oppose our playground bill. I'll wring his neck! . . . The D.A.R. are going to do another pageant. I will NOT be Martha Washington! You might be George. You have his detestable majesticness."

"Me?" as he came from his bath. "I'm a clown. Wait till you see me in Florida!"

"Yes. Pitching horseshoes. I wouldn't put it past you, my beloved! . . . Huh! It says here the Candlelight Club expect to have Hugh

9

Walpole lecture, next season. I'll see our program committee pinches him off 'em."

He was slowly dressing. He always wore large grave suits, brown or gray or plain blue, expensively tailored and not very interesting, with decorous and uninteresting ties of dull silk and no jewelry save a watch-chain. But though you were not likely to see what he wore, you noted him as a man of importance, as an executive, tall, deep-chested, his kind eyes never truculent, but his mouth serious, with crescents of wrinkles beside it. His gray-threaded brown mustache, trimmed every week by the best barber at the best hotel, was fully as eccentric and showy as a doormat.

He made his toilet like a man who never wasted motions--and who, incidentally, had a perfectly organized household to depend upon. His hand went surely to the tall pile of shirts (Fran ordered them from Jermyn Street) in the huge Flemish armoire, and to the glacial nest of collars, always inspected by the parlor maid and discarded for the slightest fraying. He tied his tie, not swiftly but with the unwasteful and extremely unadventurous precision of a man who has introduced as much "scientific efficiency" into daily domesticity as into his factory.

He kissed her and, while she nibbled at sweetbreads and drank her coffee in bird-like sips and furiously rattled the newspaper in bed, he marched down-stairs to the oak-beamed dining-room. Over a second copy of the Advocate, and a Chicago paper, he ponderously and thoroughly attended to orange juice, porridge and thick cream, bacon, corn cakes and syrup, and coffee in a cup twice as large as the cup which Fran was jiggling in her thin hand as she galloped through the paper up-stairs.

To the maid he said little, and that amiably, as one certain that he would be well served. He was not extraordinarily irritable even when he was informed that Emily, his engaging daughter, had been up late at a dance and would not be down for breakfast. He liked Emily's morning gossip, but he never dreamed of demanding her presence--of demanding anything from her. He smiled over the letter of his son, Brent, now a junior in Yale.

Samuel Dodsworth was, perfectly, the American Captain of Industry, believing in the Republican Party, high tariff and, so long as they did not annoy him personally, in prohibition and the Episcopal Church. He was the president of the Revelation Motor Company; he was a millionaire, though decidedly not a multimillionaire; his large house was on Ridge Crest, the most fashionable street in Zenith; he had some taste in etchings; he did not split many infinitives; and he sometimes enjoyed Beethoven. He would certainly (so the observer assumed) produce excellent motor cars; he would make impressive speeches to the salesmen; but he would never love passionately, lose tragically, nor sit in contented idleness upon tropic shores.

To define what Sam Dodsworth was, at fifty, it is easiest to state what he was not. He was none of the things which most Europeans and many Americans expect in a leader of American industry. He was not a Babbitt, not a Rotarian, not an Elk, not a deacon. He rarely shouted, never slapped people on the back, and he had attended only six baseball games since 1900. He knew, and thoroughly, the Babbitts and baseball fans, but only in business.

While he was bored by free verse and cubism, he thought rather well of Dreiser, Cabell, and so much of Proust as he had rather laboriously mastered. He played golf reasonably well and did not often talk of his scores. He liked fishing-camps in Ontario, but never made himself believe that he preferred hemlock boughs to a mattress. He was common sense apotheosized, he had the energy and reliability of a dynamo, he liked whisky and poker and pate de foie gras, and all the while he dreamed of motors like thunderbolts, as poets less modern than himself might dream of stars and roses and nymphs by a pool.

A crisis in life had been forced on him, for his Revelation Company was being absorbed by the Unit Automotive Company--the imperial U.A.C., with its seven makes of motors, its body-building works, its billion dollars of capital. Alec Kynance, president of the U.A.C., was in Zenith, and today the final transfer of holdings was to be made.

Sam had wanted to fight the U.A.C., to keep independent this creation to which he had devoted twenty-two years, but his fellow directors were afraid. The U.A.C. could put on the market a car as good as the Revelation at a lower price, and drive them from the market. If necessary, the U.A.C. could sell below cost for a year or two. But they wanted the Revelation label and would pay for it. And the U.A.C. cossacks were good fellows. They did not treat Sam like a captive, but as a fellow warrior, to be welcomed to their larger army, so at the last Sam hid from himself the belief that the U.A.C., with their mass production, would cheapen and ruin the Revelation and turn his thunderbolt into a standardized cigar- lighter, and he had agreed to their generous purchase price.

He was not happy about it, when he let himself think abstractly. But he was extremely well trained, from his first days in Zenith High School, in not letting himself do anything so destructive as abstract thinking.

Sam clumped up-stairs and found Fran, very brisk, fairly cheerful, still in her brocade dressing-gown but crouching over her desk, dashing off notes: suggestions to partisans in her various clubs, orders to the secretaries of the leagues which she supported-- leagues for the study of democracy, leagues for the blind, societies for the collection of statistics about the effect of alcohol on plantation-hands in Mississippi. She was interested in every aspect of these leagues except perhaps the purposes for which they had been founded, and no Indiana politician was craftier at soaping enemies, advising friends, and building up a political machine to accomplish nothing in particular.

She shone at Sam as he lumbered in, but she said abruptly, "Sit down, please. I want to talk to you."

("Oh, Lord, what have I done now?") He sat meekly in a chintz- covered overstuffed chair.

"Sam! I've been thinking lately. I didn't want to speak to you about it till you had the U.A.C. business all finished. But I'm afraid you'll get yourself tied up with some new job, and I want to go to Europe!"

"Well--"

"Wait! This may be our only chance, the only time you'll be free till we're so old we won't enjoy wandering. Let's take the chance! There'll be time for you to create a dozen new kinds of cars when we come back. You'll do it all the better if you have a real rest. A real one! I don't want to go just for a few months, but for a solid year."

"Good Heavens!"

"Yes, they are good! Think! Here's Emily going to be married next month. Then she won't need us. Brent has enough friends in college. He won't need us. I can chuck all these beastly clubs and everything. They don't mean anything; they're just make- believe, to keep me busy. I'm a very active female, Sam, and I want to do something besides sitting around Zenith. Think what we could do! Spring on the Italian Lakes! Motoring through the Tyrol! London in the Season! And I've never seen Europe since I was a girl, and you've never seen it at all. Let yourself have a good time for once! Trust me, can't you, dear?"

"Well, it would be kind of nice to get away from the grind. I'd like to look over the Rolls-Royce and Mercedes plants. And see Paris and the Alps. But a year--That's a long time. I think we'd get pretty tired of Europe, living around in hotels. But--I really haven't made any plans. The U.A.C. business was so sudden. I would like to see Italy. Those hill-towns must be very curious. And so old. We'll talk about it tonight. Auf wiedersehen, old lady."

He tramped out, apparently as dependable as an old New-foundland and as little given to worrying about anything more complex than the hiding-places of bones. But he was fretting as he sat erect in his limousine, while Smith drove him into town.

These moments of driving were the only times when he was alone. He was as beset by people--his wife, his daughter, his son, his servants, his office-staff, his friends at lunch and on the golf course--as in his most frenziedly popular days at college, when it had been his "duty to old Yale" to be athletic and agreeable, and never to be alone, certainly never to sit and think. People came to him, swarmed about him, wanted his advice and his money and the spiritual support which they found in his ponderous caution. Yet he liked to be alone, he liked to meditate, and he made up for it on these morning rides.

"She's right," he worried. "I'd better not let her know how right she is, or she'll yank me off to London before I can pack my flask. I wonder--Oh yes, of course, she does care for me, a lot. But sometimes I wish she weren't quite so good a manager. She just tries to amuse me by playing at being a kitten. She isn't one, not by a long shot. She's a greyhound. Sometimes when I'm tired, I wish she just wanted to cud-dle up and be lazy with me. She's quicksilver. And quicksilver is hard, when you try to compress it!

"Oh, that's unfair. She's been the best wife--I haven't given enough time to courting her, what with all this cursed business. And I'm tired of business. Like to sit around and chat and get acquainted with myself. And I'm tired of these streets!"

The limousine was laboring through a gusty snowstorm, skid-ding a bit on icy asphalt, creaking and lumbering as it climbed over drifts. The windows of the car were frost-emblazoned. Sam impa-tiently cleared a peep-hole with the heel of his glove.

They were creeping along Conklin Avenue, where the dreary rows of old red brick mansions, decayed into boarding houses, the cheap grocery shops and dirty laundries and gloomy little "undertaking parlors" and lunch-rooms with the blatant sign "Eats," not very entrancing at any time, were turned by the rags of blown snow into the bleakness of a lumber-camp, while the breadth of the street made it only the more shelterless and unintimate. On either side were streets of signboards advertising oil and cigarettes, of wooden one-story shacks between old-fashioned yellow brick tenement-houses gloomy in the sunless snow; a region of poverty without picturesqueness and of labor without hope.

"Oh, Lord, I'd like to get away from it! Be nice to see the Mediterranean and a little sunshine," Sam muttered. "Let's go!"

The General Offices of the Revelation Motor Company were in an immense glass and marble building on Constitution Avenue, North, above Court House Square, opposite the flashing new sky-scraper of the Plymouth National Bank. The entrance to the floor given to executive offices was like the lobby of a pretentious hotel--waiting-room in brocade and tapestry and Grand Rapids renaissance; then something like an acre of little tables with typists and typists and typists, very busy, and clerks and clerks and clerks, with rattling papers; and a row of private offices resembling furniture showrooms, distinguished by enormous desks in imitation of refectory tables, covered with enormous sheets of plate glass, and fanatically kept free of papers and all jolly disorder.

The arrival of President Dodsworth was like that of a General Commanding. "Good morning!" rumbled the uniformed doorman, a retired sergeant. "Good MORNING!" chirped the girl at the inquiry desk, a charming girl whose gentleman-friend was said to be uncommonly high up in the fur business. "Good morning!" indicated the typists and clerks, their heads bowing like leaves agitated by a flitting breeze as he strode by them. "GOOD morning!" caroled Sam's private stenographer as he entered his own office. "GOOD MORNING!" shouted his secretary, an offensively high-pressure young slave-driver. And even the red-headed Jewish office boy, as he took Sam's coat and hung it up so that it would not dry, condescended "Mornin', boss."

Yet today all this obsequiousness, normally not unpleasant to the Great Man, annoyed him; all this activity, this proof that ever so many people were sending out ever so many letters about things presumably of importance, seemed to him an irritating fussiness. What

14

did it matter whether he had another hundred thousand dollars to leave to Brent? What did it matter whether John B. Johnson of Jonesburg did or did not take the local Revelation agency? Why were all these hundreds of young people willing to be turned into machines for the purposes of rattling papers and bowing to the president?

The Great Man approached his desk, put on his eye-glasses, and graciously received a stock-report, as one accomplishing empires.

But the Great Man was thinking:

"They make me tired--poor devils! Come on, Fran! Let's go! Let's drift way round to China!"

Alec Kynance, president of the Unit Automotive Company, with his regiment of officers, lawyers, secretaries, was not coming for half an hour. Sam said impulsively to his stenographer, "Miss Rachman, skip down to the travel bureau at the Thornleigh, won't you please, and bring me all the steamship folders and European travel information and so on that they have there. And round-the-world."

While he waited for her he turned over the papers in the wire basket which his secretary had reverently laid on the glass-topped vastness of his desk. These matters had seemed significant a few days ago, like orders given in battle, but now that the Revelation Company was no longer his--

He sighed, he shuffled the papers indifferently: The secret report on the dissipations of the manager of the Northwestern Division. The plans of the advertising agency for notices about the union of the U.A.C. and the Revelation, which was to be announced with glad, gaudy public rejoicing. What did they MATTER, now that he was turned from a bandit captain to a clerk?

For the first time he admitted that if he went to the U.A.C., even as first vice president, he would be nothing more than an office boy. He could make no daring decisions by himself. THEY had taken from him the pride in pioneering which was one of his props in life-- and who THEY were, he didn't quite know. THEY were something more than just Alec Kynance and a few other officers of the U.A.C. THEY were part of a booming industrial flood which was sweeping over him. THEY would give him a larger house, a yacht, but THEY would not give him work that was really his own. He had helped to build a machine which was running away from him. He had no longer the dignity of a craftsman. He made nothing; he meant nothing; he was no longer Samuel Dodsworth, but merely part of a crowd vigorously pushing one another toward nowhere.

He wandered to the window. In that blast of snow, the shaft of the Plymouth National Bank Building was aspiring as a cathedral; twenty gray stories, with unbroken vertical lines swooping up beyond his vision into the snowy fog. It had nobility, but it seemed cruel, as lone and contemptuous of friendly human efforts as a forgotten tower on the Siberian steppes. How indifferently it would watch him starve and freeze!

With relief he looked at the travel brochures when his stenographer brought them in--a lively girl, shaking the snow from her little cloche hat, beaming at him, assuring him that he really did exist and was something of importance still. Then he was lost in the pictures. . . . Titanic walls of the Grand Canyon: scarlet pillars and pyramids of orange. A tawny road in Algiers, the sun baking, nodding camels, and drivers with dusky malign faces under their turbans. St. Moritz, shadowed by the mountains, and a pretty girl on a toboggan. A terrace at Cannes, where through fig-trees and palms and tumbling roses you looked on the sea with a lone felucca. A valley of colored patchwork fields seen from a harsh tor of Dartmoor. Japanese children rollicking among cherry trees beside a tiny temple. Dark wood of carven mediaeval houses looming over the Romerberg at Frankfort. The Grand Canal, with the fantastic columns of the piazzetta and the soft pink and cream of the ducal palace. The old sea-fronted walls of Ragusa. The streets of Paris--kiosks, impudent advertisements, a whisk of skirts, a whirligig of traffic, and little tables at which to loaf all day long.

"Wouldn't be so bad!" thought Sam. "I'd like to wander around a few months. Only I'm not going to let Fran coax me into being one of these wishy-washy expatriates, homeless, afraid of life, living on the Riviera as though they were in a sanatorium for neurotics. I'm going to go on doing something with life, and my place is here. We'll go abroad, only I'll make her fight for it or she'll feel she's running the whole show. Then I'll come back here, and I'll take Alec Kynance's show right away from him!"

"Mr. Kynance is here," announced his secretary.

CHAPTER 3

Mr. Alexander Kynance, president of the Unit Automotive Company, was a small bustling man with a large head, an abrupt voice, a lively mind, a magnificent lack of scruples, and a love for oratory and Corona-Coronas. He had been a section-hand and a railway superintendent, he had the best cellar of Burgundies in Detroit, and he made up for his runtiness by barking at people.

"Everything all ready? Everything all ready?" he barked at Sam Dodsworth, as the dozen representatives of the two companies settled down and rested their elbows on the gigantic mirror- surfaced table in the gold and oak directors'-room.

"I think so," Sam drawled.

"Just a few things left," said Kynance. "We've about decided to run the Revelation in between the Chromecar and the Highroad in class--drop it three hundred below your price--two-door sedan at eleven-fifty."

Sam wanted to protest. Hadn't he kept the price down to the very lowest at which his kind of car could be built? But suddenly-- What difference did it make? The Revelation wasn't his master, his religion! He was going to have a life of his own, with Fran, lovely loyal Fran, whom he'd imprisoned here in Zenith!

Let's go!

He was scarcely listening to Kynance's observations on retaining the slogan "You'll revel in a Revelation." Sam had always detested this battle-cry. It was the invention of a particularly bright and bounding young copy-writer who took regular exercise at the Y.M.C.A., but the salesmen loved it. As Kynance snapped, "Good slogan--good slogan--full o' pep," Sam mused:

"They're all human megaphones. And I'm tired."

When he had rather sadly signed the transfer of control to the U.A.C. and his lifework was over, with no chance for retreat, Sam shook hands a great deal with a number of people, and was left alone with Alec Kynance.

"Now to real business, old man," Kynance blatted. "You'll be tickled to death at getting hooked up with a concern that can control the world-market one of these days--regular empire, b' God!--instead of crawling along having to depend on a bunch of so- so assistants. We want you to come with us, of course. I haven't been hinting around. Hinting ain't my way. When Alec Kynance has something to say, by God he shoots! I want to offer you the second vice-presidency of the U.A.C., in general charge of production of all our eight cars, including the Rev. You've been getting sixty thousand salary, besides your stock?"

"Yes."

"We can offer you eighty-five, and your share in the managers' pool, with a good chance for a hundred thou in a few years, and you'll probably succeed me when the bootlegged hootch gets me. And you'll have first-class production-men under you. You can take it easy and just think up mean ideas to shove over. Other night you were drooling about how you'd like to make real Ritzy motor caravans with electric stoves and radios and everything built in. Try it! We've got the capital. And this idea you had about a motorized touring-school for boys in summer. Try it! Why, God, we might run all these summer camps out of business and make a real killing--get five hundred thousand cus-tomers--kid that hadn't gone on one of our tours, no class to him at all! Try it! And the U.A.C. getting into aeroplane manufacture. Go ahead. Draw up your plans. Yes sir, that's the kind of support we give a high-class man. When do you want to go to work? I suppose you'll have to move to Detroit, but you can get back here pretty often. Want to start right in, and see things zip?"

Sam's fantastic schemes for supercaravans, for an ambulatory summer school in which boys should see the whole country from Maine pines to San Joaquin wheat-fields, schemes which he had found stimulating and not very practical, were soiled by the lobster-faced little man's insistence on cashing in. No!

"First, I think I'll take a vacation," Sam said doubtfully. "Haven't had a real one for years. Maybe I'll run over to Europe. May stay three months or so."

"Europe? Rats! Dead's a doornail! Place for women and long-haired artists. Dead! Only American loans that keep 'em from burying the corpse! All this art! More art in a good shiny spark- plug than in all the fat Venus de Mylos they ever turned out. Naw! Go take a run through California, maybe grab a drink of good liquor in Mexico, and then come with us. Look here, Dodsworth. My way of being diplomatic is to come out flat. You necking around with some other concern? We can't wait. We got to turn out the cars! I can't keep this open, and I've offered you our pos-o-lutely highest salary. That's the way we do business. Yes or no?"

"I'm not flirting with any other company. I've had several offers and turned them down. Your offer is fair."

"Fine! Let's sign the contract right now. Got her here! Put down your John Hancock, and begin to draw the ole salary from this minute, with a month's vacation on pay! How's that?"

With the noisiness of a little man making an impression, Kynance slapped the contract on the glowing directors'-table, flourished an enormous red and black fountain pen, and patronizingly poked Sam in the shoulder.

Irritably Sam rumbled, "I can't tie myself up without thinking it over. I'll give you my answer as soon as I can. Probably in a week or so. But I may want to take a four-months rest in Europe. Never mind about the pay meanwhile. Rather feel free."

"My God, man, what do you think is the purpose of life? Loafing? Getting by with doing as little as you can? I tell you, what I always say is: there's no rest like a little extra work! You ain't tired-- you're just fed up with this backwoods town. Come up to Detroit and see how we make things hum! Come sit in with us and hear us tell Congress where it gets off. Work! That's the caper! I tell you," with a grotesque, evangelical sonorousness, "I tell you, Dodsworth, to me, work is a religion. 'Turn not thy hand from the plow.' Do big things! Think of it; by making autos we're enabling half the civilized world to run into town from their pig- sties and see the movies, and the other half to get out of town and give Nature the once-over. Twenty million cars in America! And in twenty more years we'll have the bloomin' Tibetans and Abyssinians riding on cement roads in U.A.C. cars! Talk about Napoleon! Talk about Shakespeare! Why, we're pulling off the greatest miracle since the Lord created the world!

19

"Europe? How in hell would you put IN four months? Think you could stand more'n ten art galleries? I KNOW! I've seen Europe! Their Notre Dame is all right for about half an hour, but I'd rather see an American assembly-plant, thousand men working like a watch, than all their old, bum-lighted, tumble-down churches--"

It was half an hour before Sam got rid of Kynance without antagonizing him, and without signing a contract.

"I'd like," Sam reflected, "to sit under a linden tree for six straight months and not hear one word about Efficiency or Doing Big Things or anything more important than the temperature of the beer-- if there is anything more important."

He had fallen into rather a rigid routine. Most days, between office and home, he walked to the Union Club in winter, drove to the golf course in summer. But tonight he was restless. He could not endure the fustiness of the old boys at the club. His chauffeur would be waiting there, but on his way to the club Sam stopped, with a vague notion of tasting foreignness, at a cheap German restaurant.

It was dark, quiet, free of the bouncing grandeur of Kynances. At a greasy oilcloth-covered table he sat sipping coffee and nibbling at sugar-crusted coffee-cake.

"Why should I wear myself out making more money for myself--no, for Kynance! He will like hell take my caravans away from me!"

He dreamed of a very masterwork of caravans: a tiny kitchen with electric stove, electric refrigerator; a tiny toilet with showerbath; a living-room which should become a bedroom by night-- a living-room with a radio, a real writing desk; and on one side of the caravan, or at the back, a folding verandah. He could see his caravanners dining on the verandah in a forest fifty miles from any house.

"Kind of a shame to have 'em ruin any more wilderness. Oh, that's just sentimentality," he assured himself. "Let's see. We ought to make that up--" He was figuring on a menu. "We ought to produce those in quantities for seventeen hundred dollars, and our selling- point will be the saving in hotel bills. Like to camp in one myself! I will not let Kynance have my ideas! He'd turn the caravans out, flimsy and uncomfortable, for eleven hundred, and all he'd think about would be how many we could slam on the market. Kynance! Lord, to take his orders, to stand his back-slapping, at fifty! No!"

20

The German restaurant-keeper said, as one content with all seasons and events, "Pretty bad snow tonight."

"Yes."

And to himself: "There's a fellow who isn't worrying about Doing Big Things. And work isn't his religion. His religion is roast goose, which has some sense to it. Yes, let's go, Fran! Then come back and play with the caravan. . . . Or say, for an elaborate rig, why not two caravans, one with kitchen and toilet and stores, other with living-bedroom, and pitch 'em back to back, with a kind of train-vestibule door, and have a real palace for four people? . . . I would like to see Monte Carlo. Must be like a comic opera."

His desire for Monte Carlo, for palms and sunshine and the estimable fish of the Prince of Monaco, was enhanced by jogging through the snowstorm in his car, by being held up in drifts, and clutching the undercurving seat during a rather breathless slide uphill to Ridge Crest. But when he entered the warmth of the big house, when he sat in the library alone (Fran was not yet back from the Children's Welfare Bridge), with a whisky-soda and a volume of Masereel woodcuts, when he considered his deep chair and the hearth-log and the roses, Sam felt the security of his own cave and the assurance to be found in familiar work, in his office-staff, in his clubs, his habits and, most of all, his friends and Fran and the children.

He regarded the library contentedly: the many books, some of them read--volumes of history, philosophy, travels, detective stories; the oak-framed fireplace with a Mary Cassatt portrait of children above it; the blue davenport; the Biedermeyer rug from Fran's kin in Germany; the particularly elaborate tantalus.

"Pretty nice. Hotels--awful! Oh yes, I'll probably go over to the U.A.C. But maybe take six weeks or a couple of months in Europe, then move to Detroit. But not sell this house! Been mighty happy here. Like to come back here and spend our old days. When I really make my pile, I'll do something to help turn Zenith into another Detroit. Get a million people here. Only, plan the city right. Make it the most beautiful city in the world. Not just sit around on my chair in Europe and look at famous cities, but MAKE one!"

Once a month, Sam's closest friends, Tub Pearson, his humorous classmate who was now the gray and oracular president of the

Centaur State Bank, Dr. Henry Hazzard, the heart specialist, Judge Turpin, and Wheeler, the packing-house magnate, came in for dinner and an evening of poker, with Fran as hostess at dinner but conveniently disappearing after it.

Fran whisked in from her charity bridge as he was going up to dress. In her sleek coat of gray squirrel she was like a snow- sprinkled cat pouncing on flying leaves. She tossed her coat and hat to the waiting maid, and kissed Sam abruptly. She was virginal as the winter wind, this girl who was the mother of Emily about to be married.

"Terrible bore, the bridge. I won seventeen dollars. I'm a good little bridge-player, I am. We must hustle it's almost dinnertime oh what a bore Lucile McKelvey is with her perpetual gabble about Italy I bet I'll learn more Italian in three weeks than she has in three trips come on my beloved we are LATE!"

"We are going then?"

"Going where?"

"To Europe."

"Oh, I don't know. Think how nice it would be for you to 'pitch a wicked horseshoe,' as dear Tub would say, in Florida."

"Oh, quit it!"

As they tramped up-stairs he tucked his arm about her, but she released herself, she smiled at him too brightly--smile glittering and flat as white enamel paint--urbane smile that these twenty years had made him ashamed of his longing for her--and she said, "We must hurry, lamb." And too brightly she added, "Don't drink too much tonight. It's all right with people like Tub Pearson, but Judge Turpin is so conservative--I know he doesn't like it."

She had a high art of deflating him, of enfeebling him, with one quick, innocent-sounding phrase. By the most careless comment on his bulky new overcoat she could make him feel like a lout in it; by crisply suggesting that he "try for once to talk about SOMETHING besides motors and stocks," while they rode to a formidable dinner to an elocutionary senator, she could make him feel so unintelligent that he would be silent all evening. The easy self-confidence which weeks of industrial triumphs had built up in him she could flatten in five seconds. She was, in fact, a genius at planting in him an assurance of his inferiority. Thus she did tonight, in her nicest and friendliest way, and instantly the lumbering Ajax began to look doubtfully toward the poker he had always enjoyed, to fear the opinion of Judge Turpin--an eye-glassed sparrow of a man who seemed to admire Sam, and who showed his reverence for the law by taking illicit drink for drink with him.

Sam felt unworthy and apologetic till he had dressed and been cheered by a glimpse of his daughter, Emily.

Emily, as a child, had been his companion; he had always understood her, seemed nearer to her than to Fran. She had been a tomboy, sturdy of shoulder, jolly as an old family dog out on a walk.

He used to come to the nursery door, lamenting:

"Milord, the Duke of Buckin'um lies wownded at the gate!"

Emily and Brent would wail joyously, "Not seriowsly, I trust," and he answer, "Mortually, I fear."

They had paid him the compliment of being willing to play with him, Emily more than the earnest young Brent.

But Emily had been drawn, these last five years, into the tempestuous life of young Zenith; dances, movie parties, swimming in summer, astonishingly unrestricted companionship with any number of boys; a life which bewildered Sam. Now, at twenty, she was to be married to Harry McKee, assistant general manager of the Vandering Bolt and Nut Company (considered in Zenith a most genteel establishment), ex-tennis-champion, captain during the Great War, a man of thirty-four who wore his clothes and his slang dashingly. The parties had redoubled, and Sam realized wistfully that Emily and he had no more of their old, easy, chuckling talks.

As he marched down to supervise the cocktails for dinner, Emily flew in, blown on the storm, crying at him, "Oh, Samivel, you old beautiful! You look like a grand duke in your dinner jacket! You sweet thing! Damn it, I've got to be at Mary Edge's in twenty minutes!"

She galloped up-stairs, and he stood looking after her and sighed.

"I'd better begin to dig in against the lonely sixties," he brooded.

He shivered as he went out to tell the butler-for-the-evening how to prepare the cocktails, after which, he knew, the butler would prepare them to suit himself, and probably drink most of them.

Sam remembered that this same matter of a butler for parties only had been the subject of rather a lot of pourparlers between Fran and himself. She wanted a proper butler in the house, always. And certainly they could afford one. But every human being has certain extravagances which he dare not assume, lest he offend the affectionate and jeering friends of his youth--the man who has ventured on spats dares not take to a monocle--the statesman who has ventured on humor dares not be so presumptuous as to venture on honesty also. Somehow, Sam believed that he could not face Tub Pearson if he had anything so effete as a regular butler in the house, and Fran had not won . . . not yet.

Tub Pearson--the Hon. Thos. J. Pearson, former state-senator, honorary LL.D. of Winnemac University, president of the Centaur State Bank, director in twelve companies, trustee of the Loring Grammar School and of the Zenith Art Institute, chairman of the Mayor's City Planning Commission--Tub Pearson was still as much the jester as he had been at Yale. He and his lively wife Matilde, known as "Matey," had three children, but neither viceregal honors nor domesticity had overlaid Tub's view of himself as a natural comedian.

All through the poker-game, at the large table in Sam's library, where they sat with rolled-up sleeves and loosened collars, gurgling their whisky-sodas with gratified sighs, Tub jabbed at Judge Turpin for sentencing bootleggers while he himself enjoyed his whisky as thoroughly as any one in Zenith. When they rested-- that is to say, re-filled their glasses--at eleven, and Sam suggested, "May not have any more poker with you lads for a while, because Fran and I may trot over to Europe for six months or so," then Tub had an opportunity suitable to his powers:

"Six months! That's elegant, Sambo. You'll come back with an English accent: 'Hy sye, hold chappie, cawn't I 'ave the honor of raising the bloomin' pot a couple o' berries, dear old dream?'"

"Ever hear an Englishman talk like that?"

"No, but you will! Six months! Oh, don't be a damn' fool! Go for two months, and then you'll be able to appreciate getting back to a country where you can get ice and a bath-tub."

"I know it's a heresy," Sam drawled, "but I wonder if there aren't a few bath-tubs in Europe? Think I'll go over and see. My deal."

He did not show it; he played steadily, a rectangular-faced, large man, a cigar gripped in his mouth, cards dwarfed in his wide hand; but he was raging within:

"I've been doing what people expected me to, all my life. Football in college, when I'd as soon've stuck in the physics laboratory. Make money and play golf and be a good Republican ever since. Human cash-register! I'm finished! I'm going!"

But they heard from him only "Whoop you two more. Cards?"

CHAPTER 4

It was late when Sam yawned up to bed, for their poker-game had lasted till after one. The spacious chamber was half lighted from the bathroom. The dusky light caught the yellow silk curtains by her bed, the crystal on her wide dressing-table. She had left the windows closed, and the air was not unpleasantly stuffy with cold cream, powder, and steaminess lingering from a hot bath scented with bath-salts.

He was eager for her breathing presence. His determination to escape with her had made Fran seem nearer and more desirable than in months, but as he felt guilty about awakening her, he did not admit that he was doing anything so unkind--he merely dropped his shoes loudly.

She looked startled when she awoke. How many times she had looked startled, a little incredulous, when she had stirred to discover him beside her! She turned on her bedside light, she looked at him vaguely, as though she wasn't quite sure who he was, but, after all, one had to be polite. She was incredibly young and unmarked with wrinkles, a girl in a lace nightgown edged at the neck with white fur.

He plumped down on the bed beside her, kissed her shoulder. She suffered it, unresponding, and said, too cheerily, "Please no! Not now. Listen, dear, I want to talk. Ohhhhh, gee, I'm sleepy! I tried to stay awake till you came up, but I dozed off. So 'shamed! But pull up the big chair and listen."

"Don't you want me to kiss you?"

"Why do you always ask that? In that hurt way? You're so silly! You know you've had several drinks. Oh, I don't mind--though Tub and you, for men that are responsible citizens and don't really drink at all, always do manage to tuck away a lot too much! I don't mind. But don't you think it's a little icky, this sudden passion for embracing when you're--well, exhilarated?"

"Don't you WANT me to kiss you?"

"Good Heavens, my dear man, haven't I been your wife for twenty-two years? Oh, please, dear, don't be quarrelsome! Have I done something to hurt you? I'm so, so terribly sorry! I am, truly, dear. Kiss me!"

It was the coolest, most brief of kisses that she gave him and, that chore done, most briskly she rattled, "Now pull up the big chair and listen, dear. Or would you rather wait till tomorrow?"

She added, with the imitation of baby-talk which ordinarily tickled him, "Is mos' awful' important!"

He dragged the wing-chair to her bed and decorously sat down, wagging a varnished pump, but he said testily, "Good Lord, you don't need to coax. Let's have it."

"Oh, don't be such an old grump! Now I ask you: IS that fair? Because I don't like the reek of whisky? Would you like it on my breath?"

"No. But I didn't take much. But--Never mind. Listen, Fran. I know what you want. And I've decided. Kynance tried to tie me up with a contract to go to work right away, but I refused. So we'll go to Europe, and maybe for four-five months!"

"Oh. That."

With all his experience of her zig-zag incalculability, her shreds of knowledge that seemed to have no source, her ambitions and desires that seemed not worth the pains, her veiled resentment of hurts which he had not meant to inflict, her amiability when he had expected her to be angry, he was surprised now at her indifference.

"It's more fundamental than going to Europe. See here, Sam. Even if I didn't want to, oh, kiss you--Sorry I don't seem to be more passionate. I wish I were, for your sake. But apparently I'm not. But even so, we have been happy, haven't we! We have built something pretty fine!"

"Yes, we have. What's worrying--"

"Even if we haven't been wild operatic lovers, I do think we mean something awfully deep and irreplaceable to each other. Don't we?"

His touchy ardor gave way to affection. He reached his long arm out and patted her slight, nervous fingers. "Yes. We differ on a lot of things, but I guess we've got something solid for each other that we can't find in anybody else."

"Something really permanent, Sam? Dependable? So we're like two awfully good friends backing each other in a terrible street fight?"

"Absolutely. But what's--"

"Listen. We've done the first part of our jobs. We've made enough money. We've brought up the children. You have something to show for your work--this really marvelous car that you've created. And yet we're still young, comparatively. Oh, let's not settle down into contentment with the dregs of life! Let's have a new life, all over, and not worry any more about duties (and I've had my own, young man--if you think it's easy to run a house like this, and entertain everybody!). Let's--oh, it's hard to express it, but I mean: let's not tie ourselves down to saying we'll come back from Europe (but it was sweet of you, dear, to consent without making me beg), but I mean: let's not insist that we HAVE to be back from Europe in four months--yes, or four years! On the other hand, if we don't like it, let's not feel we have to stay; let's take the first boat back. But let's--Oh, please now, get this! Let's start out of this stupid old town without one single solitary plan in our heads beyond landing in Europe, and coming back when we really want to, and going where we please when we please. Maybe we'll be back after two months on the Riviera, and then again, forty years from now, we may be living in a bamboo shack in Java and thumbing our noses at anybody who doesn't like it! Why, I'd almost like to sell this house, so we won't have anything to bind us."

"You're not serious? Good Lord, we couldn't do that! Why, it's our home! Wouldn't know what to do if we didn't have a safe harbor like this to come back to! Why, we've built ourselves into this old place, from the Radiola to the new garage doors. I guess I know every dahlia in the garden by its middle name! I love the place the way I do Emily and you and the boy. Only place where we can slam the door and tell everybody to go to hell and be ourselves!"

"But perhaps we'll get us some new selves, without losing the old ones. You'd--oh, you could be so magnificent, so tall and impressive and fine, if you'd let yourself be, if you didn't feel you had to be just an accessory to a beastly old medium-priced car, if you'd get over this silly fear that people might think you were affected and snobbish if you demanded the proper respect from them! There ARE great people in the world--dukes and ambassadors and generals and scientists and--And I don't believe that essentially they're one bit bigger than we are. It's just that they've been trained to talk of world-affairs, instead of the price of vanadium and what Mrs. Hibbletebibble is going to serve at her Hallowe'en party. I'm going to be one of 'em! I'm not afraid of 'em! If you'd only get over this naive passion for 'simplicity' and all those nice peasant virtues and let yourself be the big man that you really are! Not meekly say to His Excellency that though you look like a grand-duke, you're really only little Sammy Dodsworth of Zenith! He won't know it unless you insist on telling him! . . . And perhaps an ambassadorship for you, after you've been abroad long enough to learn the tricks. . . . Only to do all that, to grab the world, we must NOT be bound by the feeling that we're tied to this slow-pokey Zenith till death do us part from the fun of adventuring!"

"But to sell the house--"

"Oh, we don't need to do that, of course, silly--not at first. I just mean it as an example of how free we ought to be. Of course we wouldn't sell it. Heavens, we may be delighted to slink back here in six months! But don't let's plan to, that's what I mean. Oh, Sam, I'm absolutely not going to let my life be over at forty-- well, at forty-one, but no one ever takes me for more than thirty- five or even thirty-three. And life would be over for me if I simply went on forever with the idiotic little activities in this half-baked town! I won't, that's all! You can stay here if you insist, but I'm going to take the lovely things that-- I have a right to take them, because I understand them! What do I care whether some club of human, or half-human, tabby-cats in eye-glasses study dietetics or Lithuanian art next year? What do I care whether a pretentious bunch of young millionaire manufacturers have an imitation English polo team? . . . when I could have the real thing, in England! And yet if we stay here, we'll settle down to doing the same things over and over. We've drained everything that Zenith can give us--yes, and almost everything that New York and Long Island can give us. And in this beastly country--In Europe, a woman at forty is just getting to the age where important men take a serious interest in her. But here, she's a grandmother. The flappers think I'm as venerable as the bishop's wife. And they MAKE me old, with their confounded respectfulness--and their CHARMING rejoicing when I go home from a dance early--I who can dance better, yes, and longer, than any of them--"

"Now, now!"

"Well, I can! And so could you, if you didn't let business sap every single ounce of energy you have! But at the same time--I only have five or ten more years to continue being young in. It's the derniere cartouche. And I won't waste it. Can't you understand? Can't you understand? I mean it, desperately! I'm begging for life--no, I'm not!-- I'm demanding it! And that means something more than a polite little Cook's trip to Europe!"

"But see here now! Do you actually mean to tell me, Fran, that you think that just moving from Zenith to Paris is going to change everything in your life and make you a kid again? Don't you realize that probably most people in Paris are about like most people here, or anywhere else?"

"They aren't, but even if they were--"

"What do you expect out of Europe? A lot of culture?"

"No! 'Culture!' I loathe the word, I loathe the people who use it! I certainly do not intend to collect the names of a lot of painters-- and of soups--and come back and air them. Heavens, it isn't just Europe! We may not stay there at all. It's being free to wander wherever we like, as long as we like, or to settle down and become part of some community or some set if we like, and not feel that we have a duty to come back here. Oh, I could love you so much more if we weren't a pair of old horses in a treadmill!"

They sailed for Southampton in February, three weeks after Emily's wedding.

Sam was absorbed in completing the Revelation Company transfer, and in answering Fran when she complained, "Oh, work's become a disease with you! You go on with it when there's no need. Let the underlings finish up. Dear, it's because I do love you that--Do you think you'll ever learn to enjoy leisure, to enjoy just being yourself and not an office? You're not going to make me feel guilty for having dragged you away, are you?"

"By God, I'll enjoy life if it kills me--and it probably will!" he grumbled. "You've got to give me time. I've started this business of being 'free' about thirty-five years too late. I'm a good citizen. I've learned that Life is real and Life is earnest and the presidency of a corporation is its goal. What would I be doing with anything so degenerate as enjoying myself?"

CHAPTER 5

The S. S. Ultima, thirty-two thousand tons burden, was four hours out of New York. As the winter twilight glowered on the tangle of gloomy waves, Samuel Dodsworth was aware of the domination of the sea, of the insignificance of the great ship and all mankind. He felt lost in the round of ocean, one universal gray except for a golden gash on the western horizon. His only voyaging had been on lakes, or on the New York ferries. He felt uneasy as he stood at the after rail and saw how the rearing mass of the sea loomed over the ship and threatened it when the stern dipped--down, unbelievably down, as though she were sinking. But he felt resolute again, strong and very happy, as he swung about the deck. He had been sickish only for the first hour. The wind filled his chest, exhilarated him. Only now, the messy details of packing and farewells over, and the artificially prolonged waving to friends on the dock endured, did he feel that he was actually delivered from duty, actually going--going to strange-colored, exciting places, to do unknown and heroic things.

He hummed (for Kipling meant something to Sam Dodsworth which no Shelley could, nor Dante)--he hummed "The Gipsy Trail":

> *Follow the Romany patteran*
> *North where the blue bergs sail,*
> *And the bows are gray with the frozen spray,*
> *And the masts are shod with mail.*
> *Follow the Romany patteran*
> *West to the sinking sun,*
> *Till the junk-sails lift through the houseless drift,*
> *And the East and the West are one*
> *Follow the Romany patteran*
> *East where the silence broods*
> *By a purple wave on an opal beach*
> *In the hush of the Mahim woods.*

"Free!" he muttered.

He stopped abruptly by the line of windows enclosing the mu-sic- room, forward on the promenade deck, as he fumbled for the memory of the first time he had ever sung "The Gipsy Trail."

It must have been when the poem was first set to music. Any-way, Fran and he had been comparatively poor. The money that old Herman Voelker had lent them had gone into the business. (A sudden, meaningless spatter of snow, out on that cold sea. How serene the lights in the music room! He began to feel the gallant security of the ship, his enduring home.) Yes, it was when they had gone off on a vacation--no chauffeur then, nor suites at the best hotels, but Sam driv-ing all day in their shabby Revelation, with sleep in an earth-scented, wind-stirred tent. They had driven West--west, two thousand miles toward the sunset, till it seemed they must indeed come on the Pacific and junk-sails lifting against the misted sun. They had no responsibili-ties of position. Together they chanted "The Gipsy Trail," vowing that some day they would wander together--

And they were doing it!

Such exultation filled him, such overwhelming tenderness, that he wanted to dash down to their cabin and assure himself that he still had the magic of Fran's companionship. But he remembered with what irritable efficiency she had been unpacking. He had been married for over twenty years. He stayed on deck.

He explored the steamer. It was to him, the mechanic, the most sure and impressive mechanism he had ever seen; more satisfy-ing than a Rolls, a Delauney-Belleville, which to him had been the equivalents of a Velasquez. He marveled at the authoritative steadiness with which the bow mastered the waves; at the powerful sweep of the lines of the deck and the trim stowing of cordage. He admired the first officer, casually pacing the bridge. He wondered that in this craft which was, after all, but a floating iron egg- shell, there should be the roseate music room, the smoking-room with its Tudor fireplace--solid and terrestrial as a castle--and the swimming-pool, green-lighted water washing beneath Roman pillars. He climbed to the boat deck, and some never realized desire for sea-faring was satisfied as he looked along the sweep of gangways, past the huge lifeboats, the ventilators like giant saxophones, past the lofty funnels serenely dribbling black woolly smoke, to the forward mast. The snow-gusts along the deck, the mysteriousness of this new world but half seen in the frosty lights, only stimulated him. He shivered and turned up his collar, but he was pricked to imaginativeness, standing outside the wireless room, by the crackle of messages springing across bleak air-roads ocean-bounded to bright snug cities on distant plains.

"I'm at sea!"

He tramped down to tell Fran--he was not quite sure what it was that he wanted to tell her, save that steamers were very fine things indeed, and that ahead of them, in the murk of the horizon, they could see the lanes of England.

She, in their cabin with its twin brass beds, its finicking imitations of gray-blue French prints on the paneled walls, was amid a litter of shaken-out frocks, heaps of shoes, dressing gowns, Coty powder, three gift copies of "The Perennial Bachelor," binoculars, steamer letters, steamer telegrams, the candy and the Charles & Company baskets of overgrown fruit and tiny conserves with which they were to help out the steamer's scanty seven meals a day, his dress-shirts (of which he was to, and certainly would not, put on a fresh one every evening), and French novels (which she was to, and certainly wouldn't, read in a stately, aloof, genteel manner every day on deck).

"It's terrible!" she lamented. "I'll get things put away just about in time for landing. . . . Oh, here's a wireless from Emily, the darling, from California. Harry and she seem to be standing the honeymoon about as well as most victims."

"Chuck the stuff. Come out on deck. I love this ship. It's so-- Man certainly has put it over Nature for once! I think I could've built ships! Come out and see it."

"You do sound happy. I'm glad. But I must unpack. You skip along--"

It was not often, these years, that he was kittenish, but now he picked her up, while she kicked and laughed, he lifted her over a pile of sweaters and tennis shoes and bathing-suits and skates, kissed her, and shouted, "Come on! It's our own honeymoon! Eloping! Have I ever remembered to tell you that I adore you? Come up and see some ocean with me. There's an awful lot of ocean around this ship. . . . Oh, damn the unpacking!"

He sounded masterful, but it was always a satisfaction, when he was masterful, to have her consent to be mastered. He was pleased now when she stopped being efficient about this business of enjoying life, and consented to do something for no reason except that it was agreeable.

In her shaggy Burberry, color of a dead maple leaf, and her orange tam o' shanter, she suggested autumn days and brown uplands. She was a girl; certainly no mother of a married daughter. He was cumbersomely proud of her, of the glances which the men passengers snatched at her as they swung round the deck.

"Funny how it comes over a fellow suddenly--I mean--this is almost the first time we've ever really started out like lovers--no job to call us back. You were dead right, Fran--done enough work--now we'll live! Together--always! But I'll have so much to learn, to keep up with you. You, and Europe! Hell, I'm so sentimental! D'you mind? Just come out of state prison! Did twenty years!"

Round and round the deck. The long stretch on the starboard side, filthy with deck chairs, with rug-wadded passengers turning a pale green as the sea rose, with wind-ruffled magazines, cups left from teatime, and children racing with toy carts. The narrow passage aft, where the wind swooped on them, pushing them back, and the steamer dipped so that they had to labor up-hill, bending forward, their limbs of lead. But, as they toiled, a glimpse of ship mysteries that were stir-ring to land-bound imaginations. They looked down into a hatchway--some one said there were half a dozen Brazilian cougars being shipped down there--and along a dizzy aerial gangway to the after deck and the wheelhouse and a lone light in the weaving darkness. They saw the last glimmer of the streaky wake stretching back to New York.

Then, blown round the corner, released from climbing upward, a dash along the cold port side, blessedly free of steamer chairs and of lardy staring. Swinging at five miles an hour. The door of the smok-ing-room, with a whiff of tobacco smoke, a pleasant reek of beer, a sound of vocal Americans. The place where the deck widened into an alcove--thick walls of steel, dotted with lines of rivets smeared with thick white paint--and the door of the stewards' pantry from which, in the afternoon, came innumerable sandwiches and cakes and cups and pots of tea. The double door to the main stairway, where, somehow, a stewardess in uniform was always talking to a steward. The steel-gripped windows of the music room, with a glimpse of unhappy young-old women, accompanying their mothers abroad, sitting flapping through magazines. Where the deck was unenclosed, the yellow scoured rail and the white stanchions, bright in the deck light, brighter against the dark coil of sea. Always before them, the long straight lines of the decking planks, rigid as bars of music, divided by seams of glistening tar. Deck-- ship--at sea!

Then forward, and the people along the rail--bold voyagers facing the midwinter Atlantic through glass windows--honeymooners quickly unclasping as the pestiferous deck-circlers passed--aged and sage gentlemen commenting on the inferiority of the steerage passengers who, on the deck below, altogether innocent of being condescendingly observed by the gentry-by-right-of-passage-money, jigged beside a tarpaulin-covered hatch to the pumping music of an accordion, and blew blithely on frosted fingers.

And round all over again, walking faster, turning from casual pedestrians into competitors in the ocean marathon. Faster. Cutting corners more sharply. Superior to thrusting wind, to tilting deck. Gaining on that lone, lean, athletic girl, and passing her. . . .

"That's the way to walk! Say, Fran, I wonder if sometime we couldn't get away from hotels and sort of take a walking-trip along the Riviera--interesting, I should think. . . . Darling!"

Gaining on but never quite passing that monocle-flashing, tweed- coated man whom they detested on sight and who, within three days, was to prove the simplest and heartiest of acquaintances.

A racing view of all their companions of the voyage, their fellow- citizens in this brave village amid the desert of waters: strangers to be hated on sight, to be snubbed lest they snub first, yet presently to be known better and better loved and longer remembered than neighbors seen for a lifetime on the cautious land.

Their permanent home, for a week; to become more familiar, thanks to the accelerated sensitiveness which is the one blessing of travel, than rooms paced for years. Every stippling of soot on the lifeboats, every chair in the smoking-room, every table along one's own aisle in the dining salon, to be noted and recalled, in an exhilarated and heightened observation.

"I do feel awfully well," said Sam, and Fran: "So do I. So long since we've walked together like this! And we'll keep it up; we won't get caught by people. But I must arise now and go to Innisfree and finish the unpacking of the nine bean rows oh WHY did I bring so many clothes! Till dressing-time--MY DEAR!"

35

He was first dressed for dinner. She had decided, after rather a lot of conversation about it, that the belief that our better people do not dress for dinner on the first night out was a superstition. He sauntered up to the smoking-room for his first cocktail aboard, feeling very glossy and handsome and much- traveled. Then he was feeling very lonely, for the smoking-room was filled with amiable-looking people who apparently all knew one another. And he knew nobody aboard save Fran.

"That's the one trouble. I'm going to miss Tub and Doc Hazzard and the rest horribly," he brooded. "I wish they were along! Then it would be about perfect."

He was occupying an alcove with a semi-circular leather settee, before a massy table. The room was crowded, and a square-rigged Englishman, blown into the room with a damp whiff of sea air, stopped at Sam's table asking abruptly, "Mind if I sit here?"

The Englishman ordered his cocktail with competence:

"Now be very careful about this, steward. I want half Booth gin and half French vermouth, and just four drops of orange bitters, and no Italian vermouth, remember, no Italian vermouth." As the Englishman gulped his drink, Sam enjoyed hating him. The man was perfectly expressionless, like a square-headed wooden idol, colored like an idol of cedar wood. "Supercilious as the devil. Never would be friendly, not till he'd known you ten years. Well, he needn't worry! I'm not going to speak to him! Curious how an Englishman like that can make you feel that you're small and skinny and your tie's badly tied without even looking at you! Well, he--"

The Englishman spoke, curtly:

"Decent weather, for a February crossing."

"Is it? I don't really know. Never crossed before."

"Really?"

"You've crossed often?"

"Oh, perhaps twenty times. I was with the British War Mission during the late argument. They were always chasing me across. Lockert's my name. I'm growing cocoa down in British Guiana now. Hot there! Going to stay in London?"

"I think so, for a while. I'm on an indefinite vacation."

Sam had the American yearning to become acquainted, to tell all about his achievements, not as boasting but to establish himself as a worthy fellow.

"I've been manufacturing motor cars--the Revelation--thought it was about time to quit and find out what the world was like. Dodsworth is my name."

"Pleased to meet you." (Like most Europeans, Lockert believed that all Americans of all classes always said "Pleased to meet you," and expected so to be greeted in turn.) "Revelation? Jolly good car. Had one in Kent. My cousin--live with him when I'm home--bouncing old retired general--he's dotty over motors. Roars around on a shocking old motor bike--mustache and dignity flying in the morning breeze--atrocious bills for all the geese and curates he runs over. He's insanely pro-American--am myself, except for your appalling ice water. Have another cocktail?"

In twenty minutes, Sam and Major Clyde Lockert had agreed that the "labor turnover" was too high, that driving by night into the brilliance of headlights was undesirable, that Bobby Jones was a player of golf, and that they themselves were men of the world and cheery companions.

"I'll meet lots of people. And I like this ship. This is the greatest day of my life--next to my marriage, of course," Sam gloated, as the second dinner gong flooded the ship with waves of hysterical sound and he marched out to rouse Fran from her mysterious activities.

There was awaiting him in his cabin a wireless from Tub Pearson:

BON VOYAGE STOP LONDON SURE SEE MY NEPHEW JACK STARLING AMERICAN EMBASSY LIVING GEORGIAN HOUSE STOP DONT RAISE ON BOBTAILED STRAIGHTS WISH WITH YOU TUB.

He wondered about introducing Major Lockert to Fran.

He was never able to guess how she would receive the people whom he found in the alley and proudly dragged in to her. Business men whom he regarded as upstanding and vigorous, she often pronounced dull; European visitors whom he found elegant, she was

37

likely to call "not quite the real thing"; and men whom he had doubtfully presented to her as worthy but rather mutton-headed, she had
been known to consider fine and very sensitive. And for all her theo-
retical desire to make their house a refuge for him and for whomever
he liked to invite, she had never learned to keep her opinions of people
to herself. When she was bored by callers, she would beg "Do you
mind if I run up to bed now--such a headache," with a bright friendliness which fooled no one save herself, and which left their guests
chilled and awkward.

Would she find Lockert heavy?

While they sat in the music room over after-dinner coffee,
with a dance beginning in the cleared space, Lockert came ambling up
to them.

"Mr. Lockert--my wife," Sam mumbled.

Lockert's stolidity did not change as he bowed, as he sat down
in answer to a faint invitation, but Sam noted that his pale blue eyes
came quickly alive and searched Fran with approval. . . . Fran's lovely
pallor, in a robe de style such as only her slenderness could bear.

Sam settled back with his cigar and let them talk. To him, always, the best talk was no brilliance of his own, but conversation that
amused Fran and drew her out of her silken sulkiness.

"You've been long in America, Mr. Lockert?"

"Not this time. I've been living in British Guiana--plantation--
no soda for your whisky, and always the chance of finding a snake
curled up in your chair on the verandah--nice big snakes, all striped,
very handsome and friendly--don't seem to get used to 'em."

Lockert spoke to her not with such impersonal friendliness as
he had for Sam, not with the bored dutifulness which most men in Zenith showed toward any woman over a flapperish eighteen, but a
concentration, an eagerness in the presence of attractive women, an
authentic need for women, which seemed to flatter Fran and to rouse
her, yet make her timid. She had first looked at Lockert with metallic
courtesy. "Here was another of those ponderous business men that
Sam was always dragging around." Now she concentrated on him, she
forgot Sam, and murmured youthfully:

"It sounds dreadful. And yet so exciting! I think I should be
glad of a nice striped snake, for a change! I'm terribly fed up with the
sound, safe American cities where you never find anything in your

chair more thrilling than the morning paper. I think I'll go look for snakes!"

"Are you going East?"

"Don't know. Isn't it nice! No plans beyond London."

"You'll stay in London a bit?"

"Yes, if there aren't too many Americans there. Why IS it that the travelling American is such a dreadful person? Look at those ghastly people at that second table there--no, just beyond the pillar-- father with horn-rimmed spectacles, certain to be talking about either Coolidge or Prohibition--earnest mother in home-made frock out to hunt down Culture and terribly grim about it--daughter with a voice like a file. Why IS it?"

"And why is it that you Americans, the nice ones, are so much more snobbish than the English?"

She gasped, and Sam awaited a thunderbolt, which did not come. Lockert was calm and agreeable, and she astonishingly bent to his domination with a puzzled: "Are we, really?"

"Appallingly! I know only two classes of people who hate their own race--or tribe or nation or whatever you care to call it--who travel principally to get away from their own people, who never speak of them except with loathing, who are pleased not to be taken as be- longing to them. That is, the Americans and the Jews!"

"Oh, come now, that's idiotic! I'm as proud of being--No! That's so. Partly. You're right. Why is it?"

"I suppose it's because your boosters go so much to the other extreme, talking about 'God's Country'"

"But that expression is never used any more."

"It isn't? Anyway: 'greatest country on earth' and 'we won the war.' And your ghastly city-boosting tours and Elks' conventions-- people like you hate this bellowing. And then I do think the English have, as you would say, 'put something over on you'--"

"I've NEVER used the phrase!"

"--by sitting back and quietly assuming that we're the noblest and rightest people on earth. And if any man or any nation has the courage or the magnificent egotism to do that long enough, almost every one will accept it from him. Oh, the English are essentially more insufferable than the Americans--"

"But not so noisy about it," mused Fran.

39

Sam was not at all sure that he liked this discussion.

"Perhaps not," said Lockert; "though if there's anything noisier than the small even voice with which an Englishman can murmur, 'Don't be so noisy, my dear fellow--!' Physically, it may carry only a yard, but spiritually it rings clear up through the Heavens! And I'll be hearing it, now that I've become a Colownial. Even my cousin--I was speaking to your husband about him--absolute fanatic about motor transport--I'm to stay with him in Kent. And he'll be pleasant to me, and gently rebuking--And he's rather a decent old thing--General Herndon."

"General LORD Herndon? Of the Italian drive?" said Fran.

"Yes. You see, my revered great-grandfather did so well out of cotton that he was rewarded with a peerage."

"And you're so proud of it! That's why you enjoy your mock humility. You had a quite American thrill in admitting that your cousin is a lordship. It's bunk--I mean, it's nonsense, the British assertion that only Americans take titles seriously. You have as much satisfaction out of not calling your cousin 'Lord' as--"

"As any charming American woman would out of calling him 'Lord'!"

She seemed helpless against Lockert's bland impertinence; she seemed to enjoy being bullied; she admitted, "Yes, perhaps," and they smiled at each other.

"But seriously," said Lockert, "you'll be more English than I am, after you've lived there a year. I've knocked about so much in South America and Colorado and Ceylon that I'm merely a tramp. Jungle rat."

"You really think so--that I'll become English?" She was un-guardedly frank, she the ever-guarded.

"Quite. . . . I say, may I have this dance?"

Lockert, for all his squareness--he was as solid and ungrace-ful- looking as his favorite mutton-chop--danced easily. Sam drooped in his chair and watched them.

"Nice she has somebody to play with already," he insisted.

And within three days she had a dozen men to "play with," to dance and argue with, and race with around the deck. But always it was Lockert who assumed that he was her patron, who looked over her

40

new acquaintances one by one, and was not at all shy about giving his verdict on them. She became helplessly angry at his assumptions, and he apologized so affably and so insincerely that she enjoyed quarreling with him for hours at a time, snuggled in a steamer robe on deck. And when Lockert and she found that they were both devoted to dogs and they became learned about wire-haired terriers, Sam leaned back listening as though she were his clever daughter.

Between times she was gayer with him and more affectionate than she had been for years; and day by day the casualness suitable to a manufacturer like Sam broke down into surprising, uncharted emotions.

CHAPTER 6

On their last day out--they were due in Southampton at noon, tomorrow--there was on the Ultima all the kindly excitement, all the anticipation and laughter, of the day before Christmas. When the Dodsworths came up to the smoking-room for their cocktail before dinner they were welcomed by the dozen people whom Lockert, the mixer of the voyage, had attracted to the round table in the center of the room.

What delightful people! Sam glowed; what a pleasure to travel with them: Lockert, the stolidly loquacious English adventurer; the jolly and vulgar little Jewish millinery buyer from Denver, who was quite the cleverest man aboard; Lechintsky, the pianist; Colonel Endersley, American military attache at Constantinople; Sally O'Leary, the satiny movie actress, whose real name was Gwendolyn Alcovar; kindly and ruminating old Professor Deakins, the Assyriologist; Max Ristad, the Norwegian aviator; Pierce Pattison, the New York banker.

"Come on, you're late!" and "Sit down here; I've had mine," and "We missed you!" they cried. They were as friendly as a college reunion, as free of jealousy, and just as undiscriminating.

The Jewish buyer had two new anecdotes (against his own race, naturally), and they flowed down to dinner in a group.

The Captain's Dinner on the Ultima occurred on the last night of the voyage, and much was made of it. The dining salon was draped in scarlet, the stewards were in red hunting-coats, champagne was served at the expense of the Line. Even prohibitionists were betrayed into smiles which indicated that they wanted to keep up the friendships of this halcyon week. Toasts were drunk from table to table, with many bows, and the large Seattle contractor, who always overdid everything, threw confetti, and tonight no one minded his alcoholic philanthropy. The Comtesse de Val Montique, who had been born in Chicago, who owned nine million dollars, two chateaux, and part of a beautifully varnished husband, who crossed the ocean regularly twice a year and was so aristocratic that she had for friends only her servants, was moved tonight to look amiable as people passed her table. And the old captain, his beard like a whisk broom, went about the room patting shoulders and chuckling, "You cross again with Papa, eh?"

Sam was raised to a quivering sensitiveness toward all of them. He was not drunk, certainly, but after two cocktails, half a bottle of champagne, and a cognac or two, he was released from his customary caution, his habitual concentration on his own affairs. He was excited by their merriment at first; then it seemed to him pitiful that all of them, and he himself, should so rarely cease thus their indignant assertion of the importance of their own little offices and homes and learnings, and let themselves rejoice in friendliness. They seemed to him like children, excitedly playing now, but soon to be caught by weary maturity. He felt a little the lacrimae rerum of the whole world. He wanted to weep over the pride of the waiters as--the one moment on the voyage when they were important and beautiful and to be noticed--they bore in the platters of flaming ice cream. He wanted to weep over the bedraggled small-town bride who for the moment forgot that she had not found honeymooning quite so glorious, nor the sea so restful. And he saw as pitiful the fact that Fran expected to find youth again merely by changing skies.

All the while he looked as little sentimental as possible, the large, grave man plodding through the courses.

That was the great dance of the trip, with Japanese lanterns making the starboard deck curiously like the verandah of the Kennepoose Canoe Club, years and years ago, when he had found Fran. But he did not explain it to her. He couldn't. He said, "I adore you! You look mighty well in that gold and ivory dress." He had, indeed, little chance for sentimental explanations. No flapper aboard had more partners than Fran; certainly none danced so smoothly. Lockert was proprietorially about her, always, and to Sam he snapped, "Want to have you at Lord Herndon's for a week-end, if you'll come, and I'd like to show you a bit of London. We'll dine at Claridge's."

Sam was not at all sure that Lockert would do anything of the kind; he suspected that Lockert could forget people as quickly as he picked them up; yet it gave him a feeling of belonging a little to England. And there was Tub Pearson's nephew at the American Embassy, and of course Hurd, the manager of the London Revelation agency. He belonged!

He was emboldened to ask for a dance with Sally O'Leary, the movie queen who had made seduction famous.

"I'm not much good at this," he grumbled, as the steamer rolled and they struggled to dance up-hill. "You ought to be dancing with one of these young fellows."

"Don't be silly! You're a lovely partner. You're a man, not one of these gigolos, or whatever the damn' word is. If you didn't have such a lovely wife, I'd probably lay my head on your lovely big chest and ask you to go out to Hollywood and kill a coupla lovely beauty-parlor cowboys for me!"

He was pleased to believe that she meant it. His heightened sensitiveness, his wistful perception of the loneliness of the world, was gone in a boisterous well-being. When he danced with Fran and she dutifully pointed out his roughness, he laughed. Always she had a genius for keeping herself superior to him by just the right comment on his clumsiness, the most delicate and needle- pointed comparison of him with defter men. But tonight he chuckled, "I'm no Nijinsky, but I'm enjoying myself so much that even you can't make me mad!" He whirled her again, mercilessly; he slid gloatingly down the long deck, and marched her back to their table.

And, when Fran assured him they needed no more wine, there were joyful invasions of the smoking-room, where tablefuls of the shamelessly happy greeted him, "Come sit down!"

They liked him! He was Somebody! Not just as the president of the Revelation but in himself, in whatever surroundings!

He did sit down; he wandered from table to table in an ecstasy of friendliness . . . which became a little blurred, a little dizzy. . . . But they were the best company he'd ever known, everybody on board, all of 'em. . . . But he'd better watch out; he was slightly lit. . . . But they were the BEST folks--

He went out on deck, to clear his head; he swayed up to the boat deck. Then he stood fixed, and all his boisterousness vanished in a high, thin, clear ecstasy.

On the horizon was a light, stationary, ON LAND, after these days of shifting waters and sliding hulls. He waited to be certain. Yes!

It was a lighthouse, swinging its blade of flame. They had done it, they had fulfilled the adventure, they had found their way across the blind immensity and, the barren sea miles over, they had come home to England. He did not know (he never knew) whether the light was on Bishop's Rock or the English mainland, but his released imagination saw the murkiness to northward there as England itself. Mother England! Land of his ancestors; land of the only kings who, to an American schoolboy, had been genuine monarchs--Charles I and Henry VIII and Victoria; not a lot of confusing French and German rulers. Land where still, for the never quite matured Sammy Dodsworth, Coeur de Lion went riding, the Noir Faineant went riding, to rescue Ivanhoe, where Oliver Twist still crept through evil alleys, where Falstaff's belly-laugh discommoded the godly, where Uncle Ponderevo puffed and mixed, where Jude wavered by dusk across the moorland, where Old Jolyon sat with quiet eyes, in immortality more enduring than human life. And his own people--he had lost track of them, but he had far-off cousins in Wiltshire, in Durham. And all of them there--in a motor boat he could be ashore in half an hour! Perhaps there was a town just off there--He saw it, from pictures in Punch and the Illustrated London News, from Cruikshank illustrations of his childhood.

A seaside town: a crescent of flat-faced houses, the brass-sheathed door of a select pub and, countrywards, a governess-cart creeping among high hedges to a village green, a chalky hill with Roman earthworks up to which panted the bookish vicar beside a white-mustached ex-proconsul who had ruled jungles and maharajahs and lost temples where peacocks screamed.

Mother England! Home!

He dashed down to Fran. He had to share it with her. For all his training in providing suitable company for her and then not interrupting his betters, he burst through her confidences as Lockert and she stood aloof from the dance. He seized her shoulder and rumbled, "Light ahead! We're there! Come up on the top deck. Oh, hell, never MIND a coat! Just a second, to see it!"

His insistence bore Fran away, and with her alone, unchaperoned by that delightful Major Lockert, he stood huddled by a lifeboat, in his shirtsleeves, his dress coat around her, looking at the cheery wink of the light that welcomed them.

They had full five minutes of romancing and of tenderness before Lockert came along, placidly bumbling that they would catch cold . . . that they would find Kent an estimable county . . . that Dodsworth must never make the mistake of ordering his street-boots and his riding-boots from the same maker.

The smell of London is a foggy smell, a sooty smell, a coal-fire smell, yet to certain wanderers it is more exhilarating, more suggestive of greatness and of stirring life, than springtime hillsides or the chill sweetness of autumnal nights; and that unmistakable smell, which men long for in rotting perfumes along the Orinoco, in the greasy reek of South Chicago, in the hot odor of dusty earth among locust-buzzing Alberta wheatfields, that luring breath of the dark giant among cities, reaches halfway to Southampton to greet the traveler. Sam sniffed at it, uneasily, restlessly, while he considered how strange was the British fashion of having railway compartments instead of an undivided car with a nice long aisle along which you could observe ankles, magazines, Rotary buttons, clerical collars, and all the details that made travel interesting.

And the strangeness of having framed pictures of scenery behind the seats; of having hand straps--the embroidered silk covering so rough to the finger tips, the leather inside so smooth and cool-- beside the doors. And the greater strangeness of admitting that these seats were more comfortable than the flinty Pullman chairs of America. And of seeing outside, in the watery February sunshine, not snow-curdled fields but springtime greenness; pollarded willows and thatched roofs and half-timbered facades--

Just like in the pictures! England!

Like most people who have never traveled abroad, Sam had not emotionally believed that these "foreign scenes" veritably existed; that human beings really could live in environments so different from the front yards of Zenith suburbs; that Europe was anything save a fetching myth like the Venusberg. But finding it actually visible, he gave himself up to grasping it as enthusiastically as, these many years, he had given himself to grinding out motor cars.

CHAPTER 7

Not the charge and roaring of the huge red busses, not the glimpse of Westminster's towers beside the Thames, not the sight of the pale tall houses of Carlton House Terrace, so much delighted Sam and proved to him that incredibly he was in London as did a milk cart on its afternoon delivery--that absurd little cart, drawn by a pony, with the one big brassy milk container, instead of a truck filled with precise bottles.

"That certainly is old-fashioned!" he muttered in the taxicab, greatly content.

They planned to stay at the Berkeley, but when Sam stood at the booking-desk, making himself as large and impassive and traveled-looking as possible, and said casually, "I'd like a suite," the clerk remarked, "Very sorry, sir--full up."

"But we wirelessed for reservations!" snapped Fran.

"Come to think of it, I forgot all about sending the radio," said Sam, looking apologetically at the clerk, apologizing for the rudeness of Fran, his child.

She breathed quickly, angrily, but never yet had she quarreled with him in public.

"You might try the Savoy, sir. Or the Ritz--just across Piccadilly," the clerk suggested.

They drooped back to the taxicab waiting with their luggage, feeling unwelcome, and when they were safely inside the car, she opened up:

"I do think you might have remembered to send that wireless, considering that you had absolutely nothing else to do aboard-- except drink! When I did all the packing and--Sam, do you ever realize that it really wouldn't injure your titanic industrial mind if you were occasionally just the least little bit thoughtful toward me, if you didn't leave absolutely everything about the house and traveling for me to do? I don't think it was very nice of you! And I'm so tired, after the customs and--"

"Hell! I suppose you got the tickets to Europe! I suppose you got our passports--"

"No. Your secretary did! I'm afraid you don't get any vast credit for that, my dear man!"

That was all the family scene for which they had time before they disembarked at the Ritz, but Fran was able to keep up quite a high level of martyrdom and bad temper, for the Ritz was nearly full, also, and they could not have a suite till the next day. Tonight, Fran had to endure a mere double bedroom with a private bath.

"I suppose," she stormed, "that I'm expected to spend my entire time in London packing and unpacking and moving and unpacking all over again! This awful room! Oh, I do think you might have remembered--"

All the gaiety was gone from Sam's large face. He held her arm, painfully, and growled, "Now that'll do! You ought to be ashamed of yourself! I always deny it, even to you, but you CAN be the nagging wife! Just the kind you hate! We've never had a better room than this, and tomorrow we'll have a suite, and you needn't unpack anything besides a toothbrush this evening--we needn't dress for dinner. You make me sick when you get this suffering, abused, tragedy fit. I know it's because you're tired and jumpy, but can't you ever be tired and jumpy without insisting that every one around you be the same way?"

"Is it necessary for you to shout at me, as a proof of YOUR calmness--your superb masculine calmness--and is it necessary to break my arm? I am not a nagger! I've never nagged you! But the fact that you, who are so fond of talking about yourself as the great executive who never forgets a detail--"

"Never say anything of the kind!"

"--could forget to send that wireless, and then you're too self-satisfied even to be sorry about it--"

"Fran!" His arm circled her; he led her to the window. "Look down there! Piccadilly! London! I've always wanted to see it, just as much as you have. Are we going to quarrel now? Do you remember the very first evening I met you, after you'd come back from Europe, and I said we'd come here together? And we have. Togeth-- Oh, I guess I sound sentimental, but to be here in England, where all our people came from, with you--"

"I'm sorry. I was naughty. I'm sorry." Then she laughed. "Only my people didn't come from here! My revered ancestors galloped around the Bavarian mountains in short green pants, and yodeled, and undoubtedly they fought your ancestors on all possible occasions!"

But her laughter was not very convincing; her restoration to happiness not complete. She said, while she was unpacking her smaller bag, gliding in and out of the bathroom--she said, in rather a lonely, discouraged way:

"Same time, my dear, you aren't always thoughtful about me. American husbands never are. You're no worse than the rest, but you're just as bad. You think of nothing beyond business and golf. It never occurs to you that a woman, poor idiot, is lots more pleased when you remember to send her flowers, or when you 'phone to her at odd hours, just to say you love her, than she would be by a new motor car. Please don't think I'm nagging--maybe I was before, but I'm not now, really! I do so want us to be happy together! And now that you don't have to think about business, don't you think it might be nice to get acquainted with me? I'm really quite a nice person!"

"Nice? Oh, Lord!"

She was cheerfuller, after their long kiss, and he--he became very busy trying to be a thoughtful husband.

And she agreed that it was jolly that they needn't dress for dinner, and then she unpacked their evening clothes.

It was toward evening; he must make her first night in London exciting; and, like most American husbands, he assumed that the best way to do it was to invite some one, if possible some one a little younger and livelier than himself, to join them.

Major Lockert?

Oh, damn Major Lockert!

They'd seen too much of him on the ship--and the patronizing way in which he'd ambled into their compartment on the boat train and thrust a Graphic and a Tatler on them--And the way he'd explained that you mustn't confuse a florin and a half-crown--

49

Still, Lockert was younger than himself--perhaps half a dozen years--and he could gabble about baccarat and Paris-Plage and other things that Fran seemed to find important--

"Let's get hold of somebody for dinner, honey," he said, "and then maybe we'll take in a show. How about it? Shall I try to get hold of Lockert?"

"Oh no!"

He was pleased; considerably less pleased when she went on, "He's been so kind to us, and so helpful, and we mustn't bother him on his first evening home. What about this young Starling, Tub's nevvy, at the American Embassy?"

"We'll try him."

The Embassy was closed, and at his bachelor apartment, Dunger, the porter, explained that Mr. Starling had gone to the Riviera for a fortnight.

"Do you remember any of the people you met here when you came abroad as a kid?" Sam asked.

"No, not really. And I haven't any relatives here--all in Germany. Hang it, I do think that after all these centuries my family might have provided me with one respectable English earl as kinsman!"

"What about Hurd, the Revelation agent? I think he came to our house once when he was in Zenith."

"Oh, he--he's a terrible person--absolute roughneck--how you ever happened to send an American like Hurd over here when you might have had a nice Englishman as London agent and--Why, don't you remember I asked you not to write him we were coming? I WON'T be the 'president's little lady' to that awful bunch of back-slapping salesmen!"

"Now Hurd's a mighty good fellow! He's cocky, and I don't suppose he's read a book since he used to look at the lingerie ads in the Sears-Roebuck catalogue as a kid, but he's a whirlwind at selling, and he tells mighty good stories, and he would know the best restaurants in London."

Softened, a bit motherly--or at least a bit sisterly--she comforted him, "You really would like to see him, wouldn't you? Well then, let's get him, by all means."

"No, this is your party. I want somebody that you'd like. Plenty of time to see Hurd; go call on him tomorrow, maybe."

"No, really, I think it would be lovely to have your Mr. Hurd. He wasn't so bad. I was exaggerating. Yes, do call him up--please do! I'd feel terrible if I felt that I'd kept you from seeing--And perhaps you do owe it to the business. He may have some cables from the U.A.C."

"Well, all right. And if I don't get him, how about trying Colonel Enderley and his wife--I thought they were about the nicest people on the boat, and they may not have a date for tonight. Or that aviator, Ristad?"

"Splendid."

Hurd's office was closed.

Hurd's home address not in the telephone book.

Colonel and Mrs. Enderley not at the Savoy, after all.

Max Ristad not in.

Who else?

How many millions of American husbands had sat on the edges of how many millions of hotel beds, from San Francisco to Stockholm, sighing to the unsympathetic telephone, "Oh, not in?" ruffling through the telephone book, and again sighing, "Oh, not in?"--looking for playmates for their handsome wives, while the wives listened blandly and never once cried, "But I don't want any one else! Aren't we two enough?"

A little melancholy at having to struggle through their Second Honeymoon unassisted, they dined at the hotel and went to the theater. In the taxicab, he had a confused timidity--no fear of violence, no sense of threatened death, but a feeling of incompetence in this strange land, of making a fool of himself, of being despised by Fran and by these self-assured foreigners; a fear of loneliness; a fear that he might never be restored to the certainties of Zenith. He saw his club, the office, the dear imprisonment of home, against the background of London, with its lines of severe facades, its roaring squares, corners clamorous with newspaper vendors, and a whole nest of streets that irritated him because they weren't reasonable--he didn't know where they led! And a tremendous restaurant that looked bigger than any clashing Childs' in New York, which was annoying in a land where he had expected to find everything as tiny and stiff and unambitious as a Japanese toy garden.

And the taxi-driver hadn't understood his pronunciation--he had had to let the hotel porter give the name of the theater--and what ought he to tip the fellow? He couldn't ask Fran's advice. He was making up for his negligence about the radiogram for hotel reservations by being brusque and competent--a man on whom she could rely, whom she would love the more as she saw his superiority in new surroundings. God, he loved her more than ever, now that he had the time for it!

And what was that about not confusing a half-crown (let's see: that was fifty cents, almost exactly, wasn't it?) and a florin? Why had Lockert gone and mixed him all up by cautioning him so much about them? Curse Lockert--nice chap--awfully kind, but treating him as though he were a baby who would be disgraced in decent English society unless he had a genteel guide to tell him what he might wear and what he might say in mixed society! He'd managed to become president of quite a fair-sized corporation without Lockert's aid, hadn't he!

He felt, at the theater, even more forlorn.

He did not understand more than two-thirds of what the actors said on the stage. He had been brought up to believe that the English language and the American language were one, but what could a citizen of Zenith make of "Ohs rath, eastill in labtry"?

What were they talking about? What was the play about? He knew that in America, even in the Midwestern saneness of Zenith, where the factories and skyscrapers were not too far from the healing winds across the cornfields, an incredible anarchy had crept into the family life which, he believed, had been the foundation of American greatness. People that you knew, people like his own cousin, Jerry Loring, after a decent career as a banker had taken up with loose girls and had stood for his wife's having a lover without killing the fellow. By God if he, Sam Dodsworth, ever found HIS wife being too friendly with a man--

No, he probably wouldn't. Not kill them. She had a right to her own way. She was better than he--that slender, shining being, in the golden frock she had insisted on digging out of a wardrobe trunk. She was a divine thing, while he was a clodhopper--and how he'd like to kiss her, if it weren't for shocking all these people so chillily calm about him! If conceivably she COULD look at another man, he'd just leave her . . . and kill himself.

But he must attend to the play, considering that he was being educated, and so expensively.

He concluded that the play was nonsense. In America there was a criminal amount of divorcing and of meriting divorce, but surely that collapse of all the decencies was impossible in Old England, the one land that these hundreds of years had upheld the home, the church, the throne! Yet here on the stage, with no one hissing, an English gentleman was represented as being the lover of a decent woman, wife of a chemist, and as protesting against running away with her because then they would be unable to continue having tea and love together at the husband's expense. And the English audience, apparently good honest people, laughed.

The queer cold bewilderment crept closer to him in the entr'acte, when he paced the lobby with Fran. The people among whom he was strolling were so blankly indifferent to him. In Zenith, he would have been certain to meet acquaintances at the theater; even in New York there was a probability of meeting classmates or automobile men. But here--He felt like a lost dog. He felt as he had on the first day of his Freshman year in college.

And his evening clothes, he perceived, were all wrong.

They went to bed rather silently, Sam and Fran. He would have given a great deal if she had suggested that they take a steamer back to America tomorrow. What, actually, she was thinking, he did not know. She had retired into the mysteriousness which had hidden her essential self ever since the night when he had first made love to her, at the Kennepoose Canoe Club. She was pleasant now--too pleasant; she said, too easily, that she had enjoyed the play; and she said, without saying it, that she was far from him and that he was not to touch her body, her sacred, proud, passionately cared- for body, save in a fleeting good-night kiss. She seemed as strange to him as the London audience at the theater. It was inconceivable that he had lived with her for over twenty years; impossible that she should be the mother of his two children; equally impossible that it could mean anything to her to travel with him--he so old and tired and aimless, she so fresh and unwrinkled and sure.

Tonight, she wasn't forty-two to his fifty-one; she was thirty to his sixty.

He heard the jesting of Tub Pearson, the friendliness of his chauffeur at home, the respectful questions of his stenographer.

He realized that Fran was also lying awake and that, as quietly as possible, her face rammed into her pillow, she was crying.

And he was afraid to comfort her.

CHAPTER 8

Sam had never, for all of Fran's years of urging that it was a genteel and superior custom, been able to get himself to enjoy breakfast in bed. It seemed messy. Prickly crumbs of toast crept in between the sheets, honey got itself upon his pajamas, and it was impossible to enjoy an honest cup of coffee unless he squared up to it at an honest table. He hated to desert her, their first morning in London, but he was hungry. Before he dared sneak down to the restaurant, he fussed about, trying to see to it that she had a proper breakfast. There was a room waiter, very morose, who spoke of creamed haddock and kippers. Now whatever liberalisms Samuel Dodsworth might have about politics and four-wheel brakes, he was orthodox about American breakfasts, and nothing could have sent him more gloomily to his own decent Cream of Wheat than Fran's willingness to take a thing called a kipper.

No, said Fran, after breakfast, she thought she would stay in bed till ten. But he needed exercise, she said. Why, she said, with a smile which snapped back after using as abruptly as a stretched rubber band, didn't he take a nice walk?

He did take a nice walk.

He felt friendly with such old-fashioned shops as were left on St. James's Street; brick shopfronts with small-paned windows which had known all the beaux and poets of the eighteenth century: a hat-making shop with antiquated toppers and helmets in the window; a wine office with old hand-blown bottles. Beyond these relics was a modern window full of beautiful shiny shotguns. He had not believed, somehow, that the English would have such beautiful shiny shotguns. Things were looking up. England and he would get along together.

But it was foggy, a little raw, and in that gray air the aloof and white-faced clubs of Pall Mall depressed him. He was relieved by the sign of an American bank, the Guaranty Trust Company, looking very busy and cheerful behind the wide windows. He would go in there and get acquainted but--Today he could think of no reason; he had plenty of money, and there had been no time yet for mail to arrive--curse it!-- how he'd like a good breezy letter from Tub Pearson, even a business letter from the U.A.C., full of tricky questions to be answered, anything to assure him that he was some one and meant something, here in this city of traditional, unsmiling stateliness, among these unhurried, well-dressed people who so thoroughly ignored him.

The next steamer back--

Too late in life, now, to "make new contacts," as they said in Zenith.

He realized that Fran's thesis, halfway convincing to him when they had first planned to go to Europe, her belief that they could make more passionate lives merely by running away to a more complex and graceful civilization, had been as sophomoric as the belief of a village girl that if she could but go off to New York, she would magically become beautiful and clever and happy.

He had, for a few days, forgotten that wherever he traveled, he must take his own familiar self along, and that that self would loom up between him and new skies, however rosy. It was a good self. He liked it, for he had worked with it. Perhaps it could learn things. But would it learn any more here, where it was chilled by the unfamiliarity, than in his quiet library, in solitary walks, in honestly auditing his life, back in Zenith? And just what were these new things that Fran confidently expected it to learn?

Pictures? Why talk stupidly about pictures when he could talk intelligently about engines? Languages? If he had nothing to say, what was the good of saying it in three languages? Manners? These presumable dukes and dignitaries whom he was passing on Pall Mall might be able to enter a throne-room more loftily, but he didn't want to enter a throne-room. He'd rather awe Alec Kynance of the U.A.C. than anybody who'd only inherited the right to be called a king!

No. He was simply going to be more of Sam Dodsworth than he had ever been. He wasn't going to let Europe make him apologetic. Fran would certainly get notions; want to climb into circles with fancy-dress titles. Oh, Lord, and he was so fond of her that he'd probably back her up! But he'd fight; he'd try to get her happily home in six months.

So!

He knew now what he'd do--and what he'd make her do!

He became happy again, and considered the Londoners with a friendly, unenvious, almost superior air . . . and discovered that his hat was just as wrong as his evening clothes. It was a good hat, too, and imported; a Borsalino, guaranteed by the Hub Hatters of Zenith to be the smartest hat in America. But it slanted down in front with too Western and rakish an air.

And, swearing that he'd let no English passers-by tell him what HE was going to wear, he stalked toward Piccadilly and into a hat-shop he remembered having seen. He'd just glance in there. Certainly they couldn't SELL him anything! English people couldn't sell like Americans! So he entered the shop and came out with a new gray felt hat for town, a new brown one for the country, a bowler, a silk evening hat, and a cap, and he was proud of himself for having begun the Europeanization which he wasn't going to begin.

For lunch he invited Hurd--Mr. A. B. Hurd, manager of the London agency of the Revelation Motor Company, an American who had lived in England for six years.

Fran was fairly amiable about meeting Mr. Hurd, for the hotel management had given her the suite which she had demanded, with a vast sitting-room in blue and gold.

"I was cross, last evening," she said to Sam. "I felt kind of lonely. I was naughty, and you were so sweet. I'll be good now."

But she couldn't help being a little over-courteous to Hurd when he came in.

Mr. Hurd was a round-faced, horn-spectacled, heavy-voiced man who believed that he had become so English in manner and speech that no one could possibly take him for an American, and who, if he lived in England for fifty years, would never be taken for anything save an American. He looked so like every fourth man to be found at the Zenith Athletic Club that traveling Middlewesterners grew homesick just at sight of him, and the homesicker when they heard his good, meaty, uninflected Iowa voice. He was proud of being able to say that the "goods vans with the motors were being shunted," though if he was in a hurry he was likely to observe that the "goods vans with the autos were by God being switched."

His former awe of Sam and of the elegance of Fran was lost now in his superiority as one who certainly did know his England and who could help these untraveled friends.

He bounded into their suite, shook hands, and crowed:

"Well, by Jove, d'you know you could've doggone near knocked me down with a feather when I found you folks were in town! I say, if you'd just told us you were coming, we'd've been down to the depot with the town brass band! By golly, d'you know, Chief, I'm almost sorry we're going in with the U.A.C. It's always been a pleasure to have a straight-shooter like you for boss, and all of us hope that you're going with the U.A.C. yourself. Say, maybe we aren't shoving over what we got left of the old Series V on the Britishers, too! Now I don't know what plans you folks have, and the one thing we learn here in England about handling our guests--"

(Sam wondered if Hurd noticed the sudden rigidity with which Fran received the suggestion that she could ever be considered a guest of Mr. A. B. Hurd.)

"--is not to bother 'em, like the Americans do, but let 'em alone when they want to be let alone. Now this noon you folks come grab lunch with me at the Savoy Grill--say, I've got the waiters there trained, and I'll tell 'em they're not to treat you like ordinary Americans--they all think I'm English; they think I'm kidding 'em when I tell 'em I'm a good Yank and proud of it! And then tomorrow evening I'll get Mrs. Hurd to come in from the country--we're living at Beaconsfield, got practically an acre there--and we might all take in a show. You folks will enjoy the English stage--real highbrow actors that know how to talk the English language, not a lot of these New York roughnecks. And then maybe next week-end you might like to come down and stay with us, and I'll drive you around and show you some real English landscape, and you'll meet some of the real sure'nough English. There's a very high-class Englishman living right near us, in fact he's a knight, Sir Wilkie Absolom, the famous solicitor, that I know your good lady will fall for hard, Chief. Him and I play golf together right along, and I tell you he's a real democratic guy--he'll take you in and treat you just like you were English yourselves!"

"I THINK, Mr. Hurd," said Fran, "that we'd better be starting off and--" (So sweetly; as to a maid whom she was going to discharge come Saturday.) "--we can discuss plans on the way. You're very kind to bother with us, but I'm afraid that just these next few days we're going to be rather horribly busy. We've already, unfortunately, accepted a week-end invitation from some old friends--you see, I lived here a long time, before I was married-- and tomorrow evening we're dining out. But now let's go and have lunch, and Sam and you will have such a nice chance to discuss all the details of the U.A.C. Just forget that I'm there."

And Hurd was unconscious that anything whatever had happened.

"Huh! Guess it'd be pretty hard to ever forget YOU were around, Mrs. Dodsworth! But I certainly would like to get the real, honest-to-God low-down on the combine. And maybe you'll be able to come out to us for the week-end after that. One American thing we do stick to--real central heating! Maybe won't be as swell as some of these castles, but lot more comfy all right!"

"Oh, I'm sure of it. Shall we go now?"

Sam raged within, "I'm not going to stand her highhatting him like that! He's being as polite as he can." And, as heartily as Hurd, he shouted, "Wait there! Hold your horses, Fran! If Hurd is buying us all this expensive food, we got to give him a cocktail first. He'll be our housewarming party here."

He stamped firmly across the floor, rang for a waiter, and ordered cocktails, ignoring her flashed fury, though he knew that he would have to pay for it afterward. But he did hope that Hurd wouldn't say, drinking, "Well, here's looking at you, Chief!"

Hurd didn't. He said, "Well, here's mud in your eye! Ha, ha, ha! Say, by golly, I guess it's a year since I've heard anybody get that off! But there's a few of the good old American expressions a fellow likes to keep up, even when he's lived as long among the English as I have. Well, let's go feed the old faces. Certainly is awful' nice to have you folks here. We must see a lot of each other."

Not that Fran said anything rude at lunch. It would have been better so. She merely knotted her brows and looked suffering. Fortunately Hurd did not seem to care; probably he did not look at her; probably he was one of the American men of whom Fran had complained that they never bothered to look at a woman of over nineteen.

Hurd was unflagging. "Guess you folks would like some American grub for a change. I do myself, after all these years here," he chuckled, and ordered clam chowder, fried chicken, and sugar corn. "You folks will do fine in this burg," he said. "You'll meet some of the best. I wouldn't wonder if quite a few men in the City (that's what we call the Wall Street Section, here) have heard of you, Chief. And your good lady ought to be able to get along fine with the ladies here. . . . Oh yes, you said you were here as a girl. Well, you'll find all that coming back to you before long. Shouldn't wonder if you took to English life quicker'n I did myself, and say, I took to it like a duck to water. Of course I'm a one-hundred-per-cent. American, but I do like English ways, and this damn' Prohibition--excuse me, Mrs. Dodsworth, but I'm agin Prohibition--I guess that's about the only subject where I haven't got any come-back when my English pals razz me about the States. And the wages for servants here--Say, ain't it simply incredible, by Jove, what kitchen mechanics expect to get in America, and never do a lick of work for it! Sure, you'll like it here. But say, you must be sure to not make one mistake that even a lot of high-class Americans make when they first come over. Don't ever boast about how much money you make--"

(Surely Hurd must catch Fran's choke of rage.)

"--because the British think that's what they call putting on side. Not that you would do that, of course, but I mean--Surprise you how many of the real bon ton do. And of course I don't need to suggest to anybody with a social position like yours, Chief, that you can't just get to talking to fellows in a hotel bar here, like we would back home. Oh, you bet. I shouldn't wonder if you'd catch onto English ways even quicker than--Well, as I was saying, I don't want to intrude on you folks, but it'd be a mighty great pleasure to give you any hints I can about the British slant on things, and to start you off with a genuine English bunch of acquaintances."

"It's frightfully kind of you, and it's been such a nice lunch," said Fran. "But do you mind if we run along now? I'm afraid I'm a little late for my engagement at the hairdresser's."

When, quite wordless, they had walked through Trafalgar Square, he snarled at Fran, "Oh, SAY it!"

"Need I?"

"Better get it over!"

"You seem to be saying it to yourself, quite successfully!"

"I am. Only hurry the execution. I have too much imagination."

"Have you? If you had, would you have invited the charming and helpful and tactful Mr. A. B. Hurd to lunch with me? Couldn't you have enjoyed his highly British presence by yourself?"

"Fran, we've said all of this about so many different people-- Granted that I am a good deal of a fool about bringing the wrong kinds of people together--"

"You are, my beloved, and everybody gives you credit for being so loyal and hospitable!"

"Granted. And I admit Hurd likes himself a good deal. On the other hand, he's generous, he's honest, he's probably a man of very little home-training as a youngster. And that--No, wait now! You DON'T know what I'm going to say! In that I've expressed all our whole row, if we went on with it all afternoon. You'd just go on saying that he's a fathead, and I'd just go on insisting that he's got a kind heart. Can't you ever forego the pleasure of catching me in an error? Here we are in London, with a free afternoon ahead of us and the job of lunching with Hurd done. Must you be sulky?"

"I am not sulky! Only you can't expect me to be very radiant after an experience like that! Oh, it doesn't matter." She achieved a half-smile. "Never mind. We'll be meeting some decent people here soon. No, don't--don't tell me that Hurd is decent. Probably he is. Probably he never beats his wife. I'm sure that his playmate, Sir Toppingham Cohen, is an adornment to any salon. . . . Oh, all right, Sam; I'll be good. Only damn it, damn it, damn it, to think of wasting time like--Oh, let's go to Bond Street and buy lots of painfully expensive things."

When for two hours they had shopped up Regent Street and down Bond, Fran was in an expansive, youthful, rattling mood, and she cried, "Let's go back to the hotel--it really is a nice sitting-room-- and have tea there by our own fireplace."

On the large table in their sitting-room was a box of roses.

"Oh, and you THOUGHT of me, this morning!" she rejoiced.

He had, but he had not thought of the flowers. They were from Major Lockert.

"Oh, it doesn't matter," she said, in a tone which suggested that it decidedly did matter, and while he was being over-solicitous about the kind of cakes she'd like with tea, Lockert himself was announced.

Lockert remarked, as though he had seen them five minutes before, "It's cost me almost a bob at the club telephone to find out where you were. I say Dodsworth my cousin says you're entirely wrong about hydraulic brakes I say won't you come down to his place for the week-end awf'ly modest country cot sort of place he'd like awf'ly to have you no no tea thanks must run along forgive informality General's a widower no Lady Herndon call on you do come."

"At the same time," Sam complained, "Hurd and your friend Lockert aren't essentially different. (Oh, I don't know whether we ought to go down to Lord Herndon's or not--no reason why he should care to see me, and it'll be one of these houses with forty servants.) Oh, Lockert talks more politely than Hurd, but at bottom they're both bullies--they both want to do things for you that you don't want done. I wish Tub Pearson were here!"

"You would! Of course we're going to Herndon's. And not because he's a General and a Lord but because--Well. Yes. Because he's a General and a Lord. That's an interesting fact to discover about myself. Am I a snob? Splendid! I shall get on, if I can only be clear and resolute about it!"

CHAPTER 9

Lockert called for them in a long, sumptuous, two-seater Sunbeam which he drove himself. He insisted that there was plenty of room in the seat for the three of them, but it seemed to Sam that they were crowded, and that Fran, glossy in her gray squirrel coat and her small cloche hat, snuggled too contentedly against Lockert's shoulder.

He forgot it in the pleasure of driving from the lowering smoke of London to the winter sunshine of the country; gray fields beginning to stir with green, breathing a faint bright mist, above which, in the shining branches of the trees, the rooks were jubilant. Little villages he saw, with homely tea rooms and inn signs--"The Rose and Crown," "The Green Dragon," and "The Faithful Friend"; then thatched farmhouses, oasthouses--he could not understand what these domestic lighthouses might be--and on a ridge the splayed ruin of a castle, his first castle!

Knights in tourney; Elaine in white samite, mystic, wonderful--no, it was Guinevere who wore the white samite, wasn't it? must read some Tennyson again. Dukes riding out to the Crusades with minstrels playing on--what was it?--rebecks? Banners alive, and a thousand swords flashing. And these fairy stories really had happened, and around that wall up there, with its one broken lump of a tower! The cavalcade of knights--following this same road!-- became more real to him than the motor, for he was bored by the talk of Fran and Lockert and lost the thread of it in ancient book- colored memories which returned as desirable and somehow tragic. The other two were chattering of cricket at Lord's, of polo at Hurlingham; they were spitefully recalling the poor old rustic banker on the Ultima who came to dinner every evening in prehistoric dress clothes with the top of his trousers showing like a narrow black scarf above the opening of his baggy white waistcoat. Their superciliousness shut Sam out in the darkness along with the kindly old banker.

He wanted to escape from the hotel-and-theater London of the tourist and see the authentic English--Dorset shepherds--cotton operatives on the dole in Salford--collier captains in Bristol harbor--Cornish tin-miners--Cambridge dons--hop-pickers in Kentish pubs--great houses in the Dukeries. But they were too low or too high for Fran's attention, and was it probable, he sighed, that he would see anything that she did not choose?

A little incredulously he perceived that Fran was really attracted by Lockert--she who had not been given to even the flimsiest of tea-table flirtations, who had blushed and looked soft-eyed only at the attentions of the very best of visiting celebrities: a lecturing English novelist or a young Italian baron who was studying motor factories; she who had ever been rude with a swift cold rudeness to such flappers as were known to indulge in that midnight pawing known in Zenith as "necking." But Lockert seemed by his placid bullying to have broken her glistening shell of sexlessness. She, so touchy, so ready to take offense, accepted Lockert as though he were her oldest friend, to wrangle with, to laugh with.

"You drive much too fast," she said.

"It would be too fast for any one who wasn't as good a driver as I am."

"Oh, really! I suppose you've won races!"

"I have. With German shells. I was in the motor transport before they sent me to America. I've driven at night, on a road full of shell holes, without lights, at thirty miles an hour. . . . As I was saying, you're too American, Mrs. Dodsworth. Americans understand themselves less and are less understood by the world than any nation that's ever existed. You're excellent at all the things in which you're supposed to be lacking--lyric poetry, formal manners, lack of cupidity. And you're so timid and incompetent at the things in which you're supposed to excel--fast motoring, aviation, efficiency in business, pioneering--why, Britain has done more pioneering, in Canada and Africa and Australia and China, in any given ten years, than the States have in twenty. And you, who feel you're so European, you're so typically American! You have the most charming and childish misconceptions about yourself. You think you're an arrogant, self-contained, rational, ambitious woman, whereas actually you're warm-hearted and easily dazzled-- you're simply an eager young woman, and it's only your shyness that keeps you going about doing the starry-eyed-wonder and trusting- little-niece sort of thing."

"My dear Major Lockert, I hope that the combination of your extraordinarily careful driving and your extraordinarily generous mind-reading isn't tiring you too much!"

But she didn't, Sam realized, succeed in making it nasty.

She had turned entirely toward Lockert. She no longer noticed Sam when he mumbled, "There's a lovely old stone church," or "Guess those are hop poles"; when he wanted to hold her hand and tell her with quick little pressures that they were sharing the English country-side.

"Oh, well--" he reflected.

He recalled "Pickwick Papers," and the coach with the jovial, well- warmed philosophers swaying down the frosty roads for Christmas in the country.

"Great!" he said.

They stopped for lunch at a village inn. To Sam's alert gratification they drove under an archway into a courtyard of coaching days. He was delighted by the signs on the low dark doors beneath the archway: Coffee Room, Lounge, Saloon Bar.

They stamped their feet and swung their arms as the Pickwickians had done when they had stopped, perhaps, at this same inn. If Fran had ignored him, she took him in again and warmed him with her smile, with an excited "Isn't this adorable, Sam! Just what we wanted!" She insisted, despite Lockert's ruddy and spinsterish protests, on going into the taproom and there, with authentic- looking low rafters, paneling of black oak, floor of cherry-red tiles, they sat at a long wooden table between benches, and Sam and Lockert warmed themselves with whisky while Fran sipped half a pint of bitter out of a pewter mug-- Sam secretly bought it from the bar- maid afterward, and lost it in Paris.

The stairs to the dining-room were carpeted in warm dark red; the wall was plastered with Victorian pictures: Wellington at Waterloo, Melrose Abbey by Moonlight, Prince Collars and Cuffs, Rochester Castle; and on the landing was such a Cabinet of Curiosities as Sam had not seen since childhood: a Javanese fan, carved chessmen, Chinese coins, and a nugget of Australian gold.

The dining-room was dominated by a stone fireplace on which were carved the Tudor rose and the high-colored arms of the local

Earl. Near it, on the oak buffet, crowned with enormous silver platters, were a noble ham, a brown-crusted veal and ham pie, a dish of gooseberry tart; and at a table two commercial travelers were gorging themselves on roast beef with Yorkshire pudding.

"Great!" Sam rejoiced, and his glow continued even through watery greens and disconsolate Brussels sprouts.

Beyond Sevenoaks, Lockert played a lively tattoo with the horn, and shouted, "Almost there! Welcome to the Stately Homes of England!"

They came to an estate, high-walled, with deer to be seen through grilled gates, and the twisted Tudor chimneys of a great house visible beyond a jungle of pines.

"Oh, Lord, is this the place?" Sam privately wondered. "It'll be terrible! Ten footmen. I wonder if they do wear plush knee-pants? Whom does one tip?"

But the car raced past this grandeur, dipped into a red-brick hamlet, turned off High Street and into a rough lane gloomy between hedges, and entered a driveway before a quite new, quite unpretentious house of ten or twelve rooms. As with thousands of houses they had passed in crawling out of London, there was a glassed-in porch littered with bicycles, rubbers, and rather consumptive geraniums. At one side of the house was a tennis- court, an arbor, and the skeletons of a rose-garden, but of lawn there was scarcely a quarter-acre.

"I told you it was only a box," Lockert drawled, as he drew up with a sputter of gravel at the door.

There was a roar within. The door was opened by a maid, very stiff in cap and apron, but past her brushed the source of the roaring--a tiny, very slim image of a man, his cheeks almost too smoothly pink to be real, his mustache too precise and silvery, and his voice a parade-ground bellow too enormous to be credited in so miniature a soldier.

"How d'you do, Mrs. Dodsworth. Most awfully nice of you to come!" he thundered, and Lockert muttered, "This is the General."

If, in his quest for romance, the exterior of the house was a jar to Sam, the drawing-room was precisely what he had desired, without knowing that he had desired it. Here was definitely Home, with a homeliness which existed no longer in most of the well-to-do houses of Zenith, where, between the great furniture factories and the young female decorators with their select notions about "harmony" and "periods," any respectable living-room was as shiny and as impersonal as a new safety-razor blade. At Herndon's, blessedly, no two bits of furniture belonged to the same family or age, yet the chintzes, the fireplace, the brass fire-irons, the white paneling, belonged together. On a round table in a corner were the General's cups--polo cups, golf cups, the cup given him by his mess in India, a few medals, and a leering Siva; and through low casement windows the gray garden was seen sloping down to meadows and a willow-bordered pond. And the maid was wheeling in a tea- wagon with a tall old silver teapot, old silver slop-jar, mounds of buttered scones, and such thin bread and butter as Sam had never known could exist.

After a tea during which Herndon rumbled rather libelous stories about his fellow soldiers, they walked up the lane, across a common on which donkeys and embattled geese were grazing, past half- timbered shops with tiny windows containing a jar or two of sweets, to the fifteenth-century flint church, in itself a history of all Kent. The tower was square, crenelated, looking as though it would endure forever. In the low stone-paved porch were parish registers, and the names of the vicars of the parish since the Norman Gilles de Pierrefort of 1190. The pillars along the nave were ponderous stone; on the wall were brasses with epitaphs in black and red; in the chancel were the ancient stone shelf of the piscina of Roman Catholic days, and a slab commemorating Thos Siwickley, Kt.--all but the name and the florid arms had been worn away by generations of priestly feet.

While Herndon was lecturing them on the beauties of the church-- with rather more than a hint about the iron-bound chest in which tourists, particularly American tourists, were permitted to deposit funds for the restoration of the roof--the vicar came in, a man innocent and enthusiastic at forty-five, tall, stooped, much spectacled, speaking an Oxonian English so thick that Sam could understand nothing beyond "strawdnerly well-proportioned arches," which did not much enlighten him.

As they ambled home he saw candles in cottage windows.

They stopped to greet a porcelain-cheeked little old woman with a wreck of a black hat, a black bag of a suit, and exquisite gloves and shoes, whom Herndon introduced as Lady Somebody-or-other--

"But," Sam reflected, "it isn't real! It's fiction! The whole thing, village and people and everything, is an English novel--and I'm in it! This is Chapter Two, and it's lovely. But I wonder about Chapter

Twenty. Will there be the deuce to play? . . . Just because life is more easy and human here, I feel more out of it. So accustomed to having my office and the boys to boss around--Now that I've quit, I've got nothing but myself--and Fran, of course-- to keep me busy. These people, Lockert and Lord Herndon, they can live in themselves more. They don't need a movie palace and a big garage to be content. I've got to learn that, but--Oh, I enjoyed seeing that church, and yet I feel lonely for old Tub making a hell of a racket."

The glow in him faded as he trudged with Lockert, both of them silent, behind the chattering Fran and Herndon.

And he was irritated when Herndon turned back to crow, in the most flattering way, "You know, I should never in the world have taken Mrs. Dodsworth and you for Americans. I should have thought you were an English couple who had lived for some time in the Colonies."

Sam grumbled within, childishly, "I suppose that's an Englishman's notion of the best compliment he can pay you!"

But Herndon was so cordial that he could not hint his resentment. He would, just that moment, have preferred rudeness and the chance of an enlivening row. But his loneliness, his uncharted apprehension, vanished with the whisky and soda which both Herndon and Lockert deemed it necessary for him to take before dinner, to ward off all possible colds and other ills. As he stalked up to their bedroom (the reddest red and the shiniest brass and the most voluble little fire), Sam fretted, "I'm getting to be as touchy and fanciful and changeable as an old maid. Yet I never was cranky in the office . . . never very cranky. Am I too old to learn to loaf? I will!" And he said, as he entered the room and was startled anew at Fran's shiningness in a combination of white glove silk, "Oh, honey, speaking of old churches, you fitted into that stone aisle as if you were the lady of the manor!"

"And you were so big and straight! Lockert and the General are sweet but--Oh, you old sweet stone statue!"

He remembered for weeks their warm shared affection in the warm red room, as they laughed and dressed. His slight jealousies disappeared at the thought of Lockert off somewhere dressing alone, probably in a room as chill as the drafty corridor.

CHAPTER 10

There came in for dinner only a neighbor, whose name was Mr. Alls or Mr. Aldys or Mr. Allis or Mr. Hall or Mr. Aw or Mr. Hoss, with his wife and spinster sister. Because of the British fetish of unannotated introductions, Sam never did learn the profession of Mr. Alls (if that was his name) and naturally, to an American, the profession of a stranger is a more important matter than even his income, his opinion of Socialism, his opinion of Prohibition, or the make of his motor car. Listening to the conversation, Sam concluded at various times that Mr. Alls was a lawyer, an investment banker, a theatrical manager, an author, a Member of Parliament, a professor, or a retired merchant whose passions were Roman remains and race-track gambling.

For Mr. Alls was full of topics.

And all through the evening Sam kept confusing Mrs. Alls and Miss Alls.

They were exactly alike. They were both tall, thin, shy, pleasant, silent, and clad in lusterless black evening frocks of no style or epoch whatever. Against their modest dullness, Fran was a rather theatrical star in her white satin with a rope of pearls about her gesticulatory right arm . . . and she was also a little strident and demanding.

When Sam was introduced to Mrs. Alls (or it may have been Miss Alls), she said, "Is this your first visit to England? Are you staying long?"

Contrariwise, when he was introduced to Miss Alls (unless it was Mrs. Alls), she murmured, "How d'you do. How long are you staying in England? I believe this is your first visit."

So far as he could remember, they said nothing else whatever until they went home.

But Herndon, Lockert, Fran, and Mr. Alls made up for that silence. The General liked an audience, and considered Fran an admirable one. When she thought any one worth the trouble, she could be a clown, a great lady, a flirt, all in one. She was just irreverent enough to rouse Herndon, yet her manner hinted that all the while she really regarded him as greater than Napoleon and more gallant than Casanova. So he thundered out his highly contradictory opinions on Kaiser Wilhelm, the breeding of silver foxes, the improbabilities of Mr. Michael Arien's "The Green Hat," the universal and scandalous neglect of the back-hand stroke in tennis, the way to cook trout, the errors of Winston Churchill, the errors of Lloyd George, the errors of Lord Kitchener, the errors of Ramsay MacDonald, the errors of Lord Birkenhead, the errors of Danish butter, and the incomparable errors of Lockert in regard to emigration and dog-feeding. Otherwise, the General said scarcely anything.

"The trouble with this country is," observed Herndon, "that there're too many people going about saying: 'The trouble with this country is--' And too many of us, who should be ruling the country, are crabbed by being called 'General' or 'Colonel' or 'Doctor' or that sort of thing. If you have a handle to your name, you have to be so jolly and democratic that you can't control the mob."

"We'll try to free you from that if you come to America," said Fran, "I'll introduce you as Mr. James Herndon, the pansy-grower, and I'll tell my butler that you're so fond of rude garden life that you'd be delighted to have him call you 'Jimmy.'"

"Am I expected, Ma'am, to say that I'd be charmed by anything that YOUR butler might care to call me? As a matter of fact, I'd ask him not to be so formal, but call me 'Whiffins.' However, unfortunately, I am not named James."

"And unfortunately we haven't a butler, but only a colored gentleman who condescends to help us with the cocktails at parties, if he isn't too busy down in Shanty Town, preaching. But honestly-- Am I in bad taste? If I'm not, isn't it really rather pleasant to be known as Your Lordship?"

"Oh--I inherited the handle while a subaltern--no great day of mourning for lost dear ones, you know--I inherited from a most gloomy old uncle. I'd never been able to rebuke my colonel--tried to, in my eager boyish way, but he'd never noticed it. When I inherited, he used to go quite out of his way to rebuke ME, so I knew I'd made an impression. Fact, he was so stiff with me that I became popular with the mess. But of course you Yanks, roving your broad steppes, never dream of such puerile triumphs."

"Quite. They're too busy punching cattle," said Lockert; and Mr. Alls inquired, "Just how does one punch an unfortunate cow?"

"It's now done with automatic punching-machinery," explained Lockert. "Neat little hole right through the ear. Mrs. Dodsworth is an expert--punches six cattle simultaneously, while singing the 'Star Spangled Banner' and firing pistols."

"But my real achievement," asserted Fran, "is shooting Indians. I'd shot nine before I was five years old."

"Is it true," demanded Lord Herndon, "that the smarter American women always have girdles made of scalps?"

"Oh, absolutely--it's as de rigueur as for an Englishwoman to carry a bouquet of Brussels sprouts at a lawn-party, or--"

"Oh, what a hell of a way to talk!" fretted Sam Dodsworth.

"If they can't talk sense, why don't they dry up? What's the use of talking, anyway, beyond 'Pass the salt' and 'How much do you want a ton?' Aren't these folks ever serious?"

Suddenly they were serious, and he was even less comfortable.

"Mr. Dodsworth," asked Mr. Alls (or Mr. Ross), "why is it that America hasn't recognized Soviet Russia?"

"Why, uh--we're against their propaganda."

"But who is really responsible for the American policy? Congress or the Foreign Department?"

"I'm afraid I don't exactly remember."

It occurred to Sam that he hadn't the smallest information about Russian relations with America; only a thin memory of a conference about selling cars in Russia. He was equally shaky when they questioned him about the American attitudes toward the Allied war debt and toward Japan.

"Am I beginning to get old?" he wondered. "I used to keep up on things. Seems as though this last five years I haven't thought of anything but selling cars and playing golf."

He felt old--he felt older and older as Fran and Herndon slid over into a frivolous debate about lion hunting. He had never known that she could be so fantastic. Here she was telling some perfectly silly story about their having had a dear old lion for a pet; about Sam's kicking it downstairs one frosty night when he was in a bad temper; the poor lion slinking down the street, pursued by a belligerent black kitten, fleeing to the Zoo, and whimpering to be let into a cage. (And there wasn't even a Zoo in Zenith!)

Old! And out of it. He couldn't join in their talk, whether it was nonsense or the discussion of nationalization of mines presently set going by Herndon, who announced himself a Socialist as fervently as twenty minutes before he had announced himself a Die-Hard Tory. It was one of the few conversations in years in which Sam had not had an important, perhaps a commanding position. At dinner in Zenith, if he didn't feel authoritative when they talked of Stravinsky or the Algerian tour, soon or late the talk would return to motors and a mystery known as "business conditions," and then he would settle all debates.

He suddenly felt insecure.

As they walked to church next morning, he felt for the Kentish village a tenderness as for a shrunken, tender old grandmother. And when he noted a Revelation car parked across from the church, he was certain again that he was Somebody. But amid the politely interested, elegantly pious congregation at Morning Prayer, glancing at him over their celluloid-covered prayer books, he felt insecurity again. He was overgrown, clumsy, untutored. He wanted to flee from this traditional stillness to the anonymity and shielding clamor of London.

They rode, for the hour between church and luncheon, on ragged but sturdy horses from the village stable. Mrs. Alls had lent a wreck of a riding-habit to Fran, who looked disreputable and gay in her orange tam o' shanter--gayer than in her ordinary taut sleekness. They rode away from the village, through fields and shaggy woods, to the ridge of the North Downs.

For years Fran had ridden twice a week with an English ex-groom, turned gentleman teacher and trainer in America, his Cockney accent accepted in Zenith as the breath of British gentility. With her slim straightness she sat her aged nag like a young cavalry officer. Lockert and Lord Herndon looked at her more admiringly than ever, spoke to her more cheerily, as though she were one of their own.

Sam's riding had been a boyhood-vacation trifling; he was about as confident on a horse as he would have been in an aeroplane; he had never quite got over feeling, on a horse's back, that he was appallingly far up from the ground. Herndon had a shaky leg, and Sam and he rode slowly. Suddenly Lockert and Fran left them, in a gallop along the pleasant plateau at the top of the Downs.

"Don't you want to keep up with 'em? My leg's not up to much today," said Herndon.

"No, I'll trail," Sam sighed.

In a quarter-hour Fran and Lockert came cantering back. She was laughing. She had taken off her tam, and her hair was wild.

"Sorry we ran away, but the air was so delicious--simply had to have a scamper!" she cried and, to Sam, "Oh, was oo left alone! Poor boy!"

All the way back she insisted on riding beside him, consoling him.

A month ago he had felt that he had to protect her frailness. He was conscious now that his breath was short, that he had a corporation . . . and that Fran, turning to call back to Lockert, was bored by him.

Most insecure of all was Sam that afternoon when they motored for tea to Woughton Hall, the country place of Sir Francis Ouston, the new hope of the Liberals in Parliament. Here--so overwhelmingly that Sam gasped--was one of the great houses of which he had been apprehensive. Up a mile-long driveway of elms they came to a lofty Palladian facade, as stern as a court-house, with a rough stone wing at one end. "That's the old part, that stone--built about 1480," said Herndon.

In front was a terrace rimmed with clipped cypresses in the shape of roosters, crescents, pyramids, with old Italian wine-jars of stone. To the right, beyond a pair of tennis-courts, half a mile of lawn slipped in pale winter green toward rough meadows; to the left the stables were a red brick village. There was about the whole monstrous palace a quietness dotted only with the sound of sparrows and distant rooks. To Sam, just now, the millionaire country houses he had seen on Long Island and the North Shore above Chicago--Tudor castles, Italian villas, French chateaux, elephantine Mount Vernons, mansions which he had admired and a little coveted--were raw as new factories beside a soft old pasture.

Through a vast entrance hall with tapestries on walls of carved stucco, and high Italian candle-sticks at the foot of a walnut stairway, they were shepherded to a carved oak drawing-room high as a church, and much noisier. After that Sam knew nothing but confusion and babble. First and last there must have been fifty people popping in for tea, people with gaudy titles and cheery manners, people so amiable to him that he could not hate them as he longed to. What they were all talking about, he never knew. They spoke of Sybil, who seemed to be an actress, and of politicians (he guessed they were politicians) to whom they referred as Nancy and F.E. and Jix and Winston and the P.M. One man mentioned something called the Grand National, and Sam was not sure whether this was the name of a bank, an insurance company, or a hotel.

What could he do when a lady, entirely unidentified, asked, "Have you seen H. G.'s latest?"

"Not yet," he answered intelligently, but who or what H. G. might be, he never did learn.

And through the bright-colored maelstrom of people, his heart aching with loneliness, he saw Fran move placidly, shiningly, man-conscious and man-conquering and at home. They were all one family; they took her in; but himself, how to get in he had no notion. He had addressed conventions of bankers; he had dragooned a thousand dancing people at a Union Club ball; but here--these people were so close-knit, so serenely sure, that he was an outsider.

He escaped from the lady who knew about H. G.; he crawled through the mass of suspended tea-cups and struggled to Fran's side. She was confiding (not very truthfully) to a man with a single eyeglass that she had a high, passionate, unresting interest in polo.

When Sam had the chance, he sighed to her, "Let's get out. Too darn' many people for me!"

"They're darlings! And I've made the most terrific hit with Lady Ouston. She wants us to come to dinner in town."

"Well--I'd just like--Thought we might get a little fresh air before dinner. I feel sort of out of it here. They all chirp so fast."

"You didn't seem to be doing so badly. I saw you in the corner with the Countess of Baliol."

"Was I? Which one? All the women I talked to just looked like women. Why the devil don't they wear their coronets? Honestly,

Fran, this is too rich for my blood. I can stand meeting a couple hundred people at once, but not the entire British aristocracy. They--"

"My dear Sam, you are talking exactly like Mr. A. B. Hurd."

"I feel exactly like Mr. A. B. Hurd!"

"Are you going to demand that we take Zenith with us every place we go? Are you going to refuse to like anything that's the least bit different from a poker party at Tub Pearson's? And are you going to insist that _I_ be scared and old, too, and not reach out for the great life that I can learn to master--oh, I can, I can! I'm doing it! Must I go back with you now and sit at Lord Herndon's select villa reading the Observer or else be punished by your sulking?"

And it was she who was sulky, though he had doubtfully urged her to stay as long as she liked--or as Herndon liked. She showed a gray sulkiness all evening, but not toward Herndon, decidedly not toward Lockert. They had only a cold ham and beef supper, with no other guests, and publicly Fran was frivolous. She played the piano, played and played, and since Herndon was seized with a passion to discuss motor headlights with Sam, Lockert hung about the piano. Herndon and Sam were at the other end of the drawing-room, before the fireplace, backs to the piano, but in the Venetian mirror over the fireplace Sam could watch the others, and he did, uneasily.

Only then was he certain that Lockert aspired to considerably more than a polite friendliness with Fran.

Lockert turned her music, he kept drawling amiable insults that were apparently more fetching than flattery. His hand touched her sleeve, once rested on her shoulder. She shrugged it off and shook her head, but she was not angry. Once Sam heard her: "--don't know WHY I like you--your perfectly disconcerting admiration of yourself--
"

He felt, Sam, like a worthy parent watching his daughter and a suitor. He felt resigned. Then he began to feel angry.

"Damn it, was that why Lockert got us down here? To make love to Fran? Does he think I'm the kind that'll stand it? Does she?"

When they were going to bed, his accumulated anger came out in a chilly: "See here, my girl! All this His Lordship, Her Grace, Old England, palatial mansion stuff is fine--I've enjoyed it--but you're letting it dazzle you. You're letting Lockert be a whole lot too flirtatious.

You're off your track. At home, you'd see that he doesn't just mean to pay you pretty little compliments--"

"My dear Mr. Dodsworth, do you mean to insinuate--"

"No, I'm saying it straight! Little good home bullying!"

"Do you mean to insinuate that I'd let Major Lockert, or anybody else, make the slightest improper advances toward me? I that never tolerated loose dancing at home, that have never in my life so much as held hands in a taxi? I that--oh, it's too beautifully ironical!--that you've practically accused, time and again, of being too sexless to suit your manly ardors! Oh, it's too much!"

"Yes, at home that has been so. Though I've never accused you of sexlessness--even when I've damn' well suffered from it! I've been patient. Waited. Waited a mighty long time. That's what makes it worse now, when you've been so little attracted by me, to see you falling for this man, or at least, I mean, being obviously attracted by him, just because he's--"

"Oh, SAY it! 'Just because he's the cousin of a Lord!' Say it! Try to make me seem as contemptible a little village greenhorn as you can!"

"I hadn't intended to say anything of--Well, if I did, what I meant was: I mean, just because he's wandered enough so that he knows how to handle women by beating them. I can't. Never could beat you. Wouldn't if I could. . . . Oh, never mind. I don't mean anything serious. I just mean--Even though you are naturally something of a European, you've got to remember that this is a pretty wise and dangerous old country. But of course you've got too much sense. Sorry I said anything."

She was standing, a little rigid, in her low-necked, lace-trimmed, yellow pajamas. He lumbered toward her, his hands out bumbling, "Sorry! Kiss me!"

She shuddered. She wailed, "No, don't touch me! Oh, don't you EVER suggest things like that again! Lockert? I haven't the slightest interest in him. I'm ashamed of you! You ought to be ashamed of yourself!"

She resolutely said nothing more before they went to sleep; and in the morning she was queerly quiet and her eyes looked tired.

Lord Herndon, kindest of hosts and one of the few living men who were cheerful and full of ideas at breakfast, seemed hurt by their aloofness, but Lockert was inquisitive and slightly amused, and at the station (the Dodsworths were to return by train) he searched Fran's eyes interrogatively . . . most hopefully.

Sam was glad when the train was away, and she tried to pump up a friendly smile for him. But he was all abasement, all savage scorn of himself, that he should have spoiled the happy party of this, his child, by bucolic suspicions. She had been so innocently happy in dis-covering rural England, in sturdy friendship with Lockert, in chatter with Herndon, in a hair-blown race across the Downs, and then, he groaned, he had spoiled it all for her.

He took her hand, but it was lax--all strength gone out of the hand that yesterday had been so firm on the bridle.

CHAPTER 11

The possessions of Sir Francis Ouston were numerous and very pretty. He owned thousands of acres of Welsh coal land, he owned Woughton Hall in Kent and a tall, bleak-faced house in Eaton Square, he owned the famous mare Capriciosa III, and he owned a position in the Liberal Party immediately after that of Asquith and Lloyd George.

He himself was owned by his wife.

Lady Ouston was a beautiful woman and very commanding. She had a high, quick, passionate voice and many resolute opinions. She was firm and even a little belligerent about the preferability of Jay's to Poiret in the matter of frocks, about the treachery of the Labor Party, about the desirability (entirely on behalf of the country) of Sir Francis's becoming Prime Minister, about the heinousness of beer-drinking among the working classes, about the scoundrelism of roast chicken without a proper bread sauce, and particularly about the bad manners, illiteracy, and money-grubbing of the United States of America.

She had been born--and her father and mother before her--in Nashville, Tennessee.

She was a formidable hostess. She had a salon, and while she did explorers and chemists and the few authors who understood morning coats, she had never stooped to fill her drawing-room by exhibiting cubist painters, Hindu nationalists, American cowboys, or any of the other freaks whereby rival professional hostesses attracted the right sort of people.

And her dinners were admirable. You could be sure of Napoleon brandy, the cousin of a duke, and the latest story about the vulgarity of New York.

It was not to one of Lady Ouston's very best dinners, with a confidential cabinet minister present, that Lockert persuaded her to invite the Dodsworths, but it was quite a good, upper-middle dinner, with Clos-Vougeot and the master of a Cambridge college.

Sam was quiet, extremely observant, not extremely jolly, as he surveyed that regiment of twenty people, all nibbling so delicately at their salmon and at other people's reputations. No one seemed to have any vulgarly decided opinions, and every one desired to know of him only two things: Was this his first visit to England? and How long would he stay? And they didn't seem to care so very much about either.

He wondered how many times he himself had asked foreign visitors to the Revelation plant--Britishers, Swedes, Germans, Frenchmen-- whether this was their first visit to America, and How long did they plan to stay?

"I'll never say THAT again!" he vowed.

The dinner rather went on. Soup and a murmur about broadcasting and Bernard Shaw; salmon and a delicate murmur about Mussolini and influenza; roast mutton and an exchange of not very interested confidences about cat burglars. Sam was in a daze of gluttony and politeness when he realized that Lady Ouston was talking to him about America, and that every one at the table was beginning to pay attention. He did not know that she was born an American, and he listened to her with almost no comfort:

"--and of course none of us would ever think of classing your darling wife and you with the terrible, TERRIBLE sort of American tourists that one sees--or hears, rather--at the Cecil or in trains--where DO you suppose such Americans come from! In fact, I'm quite sure you could both be mistaken for English, if you merely lived here a few years. So it's a quite impersonal question. But don't you feel, as we do, that for all our admiration of American energy and mechanical ingenuity, it's the most terrible country the world has ever seen? Such voices--like brass horns! Such rudeness! Such lack of reticence! And such material ideals! And the standardization--every one thinking exactly alike about everything. I give you my word that you'll be so glad you've deserted your ghastly country that after two years here, you'll never want to go home. Don't you already feel that a bit?"

Sam Dodsworth had never in his life boasted of being an American nor yet apologized for it. It was amazement which made him mutter, with what sounded like humility, "Why, never thought much about America, as a whole. Sort of taken it for granted--"

"You won't long! What a land! Such terrible politicians-- positively the lowest form of animal life--even worse than Irish Republicans! And don't you rather feel ashamed of being an American when you think of America's making us pay the war debt when, after all, it was all you did contribute?"

"I do not!" Sam was suddenly and thoroughly angry; suddenly free of whatever diffidence he had before this formal society. "I never was much of a flag-waver. I don't suppose America is perfect, not by a long shot. I know we have plenty of fools and scoundrels, and I don't mind roasting them. But if you'll excuse me for differing with you--"

Lockert said pacifyingly, "You can't expect Mr. Dodsworth to agree, Lady Ouston. Remember he's--"

Sam snarled on, uncheckable: "--I suppose I have been sort of assuming that America is the greatest nation on earth. And maybe it is. Maybe because we have got so many faults. Shows we're growing! Sorry if it's bad manners not to be ashamed of being an American, but then I'll just have to be bad mannered!"

Behind his brusqueness he was saying to himself, and timidly, "Look at the dirty looks I'm getting! I've ditched things for Fran. What hell I'll get from her!"

But incredibly it was Fran herself who was attacking: "My dear Lady Ouston, out of a hundred and ten million Americans, there must be a few who have agreeable voices and who think of something besides dollars! Considering how many of us are a generation or less from England, we must have several nice people! And I wonder if every member of the British Parliament is a perfect little gentleman? I seem to have heard of rows--We probably have more self-criticism at home than any other nation--our own writers call us everything from Main Streeters to the Booboisie. But curiously enough we feel we must work out our own fate, unassisted by the generous foreigners!"

"I think Mrs. Dodsworth is quite right," said Sir Francis. "We're not at all pleased here in England when the French and Italians call us barbarians--as they jolly well do!"

Suavely he said it, and stoutly, but Sam knew that thenceforth Fran and he would be as popular in the house of Ouston as a pair of mad dogs.

Fran developed a tactful headache at a quarter after ten.

Sir Francis and Lady Ouston were very cordial at parting.

Sam and Fran were silent in the taxi till he sighed, "Sorry, honey. I was bad. Awfully sorry I lost my temper."

"It doesn't MATTER! I'm glad you did! The woman's a fool! Oh, my dear--" Fran laughed hysterically. "I can see that the Oustons and us are going to be buddies! They'll insist on our yachting round the world with them!"

"And scuttling the yacht!"

"Haven't they a dear little daughter, so Brent can marry her?"

"Fran, I'm crazy about you!"

"Du! Old grizzly! I'm glad you ARE one! Sam, a terrible thought occurs to me. I'll bet you anything that fool woman was born an American! Convert! Professional expatriate! She's much too English to be English. Not that the real English love us any too much, but she's like an Irish critic living in London, or a Jewish peer--seven paces to the right of the King. Oh, my dear, my dear, and I might have fallen into expatriate--Sam Dodsworth, if you ever catch me trying to be anything but a woolly American, will you beat me?"

"I will. But do I have to beat you very long at a time?"

"Probably. I'm rather a hussy. Only virtue is, I know it. And I did flirt with Clyde Lockert at Lord Herndon's! It flattered me to stir him out of that 'Damn your eyes' superiority of his. And I did stir him, too! But I'm so 'shamed!"

In their apartment she nuzzled her cheek against his shoulder, whispering, "Oh, I'd just like to crawl inside you and be part of you. Don't ever let me go!"

"I won't!"

The Ouston debacle considerably checked Fran's social career, though Lockert continued their mentor. He came to tea the next day, casual as ever, and drawled:

"Well, Merle Ouston was a bit of a public nuisance last night. So were you, Dodsworth!"

"Well, I couldn't sit there and listen to her--"

"You should've smiled. You Americans are always so touchy. No Englishman ever minds criticism of England. He laughs at it."

"Hm! I've heard that before--from Englishmen! I wonder if that isn't one of your myths about yourselves, like our belief that every

American is so hospitable that he'll give any stranger his shirt. Well, I've never seen any of our New York bankers down at Ellis Island begging the Polack immigrants to come stay with them till they get jobs. Look here, Lockert! The Ouston woman said all our politicians were hogs. Suppose I started making nasty cracks about the King and the Prince of Wales--"

"That's quite different! That's a question of good taste! Never mind. Herndon and I are thoroughly pro-American."

"I know," said Fran. "You love America--except for the food, the manners, and the people."

"At least, there's one American that I esteem highly!" said Lockert, and his glance at her was ardent.

Sam waited for her to rebuke Lockert. She didn't.

Lockert took them to Ciro's, to dance; he had them made members of a rackety night club called "The Rigadoon," where there was friendliness and gin and a good deal of smell. Potentates of the English motor-manufacturing companies called on them and escorted Sam to their factories. They met three or four stout matrons at a dinner given by Lord Herndon in the women's annex of the Combined Services Club, and they were again admitted to the tedious perils of occasional dinner parties.

And all the while they were as unrelated to living English life as though they were sitting in a railway station waiting for the continental train. Lockert had gone off to the Riviera, a week after the Ouston dinner. Sam was relieved--then missed him surprisingly. And with Lockert away, their invitations were few.

"Well," said Sam, "till we get acquainted with more folks here, let's do the town. Historic spots and so on."

He had studied Mr. Karl Baedeker's philosophical volume on London, and he was eager to see the Tower, the Houses of Parliament, Kew Gardens, the Temple, the Roman bath, the National Gallery; eager to gallop up to Stratford and honor Shakespeare--not that he had honored Shakespeare by reading him, these twenty-five years past; and to gallop down to Canterbury--not that he had ever gone so far as to read Chaucer.

But Fran made him uncomfortable by complaining, "Oh, good Heavens, Sam, we're not trippers! I hate these post-card places. Nobody who really belongs ever goes to them. I'll bet Clyde Lockert has never been inside the Tower. Of course galleries and cathedrals are different--sophisticated people do study them. But to sit at the Cheshire Cheese with a lot of people from Iowa and Oklahoma, exclaiming over Dr. Johnson--atrocious!"

"I must say I don't get you. What's the idea of coming to a famous city and then not seeing the places that made it famous? You don't have to send souvenir cards about 'em if you don't want to! And I don't believe the people from Iowa will bite you unless you attack 'em first!"

She tried to make clear to him the beauties of snobbishness in travel. But, in her loneliness, she did consent to go with him, even to eat lark and oyster pie at the Cheese, though she was rather snappish with the waiter who wanted to show them the volumes of visitors' names.

Ambling through London with no duty of arriving anywhere in particular, Sam came to take its somber vastness as natural; felt the million histories being enacted behind the curtained windows of the million houses. On clear days, when rare thin sunshine caressed the gray-green bricks which composed the backs of London houses, even these ugly walls had for him, in relief at the passing of the mist-pall, a charm he had never found in the hoydenish glare of sunshine on bright winter days in Zenith. He loved, as he became familiar with them, even the absurd proud little shops with their gaudy glass and golden signs: chocolate shops with pictures of Royalty on the boxes of sweets, tobacco shops with cigarette- cases of imitation silver for Sunday-strolling clerks to flourish, even the ardors and fumes of fried fish shops. He was elated at learning the 'bus lines; saying judiciously, "Let's take a 92 and ride home on top." The virility of London, town of men back from conquering savages and ruling the lone desert, seemed akin to him. . . . But Fran began to speak of Paris, that feminine and flirtatious refuge from reality.

Between explorations they tasted a loneliness they had never known in their busy domination of Zenith.

Evening on evening they sat in their suite pretending that they were exhausted after a day's "sight-seeing"; that they were exhausted, and glad they were going to stroll out for dinner alone. All the while

Sam knew that she was waiting, that he was waiting and praying, for the telephone to ring.

At their several party dinners they had met agreeable people who said, "You must come to us, soon!" and then forgot them blissfully. London's indifference to her charms depressed Fran, seemed to frighten her. She was wistfully grateful when he thought of ordering flowers, when he found some unexpected and cheery place to dine. Half the time he was pitiful that she should not be having her career; half the time he rejoiced that they had never been so close together as now, in their isolation.

She was almost timid when Jack Starling, the nephew of Tub Pearson and a secretary at the American Embassy in London, came bouncing back to town, called formally, inspected Fran's complexion and Sam's grammar, and adopted them with reserved enthusiasm. He was a pleasant, well-pressed young dancing-man, and full of ideas--not especially good ideas, but very lively and voluble. He called Sam "sir," which pleased Sam almost as much as it embarrassed him. In Zenith, no one except men who had served as officers in the Great War used "sir," save as a furious address to five-year-old boys whom they were about to beat.

And suddenly, after Starling's coming, Lockert was strolling in as though he had never been away, and Lord Herndon was in town for a month and, without any very traceable cause, the Dodsworths had more lunches, teas, dinners, dances, and theater parties than even a lady lion-hunter could have endured. Sam was so happy to see Fran excited and occupied that not for a fortnight did he admit privately that the only thing that bored him more than being an elephantine wallflower at dances was being a drowsy and food- clogged listener at dinner-parties; and that all these people whom they MUST call up, whom they simply MUSTN'T forget to invite to their own small dinners, were persons whom he could with cheers never see again. Nor could he persuade himself that their own affairs (in a private room at the Ritz, with himself pretending to supervise the cocktails before dinner and Fran making a devil of a fuss about the flowers) were any livelier than other people's. The conversation was as cautious, the bread sauce quite as bready, and the dread hour from nine-thirty to tenthirty passed on no swifter wings of laughter.

Mr. A. B. Hurd was a relief, now that Fran was busy enough so that Sam could slip away and revel with Mr. Hurd in shop gossip and motor prices and smutty stories and general American lowness.

Mr. Hurd had done his best to be hospitable, and as it had not occurred to him that there were people, like Fran, who did not wish to be hospitalitized, he had been bewildered and become shy--even his superb salesman's confidence had become shy. He had once, after innumerous telephone calls, been invited by Fran to tea, and he had brought his Oklahoma-born wife up from the country and put on his rather antiquated morning coat and very new spats.

He came into the Dodsworths' suite briskly enough, but when Mrs. Hurd crept in after her boisterous husband, Sam was so touched that he rose to the courtliness he could occasionally show. She was dressed in blue silk, with a skirt hiked up in back. Her hands looked the more rough because they had just been manicured, with rosy and pointed nails. Hurd's salary was adequate now, but Sam felt that Mrs. Hurd had for years washed dishes, diapers, muddy floors. Her lips were round with smiling, but her eyes were frightened as she shook Sam's hand in the small white-enameled foyer of the suite, and cried:

"My! I've heard so much about you, Mr. Dodsworth! Al is always talking about you and what a wonderful executive you are and what a lovely time he had with you folks when he was back in Zenith the last time and how much he enjoyed dining with you and--It's just lovely that you're here in London now and I do hope Mrs. Dodsworth and you will find time to come down to the country and see us. I know how busy you must be with parties and all but--"

Sam ushered her into the sitting-room; he tried to catch Fran's eye to warn her to be good, while he was rumbling:

"Fran, this is Mrs. Hurd. Mighty great pleasure to meet her, after we've known her husband so long."

"How d'you do, Mrs. Hurd?" said Fran, and it was worthy of Lady Ouston at her politest and rudest. Fran pronounced it "How-jDUH," and her voice rose at the end in a quiet brusqueness which finished Mrs. Hurd completely.

Mrs. Hurd fluttered, "I'm real pleased to meet you, I'm sure," then sat forward in her chair, refused the cake she most wanted, looked terrified while Fran purred about Paris. She did not venture on the invitation to the country which she had obviously come to deliver. Between Sam's heavy compliments to Hurd, Hurd's heavy compliments to Sam, and Fran's poisonously sweet manner of saying, "It was so VERY kind of you to come all this way in to see us, Mrs.--uh--

Hurd," she was bewildered, and she ventured on no conversation beyond "My, you've got such lovely rooms here. I guess you know an awful lot of English folks--lords and everything, don't you?"

After that, Hurd resentfully gave up telephoning.

But when, with Lockert and Jack Starling returned, Fran found enough of the admiration natural to her, Sam was now and then able to sneak meanly out and get hold of Hurd for odd meals.

After a fortnight Hurd suggested, at luncheon:

"Say, Chief, I'd like to pull off a bachelor dinner for you one of these evenings--some of the high-class American business men here in London--just sit around and be natural and tell our middle names. Think you could duck your good lady and have an Old Home Week? What about next Saturday evening?"

"Fine. I'll see if my wife has anything on."

"Well, I hope she has. Strict lot of police in this ole town! Ha, ha, ha, ha, ha!"

Sam was not offended. Hurd was given to smutty limericks, to guffaws about young ladies of the night, yet there was a healthy earthiness about him which to Sam was infinitely cleaner than the suave references to perversions which he had increasingly been hearing in New York and in London, and which sickened him, made him glad to be normal and provincial and old-fashioned. Hurd--hang it, he liked Hurd! The man's back-slapping was real. He could do with a little back-slapping, these days! Why should it be considered a less worthy greeting than chilly hand-shakes and fishy "Howjduh's"?

When Sam returned to the hotel, Fran was having tea with Lockert.

"I can tell that you've been seeing one of your jocund American friends again," said Lockert.

"How?"

"You have a rather decent voice when you've been under our purely insular influences for a week or so. Color in it. But the moment you slip off to America again, it sharpens and becomes monotonous."

"'S too bad!" muttered Sam, leaning against the fireplace, very tall, wondering what would happen if he threw his tea--in the cup-- at Lockert. Damn the fellow! Oh, of course he was friendly, he meant well, and probably he was right in his hints about the nice conduct of a clouded American barbarian in England. But still-- Hang it, there were some pretty decent people who seemed to like Sam Dodsworth the way he was!

He interrupted Fran's chronicle of shopping and Liberty silks to blurt, "Say, sweet, old Hurd wants to give me a bachelor dinner next Saturday evening--meet some of the American business men here. I think I ought to do it; he's tried so hard to be nice."

"And you'd like it? Be back in all the Rotarian joys of Zenith?"

"You bet your life I'd like it! We haven't a date for that evening, if I remember. Could you get up a hen party or go to the movies or something? I'd kind of like--"

"My dear, you don't have to ask permission to have an evening out!"

("The hell I don't!") "No, of course not, but I don't want you to feel stranded."

"I say, Fran," Lockert remarked, "would you care to dine with me that evening and go to the opera?"

"Well--" considered Fran.

"Fine," said Sam. "It's a go."

Jack Starling popped in just then, very cheery, and Sam was silent while the other three hilariously scoffed at America. Sam was thinking, almost impersonally. It was a new occupation for him, and he was a little confused. It had become a disease with both nations, he reflected, this discussion of Britain vs. America; this incessant, irritated, family scolding. Of course back in the cornfields of the Middlewest, people didn't often discuss it, nor did the villagers on the Yorkshire moors, nor Cornish fishermen. But the people who traveled and met their cousins of the other nation, the people who fed on newspapers on either side the water, they were all obsessed.

Fran and Lockert and Starling, chirping about it--

They found so much to laugh over--

Himself, he'd rather listen to Hurd's stories--

No. That wasn't true. He wouldn't. These Londoners (and Fran and Starling were trying to become Londoners) did talk better than the citizenry of Zenith. They were often a little silly, a little giggling, more than a little spiteful, but they found life more amusing than his business-driven friends at home.

Couldn't there be--weren't there people in both England and America who were as enterprising and simple and hearty as Mr. A. B. Hurd, yet as gay as Fran or Jack Starling, as curiously learned as Lockert, who between pretenses of boredom gave glimpses of voodoo, of rajahs, of the eager and credulous boy he had been in public school and through long riverside holidays at his father's vicarage in Berkshire?

Lockert--hang it, must Lockert always be in his thoughts?

It was true, the thing he had been trying to ignore. The beautiful intimacy which for a fortnight Fran and he had found in their loneliness, her contentment to be with him and let the world go hang, had thinned and vanished, and she was straining away from him as ardently as ever before.

Mr. Hurd's bachelor dinner for Sam was at eight-thirty. Lockert and Fran left the Ritz at seven, to dine before the opera. Sam saw them off paternally, and most filially Fran cried, "I hope you'll have a beautiful time, Sam, and do give my greetings to Mr. Hurd. I'm sure he's really quite a good soul, really." But she did not look back to wave at him as he watched them down the corridor to the lift. She had tucked her arm into Lockert's; she was chattering, altogether absorbed.

For an hour Sam tramped the apartment, too lonely to think.

Hurd's dinner was given in a private room at the Dindonneau Restaurant in Soho. There was a horseshoe table with seats for thirty. Along the table little American flags were set in pots of forget-me-nots. Behind the chairman 's table was a portrait of President Coolidge, draped with red, white and blue bunting, and about the wall--Heaven knows where Hurd could have collected them all--were shields and banners of Yale and Harvard and the University of Winnemac, of the Elks, the Oddfellows, the Moose, the Woodmen, of the Rotarians, the Kiwanians, and the Zenith Chamber of Commerce, with a four-sheet poster of the Revelation car.

Fran would have sneered. . . .

Outside was the dark and curving Soho alley, with the foggy lights of a Singhalese restaurant, a French book-shop, a wig-maker's, an oyster bar. And the room was violently foreign, with frescoes by a sign-painter--or a barn-painter: Isola Bella, Fiesole, Castel Sant' Angelo. But Sam did not look at them. He--who but once in his life had attended a Rotary lunch--looked at the Rotary wheel, and his smile was curiously timid. There was no reason for it apparent to him, but suddenly these banners made him feel that in the chill ignobility of exile he was still Some One.

He felt the more Some One as he was introduced to the guests.

They had spent from a month to thirty years in England, and they were as different one from another as the exhibits at a Zoo, with the lion beside the monkey-cage. Yet in all of them was a hint of American heartiness and of that twang which is called "talking through the nose" because it consists in failing to talk through the nose. There was Stubbs of the Haymarket branch of the Pittsburgh and Western National Bank, a gray solid man of fifty, fanatic about golf. Young Ertman, the London correspondent of the Chicago Register, once a Rhodes scholar at Oxford, very select and literary. Young Suffern of the Baltimore Eagle, very red-faced and wide-shouldered and noisy. Doblin, manager of the English agency of the Lightfoot Sewing Machine Agency, old and thread-thin and gentle. Markart of the Orient Chewing Gum and Chicle Corporation; Knabe of the Serial Cash Registers; Fish of the American Forwarding Company; Smith of the Internation Tourist Agency; Nutthal of the Anglo-Peruvian Bank--he was Lancashire born but he had lived in Omaha for eighteen years and he was three hundred per cent. American. And a throng of American motor agents.

Each of them crunched Sam's hand and growled (only the Rhodes scholar's growl was more feline than canine): "Certainly is a mighty great pleasure to meet you. Staying over here long?"

Near the door was a side-table spread with Martini cocktails, Manhattan cocktails, Bronx cocktails, and bottles of Scotch, Canadian Club, American rye and Bourbon. Sam could not escape without four cocktails, and when he wavered to his seat beside A. B. Hurd, he had altogether forgotten that he had ever been lonely, that Fran was with Lockert.

There was a deal of noisy humor at the dinner; a deal of shouting the length of the table; a number of stories beginning "Jever hear the one about the two Jews--" And it must be said that Sam, privileged now to enjoy the suburbs of correct English society, enjoyed it more than any dinner this fortnight. He enjoyed it even when cognac and whisky sodas followed the dessert and some of the guests--free for only one evening a week from the American wives whom living in England had not weakened in their view of women's right to forbid men's rights--snatched the excuse to get quite reasonably drunk and to soar into American melody: "The Old Man Came Rolling Home," and "He Laid Jesse James in His Grave" and "Way Down on the Bingo Farm," with what they conceived to be a correct Cockney version of "She Was Poor but She Was Honest," all of them leading triumphantly up to:

> *My name is Yon Yonson,*
> *I come from Visconsin,*
> *I vork on a lumberyard dere,*
> *Ven I go down de street*
> *All de people I meet*
> *Dey saaaaaaay,*
> *"Vot's your name?"*
> *And I sa-aaaay*
> *My name is Yon Yonson,*
> *I come from Visconsin--*

It seemed a good song, at a certain stage of liquor, and they kept it up for ten minutes.

But between such high lights, Sam Dodsworth got in a semi-nar of inquiries about the question that to him, also, had become a disease: Is America the Rome of the world, or is it inferior to Britain and Europe? Or confusedly both?

Out of all the thirty, there were not ten whose speech showed that they had lived abroad. If occasionally they said "braces" instead of "suspenders," or "two bob" instead of "four bits," you would have supposed that they had been reading English fiction. There were not six who would ever have been taken for Englishmen by Americans, and not three who would have been taken for Englishmen by Englishmen.

Yet there were not more than six, Sam discovered incredu-lously, who wanted to return to America for the rest of their lives.

He had understood that hybrid cosmopolites with a fancy for titles and baccarat, eccentric artists who were fond of mistresses and chess, idlers who needed some one with whom to loaf, might prefer to live abroad. But that this should be true of the gallant thirty--good salesmen, up-and-coming authorities on cash registers and motor tires--was disturbing to him, and mystifying.

90

These men believed, and belligerently announced, that America was the "greatest country in the world," not only in its resources and increasing population and incomparable comforts of daily life, not only in its energy and mechanical ingenuity, but equally in its generosity, its friendliness, its humor, its aspiration for learning. Scarce one of them, Sam judged, but longed to see his own beloved quarter of America--

New York on a winter night, with the theaters blaring and the apartment-houses along Park Avenue vanishing up into the wild sky rosy from a million lights. Vermont on an autumn afternoon, with the maples like torches. Midsummer in Minnesota, where the cornfields talked to themselves, and across miles of rolling wheatland, dimpling to the breeze, you saw the tall red wheat- elevators and the spire of the German Catholic Church. The grave silence of the wilderness: plateaus among the scarred peaks of the Sierra Nevadas, painted buttes in Arizona, Wisconsin lakes caressing in dark waters the golden trunks of Norway pines. The fan-lights above serene old Connecticut doorways in Litchfield and Sharon. Proud cold sunsets in the last five minutes of the Big Game at Thanksgiving-time--Illinois vs. Chicago, Yale vs. Harvard-- yes, and quite as aching with sentimental and unforgettable and lost sweetness, Schnutz College vs. Maginnis Agricultural School. Cities of a quarter of a million people with fantastic smoky steel works, like maniac cathedrals, which had arisen in twenty years upon unpeopled sand-barrens. The long road and a rather shaggy, very adventurous family in a squeaky flivver, the new Covered Wagon, starting out to see all the world from Seattle to Tallahassee, stopping to earn their bacon and bread and oil by harvesting; singing at night in tourist camps on the edge of wide- lawned towns--

"I certainly do like to get back to Alabama--mighty nice girls there, and you talk about your Georgia terrapin--say, listen, boy," said Stubbs of the Pittsburgh and Western National Bank, "we got the swellest food in the world in Alabama."

And Primble of the International Films Distributing Agency drawled, "Just about once a year I certainly got to get back to the Ozark Mountains and go fishing."

But except for half a dozen homesick souls, each of them admitted that he was going to go on loving, boosting, and admiring America, and remain in Europe as long as he could.

Their confessions could have been summed up in the ruminations of Doblin, pro-consul of sewing-machines, doyen of the

American business-colony, old and thread-thin and gentle, who murmured (while the others listened, nodding, nervously shaking ashes from cigarettes, or holding their cigars cocked in the corners of their mouths):

"Well, I'll tell you the way I look at it personally. Strikes me that one-half or maybe two-thirds of the American people are the best fellows on earth--the friendliest and the most interested in everything and the jolliest. And I guess the remaining third are just about the worst crabs, the worst Meddlesome Matties, the most ignorant and pretentious fools, that God ever made. Male AND female! I'd be tickled to death to live in America IF. If we got rid of Prohibition, so a man could get a glass of beer instead of being compelled to drink gin and hootch. If we got rid of taking seriously a lot of self-advertising, half-educated preachers and editors and politicians, so that folks would develop a little real thinking instead of being pushed along by a lot of mental and moral policemen. If our streets weren't so God-awfully noisy. If there were a lot more cafes and a lot less autos--sorry, Mr. Dodsworth, you being a motor-manufacturer, but that slipped out and I guess I'll just have to stand by it.

"But the whole thing, the fundamental thing, is a lot harder to express than that. Nothing like so simple as just Prohibition. . . . Golly, the number of people who think they are getting profound when they talk about that one question! . . . The whole thing--Oh, there's more ease in living here! Your neighbors don't spy on you and gossip and feel it's their business to tell you how to live, way we do at home. Not that I've got anything to hide. I haven't been drunk for thirty years. I've been true to my wife--unless you count one time when I kissed a little widow on the Baltic, and by golly that's as far as it went! But if there's one thing that would make me go out for all the vices I ever heard of, it would be the thought of a lot of morality hounds sneaking after me all the time, the way they do in the States. And you get better servants here--yes, and the servants themselves like their work a deuce of a sight better than our red-neck hired girls in America, because they're skilled, they're respected here, they're secure, they don't have the womenfolks nosing into their ice-boxes and love-letters all day long! And business--Our greatest American myth is that we're so much more efficient than these Britishers and the folks on the Continent. All this high-pressure salesmanship bunk! Why say, I'll bet that stuff antagonizes more customers than it ever catches. And over here, they simply won't stand for it! An Englishman knows what he wants to buy, and he don't intend to be bullied into buying something else. And a Scotsman knows what he doesn't want to buy! Half our efficiency is just running around and making a lot of show and wasting time. I always picture the ideal 'peppy' American business man as a fellow who spends half his time having his letters filed away and the other half trying to find 'em again. And then--Englishman don't feel he's virtuous because he spends a lot of extra time in his office not doing anything special. He goes home early and gets in some golf or tennis or some gardening. Might even read a book! And he's got a hobby, so that when he retires he has something to do; doesn't just waste away from being bored to death when he's old, the way we do.

"The Englishman will work, and work hard, but he doesn't fall for the nonsense that work--any kind of work, for any purpose--is noble in itself. Why, when I go home--Well, there's old Emmanuel White, president of my company. He's seventy-two years old, and he's never taken a vacation. He's worth two million dollars, and he gets to the office at eight, and sometimes he stays there till eleven at night and goes snooping around to see if anybody's left a light turned on. Maybe he gets some fun out of it, but he sure doesn't look like it. He looks like he lived on vinegar, and to have a conference with him is just about as pleasant as tending a sick tiger. And the fellows of forty and forty-five that never relax even when they do take an afternoon off-- they drive like hell out to a golf course. Greatest myth in the world!

"But we're beginning to learn a little bit about leisure at home, I guess. That makes me hopeful that some day we may even get cured of optimism and oratory. But I don't expect it in my time, and you bet your sweet life I'm going to stay on here in England, even after I retire. Say! I've got a little place in Surrey, with an acre of ground and a rose garden. But I'm American, just's American as I ever was. And, thank God, there's enough Americans here so I can see a lot of 'em. I admire the English, but they make me feel kind of roughneck. But LIVE here- -you bet! Say, that's one of the best proofs that America is the greatest country in the world: Paris and London have become two of the nicest of American cities! Yes sir!"

Sam was rather bewildered. Doblin was the old-fashioned, Yankee, suramerican sort whom he preferred to all the strident new evangelists of business.

He was more bewildered when Fish of the American Forwarding Company--big jovial Fish, who had played center for the University of the Western Conference--chuckled:

"You bet! First year I was here, I was homesick all the time. I went home, and I intended to stay there. Well, I lasted just one year in that dear old Chicago! God, the Loop, the elevated, driving through that traffic out to Wilmette every evening, the eternal yow-yow-yow about investments and bridge! Didn't even enjoy golf! Golly, fellows worked at it! Felt guilty as hell if they were one stroke over yesterday! And most of 'em took up playing to get acquainted with possible customers at the club--sell 'em eighteen bonds in eighteen holes. I got transferred back here. I guess I'd enlist to fight for America against any blooming country in the world, but--Maybe America will get civilized. I hope so. I'm going to send both my boys back home to American universities, and then let 'em decide whether they want to remain or come back here. Maybe we ought to stay home and fight the blue- noses, not let 'em exile us. But life's short. Want to be a good patriot, but--Say! I wish you could see my house in Chelsea-- twenty minutes from Trafalgar Square, even in one of these non- motorized London taxis, and yet it's as quiet as a hick town in Nebraska. Quieter! Because there's no kids drinking gin and hollering in flivvers, and no evangelist in the big tent raising hell. Yes SIR!"

Sam was pondering.

He was coming to like England. Perhaps he really would live here. Take an interest in some motor agency. Have an Elizabethan black- and-white house in Kent, with ten acres. Join the American Club. These were good fellows--perhaps there were three or four who would even pass the censorship of Fran. He would not be lonely here. He would learn leisure. And think of getting old Tub to come over for a while in the summer! Trot all round England and Scotland with Tub in a car--play golf at St. Andrews--

Yes.

But he recalled the horrors of an arty tea to which Jack Starling had taken them in St. John's Wood. He recalled the tedium of dinner-parties--people dining solitarily in public. He recalled his discomfort in being unable to understand the violent differences between an Oxford man and a graduate of the University of London, between a public school man and one who abysmally was not. And yet--There was SOMETHING about life here--

He didn't feel that he had to hustle, when he walked the London streets. He didn't, just now, want to return to an office in Zenith and listen to vehement young men who made Patrick Henry orations about windshield-wipers; he didn't long again to study the schedules of a company which would provide seat-upholstery at .06774 cents cheaper a yard, or to listen to Doc Wimpole, the cut- up of the golf club, in his Swedish imitations or his celebrated way of greeting you:

"Well, here's the old cut-throat! How many widows and orphans have you stuck with your rotten old Revs this week?"

No!

He went home, after tremendously cordial handshakings, more blissful about his new role of required adventurousness than ever before . . . and hoping that Fran would not say, "Did you have an agreeable time with the great American commercial intellects?"

She would! She'd wake up, no matter how softly he came into the bedroom, and she'd say--(He had it all out, there in the taxicab.) She'd say, "Well, I hope you enjoyed yourself with Mr. Hurd and all the other hearty Rotarians!"

"Now you look here! I heard more good talk tonight, more talk that really got down to cases, than I've heard at any of your dinners where gentlemen try to talk like Members of Parliament and Members of Parliament try to talk like gentlemen--"

"Why, my dear Sam, we're becoming positively literary! The influence of dear Mr. Hurd is astonishing! Was his wife there? She'd do perfectly at a bachelor dinner!"

"Now you look here! I know what a profound scholar you are, and I know I'm a roughneck business man, but may I remind you that I did go to a quite well-known institution for young gentlemen in New Haven, and I have actually read several books, and furthermore--"

It was a complete triumph, there in the taxicab.

He came radiantly into their suite. On the couch, crushing her golden evening wrap, Fran lay sobbing.

He gaped from the doorway five full seconds before he chucked his opera hat at the table, dashed to her, plumped down on the couch, and cried:

"What is it? Sweet! What is it?"

She convulsively raised her face just enough to burrow it against his knee while she whimpered:

"I've always said--oh, damn!--I've always said it was really a compliment to a woman to be what they call 'insulted.' Well, maybe it is, but oh, Sam, I don't like it! I DON'T! Oh, I want to go home! Or anyway leave England. I can't face it. Probably it was my fault that--

"No, it wasn't! I swear it wasn't! I never gave him the slightest, littlest excuse to suppose that His Grace--Oh, God, how I hate that man! He's so supercilious, and what about? I ask you, what about? What is the fool after all but a failure, an international hobo? Even if his cousin IS the real thing! What is he? I ask you!

"It was like this. Oh, Sam, Sam darling, I hate to tell you, because I must have been at fault--partly. It was after the opera. I suggested to Clyde--to Major Lockert--that we might go somewhere and dance, but he said all the good places were so noisy--couldn't we just come up here and have a drink and talk. I didn't mind; I was a little tired. Well, at first, he was awfully nice. (Oh, I can see his line so clearly now, and it wasn't so bad, considering!) He sat--he sat right there in that chair--he sat there and he talked about his boyhood and how lonely he'd been. And you know what a fool I am about children--you know how I suffer at just the least little suggestion of anybody not having a happy childhood. Of course I almost cried. And then he said he was terribly inarticulate and shy (oh yes!) but he wanted to tell me how much it'd meant to know me-- I'd been a sweet feminine influence--honestly, I think he used just those words!--of course he doesn't have a sweet feminine influence more than two or three times a week!--you can imagine the kind of Indian girls he tells that to on his plantation!--how I hate him!

"But anyway, he told me what a regular little sister I'd been to him, and--being seven kinds of a fool, as you know--I fell for it, and first thing I knew, he was sitting here on the couch beside me, holding my hand. And I confess--Oh, I'm being terribly frank! If you ever are so beastly as to go and use this against me later, I'll KILL you, I swear I will! . . . I didn't mind the hand- holding a bit. . . . Am I a hussy? I'm afraid I could become one! . . . But anyway--I mean: He has some electricity about him; he's a very educated hand-holder; not too tight, and yet he sort of makes you shudder--

"But anyway, he held my hand as though it were some particularly sacred relic. And he went on telling me that my example had persuaded him that he must stop wandering and settle down with some glorious girl like me. And I believed it all! I felt like a Sister by a dying bedside!

"But anyway, he was going to cut out all this drifting and really do something with life. He SAID that! 'Do something with life!' I might have known!

"And then--

"Oh, you know what he said! I don't have to tell you. Probably you've said it to some cutie yourself! Only, if I ever catch you doing it, I'll KILL you! You and I are the model monogamists from now on, d'you understand? Anyway, you can guess what he said. Where was he to find the admirable spouse who'd be exactly like me?

"And of course I made noises like a purr-pussy!

"And the next thing I knew, he'd thrown his arms around me, and he was trying to kiss me, and he was at the same time trying to inform me that I'd led him on--Oh, I can sound funny about it, now, or try to, anyway. But it was pretty fairly ghastly. The idiot insisted on doing a real 'Woman, you have tempted me to perdition with your poisoned smile' sort of melodrama. Oh, Sam, Sam, Sam dear--you old darling! You're so DECENT! But I mean: When he found that I was most certainly not going to be embraced, he got awfully nasty. That's one thing he does do well! He said I'd led him on. He said that among 'civilized people' there were 'rules of the game,' and the way I'd let him kiss my shoulder--Oh yes, he did that, too, in the taxicab going to dinner. Oh, I AM being frank, probably disastrously frank! But, dear, don't treasure it up and use it against a pitiful fool that thought she was a woman of the world! And honestly, I really and truly did think, when he kissed my shoulder, that if I just ignored it he'd have sense enough to see that I wasn't taking any. 'Rules of the game among civilized people!' The fool! As if I didn't understand them just as well as he does, and maybe a lot better! But anyway--

"And maybe I LIKED his kissing my shoulder! Oh, I don't know! I don't know ANYTHING, after this ghastly evening! But anyway:

"He said it was my fault, and so on and so forth--you can imagine-- and then he saw that he couldn't bully me, and he was terribly apologetic about 'showing his true feelings'--the swine hasn't got any true feelings! Anyway, he kissed my ear and my nose--a rotten marksman!--and he pleaded and--Oh, I don't know why you should have to listen to all the ghastly details! Anyway, I kicked him out, and

he--oh, he was charming, my dear!--he went back to his delightful assertion that all American women are bloodless rotters, who get a kick
out of seeing men make fools of themselves and--

"Oh, oh yes, and he also said this. This really WAS pretty, and
it'll interest you particularly! Though it certainly wasn't very consistent
with his bleat about my being a bloodless siren! He said--he made it
quite clear that he didn't merely expect a few consoling kisses, and he
said that I didn't know how much sex passion there was concealed in
me. He said that you--he was so kind as to indicate that you were a
worthy motor-pedler and quite a nice kind friend, and probably you
could defend yourself if you were attacked by bandits, but you had no
sexual fire--'spiritual fire'--I think he said, to be exact--and I was what
he called 'unawakened,' and he was willing--bless his dear, kind,
neighborly soul!--he was willing to do the awakening.

"Oh, Sam, I'm trying to be funny about it, but actually I've
never been so insulted, so hurt, so horribly misunderstood, so inno-
cent--

"Or do YOU think I led him on, too?"

Through all her vehement chronicle, Sam had been sorry for
her, most successfully; he had tried to agree with her, not very successfully; and, while he stroked her hair, he had studied a print on the
wall.

He had not, till now, been very conscious of their sitting-room.
But in these seconds he so concentrated on it that he could never forget
one minutest detail: the walls, cornflower blue; the ceiling, dull gold; a
wing chair in cretonne with cabbage roses; the mahogany escritoire,
with elegant books of English memoirs, recently purchased by Fran,
on the shelves above the writing tablet, on which she had made neat
piles of the chaste Ritz stationery and the letters which were now beginning to come from home. The low table for tea, with the old silver
tea-service which she had excitedly purchased on Bond Street. He was
touched by the homemaking which she was always doing in hotel
suites. But most of all he had been inattentively absorbed by the colored print on the wall opposite him. It wasn't any print in particular. It
was what any aged and semi-literate artist would do. Yet at this sensitive moment it was fascinating to Sam, this picture of a young gallant,
rather leggy in tights, bent over a young woman with a smile and a
flowery hat, against a background of towers and roses.

He roused himself from the study of it as he heard her demand, "Or do you think I led him on?"

"No. I'm sure you didn't, Fran. But still--"

Suddenly he had no control over what he was saying; no relation to the man who was saying it:

"Oh, God, I'm so tired! Tired!"

"If you don't think I'M tired!"

"Look here, Fran. I'm not awfully accustomed to dealing with little lovers in the home. I haven't had that sort of life. Oh, I know you never had any idea of Lockert's taking your friendliness for love-making. He was a swine. I suppose it's up to me to go out and shoot him."

"Oh, don't be silly!"

"Well, I would feel a good deal like a fool, but if you want me to--" He had been warning himself not to say what he thought. Suddenly he was saying it:

"But as a matter of fact, I don't entirely blame Lockert. You were flirting with him--you were doing it down at Lord Herndon's-- even on the steamer you acted as if he was running the whole show for you. And he had some excuse for thinking he could grab you off. You have such a nice way of bawling me out right in his presence; you say, 'Do try to remember that Lady What's-her-name isn't used to Americans, and don't talk about Zenith,' and so on and so on, until you've got me as nervous as an ammeter, till I feel like a Middlewestern bull in a Bond Street china shop, and Lockert listens to it, and naturally he supposes that you think I'm a fool, while he's ace-high and--"

"Are there any other capital crimes that I've committed?"

"Yes. A few. You enjoy highhatting Hurd and decent fellows like that--you're so blame' courteous they feel like stable-boys--you play with 'em like a cat with a mouse--and Lockert's heard you doing it, and he sees you turning toward him for approval, and he thinks you think that he's so superior to me and my friends--"

"Now you listen to ME! I deny everything you say! I have NEVER nagged you! I have NEVER said anything to embarrass you! I think even YOU will admit that in some things I have slightly more tact and patience than you have! And then out of pure friendliness, entirely for your own sake, I try to help you to understand people that you've misjudged, and you say I've bullied you! Oh, it's perfectly beastly of you! And idiotic! If you wouldn't fly off the handle so easily, if you'd listen and let me help you, perhaps you wouldn't make such perfectly appalling breaks as you did the night when you insulted Lady Ouston and made everybody so frightfully uncomfortable--"

"But you backed me up! You said I was right!"

"Naturally! I said it out of loyalty to you. I'm always loyal to you. I've never yet failed you in that--or in anything else!"

"Oh, haven't you! I suppose you call it loyalty to be constantly hinting and suggesting that I'm merely an ignorant business man, whereas anybody--ANYBODY!--that has an English or French accent, any loafer living on women, is a gentleman and scholar! After all, I have managed to deal with a few European importers without feeling--"

"Go on! Explain that you're the great Herr Geheimrat Generaldirektor! That you invented and developed the entire motor industry! It's all so new and interesting! Oh, I've never wanted to say it, Sam, but you force me to! I have no question but that you've done well. There are very few more impressive people--in Zenith! But it happens that we are not in your dear Zenith, just now, but in England, and there are several things here that you don't know so much about, and that I do know! After all, this isn't my first trip to Europe! But you're too self-important to let me teach you! I certainly do not mean to hint that you're ill bred or common, but really--I hate to have to tell you this!-- you certainly do seem vulgar and ill bred to people who don't understand you--"

"To Lockert, I suppose!"

"--and to people who venture to believe that the great tradition of Europe is slightly superior to the pep and hustle of Zenith! I could teach you that tradition, but you won't let me--"

"I suppose you're an authority!"

"I certainly am, comparatively! After all, I have been in Europe before! And my father's house was always full of Europeans. And I've read more French and German and British books, these twenty years, than you have detective stories! They accept me here. Oh, Sam, if you'd only let me help you--"

"My dear child, you can't at the same time pan me for my vulgarity and be the tender little mother! That's too damn' much to stand! And as a matter of fact, when it comes to vulgarity--Now where the devil are all the cigarettes?"

Instantly it was more important to find the cigarettes without which no real smoker can be comfortable and emotional and quarrel actively than it was to enjoy the pain of hatred. They suspended battle to join in the hunt. He turned out his dinner-jacket, rammed his hands into the pockets of his overcoat, and yanked out bureau drawers, while she popped up from the couch to look triumphantly--then bleakly--into the black and scarlet Russian box which she had bought yesterday.

"And another thing--another thing--But where ARE those cigarettes? I know I had half a package of Gold Flakes left, and some Camels," he muttered, as he searched.

It was she who thought of telephoning to the office; she who felt that she knew how to use servants, at no matter what time of night, while he would always be Americanishly shy of them.

She sat on the edge of the couch, she smoothed her skirt, she bent her head with irritating graciousness to receive a light from him when the cigarettes had come, and graciously, most irritatingly, she said:

"Sam, I hate to have to point it out again, but it really doesn't get you very far in a discussion to lose your temper and use big, strong, he-man words like 'damn' and 'the devil.' They aren't so awfully novel and startling to me! And as usual, you're merely missing the point. I'm neither 'panning' you, as you so elegantly put it, nor am I trying to mother you. I'm always willing to listen to your opinions on golf and how to invest my money. I merely expect you to admit that there may be a few things in which the poor ignorant female may know a little bit more than you do! Oh, you're like all the other American men! You speak no known language. You don't know Rodin from Mozart. You have no idea whether France or England controls Syria. You--you, the motor expert!--can never remember whether a lady should be on your right or your left in a car. You're bored equally by Bach and Antheil. You're bored by going with me to shop for the most divine Russian embroidery. You can't fence with a pretty woman at dinner. And-- But those are just symptoms! Separately, they don't matter. The thing is that you haven't the mistiest notion of what European civilization is, basically--of how the tradition of leisure, honor, gallantry, inherent cultivation, differs from American materialism. And you don't want to learn. You never COULD be European--"

"Fran! Stop sneering!"

"I am not sneer--"

"Stop it! Dear! I don't pretend to have any of these virtues. I guess it's perfectly true: I never could become European. But why should I? I'm American, and glad of it. And you know I never try to prevent your being as European as you want to. But don't take out your soreness at Lockert on me. Please!"

His encircling arms said more, and he nestled her head on his shoulder while she sobbed:

"I know. I'm sorry. But oh--"

She sat up, spoke resolutely.

"I'm terribly ashamed about this Lockert business. Shamed right down through me. I can't stand it! Sam, I want to leave England at once. I can't stand staying in this country with that man, thinking he's here laughing at me. Or else I WILL be asking you to go out and shoot him, and the law here is so prejudiced! I want to leave for France. NOW!"

"But golly, Fran, I like this country! I'm getting to know London. I like it here. France'll be so foreign."

"Precisely! I want it to be! I want to start all over. I won't make a fool of myself again. Oh, Sam, darling, let's run away, like two school-children, hand in hand! And think! The joy of seeing blue siphons and brioches and kiosks and red sashes and red- plush wall-seats and fat lady cashiers! And hearing 'B'jour, M'sieu et Madame,' the way they say it when you're leaving a shop-- like a little bell! Let's go!"

"Well, I did intend to see some aeroplane factories here. Fact I had a date--"

They went to Paris in four days.

The Channel steamer seemed to him like a greyhound--small, slim, power evident in its squat thick funnel. The delight of sea-faring which he had found on the Atlantic came to him again in the narrow gangways 'tween decks, suggesting speed in their sharp curve toward the bow. When he had established Fran in a chair on the boat deck, amid piles of snobbish blond luggage, he slipped down to the bar.

There is about a ship's bar, any bar of any ship, however small, a cheerfulness unknown elsewhere in life's dark and Methodist vale. It has the snug security of an English inn, with a suggestion of adventure as the waves flicker past the port-holes, as you speculate about the passengers--men coming from China and Brazil and Saskatchewan, men going to Italy and Liberia and Siam. As he clumped up to join Fran, Sam forgot, in waxing anticipation of the Continent, his regret for England, and he kept that anticipation even while he listened on deck to a proper cross-Channel conversation among a ripe Wiltshire vicar, his aunt, and his aunt's dear friend, Mrs. Illingworth-Dobbs:

"Oh yes, we shall stop in Florence most of the time."

"Shall you stop at the Stella Rossa ancora una volta?"

"No, I really think we shall stop at Mrs. Brown-Bloater's pension. You know we've always stopped at the Stella Rossa, but it's really too outrageous. Last year they began to charge extra for tea!"

"Extra? For TEA?"

"Yes. And it used to be quite nice there! The guests were people one could know. But now it's filled with Jews and Americans and unmarried couples and even Germans!"

"Dreadful! But Florence is so lovely."

"Charming!"

"So artistic!"

"Yes, so artistic. And Sir William is taking a villa there for the season."

"I say, that will be jolly for you."

"Si, si! Sara una cosa veramente--uh--really charming. Sir William is SO fond of the artistic. It will be quite like home, having him there. _And I have heard definitely from Mrs. Brown- Bloater that she is not charging extra for tea_!"

Sam forgot the prospect of a Continent full of Mrs. Illing-worth- Dobbses; he even forgot, in the zest of the steamer's speed, Fran's fretfulness that the boat was going up and down a good deal, for which she seemed to feel that he was to blame. The bow hit the waves like a mailed fist. There was just enough motion to show that he really was at sea, and as they left the English coast and cut into the fresh breeze, they plunged past foreign-looking craft: a French steam-trawler lurching up the Channel, with meaty little sailors in striped jerseys waving at them, a German coaster, a Dutch East Indiaman, rolling through the sun-crisped tide.

The sailors who passed their deck chairs, the officers on the bridge, they were all so sturdy, so mahogany-faced, so reliable, so British.

A man with a long blond mustache and a monocle strolled past. Fran insisted that he was Thomas Cook, of the Sons. And what was Karl Baedeker like? she speculated. Short and square, with a short square brown beard and double-thick spectacles through which he peered at menus and ruined temples and signs reading "Roma 3 chilometri."

"Yes, and what is Mr. Bass like? And the Haig Brothers? I wonder if they're like the Smith Brothers," said Sam, and, "Gosh, I'm enjoying this, Fran!"

Then he saw a pale line, which was the coast of France.

But he tramped aft, to look back toward England. He fancied that he could see the shadow of its cliffs. Doubtless it was a distant cloud-bank that he saw, but he imagined the cool and endearing hills, the welcoming crooked streets, the wholesome faces.

"England! Perhaps I'll never see it again. . . . Fran and Lockert, they've taken it from me. . . . But I love it. America is my wife and daughter, but England is my mother. And these fools talk about a possible war between Britain and America! If that ever came--I thought Debs was foolish to go to jail as a protest against war, but I guess I understand better how he felt now. 'If I forget thee, O England, let my right hand forget her cunning, if I do not remember thee, let my tongue cleave to the roof of my mouth.' How did that go, in chapel? Oh yes: 'If I prefer not Jerusalem--London--above my chief joy'! Well. I never could prefer England above America. But next to America--Oh, Lord, I'd liked to've stayed there! The Dodsworths were in England three thousand years, maybe, where they've been in America only three hundred.

"England!"

Then he turned eagerly toward France.

They crept into harbor, past the breakwater with its tiny lighthouses, bumped along a rough stone pier, saw advertisements of strange drinks in a strange language, and were flooded with small, shrieking, blue-bloused porters; heard children speaking French as though it were a natural language; and for the first time in his life Samuel Dodsworth was in the grasp of a real Foreign Land.

CHAPTER 12

Sam had remained calm amid the frenzy of a Detroit Automobile Show; he had stalked through the crush of a New Year's Eve on Broadway, merely brushing off the bright young men with horns and feather ticklers; but in the Calais customs-house he was appalled. The porters shrieked ferocious things like "attonshion" as they elbowed past, walking mountains of baggage; the passengers jammed about the low baggage platform; the customs inspectors seemed to Sam cold-eyed and hostile; all of them bawled and bleated and wailed in what sounded to him like no language whatever; and he remembered that he had four hundred cigarettes in his smaller bag.

The porter who had taken their bags on the steamer had shouted something that sounded like "catravan deuce"--Fran said it meant that he was Porter Number Ninety-two. Then Catravan Deuce had malignantly disappeared, with their possessions. Sam knew that it was all right, but he didn't believe it. He assured himself that a French porter was no more likely to steal their bags than a Grand Central red-cap--only, he was quite certain that Catravan Deuce had stolen them. Of course he could replace everything except Fran's jewelry without much expense but--Damn it, he'd hate to lose his old red slippers--

He was disappointed at so flabby an ending when he found Catravan Deuce at his elbow in the customs room, beaming in a small bearded way and shouldering aside the most important passengers to plank their baggage down on the platform for examination.

Sam was proud of Fran's French (of Stratford, Connecticut) when the capped inspector said something quite incomprehensible and she answered with what sounded like "ree-an." He felt that she was a scholar; he felt that he was untutored and rusty; he depended on her admiringly. And then he opened the smaller bag and the four hundred cigarettes were revealed to the inspector.

The inspector looked startled, he gaped, he spread out his arms, and protested in the name of liberty, equality, fraternity, and indemnities. Fran tried to answer, but her French stumbled and fell, and she turned to Sam, all her airy competence gone, wailing, "I can't understand what he says! He--he talks patois!"

At her appeal, Sam suddenly became competent, ready to face the entire European Continent, with all appertaining policemen, laws, courts, and penitentiaries.

"Here! I'll get somebody!" he assured her, and to the customs inspector, who was now giving a French version of the Patrick Henry oration, he remarked, "Just a MO-ment! Keep your shirt on!"

He had a notion of finding the English vicar to whom he had listened on the Channel steamer. "Fellow seems to know European languages." He wallowed through the crowd as though he were making a touch-down, and saw on a cap the thrice golden words "American Express Company." The American Express man beamed and leaped forward at something in the manner with which Mr. Samuel Dodsworth of the Revelation Motor Company suggested, "Can you come and do a little job of interpreting for me?" . . . Sam felt that for a moment he was being Mr. Samuel Dodsworth, and not Fran Dodsworth's husband. . . . And for something less than a moment he admitted that he was possibly being the brash Yankee of Mark Twain and Booth Tarkington. And he could not successfully be sorry for it.

The American Express man saw them on the waiting train (a very bleak and tall and slaty train it seemed to Sam); he prevented Sam from tipping the porter enough to set him up in a shop. And so Sam and Fran were alone in a compartment, safe again till Paris.

Sam chuckled, "Say, I guess I'll have to learn the French for two phrases: 'How much?' and 'Go to hell.' But--Sweet! We're in France--in Europe!"

She smiled at him; she let him off and didn't even rebuke him for his Americanism. They sat hand in hand, and they were more intimately happy than since the day they had sailed from America. They were pleased by everything: by the battery of red and golden bottles on their table at lunch, by the deftness with which the waiter sliced the cone of ice cream, by the mysterious widow who was trying to pick up the mysterious Frenchman who combined a checked suit and a red tie with a square black beard--such a beard, murmured Fran, as it was worth crossing the Atlantic to behold.

He was stimulated equally by the "foreignness" of the human spectacle flickering past the window of their compartment--women driving ox-carts, towns with sidewalk cafes, and atrocious new houses of yellow brick between lumpy layers of stone picked out in red mortar--and the lack of "foreignness" in the land itself. Somehow it wasn't quite right that French trees and grass should be of the same green, French earth of the same brown, French sky of the same blue, as in a natural, correct country like America. After the tight little fenced fields of England, the wide Picardy plains, green with approaching April, seemed to him extraordinarily like the prairies of Illinois and Iowa. If it was a little disappointing, not quite right and decent after he had gone and taken so long and expensive a journey, yet he was pleased by that sense of recognition which is one of the most innocent and egotistic of human diversions, that feeling of understanding and of mastering an observation. He was as pleased as a side-street nobody when in his newspaper he sees the name of a man he knows.

"I'm enjoying this!" said Sam.

He had been accustomed to "sizing up" American towns; he could look from a Pullman window at Kalamazoo or Titus Center and guess the population within ten per cent. He could, and with frequency he did; he was fascinated by figures of any sort, and for twenty years he had been trying to persuade Fran that there was nothing essentially ignoble in remembering populations and areas and grade- percentages and the average life of tires. He had been able to guess not too badly at the size of British towns; he had not been too greatly bewildered by anything in England, once he was over the shock of seeing postmen with funny hats, and taxicabs with no apparent speed above neutral. But in Paris, as they bumped and slid and darted from the Gare du Nord to their hotel, he could not be certain just what it was that he was seeing.

Fran was articulate enough about it. She half stood up in the taxi, crying, "Oh, look, Sam, look! Isn't it adorable! Isn't it too exciting! Oh, the darling funny little ZINCS! And the Cointreau ads, instead of chewing gum! These bald-faced high white houses! Everybody so noisy, and yet so gay! Oh, I ADORE it!"

But for Sam it was a motion picture produced by an insane asylum; it was an earthquake with a volcano erupting and a telephone bell ringing just after he'd gone to sleep; it was lightning flashes and steam whistles and newspaper extras and war.

Their taxicab, just missing an omnibus, sliding behind its rear platform. A policeman, absurdly little, with an absurd white baton. Two priests over glasses of beer at a cafe. Silver gray everywhere, instead of London's golden brown. Two exceedingly naked plaster ladies upholding a fifth-story balcony. Piles of shoddy rugs in front of a shop, and beside them a Frenchman looking utterly content with his little business, instead of yearning at the department store opposite and feeling guilty as he would in New York or Chicago or Zenith. Fish. Bread. Beards. Brandy. Artichokes. Apples. Etchings. Fish. A stinking-looking alley. A splendid sweeping boulevard. Circular tin structures whose use he dared not suspect and which gave him a shocking new notion of Latin proprieties and of the apparently respectable and certainly bearded gentlemen who dashed toward them. Many books, bound in paper of a thin-looking yellow. An incessant, nerve-cracking, irritating, exhilarating blat-blat-blat of nervous little motor horns. Buildings which in their blankness seemed somehow higher than American skyscrapers ten times as high. A tiny, frowsy, endearing facade of a house which suggested the French Revolution and crazed women in red caps and kirtled skirts. A real artist (Sam decided), a being in red beard, wide black hat, and a cloak, with a dog-eared marble-paper-covered portfolio under his arm. Gossiping women, laughing, denouncing, forgiving, laughing. Superb public buildings, solid-looking as Gibraltar. Just missing another taxi, and the most admirable cursing by both chauffeurs--

"This certainly is a busy town. But not much traffic control, looks to me," said Samuel Dodsworth, and his voice was particularly deep and solemn, because he was particularly confused and timid.

It was at the Grand Hotel des Deux Hemispheres et Dijon that he was able to reassume the pleasant mastery with which (he hoped) he had been able to impress Fran at the Calais customs. The assistant manager of the hotel spoke excellent English, and Sam had never been entirely at a loss so long as his opponent would be decent and speak a recognizable language.

Lucile McKelvey, of Zenith, had told Fran that the Hemispheres was "such a nice, quiet hotel," and Sam had wired for reservations from London. By himself, he would doubtless have registered and taken meekly whatever room was given him. But Fran insisted on seeing their suite, and they found it a damp, streaked apartment looking on a sunless courtyard.

"Oh, this won't do at all!" wailed Fran. "Haven't you something decent?"

The assistant manager, a fluent Frenchman from Roumania via Algiers, looked them up and down with that contempt, that incomparable and enfeebling contempt, which assistant managers reserve for foreigners on their first day in Paris.

"We are quite full up," he sniffed.

"You haven't anything else at all?" she protested.

"No, Madame."

Those were the words, but the tune was, "No, you foreign nuisance-- jolly lucky you are to be admitted here at all--I wonder if you two really ARE married--well, I'll overlook that, but I shan't stand any Yankee impertinence!"

Even the airy Fran was intimidated, and she said only, "Well, I don't like it--"

And then Samuel Dodsworth appeared again.

His knowledge of Parisian hotels and their assistant managers was limited, but his knowledge of impertinent employees was vast.

"Nope," he said. "No good. We don't like it. We'll look elsewhere."

"But Monsieur has engaged this suite!"

The internationalist and the provincial looked at each other furiously, and it was the assistant manager whose eyes fell, who looked embarrassed, as Sam's paws curled, as the back of his neck prickled with unholy wrath.

"Look here! You know this is a rotten hole! Do you want to send for the manager--the boss, whatever you call him?"

The assistant manager shrugged, and left them, coldly and with speed.

Rather silently, Sam lumbered beside Fran down to their taxi. He supervised the reloading of their baggage, and atrociously overtipped every one whom he could coax out of the hotel.

"Grand Universel!" he snapped at the taxi-driver, and the man seemed to understand his French.

In the taxi he grumbled, "I TOLD you I had to learn the French for 'Go to hell.'"

A silence; then he ruminated, "Glad we got out of there. But I bullied that poor rat of a clerk. Dirty trick! I'm sorry! I'm three times as big as he is. Stealing candy from a kid! Dirty trick! I see why they get sore at Americans like me. Sorry, Fran."

"I adore you!" she said, and he looked mildly astonished.

At the Grand Universel, on the Rue de Rivoli, they found an agreeable suite overlooking the Tuileries, and twenty times an hour, as she unpacked, Fran skipped to the window to gloat over Paris, the Casanova among cities.

Their sitting-room seemed to him very pert and feminine in its paneled walls covered with silky yellow brocade, its fragile chairs upholstered in stripes of silver and lemon. Even the ponderous boule cabinet was frivolous, and the fireplace was of lively and rather indecorous pink marble. He felt that it was a light-minded room, a room for sinning in evening clothes. All Paris was like that, he decided.

Then he stepped out on the fretted iron balcony and looked to the right, to the Place de la Concorde and the beginning of the Champs Elysees, with the Chamber of Deputies across the Seine. He was suddenly stilled, and he perceived another Paris, stately, aloof, gray with history, eternally quiet at heart for all its superficial clamor.

Beneath the quacking of motor horns he heard the sullen tumbrils. He heard the trumpets of the Napoleon who had saved Europe from petty princes. He heard, without quite knowing that he heard them, the cannon of the Emperor who was a Revolutionist. He heard things that Samuel Dodsworth did not know he had heard or ever could hear.

"Gee, Fran, this town has been here a long time, I guess," he meditated. "This town knows a lot," said Samuel Dodsworth of Zenith. "Yes, it knows a lot."

And, a little sadly, "I wish I did!"

There are many Parises, with as little relation one to another as Lyons to Monte Carlo, as Back Bay to the Dakota wheatfields. There is the trippers' Paris: a dozen hotels, a dozen bars and restaurants, more American than French; three smutty revues; three railroad stations; the Cafe de la Paix; the Eiffel Tower; the Arc de Triomphe; the Louvre; shops for frocks, perfumes, snake-skin shoes, and silk pajamas; the regrettable manners of Parisian taxi-drivers; and the Montmartre dance-halls where fat, pink-skulled American lingerie-buyers get drunk on imitation but inordinately expensive champagne, to the end that they put on pointed paper hats, scatter confetti, conceive themselves as Great Lovers, and in general forget their unfortunate lot.

The students' Paris, round about the Sorbonne, very spectacled and steady. The fake artists' Paris, very literary and drunk and full of theories. The real artists' Paris, hidden and busy and silent. The cosmopolites' Paris, given to breakfast in the Bois, to tea at the Ritz, and to reading the social columns announcing who has been seen dining with princesses at Ciro's--namely, a Paris whose chief joy is in being superior to the trippers.

There is also reported to be a Paris inhabited by no one save three million Frenchmen.

It is said that in this unknown Paris live bookkeepers and electricians and undertakers and journalists and grandfathers and grocers and dogs and other beings as unromantic as people Back Home.

Making up a vast part of all save this last of the Parises are the Americans.

Paris is one of the largest, and certainly it is the pleasantest, of modern American cities. It is a joyous town, and its chief joy is in its jealousies. Every citizen is in rivalry with all the others in his knowledge of French, of museums, of wine, and of restaurants.

The various castes, each looking down its nose at the caste below, are after this order: Americans really domiciled in Paris for years, and connected by marriage with the French noblesse. Americans long domiciled, but unconnected with the noblesse. Americans who have spent a year in Paris--those who have spent three months--two weeks--three days--half a day--just arrived. The American who has spent three days is as derisive toward the half-a- day tripper as the American resident with smart French relatives is toward the poor devil who has lived in Paris for years but who is there merely for business.

And without exception they talk of the Rate of Exchange.

And they are all very alike, and mostly homesick.

They insist that they cannot live in America, but, except for a tenth of them who have really become acclimated in Europe, they are so hungry for American news that they subscribe to the home paper, from Keokuk or New York or Pottsville, and their one great day each week is that of the arrival of the American mail, on which they fall with shouts of "Hey, Mamie, listen to this! They're going to put a new heating plant in the Lincoln School." They know quite as well as Sister Louisa, back home, when the Washington Avenue extension will be finished. They may ostentatiously glance daily at Le Matin or Le Journal, but the Paris editions of the New York Herald and the Chicago Tribune they read solemnly, every word, from the front page stories-- "Congress to Investigate Election Expenses," and "Plans Transatlantic Aeroplane Liners" to the "News of Americans in Europe," with its tidings that Mrs. Witney T. Auerenstein of Scranton entertained Geheimrat and Frau Bopp at dinner at the Bristol, and that Miss Mary Minks Meeton, author and lecturer, has arrived at the Hotel Pedauque.

Each of these castes is subdivided according to one's preference for smart society or society so lofty that it need not be smart, society given to low bars and earnest drinking, the society of business exploitation, or that most important society of plain loafing. Happy is he who can cleave utterly to one of these cliques; he can find a group of fellow zealots and, drinking or shopping or being artistic, be surrounded with gloriously log- rolling comrades.

But Sam Dodsworth was unfortunate, for his wife panted to combine smartness with an attention to Art, while he himself preferred business and the low bars.

For all of Fran's superiority to "sight-seeing," they were at first lonely in Paris, and Sam was able to drag her to all the places mentioned in the guide-books. They danced at Zelli's; they went up the Eiffel Tower and she came near to being sick in corners; thrice they went to the Louvre; and once he cajoled her into the New York Bar for a whisky and soda and spirited conversation with an unknown man about skiing and the Bronx. She showed even more zest than he in finding new small restaurants--he would have been content to return every night to the places in which he had conquered the waiters and learned the wine-list.

And, curiously, he enjoyed galleries and picture-exhibitions more than she.

Fran had read enough about art; she glanced over the studio magazines monthly, and she knew every gallery on Fifth Avenue. But, to her, painting, like all "culture," was interesting only as it adorned her socially. In story-books parroting the Mark Twain tradition, the American wife still marches her husband to galleries from which he tries to sneak away; but in reality Sam's imagination was far more electrified by blue snow and golden shoulders and dynamic triangles than was Fran's. Probably he would have balked at the blurs of Impressionism and the jazz mathematics of Cubism, but it chanced that the favorite artist just this minute was one Robinoff, who did interiors pierced with hectic sunshine hurled between the slats of Venetian blinds, or startling sun-rays striking into dusky woodlands, and at these (while Fran impatiently wanted to get on to tea) Sam stared long and contentedly, drawing in his breath as though he smelled the hot sun.

In every phase Fran was as incalculable about "sight-seeing" as about liking his business associates. One day she was brazen enough to be discovered with the tourists' badge, the red Baedeker, unconcealed; the next she wouldn't even sit with him at a sidewalk cafe--at the Napolitain or the Closerie-des-Lilas.

"But why not?" he protested. "Best place to see the world go by. Everybody goes to 'em."

"Smart people don't."

"Well, I'm not smart!"

"Well, I am!"

"Then you ought to be smart enough to not care what anybody thinks!"

"Perhaps I am. . . . But I don't care to be seen sitting with a lot of trippers in raincoats."

"But you sat in a cafe yesterday, and enjoyed it. Don't you remember the beggar that sang--"

"Exactly! I've had enough of it! Oh, if you want to go and yearn over your dear American fellow tourists, by all means go, my dear Samuel! I am going to the Crillon and have a decent tea."

"And yearn over the dear fellow American tourists that happen to be rich!"

"Is it necessary for you always to quarrel with me because I want to do what I want to do? I'm not keeping you from sitting on your sidewalks. Don't go to the Crillon! Go to one of your beloved American bars, if you want to, and scrape up acquaintance with a lot of drunken business men--"

They compromised on going to the Crillon.

He puzzled over her feeling that it was a duty to keep herself fashionable in the eyes of the choice people who did not know that she existed. He could understand that back in Zenith she might have a good human satisfaction in being more snobbish than the matron across the street, in the ancient sport of "putting it over on the neighbors." He had been unrighteously pleased when he had seen her better dressed than her dear friend and resented rival, Lucile McKelvey. "Good girl," he had crowed; "you were the best- dressed wench in the room!"

But why should it matter to Fran that a strange Parisian aristocrat passing in a carriage might some day see them sitting contentedly at a cafe and arch her brows at them?

He admitted that the serene and classic Place des Vosges with the Carnavalet Museum was perhaps more select than Pat's Chicago Bar; that caneton presse might be a more elegant food than corn fritters at the Savannah Grill. "But," he fretted, "why can't you enjoy both--as long as you DO enjoy 'em? Nobody's hired us to come here and be stylish! We haven't got any duty involved! Back home there may have been a law against enjoying ourselves the way we wanted to, but there's none here!"

"My dear Sam, it's a matter of keeping one's self-respect. It's like the Englishman, all alone in the jungle, who always dresses for dinner."

"Yes, I've read about him! In the first place, he probably didn't do it, and in the second place, if he did he was a chump! That's how I've always figured it."

"You would! You couldn't understand what it meant to him--"

"Well, if all that stood between him and losing his self-respect was a hard-boiled shirt-front, I guess he might as well have let it slide! If I can't be self-respectful in a flannel shirt, I'm about ready to jump off the dock and--"

"Oh, you simply can't UNDERSTAND!"

They had never had much time in Zenith for a serious attention to quarreling and being domestically vulgar. All day he had been at the office; most evenings they had seen other people; on Sunday there had been golf and relatives. They had time a-plenty now, equally for quarreling and for intimate and adventurous happiness together. One day they wrangled--and endlessly, because they were not quarreling over any one thing in particular but over the differences in their philosophies of life; the next they went off (and sometimes she was simple and gay enough to let him carry sandwiches somewhat mussily in his pocket) to explore the Forest of Fontainebleau, and they laughed as they walked through groves shivering with April.

He was becoming acquainted with her and, sometimes, slightly, with himself.

He saw little enough of Frenchmen outside of hotel-servants, waiters, shopmen, but what he did see of them, what he saw of the surface of French life, puzzled him. Many travelers in like case take out their confusion in resentment, and damn the whole nation as trivial and mad. But there was in Sam a stubborn wish to get in behind any situation that he came across. He was not one to amuse himself by novelties, by making scenes, by collecting curious people, even overmuch by travel, but once he was dragged into something new he wanted to understand it, and he had a touch of humility, a deep and sturdy recognition of his own ignorance, whenever he could not understand.

And he could not understand these Frenchmen.

He watched them in cafes, at the theater, in shops, in trains to Tours and Versailles. How was it that they could sit, not restless, playing dominoes or chattering, over nothing more beguiling than glasses of coffee (and why was it that they drank coffee in glasses, anyway, instead of in cups)?

They liked talking so much. What the deuce did they find to talk about, hour on hour? How could they stand it without something to DO?

Why were there so few grassy yards about the houses? How was it that the most respectable old couples, silvery old men and crouched little old women, were willing to be seen at ordinary cafes in the evening, when their counterparts back home considered the saloon, the cafe, as the final haunt of the abominable? He saw the French people being gracious in shops, beaming on the babies in the Luxembourg Gardens, laughing together as they paraded the streets, and he decided that they were the soul of kindliness. He saw a Frenchman scowl at American barbarians for daring to enter his quarter-filled railway compartment, he heard Fran being atrociously denounced by a recently smiling, buxom, clean, wholesome shop-woman when Fran insisted that she had been overcharged ten centimes for dry-cleaning a pair of gloves, and he decided that the French were rude and mean to a point of hatefulness . . . and that his Fran showed an enjoyment of squabbling which was a little disturbing to him.

He saw the Louvre, the silks in shops on the Place Vendome, the trimness of their own apartment at the Grand Universel, and he decided that the French had the best taste in the world. He saw the department stores with their atrocious brass-fretted windows, their displays of fish and fowl and Marquise-in-a-garden chromos, of buffets carved with wooden blobs, of chairs that were even more violently high-colored than they were uncomfortable; he saw, in the haughty Parc Monceau, the imported ruins; he saw intelligent- seeming Frenchmen snickering over smutty post-cards and the eternal, unchanging pictures of naked young women in Vie Parisienne and Le Rire; and he decided that the French had no taste whatever.

But behind all his decisions was the decision that Sam Dodsworth would never be anything save bewildered by foreign ways, while Fran might, perhaps, take to them so eagerly that their companionship would be smashed forever.

CHAPTER 13

Sam was used enough to New York hotels, and he had spent occasional fortnights at summer inns of Northern Michigan, Maine, the Berkshires. But he had never known the existence of the prosperous refugees from life who cling for years to hotels and pensions, who are mothered by chambermaids, fathered by concierges, befriended only by room-waiters--if they find any waiters kind enough and idle enough to be patient with their longing to gossip.

And he did not like it.

He felt as though he were living in an Old People's Home. The attention of the servants made him feel old; the elevator man infuriated him by placing a hand under his arm to help him out of an elevator which had stopped a whole inch above the floor; the page boy in the lobby infuriated him by spinning the revolving door--and usually spinning it so artfully that one blade just missed Sam's nose; the head waiter infuriated him by inquiring, as though Sam had never heard of menus, "A little soup this evening, Mr. Samuels?" and most of all he was infuriated by the room-waiters who were each morning astonished that he should desire eggs in addition to his Continental Breakfast, who fussed over knives and forks, who pushed up chairs and snatched away the pleasant litter of newspapers, and who held out his napkin as though he were too feeble to lift it for himself.

Yet he was dependent on them. Though Fran was making much now of reading the Matin daily and of knowing all about art exhibitions and the hours when theaters began, she had to turn to the tall and patronizing concierge for information about what train to take to Versailles--where to buy slippers--who was the best American dentist--how much one ought to pay for a lacquered Japanese cigarette case--why the deuce Mathilde et Cie. hadn't delivered the evening scarf they'd promised for this afternoon--and just what WAS the general reputation of Mathilde et Cie. for delivering things and for overcharging?

He sank heavily into accepting the hotel as his natural dwelling, as a prisoner sinks into accepting a jail. Presently he was not bothered by the devious way from the elevator to their suite--to the right, sharp turning right again, turning left by that dusty old trunk with the red and green stripes which had apparently stood there in the corridor forever, then seventh door on the left--the door with the long scratch under the knob. He came to accept it as any other peasant accepts the long way to his hut, dark and meaningless and weary to tired legs. He was no longer annoyed by the too open-work and too generally brassy and light-minded appearance of the French elevator; he learned that the elevator was the "lift" or the "ascenseur" or indeed almost anything except the "elevator"; he learned that the room service-bell never worked and that the best way to get a waiter was to stand in the door and bellow "Gar-song"; and he learned that the Mr. Samuel Dodsworth who once had been received with a certain deference in the General Offices of the Revelation Motor Company in Zenith was fortunate here when the Greek boots nodded to him in the hall.

He even got used to living in a lack of privacy like that of a monkey in a Zoo. After a time he could without self-consciousness sit and read the Paris editions of the American papers in the old- fashioned lounge of the hotel--he went there daily, despite having a drawing-room of his own, in a sneaking, never-admitted hope that some day he would be recognized and picked up by a fellow American exile. The lounge was modern in its small and hideous tables covered with pebbled beaten brass, its fountain, with Neptune undistinguishable from any other marble tombstone, and the number of cocktails gulped daily at five o'clock by young ladies who spoke Chicagoese with a very fair imitation of a French accent. But the modernity of the lounge had not run to new chairs; they were of red and golden plush, made delicate and chaste with antimacassars, and looking rather as though they had been dedicated by Napoleon III.

It had not been easy for Sam to get used to reading in the lounge, to dressing his mind in public. He was accustomed to the communism of clubs, but there, no one paid attention to any one else. In the lounge, no one had very much to do except to pay attention. They stared, and always resentfully. The English mother and daughter who were the most exclusive and the most resentful toward strangers were precisely the people who spent the most time in the lounge being exclusive and resentful. The French provincial magnate who had arrived just that morning was precisely the person who looked with the greatest irritation at a veteran like Sam, now settled here two whole weeks, when Sam annoyed him by taking the next chair and moving it two inches. And there were always elderly, slightly belching, very hairy couples who spent all their time catching his eye and then looking indignant because he had caught their eyes.

But after a fortnight he could enter the lounge, ignore the human furniture, and rustle his newspaper with almost as much relaxation as he had felt in his library in Zenith.

He was becoming accustomed to the home of the homeless.

He discovered slowly, and always with a little astonishment, that the French were human, even according to the standard of the United States of America.

He found that in certain French bathrooms one can have hot water without waiting for a geyser. He found that he needn't have brought two dozen tubes of his favorite (and very smelly) toothpaste from America--one actually could buy toothpaste, corn- plasters, New York Sunday papers, Bromo-Seltzer, Lucky Strikes, safety-razor blades, and ice cream almost as easily in Paris as in the United States; and a man he met at Luigi's Bar insisted that if one quested earnestly enough, he could find B.V.D.'s.

And he discovered that French chauffeurs drove better than Americans.

He meditated on it, alone with a cognac and soda (he had learned to say "Une fine a l'eau de seltz," and often the waiters understood him) in front of Weber's, during a not ungrateful hour of freedom when Fran was trying on hats.

"Just what did I expect in France? Oh, I don't know. Funny! Kind of hard to remember now just how I did picture it. Guess I thought there wouldn't be any comforts--no bathrooms, and everybody taking red wine and snails for breakfast, and no motor 'busses or comfortable trains, and no cocktails, and all the men wearing waxed mustaches and funny beards. And saying, 'Ze hired girl iz vun lofely girl--oo la la--'

"And then these young Frenchmen, in London clothes, driving Hispano-Suizas at a hundred kilometers an hour--And you hear 'em at the Ritz, talking perfect English, talking about English stainless steel and about building bridges in the Argentine and the influence of the Soviets in China and--

"I suppose I felt that the entire known world revolved around the General Offices of the Revelation Motor Company, Constitution Avenue, Zenith, and all the time--Towers and cathedrals and alleys, and Europe not caring what Sam Dodsworth thought about making the 1928 models a Delft blue--

"It seemed so important!

"But, mind you, I am glad I'm an American! But--

"Life was a lot simpler then. We knew we were It! We knew that all of Europe was unbathed and broke, and that America was the world's only bulwark against Bolshevism and famine. They lie so! These speakers at club meetings, and these writers in the magazines! They tell us that no European has ever played tennis or taught the Ten Commandments to his kids or built a railroad, and that the only thing that keeps Europe from reverting to the caveman is American cash.

"Rot!

"And yet, I'm never going to be European! Fran might--Oh, Fran, my darling, are you going to drift away from me? Every day you get snootier about my poor old provincial Americanism! You're just waiting for some really slick European to come along--And, by God, there's one thing I won't stand--her telling me how inferior I am to some gigolo--

"Fool! Of course the girl--Say! That's what she still is; she's still a girl! Little older than Emily, but not so sensible. Of course she gets excited by Europe. She's done her job, hasn't she? She's run the house and brought Emily and Brent up, hasn't she? I've got to be patient.

"But falling for a feather-weight like Lockert--

"Hell! I wish Tub were here. Fran and I haven't got anybody--

"And you're still dodging the issue, my lad!

"What is Sam Dodsworth going to do about the fact that he's as provincial as a prairie-dog, and that he's only fifty-one, with a chance of another thirty years, and that he's discovered a world--

"Nothing, I guess! Too late. I'd be a pretty spectacle, now wouldn't I, as one of these American business-men that come over here and try to hide the fact that they made their coin out of soap or pork--And so they collect first editions and apologize for being them-selves! But just now and then I'll learn to sit still like this, and not feel I have to be efficient and hustle--

"My God! Five o'clock! I've got to hustle and meet Fran!"

But he had one comfort, given to him by his wife. He had been uncomfortably impressed by the fact that Mathieu, his customary room-waiter at the Grand Universel, a fat, curly-haired, and unctuous person with fascinatingly different spots on his dress- suit lapels every day, spoke English so perfectly.

According to the good American custom, Sam had said to him at his very first breakfast, "Where'd you learn your English?"

Mathieu chuckled, "I wass fife years in Tchicago."

Mathieu was rather more colloquially American than Sam in his suggestions for breakfast, or for lunch when it was too rainy for them to go out, or when there was a glorious American mail. "How about a nice little minute steak?" he would say, in the very accent of Chicago; or "Say, boss, there's some nice caviare just come in from Rooshia."

Whence it happened that Sam believed Mathieu spoke the American language.

But on the third day, at breakfast, Fran said, "Mathieu! Do you happen to know where these movie theaters are on the Left Bank that are putting on modernistic films?"

Mathieu stared.

"Pardon, Madame!" he said.

"Theaters--modern films--cinemas--oh, whatever you call 'em--!"

Fran slipped across the room to the bottle-green-and-golden dictionary on the flimsy desk.

"Le--cinematograph moderne--est-ce qu'il y a--I mean, are there any on the Left Bank?"

Mathieu looked at her with a most superior intelligence:

"Oh yez. You ask the concierge. He tell you! De veal steak iss fine today--just like Tchicago!"

When Mathieu had gone out to fetch the veal steak that was so fine today, Fran murmured, "I have made a great discovery! Aside from food-vocabulary, the Mathieus speak English no better than we do French! We're not so bad, my beloved!"

"You're not, of course. But I'm terrible!"

"Don't be silly! Yesterday you said 'A quelle heure est le Louvre ferme?'--as a matter of fact, I think you did say 'est le Louvre closed?' but the taxi-driver understood it perfectly, and I know you'd learn to speak a really splendid French, if you gave your mind to it."

"Honestly?" said Sam.

CHAPTER 14

They had ventured to the Left Bank for an evening at the Cafe Novgorod, the favorite of the more arty Americans. The cafe seemed to Sam less related to Paris than he was himself. . . . The French street: bourgeois fathers strolling with their brood; dark-eyed men jesting with girls in red kerchiefs; an old woman crawling along muttering to herself. But here, in the Cafe Novgorod, under the awning, a bumble of American voices:

"--get a little Citroen and tour Normandy--"

"--a complete meal for six francs, with lovely roast beef, though prob'ly it's horse-meat--"

"--that Elliot Paul is the only really distinguished essayist in--"

The young Americans there were so dispositive. Sam heard them, at the tables about, dispose of Californian scenery, the institution of marriage, Whistler, corn fritters, President Wilson, cement roads, and the use of catsup. He became gloomier than at the thickest dinner-party in London, and he was thinking of bed when his gloom was interrupted by a voice like that of a female impersonator.

Lycurgus Watts (only he liked to be called "Jerry") was standing by their table and beaming in fondest affection.

Lycurgus (or Jerry) Watts was the professional amateur of Zenith. He was a large-faced man, as wide as a truck-driver, but he had a whiney, caressing voice, and he giggled at his own jokes, which were incessant and very bad. He was reputed to be fifty years old, and he looked anywhere from twenty-five to a hundred. He came from what was known as a "good family"--anyway, it was a wealthy family. His father had died when he was ten. He had lived and traveled with his widowed mother till he was forty-three, and he told every one that she was the noblest character he had ever known. Compared with her, all young women were such hussies that he would never marry. But he made up for it by a number of highly confidential friendships with men whose voices and matriolatry were like his own.

He wandered much, in Europe and Asia, but always he came back to the flat he kept in Zenith. It was so filled with his collections of lace, wrought-iron keys, and editions of Oscar Wilde, that there was scarcely room for his genuine Russian samovar and his bed with a cover of black and gold. He spent much of his time in Zenith in denouncing the tradesmen who manufactured soap and motor cars instead of collecting lace, and in checking up his profitable holdings in soap and motor cars. He got up the first exhibition of Slavic embroidery in the state, he read poetry aloud, and he talked a good deal about starting a new magazine of the new poetry and the new prose.

Whenever Sam had met Jerry Watts in Zenith, he had grumbled to Fran on the way home, "Why the devil did they invite that white grub? He makes me sick!" But as Jerry had invariably told Fran in three languages that she was the loveliest lady in town, she turned on Sam with "Oh, of course! Just because Jerry is really cultured, because he has brains enough to cultivate a fine leisure instead of grubbing in a dirty office, all you noble captains of industry look down on him as a dray-horse might look down on a fine race-horse!"

She even had Jerry for dinner. In fact, Sam had been led to hate Jerry with considerable heartiness.

But in the oppressive strangeness of Paris, any familiar face would have been exciting, and for five minutes Sam believed that he was glad to see Jerry Watts.

Jerry sat down; he giggled, "I TOLD you you'd escape from that dreadful Middlewest, Fran, and come to a civilized country! Don't you just ADORE the Novgorod? Such darling roughnecks! Such delectable poses! Oh, my DEARS, I heard the best one here last evening! Tommy Troizka--he's the dearest Finn boy, and a great water-colorist, speaks English perfectly, oh, too simply divinely, and Tommy said, 'The trouble with your American intelligentsia is that most of you don't know how to TELL A GENT when you see him!' Isn't that precious! Oh, you'll adore being here in Paris! Don't you, Dodsworth?"

"Yeah, great town," said Sam.

"Have you been to the Lion d'Or yet?"

"Oh yes," said Fran.

"Have you tried the rognons de la maison at Emil's?"

125

"Yes."

"And of course you've been to the L'Ane Rouge and the Rendezvous des Mariniers?"

"Yes."

"And the Chemise Sale?"

"No, I don't think--"

"You haven't been to the Chemise Sale? Oh, Fran! Why, good Heavens! Don't you realize that the Chemise Sale is the duckiest little restaurant in Paris?"

Fran was annoyed.

It was not that she was given to ducky little restaurants or any other phase of synthetic Bohemianism, but that any other citizen of Zenith should know more about Paris than she was intolerable. She glared slightly when Jerry seized his advantage and laid down the rule that it was vulgar to go to Versailles but that they MUST see the exhibition of the Prismatic Internists. Sam felt patiently that she would presently despatch Jerry. Yet she looked pleased when Jerry piped:

"Have you met Endicott Everett Atkins? He's coming to tea at my place next Saturday afternoon--I have such a dusky little studio on the Rue des Petits-Champs. You and your husband must come."

"We'll be glad to," said Fran, to Sam's considerable discouragement.

Sam grunted, in the taxicab, "What do you want to go there for? Who's Endicott Everett Atkins? Sounds like a business college yell. He another lily like Watts?"

"No, he really is somebody. Dean of the American literary colony here--writes about French novelists and Austrian peasant furniture and Correggio and English hunting and Heaven knows what all."

"But I don't have to learn about peasant furniture, too, do I?" Sam said hopefully.

Mr. Endicott Everett Atkins was reputed to resemble Henry James. He had the massive and rather bald head, the portly dignity. He spoke--and he spoke a good deal--in a measured voice, and he had a small bright wife who was believed to adore him. He also was blessed, and furthered in his critical pursuits, by having no sense of humor

126

whatever, though he knew so many sparkling anecdotes that one did not suspect it for hours. He came from South Biddlesford, Connecticut, and his father, to whom he often referred as "that dear and so classical a bibliophile," had been an excellent hat- manufacturer. He owned a real house in Paris, with an upstairs and down, and he spoke chummily of the Ambassador.

He did actually, against any expectation, keep his promise and appear at the tea in Mr. Jerry Watts's studio--an apartment with a scarlet-fever of Spanish altar-cloths, embroidered copes, and Mandarin robes. The only apparent reason for calling it a studio was that it had a north window, and that Mr. Jerry Watts naturally would call it a studio. "I just can't make love except by a north light!" he nickered to Fran.

On the refectory table was a small teapot, a small plate of limp cakes, and an enormous bowl of punch. After every one had had three glasses of the punch, the conversation became very agitated. There were massed about the table, screaming, some thirty people. Sam never remembered any of them, save Endicott Everett Atkins. The rest seemed to him as indistinguishable as separate mosquitoes in a swarm, and rather noisier. But there was nothing noisy about Mr. Endicott Everett Atkins. He had so developed poise, an appalling, reproving, Christian Science sort of poise, that Sam felt toward him as he once had toward the professor of Greek drama at Yale.

Mr. Atkins could purr at the thought of particularly pleasant and beautiful things--a Greek coin, a Javanese dancing girl, a check from his publisher--but in crowds he stood calm and expansive as an observation balloon in windless air. In the quietest corner of the apartment he held forth on the Italian Renaissance, the superiority of Parliament to Congress, the future of Anglo-Catholicism, the letters of Horace Walpole, and the perfection of anarchism as a theory--he had actually attended an anarchist meeting in Milan in 1890, as an ardent young traveler. You never remembered what he had said, but you felt that he had been tremendously sound, and you sighed, uneasily running your forefinger between collar and neck, "He has such a fund of knowledge--"

Mr. Atkins pounced on Fran, and if he did not also exactly pounce on Sam, he tolerated him. He took in Fran's shining hair, her freshness, her slim quickness. He brought her a cup of punch, bowing like Louis XIV. He won Sam by telling him of meeting Dr. Carl Benz, the father of the motor car, at Mannheim, back in 1885, and of seeing his first horseless carriage--it was, said Atkins, a wire-wheeled tricycle with a chain drive like a bicycle, a handle for steering, and under the seat a mass of machinery as wild- looking as a gutted alarm clock.

"Like to've seen it!" murmured Sam. "Happen to know what the horse-power was?"

Mr. Endicott Everett Atkins looked at him benevolently, his glossy baldness rose-hued in the red-shaded lamps. "It was three and a quarter," he said.

(It was not for sixty hours that, lying awake in the early morning, Sam realized that Atkins hadn't had the smallest notion what the horse-power of the Benz really was.)

With men, Mr. Endicott Everett Atkins rarely let down, but with slim and glistening women he came near to being human. He indicated to Fran that this was only a merry slumming prank of his to come to the studio of Mr. Lycurgus Watts--normally he moved only in the loftiest circles, among the loveliest ladies, the wittiest and bravest men, the rarest first editions, and he longed to introduce her to all of them.

She loved it.

He told her the delightful anecdote which he had heard from Andre Sorchon, who had it from E. V. Lucas, who had it from Henry James, who had it direct from Swinburne. He told her that her husband (Mr. Samuel Dodsworth) was extraordinarily like the late Duc de Malmaison, but that she was ever and ever so much nicer than the Duchesse. He told her that her ash-blond hair was astonishingly like that of Madame Zelie du Strom, the Swedish tragedienne who, Mr. Atkins agreed with himself, was greater than Bernhardt, Duse, and Modjeska put together--

Sam sat back, as so often he had sat back at directors' meetings, content to let others do the talking if he could do the plotting, and tried to make out the purposes of Mr. Endicott Everett Atkins.

"This fellow knows a lot. Well, at least he's read a lot. Well, if he hasn't read so much, he remembers all he has read. Here he's making love to Fran--telling her what a wonder she is--and she's lapping it up. Bless her! Let her have her fling--if the fling ain't any more dangerous than old Atkins! Wonder if I'll be as dry a bladder as he is in fifteen years? If I am, I'm going to retire to a log cabin and grow corn!"

"I really can't tell you," Mr. Endicott Everett Atkins was moaning at Fran, "how very, very much I admire your wisdom in coming to Europe in a really leisured pilgrimage. And I wonder if you realize you're doing a patriotic American duty--showing Europe that we have poised and exquisite creatures like yourself, if you'll permit the familiarity from an aged bookworm, as well as these Yankee tourist women--oh, these dreadful bouncing females, with their shrill voices, their ignorance of all gentle usages--and the way they frequent horrible American bars and dance in dreadful places--"

"Why shouldn't the 'Yankee tourist women' go and dance in Montmartre, if they enjoy it?" Sam meditated. "Does Atkins think the pretty buyer from Detroit comes here to please him? The American highbrow abroad is just like the Puritan back home--the Puritan says that if you drink anything at all, he'll disapprove of you, and the expatriate here says that if you drink anything but Chateau Haut Something-or-other at just the right temperature, HE'LL disapprove of you and--

"I will get back for my class reunion this June! Thirtieth reunion! Am I that old?

"Think of seeing Tub again and Poodle Smith and Bill Dyers and--Now what the devil was the name of that big fellow with the red hair that played center? Florey--Floreau--Flaherty? Corking fellow!

"And Atkins goes on. I'd better listen and get what wisdom I can, because I think our 'really leisured pilgrimage to Europe' is drawing to a close!"

"--though I'm afraid, Mrs. Dodsworth, that you'll find our house too dreadfully bookish. Beautiful people like you are superior to books. You ought never to read anything--you ought only to live. You ought to exist imperishably on some Grecian isle amid the wine- dark sea, dancing in the sunshine. But if your husband and you will delight us by coming to lunch next Sunday, at least I may be able to show you one or two intaglios--"

At lunch at the Atkinses', on Sunday, Sam met his first Princess, Madame Maravigliarsi. Not that he knew at first that she was a

Princess; in fact he supposed her to be a nice, rather shabby little Poor Relation. But Atkins revealed her princessity in a dramatic aside, and Sam was as impressed as any other proper democratic American.

And she was, Fran carefully ascertained, quite a good, high-ranking Princess, and only one-quarter American.

Sam sat next to her, at lunch in the tall cool room with its Venetian glass and the serene bust of Plato; and while he made a respectable show of not being humble, the boy who had read "Ivanhoe" and Shakespeare and "The Idylls of the King" was gloating, "I'm sitting next to a Princess!"

The Princess prattled of what she had said to Mussolini and what His Eminence the Secretary to the Pope had said to her, and for ten minutes Sam desired to know the renowned of the world. He remembered--what was it?--something that Fran had said to the effect that with his tall dignity and his experience as executive, he might become an ambassador, and be intimate with ever so many people who had said things to Mussolini and had Eminences say things to them--

But he wearied of Princess Maravigliarsi's chatter. It was SO important that he see Trouville and Biarritz; it was SO important that he properly hate the Bolsheviks; SO important that he go to tea at Lady Ingraham's. ,

He dreaded these new obligations.

"So far as I can see," he brooded, "travel consists in perpetually finding new things that you have to do if you're going to be respectable."

Fran was polite to the Princess Maravigliarsi with a cold politeness which indicated to Sam that she was impressed. But it was to a certain Madame de Penable that she gave most of her attention. Madame de Penable was a red-headed, white-skinned, rather plump woman who seemed to specialize on knowing everybody of influence in every land. The Dodsworths never learned whether she was born in Poland, Nebraska, Africa, the Dordogne, or Hungary. They never learned just who Monsieur de Penable was, if there ever had been a Monsieur de Penable. They never learned whether she was in trade, living on alimony, or possessed of a family income. Sam suspected that she was an international spy. She was a pleasant woman, and very clever. She talked about herself constantly, and never told anything whatever about herself. She spoke English, French, German, and Italian perfectly, and at restaurants, with waiters as mysterious as herself, she went off into tongues which might have been Russian, Lancashire, or Modern Greek.

Apparently she fancied the Dodsworths as additions to her circle. Sam heard her inviting Fran and himself to lunch at the Ermitage.

"Fran is launched," he sighed. "At last we'll be gay and cosmopolitan! I wonder how much I'll be able to win from Tub at poker, now that I've had my style of playing perfected by European culture?"

CHAPTER 15

They ceased to be children exploring together, rather happy in their loneliness. They were dominated by Endicott Everett Atkins and Madame de Penable and their smart groups. Madame de Penable saw that because in her fresh, keen, naive way Fran was different from European women, she was the more novel and attractive to the innumerable European men whom the De Penable always had about her, running her errands, drinking her excellent Moselle, listening to her scandalous anecdotes; she saw also that Sam was likely to keep Fran from snatching such of these men as the De Penable wanted to hold for her own.

She cultivated the Dodsworths enthusiastically.

Fran's life became hectic as life can be only in Paris: a ride in the Bois, lunch, shopping, tea, bridge, cocktails, dressing, dinner, the theater, dancing at such icily glittering haunts as the Jardin de Ma Soeur, cold cream and exhausted sleep. In between she managed to fit three hours a week of French lessons.

And Sam--he came along.

He enjoyed it, for a month. There was color to this life, and motion, like waves under the gray cliff that was Paris. There were pretty women who took him seriously, as one of the financial captains of America (he suspected, with an inward chuckle, that they thought him far richer than he was). There were gorgeous clothes and marvelous food. He learned something of the art of wine. He had long known that Rhine wines should be cold; that Burgundy is better than that womanish drink, champagne. But now, meeting people who took wine as seriously as he had motor engines, and listening to their reverent discussion of it, he learned the epochal differences between the several Burgundies--between Nuits St. Georges and Nuits-Premeaux; the cataclysmic differences between vintages--between the lordly crop of 1911 and the mediocre product of 1912. He learned that it was a crime to dull the palate with a cocktail before a sacred bottle of good wine, and that it was bloody treason to heat Burgundy suddenly by plunging it in the hot water, instead of decently decanting it hours before drinking and letting--it--come--SLOWLY (the connoisseurs breathed)--to--room-- temperature.

It interested him, this cyclone of new excitements. And Fran was, for the first time in years, altogether satisfied.

Between them, Atkins and the De Penable knew a dozen sets. Atkins fished for portrait painters, French critics, American ladies from the choicer portions of Back Bay and Rittenhouse Square, English poets who pretended to be biologists and English biologists who were flattered at being taken for poets. Madame de Penable went in for assorted titles--a judicious mixture of Italians, French, Roumanian, Georgian, Hungarian--and she always had one sound, carefully selected freak: a delightfully droll pickpocket or a minor Arctic explorer.

The man out of all this boiling whom Fran most liked was an Italian aviator, Captain Gioserro, a bright-eyed, very smiling man, ten years younger than herself. He was dazzled by her; bewildered by her quick speech. He said that she was the Norse goddess, Freya, that she was an Easter lily, and a number of other highly elegant things, and she liked it and went riding with him.

Sam hoped that there was not going to be another Lockert explosion. He believed her when she insisted that she considered Gioserro a "mere boy." But alone, brooding, he was worried. He wondered if her rigid distaste for flirtation had existed only because she had not found American men attractive. She seemed softer, more relaxed, more lovely, and considerably less dependent on him. She was surrounded by amusing men, and warmed by their extravagant compliments. His conscious self declared that she couldn't possibly be tempted, but his sub-conscious self was alarmed.

And presently he became weary of their insane dashing. The voices-- the voices that never ceased--the high thin laughter--the reference to Mike This and Jacques That and the amours of Lady the Other--the duty of being seen at every exhibition, every select tea, every concert--

Fran had sharply dropped for him the people they knew, all the low adventurers who sat about bars, the couples from Zenith whom they had met at the hotel, even the unfortunate Jerry Lycurgus Watts, once Jerry had served his biological purpose by producing Endicott Everett Atkins. And so Sam became exceedingly hungry for a good wholesome lowness; for poker, shirt-sleeves, sauerkraut, obscene vaudeville, and conversation about motor sales and Zenith politics.

Fran was having her portrait painted, glossily and very expensively, by a Belgian whose manner of serving tea and commenting on new frocks had enabled him to capture a number of rich American women. With him, painting was a social function; while he worked he was surrounded by the most decorative human parrots and peacocks, shrieking their admiration of his craftsmanship, which was excellent. He managed to add the muzziness of a Laurencin to the photography of a Sargent; he made his women look rich, and all alike.

Madame de Penable had insisted on Fran's going to this good man, and when Sam learned that the De Penable had also insisted on a number of other women benefiting by the Belgian's gifts, he wondered if possibly the lively De Penable might not have some interest in the business. But Fran was magnificently offended when he made the hint.

"It may interest you to KNOW," she raged, "that M. Saurier wanted to paint me for NOTHING, because he said I was the most perfect type of American beauty he had ever seen! But of course I couldn't let him do that. Of course you wouldn't have noticed that certain Europeans think I'm rather good-looking--"

"Don't," said Sam mildly, "be a damn' fool, my darling."

He went once to the orgy of her sittings; and he, the rock of ages in business crises, wanted to scream as he heard Madame de Penable, and six women, who spoke all languages, except French, with a French accent, lilting that "le Maitre" was at least a genius, and that he was particularly historic in the matter of "flesh tints."

He did not go again.

He came to like the affabilities of Endicott Everett Atkins even less than the expensive sunset-hues of Madame de Penable. The De Penable was surrounded by gay people. "Not so bad," Sam considered, "to have a cocktail with a pretty girl that tells you that you look like a cross between Sir Lancelot and Jack Dempsey." But Mr. Atkins had not yet heard of cocktails. And Mr. Atkins held forth. He had been everywhere, and he could make everywhere sound uninteresting. He would look at you earnestly and demand to know whether you had made a pilgrimage to Viterbo to see the Etruscan remains, and he made it sound so nagging a duty that Sam vowed he would never let himself be caught near Viterbo; he was so severe about American music that he made Sam long for the jazz which he had always rather irritably detested.

Toward the seven deadly arts Sam had had the inarticulate reverence which an Irish policeman might have toward a shrine of the Virgin on his beat . . . that little light seen at three of a winter's morning. They were to him romance, escape, and he was irritated when they were presented to him as a preacher presents the virtues of sobriety and chastity. He hadn't the training to lose himself in Bach or Goethe; but in Chesterton, in Schubert, in a Corot, he had been able to forget motors and Alec Kynance, and always he had chuckled over the gay anarchy of Mencken. But with rising stubbornness he asserted that if he had to take the arts as something in which he must pass an examination, he would chuck them altogether and be content with poker.

As Fran had both a sitting and a fitting that afternoon (to Sam they seemed much the same, except that Fran's costumer was more virile and less grasping than her portrait-painter) he had a whole afternoon off.

Secretly, a little guiltily, he reflected, "I've done Notre Dame right, with Fran. Now I think I'll sneak off and see if I really like it! You can't tell! I might! Even though old Atkins says I have to. . . . Hell! I wish I were back in Zenith!"

Solemnly, his Baedeker shamelessly in hand, Sam lumbered out of his taxi before Notre Dame, and quite as shamelessly slipped off across the river to a cafe facing the cathedral. There, quietly, without Fran's quivers of appreciation, he began to feel at home.

He admitted the cathedral's gray domination. There was strength there; strength and endurance and wisdom. The flying buttresses soared like wings. The whole cathedral expanded before his eyes; the work of human hands seemed to tower larger than the sky. He felt, dimly and disconnectedly, that he too had done things with his hands; that the motor car was no contemptible creation; that he was nearer to the forgotten, the anonymous and merry and vulgar artisans who had created this somber epic of stone, than was any Endicott Everett Atkins with his Adam's apple ecclesiastically throbbing as he uttered pomposities about "the transition in Gothic motifs." How those cheery artisans would have laughed--drinking their wine, perhaps, at this same corner!

He read in the Book of Words. (Did Ruskin and Cellini and Dante actually travel without Baedekers? How strange it seemed, and new!)

"Notre Dame . . . in early Roman times the site was occupied by a temple of Jupiter. The present church was begun in 1163."

He laid the book down and drifted into the pleasantest dreaming he had known for all the fatal weeks since he had been adopted by the Right People.

A temple of Jupiter. Priests in white robes. Sacrificial bulls with patient wondering eyes, tossing their thick garlanded heads. Chariots pounding across the square--right across the river there! The past, which had been to the young Sam Dodsworth playing football, to the man harassed by building motor cars, only a flamboyant myth, was suddenly authentic, and he walked with Julius Caesar, who in that moment ceased to be merely a drawing in a school-book, a ventriloquist's dummy talking the kind of overgrammatical rot that only school-masters could understand, and became a living, lively, talkative acquaintance, having a drink here with Sam, and extraordinarily resembling Roosevelt off-stage.

Heavy with meditation, happy in being unobserved and not having to act up to the splendors of Fran, he paid his bill and ambled across the bridge and into the cathedral.

It bothered him, as always, that there were no prim and cushioned pews such as he knew in Protestant churches in America; it made the cathedral seem bare and a little unfriendly; but beside a vast pillar, eternal as mountains or the sea, he found a chair, tipped a verger, forgot his irritation with people who buzzed up and wanted to guide him, and lost himself in impenetrable thoughts.

He roused himself to read, patiently, in Baedeker: "Geoffrey Plantagenet, son of Henry II of England, was buried beneath the high altar in 1186. In 1430 Henry VI of England was crowned king of France and in 1560 Mary Stuart (afterward Mary Queen of Scots) was crowned as queen-consort of Francis II. The coronation of Napoleon I and Josephine de Beauharnais by Pope Pius VII (1804) . . . was celebrated here with great ceremony."

(And in Saurier's studio brassy women were chattering about the races!)

Plantagenet! Rearing lions on scarlet banners edged with bullion. Mary Stuart and her proud little head. Napoleon himself--here, where Sam Dodsworth was sitting.

"Humph!" he said.

He stared at the Rose Window, but he was seeing what it meant, not what it said. He saw life as something greater and more exciting than food and a little sleep. He felt that he was no longer merely a pedler of motor cars; he felt that he could adventure into this Past about him--and possibly adventure into the far more elusive Present. He saw, unhappily, that the Atkins and De Penable existence into which Fran had led him was not the realization of the "great life" for which he had yearned, but its very negation-- the bustle, the little snobberies, the cheap little titles, the cheap little patronage of "art."

"I'm going to get out of this town and do something--Something exciting. And I'll make her go with me! I've been too weak with her," he said weakly.

His longing for low and intelligent company could not be denied. He went to the New York Bar. Through the correspondent of a New York newspaper whom he had known as a reporter in Zenith, Sam had met a dozen journalists there, and he felt at home with them. They did not heap on him the slightly patronizing compliments which he had from the women in Madame de Penable's den of celebrities. He was stimulated by what was to the journalists only commonplace shop-talk: how Trotsky really got along with Stalin--what Briand had said to Sir Austen Chamberlain--what was the "low-down" on the international battle of oil.

This afternoon he met Ross Ireland.

Sam had heard of Ireland, roving foreign correspondent of the Quackenbos Feature Syndicate, as one of the best fellows among the American journalists. The former Zenith reporter introduced Sam to him. Ross Ireland was a man of forty, as large as Sam, and in his oversized rimless spectacles he looked like a surgeon.

"Pleased to meet you, Mr. Dodsworth," he said, and his voice still had all the innocence of Iowa. "Staying over here long?"

"Well, yes--some months."

"This your first trip across?"

"Yes."

"Say, I've just been driving one of your Revelation cars in the jungle in India. Great performance, even in rough going--"

"India?"

"Yes, just back. Real Kipling country. Oh, I don't know as I saw any Mowglis gassing with tigers and sixteen-foot snakes, and I heard more about jute and indigo than I did about Mrs. Hauksbees, but it certainly knocks your eye out! That big temple at Tanjore-- tower eleven stories high, all carved. And the life there-- everything different--SMELLS different (and sometimes not so good!)--and the people still in masquerade costumes, and queer curry kind of grub, and Eurasian shops where the Babus will tell you grand lies--every one good for a mail-story. You ought to get out there, if you can take the time. And then beyond India, Burma-- take a river-boat--regular floating market-place, with natives in funny turbans squatting all over the decks--go up the Irrawaddy to Mandalay and on to Bhamo. Or you can get steamers at Rangoon for Penang and Sandoway and Akyab and Chittagong and all kinds of fancy places."

(Rangoon! Akyab! Chittagong!)

"And then around to Java and China and Japan, and home by way of California."

"I'd like to do it," said Sam. "Paris is a lovely city, but--"

"Oh, Paris! Paris is nothing but a post-graduate course in Broadway."

"Looks good to me," said the ex-Zenith-newspaperman.

"It would! Paris is a town for Americans that can't stand work," said Ross Ireland. "I'm keen to see America; tickled to death I'm going back in June. I've been away three years--first time I've ever been away. I'm homesick as the devil. But I like my America straight. I don't want it in the form of a lot of expatriates sitting around Paris cafes. And when I want to travel, I want to TRAVEL! Say, you land in Bangkok, with that big gold temple rising over the town, and the boatmen singing in--whatever it is that they DO sing in--or you go to Moscow and see the moujiks in felt boots and sheepskin coats, with the church spires absolutely like white and gold lace-work against the sky--Say, that's travel!"

Yes. That's the stuff! Sam was going to travel like that. He'd go--Oh, to Constantinople, back through Italy or Austria, and home for his thirtieth class reunion--just time to do it now, if he hustled. Then Fran and he might start out again next autumn and see Egypt and Morocco--Yes.

It is a favorite American Credo that "if the acting is good enough, you can enjoy a play in a language you don't understand as well as in English." Fran held to that credo. Sam urgently did not. He hated to sit through French plays, and when he returned to the hotel from the New York Bar and Ross Ireland--from the Irrawaddy River and Chittagong--he found Fran with tickets for "Le Singe qui Parle," a slightly bad temper, and the aviator Gioserro.

"You smell of whisky! Atrociously! Now please hurry and dress! Captain Gioserro and you and I are going to the theater. Now please hurry, can't you? I'll order the cocktails meanwhile. As you see, I'm all ready. After the theater, we'll meet Renee de Penable and some other people and dance."

As he dressed, Sam fretted, "French play! Humph! I won't know which is the husband and which is the lover for at least the first two acts!"

If he slept at the play, he did it ever so modestly and retiringly, and he was unusually polite to Madame de Penable. Fran was approving on their way home, and quite as easily as though they were back in Zenith, he asserted while they were undressing:

"Fran, I've got an idea that--"

"Just unfasten this snap on my shoulder-strap, would you mind? Thanks. You were so nice tonight. Much the best-looking man in the room!"

"That's--"

"And I'm so glad you've come to like Renee de Penable. She's really a darling--so loyal. But, uh--Sam, I do wish you hadn't brought up that question as to what right the French have in the Riff."

"But, my God, they talked about us in Haiti and Nicaragua first!"

"I know, but that's entirely different. This is an ANCIENT question, and of course Renee was shocked, and so was that English woman, Mrs. What's-her-name. But it doesn't matter. I just thought I'd mention it."

And he'd thought he'd behaved so beautifully tonight!

"But," he went on heavily, becoming dimly irritated as he noted how little she heeded him while she brushed her hair, "I wanted to suggest that--Look here, Fran, I've got kind of an idea. It's almost May, but we could get in a month or more on the Mediterranean and still have time to get home late in June, and then I could go to my class reunion--thirtieth--"

"Really? THIRTIETH?"

"Oh, I'm not so old! But I mean: we haven't talked especially about when we would go home--"

"But I want to see a lot more of Europe. Oh, I haven't started!"

"Neither have I. I agree. But I just mean: there's several business things I ought to settle up at home, and there's this reunion, and I'd like to see Emily and her new home, and Brent--"

"But perhaps we could get them to come over here this summer. Would you mind handing me the cold cream that's in the bathroom-- no--no--I think it's on the bureau--oh, thanks--"

"I thought we could go home for just a couple months, or maybe three, and then start out again. Say go West this time, and sail for China and Japan and round to Rangoon and India and so on."

"Yes, I'd like to do that sometime. . . . Oh, dear, how sleepy I am! . . . But not now, of course, now that we know nice people here."

"But that's just what I mean! I don't--Oh, they're a lively bunch, and lots of 'em good families and so on, but I don't think they ARE nice."

"What do you mean?"

"I mean they're a bunch of wasters. All they do, Penable and her whole gang, and Atkins's hangers-on aren't much better, all they do is just dance and chatter and show off their clothes. Their idea of a good time is just about that of a chorus-girl--"

Fran had been inattentive. She wasn't now. She snatched up a lace wrap, slapped it about her shoulders over her nightgown, and faced him, like a snarling white cat:

"Sam! Let's get this straight. I've felt you've been sulking, that you've been too afraid to--"

"Too polite!"

"--say what you thought. Well, I'm sick and tired of having to apologize, yes, to APOLOGIZE, for the crime of having introduced you to some of the nicest and most amusing people in Paris, and for having backed you up when they were offended by your boorishness! Am I to understand that you regard Madame de Penable and her whole GANG, as you so elegantly call it, as simply rotters? May I point out to you that if I don't have quite so lively an appreciation of such nature's noblemen as Mr. A. B. Hurd--"

"Fran!"

"--yet possibly I may be a little better equipped to understand really smart, cosmopolitan people than you are! Kindly let me remind you that Renee de Penable is the intimate friend of the most exclusive aristocracy of the ancien regime here--"

"But is she? And what of it?"

"Will you KINDLY stop sneering? You that are so fond of accusing ME of sneering! And, my dear Samuel, you really don't do it so very well! Delicate irony isn't your long suit, my dear good man!"

"Damn it, I won't be talked to like a stable boy!"

"Then don't act like one! And if I may be permitted to go on and answer the charges which YOU brought up, not I--the whole subject is thoroughly distasteful to me--and oh, Sam, so vulgar, so beastly vulgar!" For a second she was dramatically mournful and hurt, but instantly she was a charging Cossack again: "But when you attack any one that's been as sweet to me as Renee, all I can say is--Do you happen to realize that she is the dearest friend of the Duchesse de Quatrefleurs--she's promised to take me down to the Duchesse's chateau in Burgundy--"

"She's never done it!"

"As it HAPPENS, the Duchesse is ill, just at the moment! And your charming remark illustrates perfectly what I mean by your sneering! . . . Or, to take the example of Renee's friend, Mrs. Sittingwall. She's the widow of a very distinguished English general who was killed in the war--"

"He wasn't a general--he was a colonel--and now the woman is engaged to that old rip of a French stock-broker, Andillet."

"What of it? M. Andillet does dress too loudly, and he drives a car too fast, but he's a most amusing old dear, and he orders the best meal in Paris. And knows cabinet ministers--bankers-- diplomats-- everybody that's influential."

"Well, he looks to me like a crook. And what about the young gigolos that are always hanging around Mrs. Penable?"

"I do think it's too gracious of you to take the word 'gigolo,' which I taught you in the first place--"

"You did not!"

"--and use it against me, my dear polylingual Sam! I suppose you are referring to boys like Gioserro and Billy Dawson. Yes, they're not at all like American business men, are they! They actually enjoy being charming to women, they enjoy sharing their leisure with women, they dance beautifully, they talk about something besides the stockmarket--"

"Oh, they enjoy leisure, all right! Oh, now, Fran, I don't mean to be nasty about them, but you know they graft on women--"

"My dear man, Captain Gioserro (and he could call himself Count Gioserro, if he wanted to!) has a perfectly good family income, as his people have had before him, for generations--"

"Whoa now! Hold up! I question his having a very GOOD family income. I notice that whenever he's with us, he always manages to let me pay. Not that I mind, but--Why say, I've never seen him spend a cent except tonight, when he gave ten centimes to the fellow that opened the cab door. Now please listen, Fran, and don't go off into a tantrum. Don't you and Mrs. Penable almost always pay the bills--for feeds, for taxis, for tips, for tickets-- for Gioserro and young Dawson and most of these other slick young men that she has hanging around?"

"What of it? We can afford it. (The name, by the way, as I have remarked several hundred times before, is MADAME DE PENABLE!) Or are you--" She became regally outraged and deliberate. "Are you perhaps hinting that because you so generously support me, you have the right to dictate on whom and for what I spend every cent? Do you desire me to give you a detailed account of my expenses, like an office boy? Then let me remind you--oh, this is SO distasteful to me, but I must remind you that I have twenty thousand a year of my own, and now that I have a chance to be happy, with amusing people--"

She was sobbing. He caught her shoulders, and demanded, "Will you stop self-dramatizing yourself, my young lady? You know, and you know good and well, that I'm criticizing these young men for grafting just because I want to point out that they're no good; nothing but a lot of butterflies."

She broke away from his grasp and from her own sobs, and she was tart again: "Then thank God for the butterflies! I'm so tired of the worthy ants! . . . Sam, we might just as well have this out . . . if we're going on together."

The last five words chilled him. He was incredulous. She seemed a little to mean it, and she went on resolutely:

"Let's get it straight--just what we are up to; what we want. Now that we are meeting them, do you appreciate people with wit and elegance, or have you already had enough of them? Are you going to insist on returning to--oh, decent enough people, but people that can't see anything in life more amusing than poker and golf and motoring, that are afraid of suave manners, that think to be roughneck is to be strong? Does the accumulated civilization of two thousand years of Europe mean something to you or--"

"Oh, come off it, Fran! I'm not a roughneck and you know it. And I'm not uncivilized. And I like nice manners. But I like nice manners in people that are something more than amateur head-waiters and--And after all, a rock takes a better polish than a sponge! These people, even Penable herself, are parrots. What I'd like to meet--Well, you take the colonial administrators and so on out in the British possessions. People that are doing something besides going night after night to these restaurants where your gigolos hang out--"

"Sam, if you don't mind, I think I've stood all the insults to my friends that I can for one night! You can think up a few new ones for tomorrow. I'm going to sleep. And now."

Whether she slept or not, she was rigidly silent, her face turned from him.

He expected her to be soft, fluttery, apologetic, in the morning. But, awakening at nine, she looked unrepentant as steel. He trundled out talk about breakfast, about the laundry, then he grumbled, "I don't know that I made myself quite clear last evening--"

"Oh yes, you did! Thoroughly! And I don't think I care to discuss it. Shall we not say anything more about it?" She was so brightly forgiving and superior that he was infuriated. "I'm going out now. I'll be back here about twelve. I'm lunching with Renee de Penable, and if you think you can endure another hour with my degenerate friends, I should be glad to have you join us."

143

She vanished into the bathroom, to dress, and nothing more could be get out of her. When she was gone, he sat in bathrobe and slippers, over a second order of coffee.

She'd never before let a quarrel last overnight, at least when she'd been in the wrong--

Or was it possible that she had not been in the wrong in their controversy?

And (each second he was more confused) just what was the controversy about?

Anyway, she couldn't really have meant anything by her "if we're going on together." But suppose she had? Married couples did break up, quite incredibly, after years. Did he, in order to hold her, have to obey her, to associate forever with peacocks like this Mrs. Sittingwall and this fellow Andillet--who was certainly a little more than friendly with the Penable woman?

No, hanged if he would!

But if that meant losing Fran? Good God! Why, now that he had no work, he had nothing to absorb him save Fran, Emily, Brent, and three or four friends like Tub Pearson. Nor would he have anything new: he doubted if any other job could stimulate him like building up the Revelation Company; he doubted if he would make any new friends; he doubted if travel, pictures, music, hobbies, would ever be anything more than diversions interesting for an hour at a time. And of what he had left to keep life tolerable, Fran was first. She was the reason for everything! It was a second, a renewed Fran that he loved in his daughter Emily. His business and his making of money had been all for Fran--well no, maybe not all--hell! how hard it was to be honest about one's own self--maybe not all--fun putting business across, too--but she'd been the chief reason for it, anyway. As for his friends--Why, he'd've chucked even Tub, if Fran hadn't liked him!

Fran! That just the other day had been a girl, cool and sparkling and strange, on the Canoe Club porch--Good Lord, the Canoe Club had burned down twenty years ago.

In the radiant May of Paris, with the horse chestnuts out on the Champs Elysees, he sat huddled, feeling cold.

He went to lunch with Fran, Madame de Penable, and Billy Dawson, a young American who was the airiest and most objectionable of the De Penable's gentlemen valets. Sam was gravely polite. For two weeks he went with Fran and the De Penable's court to all sorts of restaurants reeking with cigarette smoke and expensive perfume and smart scandal. Between times, he sneaked off, like a small boy going to the circus, to low places, looking particularly for the roving correspondent, Ross Ireland, and when he found that Ireland was sailing on June fifteenth on the Aquitania, which would arrive in time for Sam's thirtieth reunion at Yale, he anxiously engaged a stateroom for "self & wife." He liked Ross Ireland; he found particularly amusing, very like his own cultural pretenses, the fact that since Ireland was totally unable to learn any language save Iowan, he thundered that English was "enough to take anybody anywhere" and that "these fellows that talk about your having to know French if you're going to do political stuff in Europe are just trying to show what smart guys they are." And he liked the way in which Ireland mingled stories of Burmese temples with stories of Old Doc Jevons back t' home in Ioway.

This lowness Sam hid from his wife, and hid the fact that he was agonizingly bored by not having enough to do. Yet his devotion did not win her back. There was a courteous coolness about her, always.

When he had definitely to know about returning to America, she answered briskly:

"Yes, I've thought it over. I can understand that you need to go back. But I'm not going. I've practically promised Renee de Penable to take a villa with her near Montreux for the summer. But I want you to go and see Tub and every one and thoroughly enjoy yourself, and then come back and join me in the late summer, and we'll think about the Orient."

But when she saw him off at the Gare St. Lazare she was suddenly softened.

She cried; she clung; she sobbed, "Oh, I didn't realize how much I'll miss you! Perhaps I'll come join you in Zenith. Do have the very best time you can, darling. Go camping with Tub--and give him my love--and tell him and Matey I hope they'll come over here--and try to get Em and Brent to come. Oh, my dear, forgive your idiotic, feather-brained wife! But let her have her foolish fling now! I did make a real home for you, didn't I? I shall again. Take care of yourself, my dear, and write me every day, and don't be angry with me--or do be angry, if it'll make you any happier! Bless you!"

And the first day out she sent him a radio: "You are a big brown bear and worth seventy-nine thousand gigolos even when their hair greased best butter stop did I remember to tell you that I adore you."

CHAPTER 16

With Ambrose Channel ahead of them, Sam Dodsworth and his friend Ross Ireland spent a considerable part of their time in the smoking-room of the Aquitania arguing with other passengers about the glories of America. Sam was appreciative enough, but Ross was eloquent, he was lyric, he was tremendous.

At praise of Paris, Cambodia, Oslo, Glasgow, or any other foreign pride, he snorted, "Look here, son, that's all applesauce, and I KNOW! I've been hiking for three years. I've interviewed Count Bethlen and I've paddled up the Congo; I've done a swell piece about the Lena Gold Fields and I've driven three thousand miles in England. And believe me, I'm glad to be getting back to a real country, buddy!

"New York? Noisy? Say, why wouldn't it be noisy? It's got something going on! Believe me, they're remodeling all the old parts of Heaven after New York skyscrapers! Say, if we get past the perils of the deep and I have the chance to hang my hat up in Park Row again, you'll never get me farther away than an Elks' Convention at Atlantic City! And don't let anybody tell you that the Elks and the Rotarians and the National Civic Federation are any more grab-it-all than the English merchant, who hates our dollar-chasing so much that he wants to keep us from it by copping all the dollars there are to chase, or the elegant highbrow Frenchman who doesn't love the franc any more than he loves God. Why say, even about drinking--I'll admit I like a sidewalk cafe better than I do a speak-easy, but once I round up my old bunch at Denny's and have a chance to stick my legs under the table with a lot of real home-baked he-Americans instead of these imitation-Frog Americans that loaf around abroad--Boy!"

Sam discovered, dropping into Ross Ireland's stateroom, that Ross was guilty of secret intellectual practises. Except when, in morning clothes, he was interviewing Lord Chancellors and Generals Commanding, Ross felt that he must prove his sturdy independence by saying "Buddy," "Where d'you get that stuff," and "Oh, bologny." He was never, by any chance, "doing an analytical study"--at most he was "writing a little piece." He addressed English stewards as "Cap'n," he asked the Cockney smoking-room steward for his "check," and almost his only French expression was "viskey-soda." He announced, widely and loudly, that any newspaperman who called himself a "journalist" was a Big Stiff, a Phoney Highbrow, and an Imitation Limey. He said that any foreign correspondent who read history, went to concerts, or wore spats was "showing off."

But Sam discovered that Ross Ireland was guilty of reading vast and gloomy volumes of history; that he admired Conrad more than Conan Doyle; that he had a sneaking preference of chess to poker; and that he was irritably proud of having his evening clothes made in London.

That such a man, violently American yet not untraveled in distant coasts, should so rejoice at going back made Sam the more convinced about returning to his own. Of the vast and polished elegancies of the Aquitania he had little impression, none of the excitement about the steely resolution of ships which he had known on the Ultima, because all his excitement was focused on the blessed people he was going to see.

Tub Pearson--

He heard himself saying, "Well, you fat little runt! You horse-thief! Golly, I'm glad to see you!"

He stood forward on the promenade deck, fancying that his heart beat in rhythm with the rise and the fall of the prow, exulting as the ship slashed through the miles between him and home. He seemed a kindly but stolid figure there, a big man in a gray Burberry and a gray cap, a competent and unsentimental man. But he was boiling with sentiment. Once at night, when he saw the lights of a ship ahead, he pretended that they were the shore lights of Long Island, and he ardently imagined the dear familiarities--wide streets, clashing traffic, brick garages, the insolent splendor of skyscrapers and, toward the country, miles of white and green little houses where the sort of men he understood played games he understood, poker and bridge, and listened on the radio to the sort of humor and music that he understood. And before every other bungalow was a Revelation car.

"--and I'm going to STAY!" he exulted.

All the way over, Ross Ireland and he had boasted to such passengers as had never seen America that they would not "be able to believe their eyes" when they steamed up North River. Ross chanted, "Greatest sight in the world--skyscrapers one after another--thirty, forty, fifty stories high, and beautiful--say! they make Cologne Cathedral look like a Methodist chapel and the Eiffel Tower look like an umbrella with the cover off!"

They both, indeed, made so many protestations about the sight of New York harbor that Sam began to wonder whether he really was going to be as thrilled as he was going to be thrilled. He remembered how, after the most conversational anticipation with Fran, he had been disappointed by his first sight of Notre Dame. It had seemed low and hulking--not half so impressive as the lath- and-plaster Notre Dame in the movie film. He managed to fret rather ardently. He hoped to be uplifted by New York as a young lover hopes to be enraptured by the sight of his lady.

They came through the Narrows, into New York harbor, early in the June morning. Sam was up at five, delighted by the friendly green of the lawn at Fort Hamilton, after the shifting sea. It was extraordinarily hot for early summer, a bit uncomfortable even on deck, and a fog hid the horizon. Sam was afraid that he was not to have his rediscovery of New York. After quarantine, as they trudged from Staten Island toward North River, he could see only anchored tramp steamers, and a huge water-beetle of a ferry boat, hoarse-voiced and insulting. Then the fog lifted, and he cried "My God!" High up shone the towers and spires of an enchanted city floating upon the mist, pyramids and domes glistening in the early sun, vast walls studded with golden windows, spellbound and incredible.

Ross Ireland, beside him, muttered "Gee!" and then, "Say, does it make you proud to be coming home to that?"

It is true that when they swaggered up North River, the debris of docks and warehouses and factories on the riverbank seemed rather littered. The thickening heat glared round them, and the river was greasy with swirls of fantastically colored oil films. But as they were cumbersomely warped into the dock, as Sam heard the good American shouts from the dark hedge of people waiting on the pier; "Attaboy!" and "Where'd you get the monocle?" and "How'd you leave Mary?" and "Oh, come on--have a heart!--sneak me ONE bottle ashore!"--he muttered over and over, "It's kind of nice to be home!"

Then there were the customs.

Not that the inspectors were so impolite as is fabled, but it is irritating to be suspected of smuggling liquor, particularly when, like Sam, you are smuggling liquor. He had a quart of pre-war Scotch among the suits in a wardrobe trunk, and the inspector found it, immediately.

"What's this? What d'you call this?"

"Why! It looks like a bottle!" said Sam, affably. "I can't imagine how it got there! Let me present it to you."

And they fined him five dollars. But what was worse was that being destitute of liquor caused in Sam a most indignant thirst--Sam Dodsworth, who had never in his life taken a drink before noon, except once after a certain football game in New Haven. He HAD to have--

The taxi-driver--Sam came to him after hours of paying customs- fees, of getting necessitous porters, in a high state of boredom, to trundle his luggage along the immensity of cement floor and through to freedom, of seeing it shot perilously down the most efficient and disconcerting moving belt, and of having it and himself thrown gasping into the lions' den of New York traffic-- the taxi-driver gave Sam his first welcome to America.

"Wherejuh wanna go?" he growled.

It shocked Sam to find how jarred he was by this demonstration of democracy. Like most Americans in Paris, he had been insisting that all French taxi-drivers were bandits, but now they seemed to him like playful and cuddling children.

It was achingly hot in the side streets leading from the piers, and appallingly dirty. In front of warehouses and mean brick houses turned into tenements were flying newspapers, piles of bottles and rags and manure. Gritty clouds of ashes blew from open garbage cans, and tangled with the heat was New York's summertime stench of rotten bananas, unwashed laundry, ancient bedding, and wet pavements. In front of the taxicab, making Sam's heart stop with fear, darted ragged small boys (quite cheerful, and illogically healthy); and on the flimsy iron balconies of fire-escapes sat mothers with hair dragging across their eyes, nursing babies who in between sups wailed against the unjust heat. It was, Sam felt, a city nervous as a thwarted woman. (Sam still believed in male strength and female weakness.) It seemed so masculine in its stalwart buildings, but there was nothing masculine in its heat- shocked, clamor-maddened nerves. The traffic policemen raged at Sam's taxi-driver, the taxi-driver cursed all the truck-drivers, and, above the roaring of their engines, the truck-drivers cursed everybody on the street.

Ninth Avenue was insane with the banging of the Elevated; Eighth Avenue was a frontier camp of little shops; Seventh Avenue was a bedlam of traffic between loft buildings with enormous signs-- "Lowenstein & Putski, Garments for Little Gents," and "The Gay Life Brassiere, Rothweiser and Gitz"; Sixth Avenue combined the roar of Ninth with the nastiness of Eighth and the charging traffic of Seventh; and when in relief Sam saw the stateliness of Fifth Avenue, there was an inhuman mass of shiny cars from curb to curb.

The Sam Dodsworth who considered himself tireless was exhausted when he crawled into the cool refuge of his hotel. He sat by the window in his room, looking at the sullen stretch of the lofty office-building opposite, and longed for a drink.

"Conservatively, I'd give twenty-five dollars right now for the bottle of Scotch that the customs man took away from me. . . . Oh, Lord! . . . I don't like New York so well, in weather like this. I'll be glad to get out into the country. That's the real America. . . . I hope it will be! . . . I can see where I'm not going to complain about having too much leisure, the way I did in Paris! And I want that drink!"

It did not improve his opinion of Prohibition--it made the whole business seem the more imbecile and annoying and hypocritical--that after a telephone call, within half an hour he had a case of whisky in his room, and that he was taking a drink far earlier in the day than he would ever have done in Paris.

He had many people to see in New York before he went to New Haven for his class reunion. But he telephoned to no one--with the exception of the bootlegger. He had only the energy to sit by the window, getting what breeze there was, trying to ignore the ceaseless menace of the city roar, feeling more homeless than in Europe, trying to compose a lively cable to Fran and to get Brent, in New Haven, on the telephone.

He had not cabled Brent his date of sailing. "Boy's probably tied up with a lot of exams and things; when I land in New York I'll find out by 'phone when it's convenient for him to come down to New York." Brent was not to be found now by telephone. Sam sent him a telegram, and that was quite all that he felt like doing. He rested till one, till half-past. He had a small lunch, in his room, and the joy of having proper American sugar corn almost revived him, but afterward he sat by the window again till three, brooding. Lassitude bound him like a vast cobweb.

What was he doing here in New York? What was he doing anywhere? What reason had he for living? He was not necessary to Fran in Paris. And the motor-car industry seemed to be spinning on quite cheerily without him.

He faced his discovery--the incident had happened at his entrance to the hotel, but he had not admitted it to his consciousness till now. Alighting from his taxicab he had seen the new model Revelation car, as produced by the Unit Automotive Company, at three hundred dollars less than Sam's former price. He had wanted to hate it, to declare that it was tinny and wretched, but he had had to admit that it was a marvel of trimness, with the body swung lower, the windshield more raking. He felt antiquated. The U.A.C. had created this new model in six months; with his own organization he could not have produced it in less than a year. And he would have held it till the autumn motor shows and brought it out pompously, as though he were a priest grudgingly letting the laity behold his mysteries. Were the U.A.C. making light of seasons and announcement-dates--just tossing off new models as though they were cans of corn?

It came to him that he had not known when the new Revelation would be out. For the first months of his absence he had heard often from Alec Kynance, received all the gossip, with many invitations to return. He had heard but little the past three months. Was he out of it--perhaps forever?

He had come back to America feeling that the world of motors longed for him; he felt, this hot confused afternoon, that no one cared. . . . It was true that, to keep his time free, he had told no one he was arriving, but confound it, they might have found out somehow--

Come to think of it, not one of the reporters who had boarded the Aquitania and hunted down incoming celebrities--the Polish tennis champion, the famous radio-announcer who had been perfecting his art in Berlin, the latest New York-Paris divorcee--had paid attention to him. Yet when he had gone abroad, they had interviewed him as a Representative American Business Man--

He was frightened by his drop into insignificance.

At half-past three he was startled and cheered by a telephone-call:

"Hello? Dodsworth? This is Ross Ireland. Say, I'm in the same hotel. Doing anything? Mind if I run up for a minute?"

Ireland burst in, red, collar wilted, panting.

"Say, Dodsworth, am I crazy? Do I look crazy?"

"No, you look hot."

"Hot? Hell! I've been hot in Rangoon. But I sat back in a nice carriage, in my pretty little white suit and my sun helmet, and took it easy. I didn't feel as though I'd been in two hundred and twenty-seven train collisions, one right after another. Do you know what I've found out? I hate this damn' town! It's the dirtiest, noisiest, craziest hole I was ever in! I hate it--me that's been going up and down the face of the earth for the last three years, shooting my face off and telling every-body what a swell capital New York is.

"What you got to drink? Oh, God, only whisky? Well, let's have a look at it.

"Well, this morning I didn't even stop to unpack. I was going to see the dear old home town--the dear old neighbors, by heck, down on Park Row. I got down to the Quackenbos office, and the office boy hadn't ever heard my name--I've only been sending in three columns a week, signed, for three years! But he found a stenographer who thought she'd heard of me, and they actually let me in to see the old man--mind you, to get in to see him was sixteen times harder than it would be to see King George at Buckingham Palace, and when I did get in, there he was with his feet in a desk drawer reading the jokes in the New Yorker. Well, he was all right. He jumped up and told me I was the white-haired boy, and the sight of me'd just about saved him from typhoid, and we talked a whole half hour, and then made a date to finish up our business at lunch, tomorrow! Oh no, he didn't have one minute till then! Tonight--God, no, he had to help open up a new roof garden.

"Oh, I've been the boiled mutton-head! I've been going around Europe and Asia telling the heathen that the reason we hustle so in New York is because we get so much done. I never discovered till to-day that we do all this hustling, all this jamming in subways, all this elbowing into elevators, to keep ourselves occupied and keep from getting anything done! Say, I'll bet I accomplished more honest-to-

God work in Vienna in three hours than I will here in three days! Those Austrian hicks don't have any bright office boys or filing-systems to prevent them from talking business. So they go home for two hours' lunch. Poor devils! No chance to ride on the subway! And only cafes to sit around in, instead of night clubs. Awful life!

"Well, when I'd got this whole half hour in with the boss--he took up most of it telling a swell new smutty story he'd just heard--one I used to tell back in Ioway in 1900--I drifted over to the Chronicle to see the bunch I used to work with. . . . I was city editor there once! . . . Half of the bunch were aus. Gone into politics, I guess. . . . The other half were glad to see me, so far as I could figure out, but they'd gone and got married or learned to play bridge or taken to teaching Sunday School or some immoral practise like that, and by golly not one of 'em could I get for dinner and a show tonight. By the way, you don't happen to be free for tonight, Dodsworth, do you? Grand! Tickled to death!

"Well, I went out to lunch with one of the fellows on the Sunday edition. He suggested some whisky, but I wanted something cool. He said he knew a place where we could get some real genuine Italian Chianti--and say, he called it 'genuwine Ytalian' too. As a joke. I believe he taught English in Harvard for a year. But being a hard-boiled newspaperman, of course he had to be a roughneck, to show he wasn't pedantic. . . . Like me, I guess. I've been pulling that same lowbrow pose myself.

"But anyway: we look up this genuwine Ytalian dump--I guess, from the smell, they used it as a laundry till it got too dirty--and the Wop brought on a bottle of something that was just about as much like Chianti as I'm like a lily of the valley. Honestly, Sam, it tasted like vinegar that'd been used on beets just once too often.

"And then--Oh, I suppose, being just back after my first long hike, I felt I had a Chautauqua message for Young America--I suppose I felt I was a Peary bringing home the Pole under my arm. I tried to tell this chap how much I knew about Burma, and how chummy I was with Lord Beaverbrook, and all the news about the land problem in Upper Silesia, and was he interested? Say, he was about as much interested as I'd be in a chatty account of the advancement of Christian Science in Liberia! But he had a lot of important news for me. Golly! Bill Smith'd had a raise of twenty bucks a week! Pete Brown is going to edit the hockey gossip, instead of Mike Magoon! The Edam Restaurant is going to have a new jazz orchestra! The Fishback Portable

Typewriter has gone up five dollars in price! Ellen Whoozis, the cocktail-party queen, who writes the Necking Notes, is going to marry the religious editor!

"Say, it was exactly like going back to the dear old Home Town in Ioway, after my first three years in New York! That time I wanted to tell the home-town boys all the news about the Brooklyn Ridge and immorality, and they wanted to talk about Henry Hick's new flivver!

"Well, I guess it's all about alike, really--Buddhism in Burma and Henry's flivver. It's all neighborhood gossip, with different kinds of neighbors. Only--

"But it isn't the same! I've seen--oh, God, Sam, I've seen the jungle at dawn, and these fellows have stayed here, stuck at little desks, and never drifted five steps away from their regular route from home, to the office, to the speak-easy, to the office, to the movie, to home. I was on a ship afire in the Persian Gulf--

"I know it's just vanity, Sam, but there ARE things outside America--Whether they're ever going to have sense enough to make a Pan-Europa there--whether Britain is going to recognize Russia, and who's going to get Russian oil--what will become of Poland--what Fascism really means in Italy; things that ought to be almost as interesting as the next baseball game. But these lads that've stuck here in New York, they're so self-satisfied (like I was once!) that they don't care a hang for anything beyond the current price of gin! They don't know there is a Europe, beyond the Paris bars. Why even in my shop-- I carry on in Europe as though I were the great, three-star, two-tailed special foreign correspondent but here (it's a fact!) the fellow that does the weekly cartoon about Farmer Hiram Winterbottom gets three times my salary--say, if HE came into the office, old Quackenbos would give him the whole day!

"Well, now that I've told you what a nice, lace-collared, abused darling I am, let's--

"But this town, that I've been looking forward to--(Man, do you realize we could sail back on the Aqui in a week? Think of that nice cool corner in the smoking-room!) I've found that the one and only up-to-date, new, novel, ingenious way of getting anywhere in this burg, if you want to GET there, is to walk! It takes a taxi, in this traffic, ten minutes to make ten blocks. And the subway-- How many years since you've been in the subway? Well, don't! I thought I was a pretty big guy, and fairly husky, but say, the subway guard at the Grand Central just stuck his knee in the middle of my back and rammed me into a car that was already plumb-full like I was a three-year-old child! And I stood up as far as Brooklyn Bridge, with my nose in the neck of a garbage-wholesaler! Say, I feel like an anarchist! I want to blow up the whole town!

"Then, after lunch, I wanted to buy a few real first-edition suits of American athletic underwear, so I went to Mosheim's department store. Seen their new building? Looks like a twenty-story ice-palace. Windows full of diamonds and satins and ivory and antique Spanish furniture, and lingerie that would make a movie-actress blush. 'City of luxury--Europe beat a mile!' says I. 'Extra! Pleasure Capital of the World Discovered by H. Ross Ireland!' And then I tried to get into the store. Honestly, Sam. I'll be quite a husky fellow when I get my strenth. I used to play center and wrestle heavyweight in the University of Iowa. But, by golly, I couldn't hardly wedge my way in through the doors. There was one stream of maniacs rushing out and another rushing in, as though it was a fire, and every aisle was jammed, and then when you got to the proper counter--

"Well, I've got good and plenty sore at the way the hired help treat you abroad. I've had a Turkish rug-vendor go crazy when I didn't want to pay more'n twice the price of a rug; I've had a hard-boiled Greek mate bawl hell out of me because he tripped over me on deck; I've had a gondolier say what he thought of my tip. But anyway, those fellows treated you as though you were almost their equals. It's like Chesterton says--if a fellow kicks his butler down-stairs, it doesn't show any lack of democracy; it's only when he feels too superior to his butler to touch him that he's really snooty. And that's how the nice bright young gent at the underwear-counter treated me. He had about six people to wait on, and unless I spoke quick and took what he gave me, he wasn't going to waste time on me, and he kept looking at me with a 'You big hick, don't try to fool me, that ain't no real New York suit you got on--back to Yankton.'

"Then I tried to get out of the store. One fellow elbowing you in the stomach and another jabbing you in the back, and the elevator man hollering 'Step lively, please,' till you wanted to sock him in the nose. Honestly, I felt like a refugee driven by the Cossacks-- no, I didn't feel that human; I felt like I was one of a bunch of steers driven down the runway to the slaughter-house. God, what a town! Luxury! Gold! Everything but self-respect and decency and privacy!

"And what an oration! That's the longest speech I've made since I caught my No.1 Boy in Burma wearing my best pants!"

"Well," Sam soothed, "it'll be better when you get out into the country."

"But I don't like the country! Being a hick by origin, I like cities. I had enough cornfields and manure-piles before I ran away, at fourteen. And from what I heard at lunch, all the other towns in America are becoming about as bad as New York--traffic jams and big movie theaters and radios yapping everywhere and everybody has to have electric dish-washers and vacuum cleaners and each family has to have not one car, by golly, but two or three-- and all on the installment plan! But I guess any of those burgs would be better than this New York monkey jungle.

"And I thought I knew this town! Ten years I put in here! But honestly, it's sixteen times as bad as it was three years ago, seems to me. Ought to be lovely three years from NOW! And foreign--say, when you see a real old-fashioned American face on the street, you wonder how he got here. I think I'll go back to London and see some Americans!"

Ross, Sam felt, was exaggerating. But when Ross had gone and he had roused himself from his lassitude for a walk--for a hot crawl-- he felt lost and small and alien in the immense conflict of the steaming streets.

And he had no place to go. He realized that this capital, barbaric with gold and marble, provided every human necessity save a place, a cafe or a plaza or a not-too-lady-like tea-shop, in which he could sit and be human. Well! He could go to the Metropolitan Art Gallery, the Aquarium, the dusty benches of Central Park, or sit gently in a nice varnished pew in a Protestant Church.

People running with suit-cases nicked his legs, small active Jews caromed into him, flappers with faces powdered almost purple looked derisively at his wandering and bucolic mildness, a surf of sweaty undistinguishable people swept over him, shop-windows of incredible aloof expensiveness stared at him, and at every street-crossing he was held up by the wave of traffic, as he crept over to Fifth Avenue, down to Forty-second, past leering cheap-jack shops and restaurants, over to Sixth and back again to the Grand Central Station.

He stood contemplatively (he who a year ago would never have stood thus, but would have rushed with the most earnest of them) on the balcony overlooking the shining acres of floor of the Grand Central Station, like a roofed-over Place de la Concorde. Why, he wondered, was it that the immensity of Notre Dame or St. Paul's did not dwarf and make ridiculous the figures of the worshippers as this vastness did the figures of travelers galloping to train- gates? Was it because the little people, dark and insignificant in the cathedrals, were yet dignified, self-possessed, seeking the ways of God, whereas here they were busy with the ludicrous activity of insects?

He fancied that this was veritably the temple of a new divinity, the God of Speed.

Of its adherents it demanded as much superstitious credulity as any of the outworn deities--demanded a belief that Going Some- where, Going Quickly, Going Often, were in themselves holy and greatly to be striven for. A demanding God, this Speed, less good- natured than the elder Gods with their faults, their amours, their vanity so easily pleased by garlands and flattery; an abstract, faultless, and insatiable God, who once he had been offered a hundred miles an hour, straight-way demanded a hundred and fifty.

And with his motor cars Sam had contributed to the birth of this new religion, and in the pleasant leisure of Europe he had longed for its monastic asperities! He blasphemed against it now, longing for the shabbiest bar on the raggedest side street of Paris.

He shook his great shaggy head as he looked down on travel- ing- salesmen importantly parading before bag-laden red-caps, on fagged brokers with clanking bags of golf sticks, on fretful women, contemptuous overdressed women, and sleek young men in white knickerbockers. They seemed to him driven to madness by the mad God of Speed that themselves had created--and Sam Dodsworth had created.

Sam and Ross Ireland foolishly tried to take a taxicab to the theater. When they were already half an hour late, they got out and walked the last six blocks. They saw a number of delightful and naked young women, as naked as they would have been at Folies- Bergere.

"From the breaths around us, I guess there's a few New York- ers who haven't heard about Prohibition," sighed Ross, as they paced the street in the entr'acte. "Well, fortunately, the preachers haven't enough influence with God yet to keep the girls from being naked. They'll have to fix that up as soon as Prohibition really goes over-- arrange to have the girls born with flannel nighties on. . . . Honestly, Sam, I don't get these here United States. We let librarians censor all the books, and yet we have musical comedies like this--just as raw as Paris. We go around hollering that we're the only bona fide friends of democracy and self-determination, and yet with Haiti and Nicaragua we're doing everything we accused Germany of doing in Belgium, and--you mark my word--within a year we'll be starting a Big Navy campaign for the purpose of bullying the world as Great Britain never thought of doing. We boast of scientific investigation, and yet we're the only supposedly civilized country where thousands of supposedly sane citizens will listen to an illiterate clodhopping preacher or politi- cian setting himself up as an authority on biology and attacking evolution."

It was after the wearisome glare of the musical comedy, at a speak- easy which was precisely like an old-fashioned bar except that the whisky was bad, that Ross Ireland raged on:

"Yes, and to have a little more of our American paradox, we have more sentimental sobbing over poor de-uh mother in the movies, and more lynching of negroes, than would be possible anywhere else in the world! More space, and more crowded tenements; more hard- boiled pioneers, and more sickly discontented wives; more Nancies among young men; more highbrow lectures, and more laughing-hyena comic strips and more slang--Well, take me. I'm supposed to be a newspaperman. I've seen a lot--and read a whale of a lot more than I ever admit. I have ideas, and I even have a vocabulary. But I'm so American that if I ever admit I'm interested in ideas, if I ever phrase a sentence grammatically, if I don't try to sound like a longshoreman, I'm afraid that some damned little garage-proprietor will think I'm try- ing to be pedantic! Oh, I've learned a lot about myself and my beloved America today!"

"Just the same, Ross, I prefer this country to--"

"Hell, so do I! Things I can remember, people I've talked to, knocking around this country, High Sierras to the Cape Cod cranberry- bogs. Old Pop Conover, that used to be a Pony Express Rider, going lickety-split, risking his life among the Indians--I remember him at eighty, the whitest old man you ever saw; lived in a little shack in my town in Iowa, baching it--had an old chair made out of a flour-barrel.

159

Say, he'd tell us kids stories by the hour; he'd put up a tramp for the night; and he'd've received a king just the same way. Never occurred to him that he was any better than the tramp or any worse than a king. He was a real American. And I've seen the bunch at football games--nice clean youngsters. But we're turning the whole thing into a six-day bicycle race. And with motor-cycles instead of the legs that we used to have once!"

With Ross Ireland talking always--assailing the American bustle except at such times as Sam complained of it, whereupon Ross would defend it furiously--they ambled to a Broadway cabaret.

It was called "The Georgia Cabin," it specialized in Chicken Maryland and yams and beaten biscuit, and the orchestra played "Dixie" every half hour, to great cheering. Aside from Ross and Sam, everybody in the place was either a Jew or a Greek. It was so full of quaintness and expensiveness. The walls were in monstrous overblown imitation of a log cabin; and round the tiny fenced dancing-floor, so jammed that the dancers looked like rush-hour subway passengers moving in sudden amorous insanity, was the Broadway idea of a rail-fence.

The cover charge was two dollars apiece. They had two lemonades, at seventy-five cents each, with a quarter tip to the Hellenic waiter--at which he grumbled--and a quarter to the trim and cold- eyed hat-girl--at which she snapped, "Another pair of cheap skates!"

They said little as they marched toward their hotel. Over Sam, thick, palpable, like a shroud, was the lassitude he had felt in Paris. He was in a dream; nothing was real in all this harsh reality of trolley bells, furious elevated trains, swooping taxicabs, the jabbering crowds. The heat was churning up into a thunderstorm. Lightning revealed the cornices of the inhumanly lofty buildings. The whole air was menacing, yet he felt the menace indifferently, and heavily he said good night to Ross Ireland.

The storm exploded as he stood at the window of his hotel room. Every lightning flash threw into maniacal high relief the vast yellow wall of the building opposite, and its innumerable glaring windows; and in the darknesses between flashes he could imagine the building crashing over on him. It was terrifying as a volcanic eruption, even to Sam Dodsworth, who was not greatly given to fear. Yet terror could not break up the crust of dull loneliness which encased him.

He turned from the window with a lifeless step and went drearily to bed, to lie half awake. He muttered only, "This hustle of American life--regular battle--is it going to be too much for me, now I'm out of the habit?"

And, "Oh, God, Fran, I am so lonely for you!"

CHAPTER 17

But it was a pleasanter and more kindly America that he found the next evening, when he sat with Elon Richards, chairman of the board of the Goodwood National Bank, on the terrace at Willow Marsh, Richards' place on Long Island.

In the morning, Sam's son, Brent, telephoned from New Haven that he would finish his examinations in two days and be down for a real bender with his father. In the afternoon Sam labored mightily with Alec Kynance in the New York office of the U.A.C. He was again offered a vice presidency of the U.A.C. and again he refused.

He was vague about his refusal.

"Alec, it's hard to explain it--just feel that I've given most of my life to making motor cars, and now I'd like to sit around and visit with myself and get acquainted. Yes, I was lonely in Paris. I admit it. But it's a job I've started, and I'm not going to give it up yet."

Kynance was sharp.

"I don't know's I can ever make this offer again."

Sam scarcely heard him. He--of old-time the steadily attentive-- was wool-gathering: "I'll never be good for anything BUT business, but why not have a little fun and try something new--big orange- grove in Florida, or real estate?"

When Sam telephoned to Richards of the Goodwood National, Richards insisted on his coming out to Long Island for the night.

Sam was relaxed and cheered by the drive, in the Hispano-Suiza which Richards' daughter, Sheila, had invited her father to buy the moment she had read the novels of Michael Arlen. They slipped through the vicious traffic of the Grand Central district, turned up First Avenue with its air of a factory village, crossed the superb arch of the Fifty-ninth Street Bridge, from which they looked down to towers looming over docks for steamers from Rio de Janeiro and Barbados and Africa.

They shot through a huddle of factories and workers' cottages, and fled along a road which followed the shore-line, with a salt breeze whispering through the open windows of the great car; they came into pleasant suburbs, and turned off on a country lane among real farms. Sam's slightly battered Americanism rose exultantly as he saw corn-fields, pumpkin vines, white farm-houses with piles of poplar stove-wood.

And the talk was good.

Sam had never been such a fool as to assert that virile citizens talked only of bonds and prize-fighting, and that any one who pretended to an interest in Matisse or the Ca' d' Oro was an effeminate pretender. Only, he had pled with Fran, he himself had as much right to be interested in bonds and bored by Matisse as a painter had to be interested in Matisse and bored by bonds. Of course bonds had been important enough to Alec Kynance, that afternoon. Yet Alec's talk had not been good, because the little man could never keep his role of Napoleon of Commerce to himself, but insisted on treating every one he met as either a Faithful Guardsman whose ear he could tweak, or as a Faithful Field Marshal who was gaping to receive (from Alec) a new baton.

But Elon Richards talked of consolidations and investments and golf and the more scandalous divorces of bankers with the simplicity and impersonality of a dairyman discussing cattle-feed. He announced (while the car slipped past the little farms and into a region of great estates) that the K. L. and Z. would be bankrupt within two months, that there really was something to this company that was going to grow 1,000,000 reindeer in Alaska, that Smith Locomotive Common wouldn't be such a bad buy, and that it was perfectly true that the Antelope Car was going to announce safety windshield glass as a standard accessory.

The great house at Willow Marsh stood on a bluff looking over marshes to Long Island Sound. They dined on a brick terrace, at a little table with quivering candles, round it three wicker chairs with Sam, Richards, and his daughter, Sheila. It was Sheila who six months ago had demanded the Hispano-Suiza, but this summer she was in a socialist stage. Sam was a little annoyed because all through dinner she kept asking why the workers should not take from Sam and her father all their wealth.

163

Richards, to Sam's incredulity, encouraged Sheila by teasing her:

"If you can get a really first-class leader, like Lenin, who's strong enough to take the money away from me in the first place and to construct a practical working state in the second, I shan't worry--just as soon work for him and his gang as for our stockholders. But if you think, my impudent young daughter, that because a lot of socialist journalists yap that maybe, possibly, some day, the working-class may get educated up to the point of running industry and therefore I ought to join 'em--well, let 'em MAKE me!"

So for an hour.

After twenty-five years of big industry, Sam Dodsworth still believed, in an unformulated and hazy way, that socialism meant the dividing-up of wealth, after which the millionaires would get it all back within ten years. He still half believed that all Bolsheviks were Jews who wore bushy beards, carried bombs, and were hardly to be distinguished from anarchists. He didn't completely believe it, because in his office he had met suave and beardless Soviet agents who had talked competently about importing Revelation cars. But to take so-cialism seriously--

It annoyed him.

Why had he ever gone abroad? It had unsettled him. He had been bored in Paris, yet he liked crepes Susette better than flapjacks; he liked leaning over the bridges of the Seine better than walking on Sixth Avenue; and he couldn't, just now, be very excited about the new fenders for the Revelation car. How was it that this America, which had been so surely and comfortably in his hand, had slipped away?

And here was the daughter of an Elon Richards, most safely conservative of bankers, contaminated with a lot of European social-ism. Was life really as complicated as all that?

It was simpler when Sheila had left them. The June twilight was tender, and across the mauve ribbon of Long Island Sound unseen villages sprang to life in soft twinkling. On the cool terrace, after two choked days in New York, Sam relaxed in a wicker chair, shoulders moving with contentment. Richards' cigars were excellent, his brandy was authentic, and now that Sheila was away, driving her own car off to a dance, his talk was again reasonable.

But it came again--

"Curious, Richards," Sam pondered aloud. "Since I landed in New York yesterday, I've hated the whole rush and zip of it--till this evening, when I've had a chance to sit down in the country and feel human. Course it was probably just the hot weather. Only--Do you know, I had a feeling of leisure in France and in England. I felt there as though people made their jobs work for them; they didn't give up their lives to working for their jobs. And I felt as though there was such a devil of a lot to learn about the world that we're too busy to learn here."

Richards puffed comfortably; then:

"Did you know I was reared in Europe, Sam?"

"No! Fact?"

"Yes. My father and mother were devoted to Europe. We wandered. I spent fourteen out of the first sixteen years of my life in schools in France and England and Switzerland, and I went back there every summer while I was in Harvard--except the last vacation, after Junior year. Then my father had a brain-wave, and sent me out to Oregon to work in a lumber camp. I was crazy about it! I was so sick of pensions and cafes and the general European attitude that, for an American, you weren't such a bad egg. In Oregon I got beaten up by the lumberjacks three times in seven days, but at the end of the summer I was ardently invited to stay on as straw boss of the camp. I loved it! And I've gone on loving it ever since. I know that plenty of French financiers are more elegant and leisurely than your flat-footed friend Alec Kynance, but I get more fun out of fighting Alec!

"Sam, it's a battle here, the way it is in Russia and China.. And you, Sam, you old grizzly, can never be a contemplative gazelle. You've got to fight. And think of it! Maybe America will rule the world! Maybe in the end we'll be broken up by Russia. But isn't a world-fight like that better than sitting around avoiding conversational errors and meditating on the proper evening waistcoats? Life!"

Sam meditated, silently and long.

"Elon," said he, "there was a time when I knew my own mind. I didn't do whatever my latest stenographer suggested. But I've seen too many things, recently. If Fran were here--my wife--I'd probably be pro-Europe. You make me pro-America."

"Why be pro-anything? Why not dive head-first into whatever battle seems most interesting? You can be sure of this: the result won't mean anything. My girl, Sheila, informs me that a judicious use of eugenics, Karl Marx, and tennis would turn us all into a bunch of beneficent Apollos in five generations. God forbid! I have a sneaking suspicion that none of us poor vertebrates want perfection, really! But I mean: You're one of these kind-hearted, dutiful Americans who feels apologetic and inferior the moment he retires, and who'll spend the rest of his life trying to satisfy everybody he meets: his 'wife and his mistress--"

"Not yet!"

"Wait!--and his friends. Sam, I'm such an idealist that I'd like to start an Association for the Hanging of All Idealists. For Heaven's sake decide whether you, your own self, are happier in America or in Europe, and then stick there! Me, I'm glad to have European bankers coming to me begging for loans instead of my going to European cafes and begging waiters for a table in the sun! Sam, this American adventure--Because it is an adventure that we have here--the greatest in the world--and not a certainty of manners in an uncertainty of the future, like all of Europe. And say, do you know, our adventure is going to be the bigger because we DO feel that Europe has a lot we need. We're no longer satisfied with the log cabin and the corn pone. We want everything that Europe has. We'll take it!"

"Um," said Sam.

That night he slept child-like, in a breeze from the Sound. He awoke at five, to sit on the edge of his bed, bulky in his rather touseled silk pajamas, meditating while he looked down on the marshlands smoking with morning, and the Sound, like whirls of cobweb over bright steel.

If he were fifty miles farther out on Long Island, perhaps he could see across to the Connecticut shore and New Haven.

He realized that this was grotesquely like a day in spring of his senior year in Yale when from East Rock he had looked across the Sound to Long Island, and in that distant shore beheld romantic harbors. He was separated from the boy who had sat on East Rock only by Long Island Sound, and thirty years, and that boy's certainty that he would "do something worth while." Today he could think of things far more interesting to attempt than in those solemn important days when he had been a football star weighed down with the monastic duties of an athlete. It was not, now, ridiculous to consider being a wanderer in Japan, a proponent of Sheila Richards' socialism or its crusading foe, or, twenty years hence, merely an old man with a pipe, content among apple trees on a hill above the Ohio River. But also it was obvious now that he was chained by people and strengths and weaknesses which he had not recognized in his young hour of vision on East Rock.

He could not return to a completely simple and secure life in America because of Fran's dislike for it, and without the habitual titillation of Fran's gaieties and bad temper, life was inconceivable. He could not become an elegantly lounging cosmopolitan because--his thought stumbled and growled--oh, because he was Sam Dodsworth!

He was chained by every friend who had made life agreeable-- bound not to shock or lose them. He was chained by every dollar he had made, every automobile he had manufactured--they meant a duty to his caste. He was chained by every hour he had worked--they had left him stiff, spiritually rheumatic.

He still wanted the world . . . but there was nothing specific in the world that he wanted so much as, thirty years ago, he had wanted to be a Richard Harding Davis hero.

Then it came to him.

He marveled, "No, the trouble is that, aside from keeping in with Fran and the children and a few friends, I don't want anything enough to fight for it much. I've done about all I ever imagined-- got position, made money, met interesting folks. I'd be a lot luckier if I were a hobo that hadn't done any of the things he wanted to. Oh, hang it, I don't much care. Maybe I didn't hitch my wagon to a high-enough star! This one don't look very good!

"Rats! When I get out of this crazy New York district and meet real, simple, hearty fellows back in Zenith--yes, sure, and at my re-union--I'll get over this grouch.

"But what's it all about, this business of life?

"I'd give my left leg if I could believe what the preachers say. Immortality. Serving Jehovah. But I can't. Got to face it alone--

"Oh, for God's sake, quit pitying yourself! You're as bad as Fran--

"Fran! She's never bad. Not really. Did I ever happen to re-member to tell you that I adore you, Fran?"

Four hours later, at breakfast, he was an unsentimental Captain of Finance, attentive only to waffles.

167

He stood at a gate in the Grand Central Station watching his son lope up the inclined cement runway from the New Haven train.

"If there's anything finer than him at Oxford or in France--" he gloated, and "More Fran's boy than mine, though; got her good looks and quickness."

Brent was like a young race horse, his pale face and high thin forehead almost too bred-down, too refined. But there was health and buoyancy in his humorous eyes, his shout of "Hello, Dad! Swell to see you again. Good crossing?"

"Yes. Fair. Nice to see you, boy. How long can you stay?"

"Have to be back in the morning. Catch the milk-train."

"Too bad. Here, give your bag to a red-cap."

"And pay a quarter? Not a chance--not with corn whisky costing what it does."

"Um. I wouldn't drink much of that. But I guess you know that. Where'd you like to dine tonight? Ritz, or some hell-raising place?"

"I'll show you a real joint with real German beer."

"Fine. Uh--"

Sam looked shyly down at the shy boy, and blurted, "Mighty proud of you for making both Bones and Phi Beta Kappa."

"Oh, thanks. Gosh, you're looking fine, sir."

He found that though Brent would be in New York for only twelve hours, he had brought dinner clothes.

"Fran's boy, all right," he reflected, and somehow he was a bit lonely. He wished that he could give this nervous youngster something more than an allowance--some strength, some stability.

While they dressed, Brent recovered from his filial shyness enough to chatter about the miracles performed by Chick Budlong as a pole- vaulter, about the astounding fact that after being a perfectly good egg for over two years, Ogden Rose had turned literary and heeled the Lit., about the "bum body job" of the new U.A.C. Revelation. He was emerging as the young elegant, slim in dinner clothes, and he belonged to a world which would resent Sam's intrusion, which desired no strength nor stability . . . even if, Sam considered, he had any to give.

The "German restaurant" to which Brent led him was altogether imitation: beer mugs made in Pennsylvania; beams stained to look old; colored glass windows which, if they could have been opened, would have been found to look on nothing but a plaster wall; and beer that was most deplorably and waterily imitation.

Against this soiled and tawdry background, against the soiled and insolent and rather pathetic Polish waiters, Brent was real as a knife-blade, and as shining.

Sam had had a notion that now, two men together, his son and he could be intimately frank. He would talk to Brent about drinking, gambling, the value of money as a means and its worthlessness as an end, and most of all, about women. Oh, he wouldn't snoop and paw-- he'd just give his own notions of a life neither Puritanical nor licentious; be awfully frank about the danger of the daughters of the street, while admitting, like a man of the world, the compulsion of "sex"; and if Brent should be moved to give any confidences, he would treat them casually, sympathetically--

That warm rejoicing idea had been chilled the moment he saw Brent's self-confident figure. Why, the boy might think he was in Bad Taste, and next to the affection of Fran and Emily, he wanted Brent's affection and respect more than that of any one in the world. So, in parental fear, while he would have liked to expose his soul, he droned about Lord Herndon, Gioserro the aviator, the palace at Versailles--

But there was one intimate thing of which he could talk:

"Son, have you decided whether you'll go to Harvard Law School when you finish Yale?"

"I haven't quite decided, sir."

"Don't call me 'sir'! Look here, Brent; I have a notion--If your Mother and I are still abroad when you graduate, how would it be for you to come and join us for a year or so? Maybe between us, we could get her to chase off to Africa and India and China and so on. Just now she's stuck on Paris. I've been finding out there's a devil of a lot to see in this world. There's no hurry about your getting down to earning money."

"But you went to work early, sir."

"Don't call me 'sir'--I'm still under the age for it--I hope! And I think that maybe I got to work too early. Rather wish, now, I'd bummed around the world a little first. And after all these years you've been studying, to go right on to your law books--"

"Well, you see, sir, I'm not sure I'll go out for law."

"Um. What you thinking of? Medicine? Motors?"

"No, I--You know my roommate, Billy Deacon, his dad is president of Deacon, Iffley and Watts, the bond-house; and Billy wants me to come in with him selling bonds. I think probably I could be making twenty-five thousand a year in ten years, and in the law, if I went into a really tophole New York firm, I'd only be a clerk then. And some day I'll be in the hundred and fifty thousand a year class."

Brent said it with the modest confidence, the eager eyes, of a young poet announcing that he was going to write an epic.

Sam spoke doubtfully:

"May sound like a funny thing from a man that's always captured every dollar he could lay his hands on, but--Brent, I've always wanted to build things; to leave something besides a bank balance. Afraid you wouldn't be doing that, just selling bonds. Not that I've anything against bonds, you understand! Nice handsome engravings. But are you going to need to make money so fast--"

"Life's a lot more expensive than when you started, Dad. Fellow has to have so many things. When I was a kid, a man with a limousine was a little tin god, but now a fellow that hasn't got a yacht simply isn't in it. If a fellow makes his pile, then he can lay off and have a hobby--see Europe and go out for public spirit and all that stuff. I believe I've got a swell chance with Bill Deacon and his bunch."

"Well. Course you've got to decide for yourself. But I wish you'd think it over--about really building things."

"Sure. I certainly will, sir."

Brent was bright with compliments about Sam's knowledge of Europe; he remarked that Sam's football glories were still remembered at Yale.

And Sam sighed to himself that he had lost the boy forever.

CHAPTER 18

Sam was packing, to go to New Haven for his thirtieth class reunion, when the mild little knock came at the door. He roared "Come in," and at first did not look to see who his visitor might be. The silence after the opening of the door made him turn.

Tub Pearson was on the threshold, grinning.

"Well, you fat little runt!" said Sam, which meant, "My dear old friend, I am enchanted to see you!" And Tub gave answer, "You big stiff, so they couldn't stand you in Yurrup any more, eh? So you had to sneak back here, eh? You big bum!" Which signified, to one knowing the American language, "I have been quite distressingly lonely for you in Zenith, and had you not returned, I should probably have given up the Reunion and gone to Europe to see you-- I would, really."

"Well, you're looking fine, Tub." And they patted each other's arms, curtly.

"So are you. You look ausgezeichnet. I guess Europe agreed with you. Didn't bring me home a little of that swell French wine, did you?"

"Sure, I've got a whole case of it in my collar box."

"Well, bring it out. Let's not put off the fatal hour."

From behind a trunk (where, under the new American dispensation, all hotel guests hide the current bottle of whisky, to make it easier for the hotel servants to find it) Sam produced something, chuckling, "Now this may just look like plain Methodist bootlegged corn to you, Tub, but remember you ain't traveled expensively and got educated, the way I have. Say when. . . . Oh, say, Tub, I got a bottle of the real thing--pre-war Scotch--taken off me here at the docks."

"Oh, my God! What a sacrilege! Well now, tell me, what kind of a time d'you really have?"

"Oh, fine, fine! Paris is a fine city. Say, how's Matey and your kids?"

"Fine!"

"How's Harry Hazzard?"

"He's fine. He's got a grand-daughter. Say, they whoop it up all night long in Paris, don't they?"

"Yeh, pretty late. Have you seen Emily lately?"

"Just the other day at the country club. Looked fine. Oh, say, Sambo, can you explain one thing to me? Is there any chance the Bolsheviks will pay the Czarist debts to France? And what kind of a buy are French municipals?"

"Well, I didn't find out much about--Oh, I met some high-class Frogs--fellow named Andillet, stock-broker, pretty well heeled I guess. But it isn't like with us. Hard to get those fellows down to real serious talk, out of the office. They want to gas about the theater and dancing and horse-racing all the time. But say, I did learn one mighty interesting thing: the Citroen people in France and the Opel people in Germany are putting up low-priced cars that'll give the Ford and the Chev a mighty hard run for their money in European territory and--Oh! Say! Tub! Can you tell me anything about the rumors that Ford is going to scrap Model T and come out with an entirely new model? My God, I've tried and tried and I can't find out anything about it! I've asked Alec Kynance, and I've asked Byron Rogers of the Sherman, and I've asked Elon Richards, and if they know anything, they won't let it out and--By golly, I'd like to find out something about it."

"So would I! So would I! And I can't find out a thing!"

They both sighed, and refilled.

"They finished the new addition to the country club?" asked Sam.

"Yes, and it's a beauty. They play much golf in France?"

"I guess so, on the Riviera. Been by my house recently? Everything look all right?"

"You bet. I stopped and spoke to your caretaker. Seems like a good reliable fellow. Say, just what does a fellow DO, evenings in Paris? What kind of hang-outs do you go to? 'Bout like night- clubs here?"

"Well, a lot better wine--well no, at that, some of the places that are filled with Americans stick you and stick you good for pretty poor fizz. But on the whole--Oh, I don't know; you get tired of racketing around. All these pretty women, talking all the time!"

"Didn't pick up a little cutie on the side, did you?"

"Did you say 'cutie' or 'cootie'?"

And they both laughed, and they both sighed, and of Sam's non- existent amorous affairs they said no more.

And they found that they had nothing else to say.

For years they had shared friends, games, secret business-reports. They had been able to talk actively about the man they had seen the day before, the poker they had played two days ago, the bank scandal that was going on at the moment. But in six months, most of the citizens of Zenith whose scandals and golf handicaps had been important had been dimmed for Sam; he could not visualize them, could think of nothing to ask about them. The two men fell into an uncomfortable playing at catch with questions and answers.

Sam said, mildly, "Kind of wish I'd started going abroad earlier, Tub--kind of interesting to see how differently they do things. But it's too late now."

He struggled to make clear what had interested him in England and France--the tiny, unchartable differences of dress, of breakfast bacon, of political parties, of vegetables in market places, of the ministers of God--but Tub was impatient. What he wanted was a gloating vicarious excursion into blazing restaurants full of seductive girls, marvelous food, wine unimaginably good at fifty cents a bottle, superb drunks without a headache, and endless dancing without short breath. Sam tried to oblige but--

"Funny!" He couldn't somehow picture the dancing rendezvous he had seen only a fortnight ago. He could see the musty cupboard where the patient chambermaid of their hotel floor had sat waiting, apparently all day and all night, knitting, smelling of herring and poverty; but of the Jardin de Ma Soeur he could see nothing but tables, smooth floor, and the too darkly enraptured eyes of Gioserro the aviator, dancing with Fran.

Sam dropped so low conversationally that he asked about the well- being of the Rev. Dr. Willis Fortune Tate of Zenith.

Then Ross Ireland banged in.

"Off to Mexico to do a story on oil, gimme a drink," he said, and all was liveliness again.

Sam was distressed that he should be relieved to have his confidences with his oldest friend interrupted by this half- stranger, but he was pleased when Tub Pearson took to him. Half an hour later, when Ross had told his celebrated story of Doc Pilvins the veterinarian and the plush horse, the three of them went out to dinner, had cocktails, and became lively and content.

Only once in an evening of different night clubs, none of which were different, did Sam worry again:

"Good Lord, are all of us here in America getting so we can't be happy, can't talk, till we've had a lot of cocktails? What's the matter with our lives?"

But on the Yale campus next afternoon, with Tub, he was roaring with delight to see again the comrades of old days; the beloved classmates who stayed so unshakably in his mind that he had forgotten nothing about them save their professions, their present dwelling-places, and their names.

The 1896 division of the procession to the baseball game at Yale Field, in their blue coats and white trousers, was led by Tub Pearson, shaking a rattle and singing:

Good morning, Mr. Zip, Zip, Zip,
Got a hair-cut as short as mine?
Good morning, Mr. Zip, Zip, Zip,
I cer'n'ly am feeling fine.
Ashes to ashes and dust to dust,
If the army don't get you then the navy must--

Sam was moved to sadness and prayer by the sight of his classmates. It was one of the astonishments of the reunion how old many of them had become at fifty or fifty-two--Don Binder, for instance, in college a serious drinker, baby-faced and milky, now an Episcopalian rector who looked as though he were sixty-five and as though he carried the sins of the country on his stooped shoulders. The spectacle made Sam himself feel ancient. But as startling were the classmates who at fifty looked thirty-five, and who irritated a man like

Sam, amiable about exercise but no fanatic, by shouting that everybody ought to play eighteen holes of golf a day.

But however sheepish Sam might feel, Tub was radiant, was again the class clown during the procession. He danced across the road from side to side, shaking his rattle, piping on a penny whistle, frightening a child on the sidewalk almost into epilepsy by kneeling down and trying to be chummy.

"He's fine. He's funny," Sam assured himself. "He's a great goat. Hell, he's an idiot! WHY am I getting to be such a grouch on life? Better go back to the desk."

But whatever discomfort he had at playing the hobbledehoy, in the class reunion Sam found balm. They knew who he was! No one in Paris (except Fran, at times) knew that. But his classmates realized that he was Sambo Dodsworth, great tackle, Skull and Bones, creative engineer, president of a corporation, "prince of good fellows."

Except for a few professional alumni who at fifty could still tell what was the score in last year's Yale-Brown game, who at fifty had nothing with which to impress the world except the fact that they were Yale Men, the class had drifted far from the cheery loafing and simple-hearted idealism of college days. They were bank presidents and college presidents and surgeons and country school- teachers and diplomats; they were ranchmen and congressmen and ex- convicts and bishops. One was a major general, and one--in college the most mouse-like of bookworms--was the funniest comedian on Broadway. They were fathers and grandfathers, and most of them looked as though they overworked or overdrank. Not one of them had found life quite the amusing and triumphant adventure he had expected; and they came back wistfully, longing to recapture their credulous golden days. They believed (for a week) that their classmates were peculiarly set apart from the crooked and exasperating race of men as a whole.

And all of this Sam Dodsworth believed--for a week.

It was pleasant, on a clam bake at Momauguin, to loll in the sand with the general, a college president, and two steel kings, as though they were all of them nineteen again, to be hailed as "Old Sambo," to wrestle without thinking of dignity, and for a moment to be so sentimental as to admit that they longed for something greater than their surface successes. It was pleasant, in the rooms to which they were assigned in Harkness, to forget responsibilities as householders

175

and company managers, and to loll puppy-like on window-seats, beside windows fanned by the elms, telling fabulous lies till one, till two of the morning, without thinking of being up early and on the job. It was pleasant at dinner in a private room to sing "Way Down on the Bingo Farm" and to come out with a long, clinging, lugubrious yowl in:

Here's to good old Yaaaaaaaaaaaale
She's so hearty and so hale--

Even the men who on the first day he had not been able to remember became clear. Why yes! That was old Mark Derby--always used to be so funny the way he played on a comb and never could remember his necktie.

He was nineteen again; in a world which had seemed barren of companionship he had found two hundred brothers; and he was home, he rejoiced--to stay!

So, with Tub Pearson, he rode westward from New York to Zenith, gratified as the thunderous slots of Manhattan streets gave way to the glowing Hudson, to tranquil orchards and old white houses and resolute hills.

The breakfast-room of Harry McKee, Sam's new son-in-law, was a cheery apartment with white walls, canary-yellow curtains at the French windows, and a parrot, not too articulate, in a red enamel cage. The breakfast set was of taffy-like peasant faience from Normandy, and the electrical toaster and percolator on the table were of nickel which flashed in the lively Midwestern morning sunshine.

Sam was exultant. He had arrived late last evening, and as his own house was musty from disuse, he had come to Emily's. He had slept with a feeling of security, and this morning he was exhilarated at being again with her, his own Emily, gayest and sturdiest of girls. He had brought his presents for them down to breakfast--the Dunhill pipe and the Charvet dressing-gown for Harry, the gold and tortoiseshell dressing-table set and the Guerlain perfumes for Emily. They admired the gifts, they patted him in thanks, they fussed over his having real American porridge with real cream. In a blissful assurance of having come home forever to his own snug isle, after decades amid white-fanged seas, of having brought to his astounded tribe incredible tales of Troy and Circe and men with two heads, he began to expatiate on Paris, smiling at them, reaching out to take Emily's hand, launching into long-winded details.

"--now what I never understood about Paris," he was rumbling, "is how much of it is like a series of villages, with narrow streets and little bits of shops that don't hardly keep the proprietor busy. You always hear of the big boulevards and the wild dance halls, but what struck me was the simple little places--"

"Yes, that was so even in the war, when I was in Paris," said McKee. "But there must be a lot of difference since then. Say, Dad, I'm afraid I have to hustle to the office. Hope to sell a few million bolts to the Axton Car people today. But I want to hear all about Paris. Be home by six-thirty. Awful' good to have you back, sir. Good-bye, Emily of Emilies!"

After the kisses and flurry and engine-racings of McKee's departure, Emily beamed her way back and caroled, "Oh, don't eat that cold toast! I'll make you a nice fresh slab. You must try this lovely apricot jam. Now go on and tell me some more about Paris. Oh, it's perfectly ducky to be with you again! Harry is NEXT to the nicest man living but you're the--Oh, you MUST eat some more. Now tell me about Paris."

"Well," mildly, "I really haven't much to tell. It's hard to express how you feel about a foreign place. Something kind of different in the air. I'm afraid I'm not much on analyzing a thing like that. . . . Emily, uh--Harry doing pretty well financially?"

"Oh, splendidly! They've raised him another five thousand a year."

"You don't need a little check for yourself?"

"Oh, not a thing. Thanks, old darling. Drat him, Harry carried off the Advocate and I know you want to read it."

Sam did not hear her reference to the Advocate. Flushed, he was reflecting, "Am I trying to pay my daughter to be interested in me? Trying to buy her affection?" He scuttled away from the thought, into a hasty description of Les Halles at dawn, as he had seen them when the De Penable menagerie, with himself as an attendant keeper, had had an all-night round of cafes. He had begun to care for his own narration; he was saying, "Well, I'd never tried white wine and onion soup for breakfast, but I was willing to try anything once," when the telephone began.

"Excuse me a second, Daddy," said Emily, and for five minutes she held a lively conversation with one Mona about a tennis tournament, knitted suits, Dick, speed boats, lobster salad, Mrs. Logan, and a Next Thursday mentioned with such italicized awe that Sam felt ignorant in not knowing how it might differ from any other Thursday. He realized, too, that he did not know who Mona, Dick, or Mrs. Logan were.

The importance of having eaten onion soup for breakfast had cooled by the time Emily whisked back to the table. Before Sam had warmed up and begun the story of Captain Gioserro's hiring a vegetable wagon to drive to the hotel, the sneering telephone called Emily again, and for three minutes she dealt with a tradesman who had apparently been sending bad meat. She dealt with him competently. She seemed to know everything about cuts of steak, the age of ducklings, and the trimming of a crown roast.

She was not his rollicking helpless girl. She was a Competent Young Matron.

"She doesn't need me any more," sighed Sam.

The Dodsworths had not rented their house but had left it tenantless, save for a caretaker who maintained a creeping ashen existence in a corner of the basement, spelling out old newspapers from garbage cans all day long. The caretaker, when he had admitted Sam after five minutes of ringing, wanted to show him through the house, but Sam said abruptly, "I'll go by myself, thanks."

The hall was dim as a tomb and as airless. His foot-fall on the carpetless floor was so loud that he began to tip-toe. There were presences which threatened him as an intruder in his own house. He stood in the door of the library. The room, once warm and tranquil, was bleakly unwelcoming. It was a dead room in a dead house. The rugs were rolled up, piled in a corner, their exposed under-sides drab and pebbly. The book-shelves were covered with sheets, and the deep chairs, swathed in gray covers, were as shapeless and distasteful as the wrapper of a slovenly housewife. The fireplace had a stingy cleanness. But in a corner of it clung a scrap of paper with Fran's hectic writing. He stooped slowly to pick it up, and made out the words "--call motor at ten and--" She seemed to dash into the room and flee away, leaving him the lonelier.

He climbed heavily up the stairway, steps clattering flatly, and shouldered into their bedroom. He looked about, silent.

The canopies of their two beds had been taken down, leaving the posts like bare masts; and the surfaces of those once suave and endearing retreats were mounds of pillows and folded blankets covered with coarse sheets.

He went to the drawn window blinds.

"Blinds getting cracked. Need new ones," he said aloud.

He looked about again, and shivered. He went to the bed in which Fran had always slept, and stood staring at it. He patted the edge of the bed and quickly marched out of the room--out of the house.

Brent was to have returned to Zenith for a fortnight, and Sam had a hundred plans for motoring with him, fishing with him. But Brent telegraphed, "Invited corking yachting party Nova Scotia mind if not return," and Sam, perfectly expressionless, wrote his answer, "By all means go hope have splendid time." As he walked out of the Western Union office he sighed a little, and stood with his hands in his pockets, looking up and down the street, a man with nothing to do.

He had thought of himself, when he had been the president of the Revelation Company, as a young man at fifty. To him, then, old age did not begin till seventy, perhaps seventy-five, and he would have another quarter-century of energy. But the completeness with which Emily, at twenty-one, had matured, become competent to run her own life, made Sam feel that he belonged to an unwanted generation; that, amazingly, he was old.

It was the afternoon of Elizabeth Jane's party which made Sam so conscious that he was a stranger, unable to mix with this brisk, luxurious Young Married Set, that he politely fled from Emily's house and holed-in at the Tonawanda Country Club.

Elizabeth Jane was Harry McKee's eleven-year-old niece. Like a surprising number of other successful youngish men of Zenith, hard-surfaced, glossy, ferociously driving in business, and outside of business absorbed only in sports and cocktail-lit dancing, McKee was fanatically interested in children. He was on the Zenith school-board and the Board of Visitors of St. Mark's Town and Country School. Emily and Harry McKee made Sam blush by the cheery openness with which they informed him that they intended to have only three children, but to have those with celerity and to have them perfect. (They apparently possessed more control of Providence than was understood by such an innocent as Sam.) While they awaited the arrival of the three, they were devoted to Elizabeth Jane, a sedate, bob-haired, bookish child, who reminded Sam of a boy minstrel in a Maxfield Parrish picture. (He had always admired Parrish's dream castles, despite Fran's scoffing.)

Sam liked Elizabeth Jane. "Real old-fashioned child," he said. "So innocent and demure."

And the next day Elizabeth Jane remarked placidly, when she had invited herself to tea with Sam and Emily, "Aunty, would it be awfully rude of me if I said my teacher is a damn' fool? Would it? She's started telling us about sex, and she's so scared and silly about it, and of course all of us kids know all about it already."

"My God!" said Samuel Dodsworth to himself.

McKee and Emily celebrated Elizabeth Jane's twelfth birthday with an afternoon party for forty children. Sam knew that there were to be many dodges of a rich nature; he was aware that a red and white striped pavilion was being erected on the McKee lawn, and orders in for such simple delights as Peche Melba, Biscuit Tortoni, and Bombe Surprise, along with Viennese pastry, loganberry juice, imported ginger ale and lobster salad, and that the caterer was sending half a dozen waiters in dress suits. But he was still antiquated enough to picture the children playing Ring Around a Rosy, and Puss in the Corner, and Hide 'n' Go Seek.

He was lunching with Tub Pearson on the day of the party, and after lunch he excitedly went to the five and ten cent store and filled his pockets with dozens of pleasant little foolishnesses--false noses, chocolate cigars, tissue-paper hats--and proceeded to McKee's, planning to set all the children at the party laughing with his gifts.

He was late. When he arrived the children were decorously sitting in four rows of chairs on the lawn, watching a professional troupe from the Zenith Stock Company perform an act from "Midsummer Night's Dream." And there was a professional magician afterward-- though the young lordlings were bored by such kitchy banalities as rabbits out of silk hats--and a lady teacher from the Montessori

School, who with a trained voice-for-children and trained gestures told ever such nice Folk Tales from Czechoslovakia, Serbia, Iceland, and Yucatan. Then, unherded but politely in order, the children filed past a counter at which Harry McKee, disguised as an Arab for no perceptible reason, gave each of them a present.

They each said, "Thank you very much," tolerantly, and unwrapped their presents, showing their trained social-mindedness by depositing the wrappers in a barrel therefor provided. Sam goggled at the presents. There were French perfume and packets of a thousand stamps, riding crops and portable phonographs, engraved stationery and a pair of love-birds.

He hastily pulled out the flaps of his coat pockets lest some one see the ludicrous little gifts he had bought.

And later, "I've got to get out of this. Too rich for my blood."

It took a week of tactful hinting about needing eight hours of daily golf, but in the end he escaped to one of the chintzy bedrooms at the Tonawanda Country Club and there, in an atmosphere of golf, gin-bottles in the locker room, small dinners followed by poker, and a reading-room full of magazines which on glossy paper portrayed country houses and polo teams, he made out a lotus-eating existence, with cold cauliflower and stringy lamb-chops and bootlegged whisky for lotuses.

He persuaded himself, for minutes at a time, that business affairs demanded his staying in Zenith, and he bleakly knew, for hours at a time, that they didn't.

His capital was invested in carefully diversified ventures--in U.A.C. stock, railroad and industrial and government bonds. However often he conferred with his bankers and brokers, he couldn't find anything very absorbing to do in the way of changing investments.

But he also owned, as a more speculative interest, a share of a resort hotel near Zenith, and on his way to America he had persuaded himself that, with his newly educated knowledge of food and decoration and service, he would be able to improve this hotel.

It was quite a bad hotel, and very profitable.

He had a meal there, two days after arriving in Zenith, and it was terrible.

He told the manager that it was terrible.

The manager looked bored and resigned.

181

When Sam had persuaded him to stay, the manager explained that with the cost of materials and the salaries of cooks, he couldn't do a better meal at the price. It was all very well, the manager pointed out, to talk about the food in Paris. Only, this wasn't Paris. And furthermore, did Sam happen to know what chickens cost per pound at the present moment?

That was Sam's only achievement during his stay in Zenith. But weeks went by before he admitted, rather angrily, that business did not need him . . . just as Brent did not need him, Emily did not need him.

But certainly, he comforted himself, Fran needed him, and such friends as Tub Pearson.

CHAPTER 19

Thomas J. Pearson and Samuel Dodsworth had always been too well acquainted to know each other. They had been together since boyhood. Each was a habit to the other. It had been a habit for Tub to go once a week to Sam's for poker; a habit for Sam to telephone him for lunch every Tuesday or Wednesday. They analyzed each other, they considered each other as individuals, no more than a man considers the virtues of his own several toes, unless they hurt. Even Sam's absence from Tub at technical school, after college, had given them no understanding of each other. They were under the spell of the collegiate belief that one's classmates are the most princely fellows ever known in history.

But in Sam's six months abroad, Tub had grown into new habits. It was to the house of Dr. Henry Hazzard that Tub looked now for his weekly drug of poker. Sam saw that Hazzard was at least as necessary to Tub as himself, now, and sometimes he found himself allied against the two of them when the talk fell on labor or European alliances and they expressed the fat opinions which Sam himself had once accepted but about which he now felt shaky. He was slightly jealous, slightly critical. He noted that Tub wasn't quite so perfect as he had remembered. When Tub shrieked, during a game of poker, "'What ho' said the cat to the catamaran" or "Now is the time for all good men to come to the aid of the ante" Sam was not diverted. And he felt that Tub was as critical of him. If he hinted that the paving on Conklin Avenue was bad, or that the coffee at the country club left something to be desired, Tub scolded, "Oh, God, we expatriates certainly are a hard bunch to please!"

When Sam dined with them, he found himself turning oftener to Tub's bouncing goodwife, Matey, than to Tub.

Yet between times they played their nineteen holes happily, serene as a pair of old dogs out rabbit-hunting. If sometimes Sam found himself wishing for Ross Ireland's melodramatic talk about revolutions and lost temples, if sometimes Tub seemed rather provincial, Sam was thoroughly scandalized, and rebuked himself, "Tub's the best fellow in the world!"

It is doubtful whether he was the more disturbed by finding that he could get along without Tub or by finding that Tub could get along without him.

Believing from Sam's first enthusiastic foreign letters that he would not return from Europe this year, Tub had planned with Dr. Hazzard a month's motoring-golfing expedition. They were excited about it. They were going to play over the best courses in Winnemac, Indiana, Illinois, Michigan, and Ohio. They spoke of the charms of stumbling over new varieties of bunkers, wild grass, and rosebushes. They raved over long shots across sand dunes, and disastrous ponds in which to lose dozens of golf balls.

They had planned to go by themselves, but now they invited Sam. He hesitated. He felt unwanted.

Of course they hadn't known he would be returning--

Of course they HAD urged him to come--

Only why couldn't they have waited to see whether he would return?

He compromised by going with them for two weeks out of the month.

It was a good jaunt. They laughed, and felt free of womenfolk and nagging secretaries, retold all the dirty stories they knew, drank discreetly, drove fast, and admired the golf courses on the North Shore, above Chicago. Sam enjoyed it. But he noted that when he left they seemed cheerful enough about going on by themselves.

Brent--Emily--business--now Tub and Hazzard--they didn't need him.

All thinking about matters less immediate than food, sex, business, and the security of one's children is a disease, and Sam was catching it. It made everything more difficult.

He thought about alcohol.

He noted that most of the men of the country club set, including himself, drank too much. And they talked too much about drinking too much. Prohibition had turned drinking from an agreeable, not very important accompaniment to gossip into a craze. They were jumpy about it, and as fascinated as a schoolboy peering at obscene posters.

And he began to meditate about his acquaintances, almost frankly.

He realized, almost frankly, that he was not satisfied now by Dr. Hazzard's best limericks, Tub's inside explanations about the finances of Zenith corporations, even Judge Turpin's whispers about the ashes upon the domestic hearths of their acquaintances.

Hang it, that HAD been good talk in Paris, even when he had not altogether understood it--Atkins' rumination on painters, the gilded chatter of Renee de Penable's gang of pirates, and still more the stories of Ross Ireland. He had heard of Anastasia, who was declared to be the daughter of the Czar, of the Zinovieff letter which had wrecked the Labor Party of Britain, of the suicide of Archduke Rudolph, of the Empress Charlotte wandering melancholy mad through the haunted rooms of Castle Miramar, of systems to win at Monte Carlo, of Floyd Gibbons' plan to make a motor road from Tierra del Fuego to the Rio Grande, of Turkish women born in harems who now bobbed their hair and studied biology, of the Chinese "Christian general"--oh, a hundred stories touching great empires and hidden lands. And he had seen the King and Queen of England drive up Constitution Hill in an open motor, had seen Carpentier, the prize-fighter, dancing--a pale, solemn, unathletic-looking young man, seen Briand at the opera and Arnold Bennett at the theater.

It had been good talk and good seeing.

But even if he were articulate enough to bring home this booty to Tub and Dr. Hazzard and Judge Turpin, he felt--after a few stumbling trials he knew--that they would not be interested.

He saw that it was not a question of Ross Ireland being interested in kingdoms and of Tub being interested only in coupons and aces. He saw, slowly, that none of his prosperous industrialized friends in Zenith were very much interested in anything whatever. They had cultivated caution until they had lost the power to be interested. They were like old surly farmers. The things over which they were most exclamatory--money, golf, drinking--didn't fascinate them as brush-strokes or wood-winds fascinated the peering Endicott Everett Atkins; these diversions were to the lords of Zenith not pleasures but ways of keeping so busy that they would not admit how bored they were, how empty their ambitions. They had as their politics only a testy fear of the working class. (Why, Sam perceived uneasily, the whole country turned the dramatic game of politics over to a few seedy professional vote-wanglers!) To them, women were only bedmates, housekeepers, producers of heirs, and a home audience that could not escape, and had to listen when everybody at the office was tired of hearing one's grievances. The arts, to them, consisted only of jazz conducive to dancing with young girls, pictures which made a house look rich, and stories which were narcotics to make them forget the tedium of existence.

They did things, they rushed, they supervised, they contended--but they were not interested.

However difficult Fran might be at times, pondered Sam, however foolish Madame de Penable with her false hair and her false gigolos, however pompous and patronizing Mr. Endicott Everett Atkins, they were fascinated by everything in human life, from their own amours to soup and aeroplanes.

He would like to be one of them. There was only one thing in the way. Could he?

Thus meditated Samuel Dodsworth, alone on the porch of the country club, awaiting the return of Tub Pearson.

What the devil was he doing here? He was as dead as though he were entombed. He had to "get busy"--either go back to work, at once, or join Fran.

Which?

Then, for a week or two, he became very busy peering into the Sans Souci Gardens development.

To the north of Zenith, among wooded hills above the Chaloosa River, there was being laid out one of the astonishing suburbs which have appeared in America since 1910. So far as possible, the builders kept the beauties of forest and hills and river; the roads were not to be broad straight gashes butting their way through hills, but winding byways, very inviting . . . if one could only kill off the motorists. Here, masked among trees and gardens, were springing up astonishing houses--considerably more desirable as residences than the gaunt fortified castles of the Rhine, the magnificent and quite untenantable museums of French chateaux. They were all imitative, of course--Italian villas and Spanish patios and Tyrolean inns and Tudor manor-houses and Dutch Colonial farmhouses, so mingled and crowding one another that the observer was dizzy. They were so imitative and so standardized that it was easy to laugh at them. But they were no more imitative of Munich than was Munich of Italy or than Italy of Greece, and like the rest of the great American Domestic Architecture of this era, they were probably the most comfortable residences in the world . . . for one who didn't mind it if his Venetian balcony was only ten feet from his neighbor's Swiss chalet, and if his neighbor's washing got slightly in the way of tea on his own lawn.

Driving through the San Souci Gardens, Sam was fascinated. He liked the energy with which roads were being dug, houses rising, stone fountains from Florence being set up in squares and circles designated by arty little swinging street signs as "Piazza Santa Lucia" and "Assisi Crescent" and "Plaza Real."

That there was something slightly ridiculous about mixing up Spain and Devon and Norway and Algiers, and transplanting them to the sandy hills of a Midwestern town, where of late the Indians had trapped rabbits and the rusty-bearded Yankees had trapped the Indians, did vaguely occur to Sam, but it was all a fantastic play to him, very gay and bright after the solemn respectabilities and the disapproving mansard roofs of the older residential avenues in Zenith.

Here, at least, he reflected, was all the color and irregularity he had gone abroad to seek; all the scarlets and yellows and frivolous pinks, all the twisty iron-work and scalloped tiles and striped awnings and Sicilian wine-jars he could swallow, along with (he thanked Heaven) all the mass-produced American electric refrigerators, oil furnaces, vacuum cleaners, garbage incinerators, over-stuffed chairs and built-in garages which, for all of Fran's scoffing and Mr. Atkins' expatriate distress, Sam still approved.

It came to him that now there was but little pioneering in manufacturing motors; that he hadn't much desire to fling out more cars on the packed highways. To create houses, perhaps less Coney-Island-like than these--noble houses that would last three hundred years, and not be scrapped in a year, as cars were--

"That'd be interesting," said Sam Dodsworth, the builder. Of course he knew nothing about architecture. But he knew a good deal about engineering, about steel and wood and glass, about organizing companies, about getting along with labor.

"And say! Here's something that Fran would take an interest in! And she's an expert about decorations and all that stuff. . . . Might hold her here!"

187

In a leisurely way, apparently not much interested, Sam saw to it that he was introduced to the president of the Sans Souci Company and that they played golf together. He was invited to view the Gardens with the president, and afterward he spent a good deal of time walking through them, talking to architects, to carpenters, to gardeners. Otherwise he merely waited.

He was very good at waiting.

Twice a week letters from Fran had drawn him toward her and toward Europe. Her first letter had come on the day of his arrival in Zenith:

Villa Doree, Vevey, Montreux, La Suisse.

SAM DEAR, it's TOO glorious! Down the lake, the friendliest little steamers zipping by--peaks of the Dent de Midi--too perfectly SUPERB--at sunset they're clouds of gold. And I've actually been walking! (Was Fran terribly bad in Paris, always galloping out to night clubs when you'd rather have gone walking? Well, you have your revenge--AWFULLY lonely for your big bear growls and general dependability even though I am moved by beauty of this place and rather grateful for a little calm.) Walk up through vineyards to ducky little stone houses.

The villa is CHARMING--not much ground but lawns and roses and terrace for tea, right on the lake. Renee de Penable is just as glad as I am to be free for a while of all the noisy young dancing men. We've both sworn to let ourselves be old ladies with caps and knitting for a while, probably take to religion and camomile tea. I'm waiting for your letters, just had your steamer note, SO glad you enjoyed crossing with Mr. Ireland, you probably had much more fun with him than with a bad sport like me--shouldn't have said that, looks mean, and I really and truly am glad you had a nice bachelorish time. Be sure and write EVERYTHING about Brent and Emily and McKee. Give my regards to Tub and Dr. Hazzard. An astonishing big gull has just lighted on the lawn right in front of the window by which I write. We have the funniest pair of maids-- one looks like a kewpie, and I suspect the purity of her intentions toward the postman, and cook is built like a Japanese wrestler-- only more clothed, of course. I hope you will have a happy stay in Zenith. I do miss you. Come back soon and in early autumn we'll jaunt off together. I know you're a little fed up with Paris and personally I don't care if we don't get back there till

spring, we might view Egypt, Italy, etc., for six months. Renee sends
you her love and so do I, old grizzly!

Your FRAN.

Her next three letters were short, devoted to scenery and troubles. She always had troubles--always. They weren't very serious troubles, he thought: Renee had been cross, the cook had been cross-- apparently Fran herself had never been cross. The dance at the Hotel des Deux Mondes had been a bore, the rain had been wet, the English family next door had been rude, she had a toothache. Two of the letters were impersonal, almost chilling; in between was an affectionate cry for him, so that he was confused and gave a good deal of his hours of meditation to wishing that she were a little less complicated.

The fourth letter was livelier:

Wouldn't you KNOW it, Sam! After swearing that she never
wanted to see a dancing man again, or anything in the way of a male
more disturbing than a Father Confessor, Renee has already gathered
about her (which unfortunately means more or less about me too) a
brand-new horde of Apollos. How she does it _I_ don't know! There'll
be a nice young man of sixty staying with his venerable mamma at a
hotel here; somebody in Paris asks him to call on us; he comes for-
mally to tea; and the next day he's panting on the doorstep again,
bringing a pack of males ranging from sixteen to eighty and from rac-
ing models to the latest thing in hearses. Of course she knows simply
EVERYBODY--we can't go to the Deux Mondes for a cocktail without
at least one gent swooping down on her with glad whoops of alcoholic
welcome. So now the house is littered with fauns and Bacchuses, if
that's the word.

There's an English hunting man named Randall who wears
blue collars and shirts, and another Englishman picturesquely named
Smith, and an Austrian baron who, as far as I can find out, sells
clocks, and a man who seems to have leased the French Bourse, and a
rich American Jew named Arnold Israel--he's about forty and very
good- looking in a black-haired, black-eyed, beefy sort of way but a
little too gaudily Oriental for my simple taste, when he kisses your
hand he almost bites it, ugh! Of course it is nice to be able to dance
again, but I really and truly did enjoy just mouching around and being
quiet. Would you mind transferring five thousand (dollars) to my ac-

count at the Guaranty, Paris? Food here is more expensive than I had expected, and I've had to buy some more summer things--I found a shop in Montreux with simply DARLING hats, and while it's all very well to walk and to study the dear sweet smelly Common People by riding on trains, now that Renee has gone and dragged us into the Life Idiotic again we've had to hire a limousine and a chauffeur. I hope you're ever so happy, darling.

  FRAN.

It was with her next letter that he began to fret. It reached him while he was motoring and golfing with Tub Pearson and Dr. Hazzard:

Such a lovely blue and golden day! The mountains are like the pillars of heaven. A bunch of us are taking a motor boat across to the French side of the lake. Arnold--Arnold Israel, an American here, I think I spoke of him--he has discovered a marvelous little inn where we can lunch--under the vine and fig tree sort of thing. He's really an awfully nice person, one of these extraordinary international Jews who can do everything and knows everything-- rides like an angel, swims seven miles, tells the funniest living stories, knows more about painting than old Atkins and more about biology and psychology than sixteen college professors and I must say he dances like Maurice himself! And he is an American. It's funny, I know I'm playing into your hands but I must admit this, much though I admire Europeans, it IS nice to rest one's self after even Renee's best cut-glass wit, etc., etc., by being simple and natural with a fellow countryman--one who will UNDERSTAND when you say, "She must have gotten that hat from the five and ten cent store," or even, "Attaboy." I find that with you away, you dear darling old vulgarian, I have positive joy in hearing some-body say, "Oh, hell." Makes me almost homesick. Oh yes, I guess I am American all right! Must hurry now, lots of love,

  F.

For ten days, no letter, then two together:

You would approve of your bad Fran thoroughly if you knew what a healthful life she is leading. Of course sometimes I do stay up a bit late at dances--we've met an awfully nice American Jewish family here named, of all things, Lee, friends of Arnold Israel-- they have rented a wonderful old castle back from the lake above Glion, and they do give the most gorgeous parties. But otherwise I'm outdoors most of the time--riding, swimming, tramping, motoring, tennis--the Israel man has the most terrific cannon-ball in tennis. And then he'll read Shelley aloud, like a twenty-year- old Vassar girl! What a man! And to think that he's in the jute and hemp importing business! though it's true that he merely inherited the business from his hustling old father, and that he's able to leave it four or five months every year and loaf all through Europe.

Good Heavens, this whole letter seems to be about Arnold Israel! That's only because I thought he was the person here who would interest you most. I needn't tell you that he and I are merely the most impersonal kind of friends. Oh, I suppose he would get sentimental if I'd let him but I most certainly will not, and with all his Maharajah splendors, he has the most delicate and sensitive mind. I do appreciate what you say about Brent and Emily's having really grown up and hardly needing us. Madly though I adore them and long to see them, I'm almost afraid to, they'd make me feel so old, whereas now if you could see me in white blouse, shamelessly crimson skirt, white shoes and stockings, you would say I'm a flapper, and it's beautifully quiet here by the lake at night- getting in QUANTITIES of restful sleep.

Your FRAN.

Sam dear, this isn't really a letter but just a PS. to my note of yesterday. I feel as though I wrote so much about Mr. Israel that you'll think I think too much about him. That's the unfortunate thing about letters--one just chats along and often gives a wrong impression. If I have mentioned him several times it's only because most of the other people, no matter how well they may dance or swim, are really pretty dull, while he is a nice person to talk to, and of course--I needn't tell you, you old loyal darling, I have no other interest in him. Besides, Renee is crazy about him and wants to annex him for keeps, and as she's really the chef de bureau here, having found the villa, etc., even though she does pay only half the rent, if she wants her old Arnold she can certainly jolly well have him, for all I care. Hastily, F.

191

The next letter did not come for nearly a fortnight, and Sam realized, putting on his glasses to peer at the stamp, that it was not from Vevey, but from Stresa, in Italy:

Sam, the most dreadful thing has happened. Madame de Penable and I had simply the most dreadful row, she said things I simply could not forgive, and I have left the villa and come here to Lake Maggiore. It's a lovely place, but as I don't know whether I shall stay, you'd better address me c/o Guaranty, Paris. And it was all about nothing.

I've written you about a Mr. Israel we met at Vevey and how crazy Renee was about him. One evening, I hate to say this about a woman who, after all, no matter how vulgar and unscrupulous she is has given me a good time, but I really must say she'd drunk more than was good for her and after the guests had gone she suddenly turned on me like a fishwife and she used the most DREADFUL language and she accused me of carrying on an affair with Mr. Israel and of stealing him from her which was idiotic as well as false because I must say she never did have him so how could I have stolen him from her even supposing I had the slightest desire to! I've never had anybody talk to me the way she did, it was simply DREADFUL!

Of course I didn't condescend to stoop to her level and answer her, I simply said very politely, "My dear Madame de Penable, I'm afraid you are hysterical and not altogether responsible for what you are saying and I would prefer not to discuss the matter any further certainly not till tomorrow morning." But that didn't stop her and finally I simply went to my room and locked the door and next day I moved to a hotel and then came down here--it really is lovely here, with the Borromean Isles including the famous Isola Bella lying out in the lake and across the lake, behind the nice village of Pallanza, the mountains rising, quite high and villages, etc., strung along the roads up the mountains. I feel awfully lonely here and that beastly toothache I had in London is returning but, after all, anything is better than living with a brawling vulgar fool like Mme. de Penable.

I hate to 'fess up and I guess this gives you a lovely chance to crow over me, only I know you're too generous and understanding of your bad little girl to take such an advantage of her, but you certainly were completely right in what you said, or rather hinted, for you were too kind to come out and say anything rude, about the Penable woman and her dreadful vulgar friends. I'm sorry. I hope I've learned some-

thing. Only I don't want you to think that Mr. Israel is in any way to blame, like the Penable woman and her friends.

He was as innocent as I was, and he was good enough to see me off on the train at Vevey. He is a man I would like to have you meet, I think you would find in him all the nice, jolly, companionable, witty things you find in Ross Ireland and at the same time a subtlety and good taste that I'm sure you will admit with all his fine qualities Mr. Ireland lacks. Well, perhaps we will run into Arnold when you come back for I believe he is taking a whole year this time wandering around Europe.

Oh, do come soon, darling! I miss you so today! If you were here we'd take the little batello--aren't you proud of me, I've already learned ten words of Italian in one day; "Come in" is avanti and the bill is le conto or no, il conto I think it is--and we'd go scooting around the lake. If it's convenient you might send another couple of thousand, Guaranty Paris--of course I have to pay my share of the rent at the cursed villa at Vevey even though I'm not there. I suppose if I didn't, and I certainly would jolly well like not to, the De Penable woman would go around saying that I was not only a libertine and a man-snatcher but also an embezzler!

How I'd like to have you spank her for me with your big beautiful strong hand! You'd do it so calmly and so thoroughly! So of course I have to pay my share of the rent and limousine hire there and as I also have to pay now for my rooms here or wherever I may be (you better not depend on this address reaching me but address c/o Guaranty) it will make things a little more expensive than I had hoped. Oh, dear, I did hope this would be a nice economical summer, and heaven knows I tried hard enough to make it so, but I didn't expect the unexpected to unexpect quite so disastrously. I feel better now after talking to you like this--I cried almost all last night--and I shall now live the life of a nun and devote myself to the study of the Italian language and people, as befits an old lady like me.

Your rumpled and repentant Fran.

That letter had come on the day when the president of the Sans Souci Gardens Company had invited Sam to lunch.

He was very frank, the president. He was a trained architect. He astonished Sam by admitting that he thought Sans Souci rather dreadful.

"There's too much mixture of styles, and the houses are too close together," he said. "But most Americans, while they'll pay a devil of a lot for a big impressive house, don't care enough for privacy so that they'll pay for a decent-sized plot of ground. And they WANT French chateaux in a Henry Ford section! But at least we've been educating them to be willing to come out toward the country instead of huddling together in the city. And I'm planning now, if Sans Souci doesn't ruin me, a much bigger development where we won't mix the styles. Oh, I suppose we'll have to go on cribbing from Europe and Colonial America. When a natural genius comes along and creates something absolutely new in houses, only a few people really like 'em. But I picture a new development--I hope with a less agonizing name than Sans Souci Gardens, which is the invention of that grand old Frenchman, one of my partners, Mr. Abe Blumenthal--in which, at least, we can keep the thing from looking like a world's fair. For instance, one section strictly confined to houses more or less in the Tudor style, and another all Dutch Colonial, or something not warring with Dutch Colonial. Or maybe the whole development in one style. Like Forest Hills on Long Island."

But--the Sans Souci president went on--he himself was too fanciful and too impatient. And as partner he needed some one (he hinted that it might be Sam) who would take the hundred or so notions for hotels and luxurious yachting tours and chain restaurants which he conceived every month, pick out the most practical, and control the financing, the selling.

He grinned. "Doesn't sound like much of an offer. It's based on the belief that I do have some new and interesting ideas along with quite a decent knowledge of architecture and building. But--I'd like to see if it isn't possible for us to get together. While you'd been deciding that you were bored with selling cars and while you've been looking up my record for dependability--"

"Oh, you guessed that?" grunted Sam.

"Of course!"

"I'll think it over, I most certainly will," said Sam.

He returned to the country club, planning a dozen or so new kinds of real estate developments of his own, to receive Fran's distressed letter from Stresa.

It all seemed to fit in. He would bring her back; together they would look into the building of houses. He cabled her, "Too bad penable glad got rid her why don't you return zenith then abroad again in year or so."

She answered, "No want stay few more months suit self about joining."

And the great Samuel Dodsworth still had no more notion of what he was going to do than when, as a senior in college, he had sat on East Rock, looking at Long Island Sound, planning to be a bridge-builder in the Andes.

He wrote to her of the Sans Souci Gardens, and waited. He read about domestic architecture, and went to Cleveland and Detroit to inspect new developments.

Her next letter had been written some days before he had received her Stresa letter, before she had his cable. It informed him:

Yes, my dear Samivel, I am still at Stresa, though I may be off to Deauville immejit--I've always wanted to see one of those places where gloomy earls go to lose money at chemin de fer. But meantime I've been very happy here, after getting over my first hysterics at the De Penable woman's beastliness. I've had such a nice girl here to give me Italian lessons daily and with her or other acquaintances made at the hotel I've explored all the divine villages about here-- Pallanza and Baveno and Gignese, back in the hills and Cannobio, and Arona, etc. etc. I've taken a steamer clear up to Locarno, the Swiss end of the lake, and the tram up to the top of Monte Mottarone--Sam, it's so steep that when you look down at the lake below you the water seems abso-lutely to tip up like a tilted platter! So you're not to worry about me, I'm quite all right. I suppose I ought to tell you that Arnold Israel has come down here from Vevey, you remember the nice American I wrote you about, he's staying here at this same hotel.

I don't know that I ought to tell you this--even you, you old woofly-bear darling with your kind, decent, sympathetic mind might possibly misunderstand for, with all your virtues, after all you do have an American way of looking at things, but I'm afraid some gossip might come to you some day and I want you to understand. Needless to say, our relations are as innocent as though we were a boy and girl of eight and I do have such a nice happy clean time with him--Sam, Ar-nold drives a car even faster than you do, my heart almost stopped yesterday when he was driving 118 kilometers an hour, but he's such a

195

superb driver that I usually feel quite safe. Now I must hurry and dress. Bless you. I hope you're well and happy. Best love to Emily and Harry.

> *F.*

That afternoon he telephoned to the president of the Sans Souci Company that he was summoned abroad and could decide nothing for several months. He telegraphed to New York for a steamer reservation. He dashed to Emily, to Tub, to Hazzard, and said goodbye. But it was a week before he could sail, and meantime another letter had come from Fran--from Deauville:

Yes, here I am, and I don't like it much. This place is very gay but a little icky; lots of nice people but also DREADFUL ones, profiteers giving cocktail parties, race-track touts infesting the lounge. I wish I'd gone to the Lido instead. Perhaps I will. See here now, Samivel. In your letter, written to me at Vevey but received since I left, you said that you hoped I would, as you expressed it, "lay low" after my winter in Paris and "get to bed early for a while." I don't suppose you meant to be unpleasant but you couldn't realize how jumpy and hurt and bewildered I was after the horrible Penable affair, like a lost child, and how your scolding would hurt me. Am I to spend the rest of my life growing old as gracefully AND AS FAST as I can, which is apparently YOUR ideal!

You talk as though I were some hell-raising flapper instead of a woman of the world who likes civilized amusements. There! I'm sure you didn't mean to be scolding, but can't you understand how it might hit me when I was in a very high-strung condition? Really, Sam, you must be a little more thoughtful! Do try to use a little imagination, now and then! Now that's off my chest and shall we just forget it? Only I must say--Sam, you may think I'm unjust, but really it was essentially your fault that I ever had the De Penable trouble. If you hadn't insisted on running back to America for your class reunion, which wasn't so awfully necessary, after all, if you had stuck by me so that I wasn't in the anomalous and almost humiliating position of being without a husband, just like a lone adventuress, the De Penable woman would never have dared act as though I WERE an adventuress and have turned on me the way she did. I hope you'll understand that I mean this only in the kindest and sweetest way, and we are, after all, aren't we, one of the few married couples who understand each other so well that we can be frank, and next time I hope you'll try to remember. There, that's over, and now for the news.

Yes, says the hussy defiantly, Arnold Israel IS here with me, that is, as I'm sure you'll understand, he is in no sense WITH me, but he's here in Deauville. At first I wouldn't come along, but he was so thoughtful, so sweet, so understanding. He dug up somehow--I don't know how he does these things but he has what one might call the spiritual as well as the financial Midas touch, do you know that I've just discovered that while I thought he was merely loafing while he was away from his beastly old jute and hemp business, here in Europe, he's made about $40,000 by gambling in exchange and buying and selling a, well, a REASONABLY authentic Rembrandt and he wanted to give me some pearls but of course I wouldn't let him, but I'm drifting away from the thread of my story.

He found out at Stresa that a most respectable old Philadel-phia couple, real Rittenhouse Square sort only fond of gaiety, were here, and he had them invite me to come here under their wing, which made it all right and prevents any of the nasty kind of gossip such as a beast like the De Penable woman loves. After all, I thought, I'm silly about NOT coming with him. Sam will NEVER misunderstand, he has imagination, and besides, I realized, I'm not a young flittergibbet or one of these horrible female Ponce de Leons like De Penable, but a perfectly respectable matron who has brought up a son and a daughter now married, and no one would ever think of gossiping.

So here I am and while, as I say, I'm not crazy about the place, Arnold and I and his friends, a Mr. and Mrs. Doone, perfectly DARLING people and such wonderful sports though they're nearly seventy, we have gay little parties of our own and loaf around on the beach for hours nours nours at a time. Address me c/o Paris, though I'm certain to be here for at least three weeks more, as there is a mag-nificent costume ball coming off to which Arnold and I are going, most scrumptiously as the Sirocco and the North Wind, me with my nice pale Swede hair being naturally the North Wind. Lots of love,

 F.

Sam cabled, "Sailing carmania meet you paris hotel universel september two." He added "Love," and crossed it out, and put it in again.

197

Twelve days later he was looking at the long fortifications at Cherbourg, watching the voluble little Frenchmen on the tender.

On deck, by night and day, he had walked out of his system all irritation at Fran, all hatred of Arnold Israel. When he had finished her letter from Deauville, he had suddenly grasped something which he had never completely formulated in their twenty- three years of marriage: that she was not in the least a mature and responsible woman, mother and wife and administrator, but simply a clever child, with a child's confused self-dramatizations. The discovery had dismayed him. Then it had made him the more tender. His other children, Brent and Emily, did not need him; his child Fran did need him! Something in life still needed him! He thought of her, awaiting him there in Paris, as he had thought of her in the uncomplicated days of their courtship.

CHAPTER 20

Late of a cloudy afternoon, the Paris express slid through the thunderous gloom of the train shed, and Sam was jumpy with the excitement of arrival, looking down at the porters as though they were his friends, smiling at the advertisements of Cointreau and Fernet Branca, of Rouen and Avignon, on the station walls. He marched quickly out of the train, peering for Fran, anxious when he did not see her, and he felt utterly let down as he clumped after the porter with his bags.

She was at the end of the platform.

He saw her afar; he was startled to know how much lovelier she was than he had remembered. In a cool blue coat and skirt, with a white blouse, her hair, pale and light-touched as new straw, her slim legs so silken, her shoulders so confident, she was the American athletic girl, swift to dance, to play tennis, to drive like a cyclone. She was so vital, so YOUNG! His heart caught with admiration. But he was conscious that her face was unhappy, and that she looked at the approaching passengers only mechanically. Didn't she want him--

He came up to her shyly. He was confused by the rather polite smile that masked her face, but holding her by her shoulders, looming over her, he murmured, "Did I remember to write you that I adore you?"

"Why, no, I don't believe you did. Do you? That's very nice, I'm sure."

Her tone was as light and smooth and passionless, her laugh was as distant, as the banter of an actress in a drawing-room comedy.

They were strangers.

At the hotel she said hesitantly, "Uh, Sam--do you mind--I thought you'd be tired after the journey. I know I am, after coming from Deauville. So I got two single rooms instead of a double. But they're right next to each other."

Lewis

"No, maybe better rest," he said.

She came with him into his room, but she hovered near the door, saying with a dreadful politeness, "I hope you will find the room all right. It has quite a nice bathroom."

He hesitated. "I'll unpack later. Let's not hang around here now. Let's skip right out and catch us a good old sidewalk cafe and watch the world go by again!" Wretchedly he noted that she looked relieved. He had given her but a tap of a kiss. She had demanded no further caress.

She was courteous, while he gossiped of Zenith; she laughed at the right moments; and she remained a stranger, forced to entertain the friend of a friend and wanting to get the duty over. She did ask questions about Emily and Brent, but when he talked of Tub, of golfing, she did not listen.

He could not endure it, but he said only, tenderly, "What's matter, honey? You seem kind of far off. Not feeling well? Glad to see me?"

"Of course! It's nothing. It's just--I guess I didn't sleep very well last night. I'm a little nervy. But of course I'm glad to see you, dear old bear!"

And still they had not talked of Madame de Penable, of Arnold Israel, of Stresa and Deauville. He had kept from it as much as she; he had said only, "Too bad you had your trouble with Mrs. Penable, but I'm glad you had some fun after that. Your letters were great." He sounded provincial to himself as he maundered about Zenith, sounded rather dull and thick, but his senses were furiously awake. He noted how agitated she seemed. He noted that she drank three cocktails. He noted that he, Sam Dodsworth, was slowly massing for a battle, and that he dreaded it.

When they dressed for dinner, she closed the door between their two rooms.

"Let's go to Voisin's, where we can be quiet and talk," said he, when she came in to announce that she was ready.

"Oh, wouldn't you rather go some place a little more festive?"

"I would not!"

Then first was he brusque.

"I want to talk!"

200

She shrugged.

After the soup, he bumbled, "Well, I guess I've given you most of the news. Let's talk about plans. Where would you like to go, this fall? What about a good, long, easy hike through Italy and Spain and maybe over to Greece and Constantinople?"

"Why, I think that would be very nice, a little later on. But just now--After all, I've had a dreadfully rustic summer--and of course you have, you poor thing! I think we both deserve a little gaiety here in Paris before we leave. After all, when you go traveling around to assorted places, you're frightfully detached from people."

Then, very blandly, as though it wasn't at all necessary to have his agreement, "I think we might stay here three months or so, and we might take a nice apartment up near the Etoile. I'm so sick of hotels."

"Well--" He stopped; then it came in a slow tidal wave. "I don't blame you for being sick of hotels. So am I! But I certainly don't intend to spend all fall, as I spent all spring, sitting on my rear in Paris--"

"Need you be vulgar?"

"Yes, I guess I need to. I don't intend to sit around here all fall, waiting for you to go. When we first started out, I was willing either to go on living in Zenith or travel, but if I'm going to travel, I want to TRAVEL--to see things, see different kinds of people and towns. I'd like to see Venice and Madrid; I'd like to have some German beer. I don't propose to go on being sacrificed to your ambition as a social climber--"

She flared, "That is a lie, and you know it's a lie! Do you think I have to CLIMB to meet people like Renee de Penable? Climb DOWN, if anything! But I do find it rather more amusing to play with civilized people than to sit and soak at the New York Bar--yes, or go around gaping at ruins with a Baedeker! It's all very well for you, but I have to do the packing, I have to interpret for you. I have to plan the trip. Heavens, we'll GO to Venice! But is there any need of our galumphing off like a Cook's tour when we could have a charming autumn here, with our own flat and servants, and all the friends that I have here now--quite independent of the De Penable person? I'm sorry, Sam, but if you could just occasionally try to catch somebody ELSE'S point of view--I should prefer to remain right here in Paris for--"

"Fran!"

"Well?"

He hesitated. While they talked, round them flowed the amenity of good service, and if they were two volcanoes, they kept their rumblings low, and to any observer they seemed merely a large and impassive man, probably English, and a woman with a quick-changing face who was a little angry but very much in control of her anger.

"Fran! You really would sacrifice me, to stay here?"

"Don't be so melodramatic! I can't see that it's any sacrifice to remain in the loveliest city--"

"Is Arnold Israel here in Paris?"

"Yes, he is! What of it?"

"When did you see him last?"

"This noon."

"He going to stay here in Paris some time?"

"I don't know. How should I know? Yes, I suppose he is."

"He give you any ideas about a flat near the Etoile?"

"See here, my dear Samuel! Have you been reading novels? Just what is the idea of this comic returned-husband-sternly-cross- examining-loose-wife pose--"

"Fran! How far did you go with this Israel?"

"Have you any idea how insulting you are?"

"Have you any idea how insulting I'm going to be, if you don't stop this injured-innocent business?"

"And have you any idea of how angry I'm going to be if you continue to act like a barroom bully--which is what you are, essentially! I've concealed it from myself, for years, but I knew all the time- - The great Sam Dodsworth, the football player, the celebrated bruiser, the renowned bully! Why, you belong in the kitchen, with the corner policeman, not among civilized--"

"You haven't answered! How far did you go with this Israel? I'm doing you the honor of asking you, not of snooping. And you haven't answered."

"And I most certainly do not intend to answer! It's an insult to be expected--And it's an insult to Mr. Israel! He is a gentleman! I wish he were here! You wouldn't dare to talk to me as you've been talking, if he were here. He's quite as powerful as you are, my dear Samuel-- and he has brains and breeding and manners as well. Aah! 'How far did you go in sin with your hellish lover!' After all the years I've tried to do something for you, you still have the vocabulary of a Laura Jean Libbey novel! Arnold, you will be shocked to learn, is so unregenerate that he prefers Andre Gide and Paul Morand to Laura Jean Libbey, and of course it's Black Guilt for me to have found a little pleasure in talking to him instead of discussing poker with your lovely friend Mr. Tub Pearson--"

While she raced on, quietly hysterical, he knew the answer to his question, and he was astonished that he was not more astonished, shocked that he was not more shocked. He did not greatly press her. When she stopped, shaking with muted sobs which he pitied, he said, gently:

"You found him very romantic?"

"Of course! He is!"

"Perhaps I can understand that--more or less."

"Oh, Sam, please DO be human and understand! You do it so well, when you forget your Stern Man of Granite role and let yourself be sweet. Of COURSE there was nothing wrong between Arnold and me-- Isn't it funny how--I'm just as bad as I accused you of being! Using old cant phrases like that! 'Nothing wrong between Arnold and me!' After all, though, perhaps I was unjust to you; perhaps you didn't mean anything of the kind but merely--You are kind, Sam, but if you don't mind my saying so, you're just the least little bit clumsy, now and then--"

She had checked her hysteria, had become amiable and prattling and self-confident again, and all the while he was reflecting, "She's lying. She never used to lie. She's changed. This fellow is her lover."

"--and what I suppose you were really hinting at was that I may have been handsomely kissed by my ardent Jewish friend, before I left Deauville. Well, I was! And I liked it! It doesn't matter if I never see him again--Oh, Sam, if you could only UNDERSTAND how humiliating and infuriating it was of you to suggest that my desire to stay here had anything whatever to do with Arnold! But he was charming. If you could only have seen him, lolling among the sand dunes as though (I used to tell him) he were a Maharajah among gold cushions, with white flannels, and his hair wild and his shirt open at the throat-- It would've looked silly and pretentious with any other man, but on him it seemed natural. And all the while, with all his gorgeousness,

203

Lewis

talking so simply, so confidingly--really, it was touching. But haven't we talked enough of him? We must still make our plans--"

"Let's get him settled first. I've got--"

"Sam, the thing you never could realize about him, even if you met him, was how TOUCHING he was. Clever and handsome and rich and so on, and yet such a child! He needed some one like me to talk to. Oh, I was just an audience for him--nice old mother confessor. He was condescending enough to say that for a venerable dame of forty- two, I was still an excellent imitation of a pretty wench, and he'd supposed I was five years younger than himself, not two years older. And that I was the best dancer he'd found in Europe. But of course the bouquets were just preliminary to his talking about himself and his unhappy childhood, and you know what a fool I am about children--the least hint that anybody has had an unhappy childhood and I dissolve in tears! Poor Arnold! He suffered as a boy because he WAS clever and strong. Nobody could believe how sensitive he was. And his mother was a grim, relentless old dragon, who hated weakness of any kind, or what she thought was weakness, and when she'd find him daydream- ing, she'd accuse him of loafing--Oh, it must have been hell, for so fine a spirit! And then in college, the usual trouble of the too clever and too handsome Jew--high-hatted by the stupidest, drabbest, meanest Yan- kees and Middle-westerners--they looked down on him, just the way a dray-horse might look down on a fine race-horse. Poor Arnold! Of course I was touched by so proud a person as he CARING to tell me about his real self."

"Fran! You don't suppose that this is the first time your Mr. Is- rael has used the neglected-childhood approach? And apparently successfully!"

"Are you AGAIN hinting that I fell for him?"

"I am! It's rather important to know! Did you?"

"Well, then--yes. I did."

"Oh!"

"And I'm proud of it! I couldn't, once--under your heavy- handed tutelage, my dear Samuel!--have believed it possible to be an 'erring wife'! What blind hypocrites people are! And when it did hap- pen, it all seemed so right, so natural and sweet--"

While she raced on he was incredulously admitting that this abominable thing, this newspaper-headline, divorce-court, sensational- novel degradation had actually happened to him--to her-- to Emily and

204

Brent. He had a fascinated desire to know details. He pictured this Arnold Israel, this black leopard of a man--no, too big for a black leopard, but that sort of gracefulness-- returning to her Deauville hotel with her, shirt open at his too smooth throat--no, he'd be coming home with her in evening clothes, probably with a cape thrown back. He'd accompany her to her room at the hotel in Deauville; whisper, "Just let me come in for one good-night kiss." Then Fran became real. Since he had arrived, Sam's eyes had seen her but cloudily, his ears had heard her only as a stranger. Now he peered at her, was conscious of her, in black and silver, conscious of the curve from shoulder to breast; and he was raging at the thought of Israel.

All his long thinking and his wrath slid by in five seconds and he had not missed a word as she panted:

"You think it's an overwhelming attack on Arnold to suggest that he's used the same tactics before! Of course he has--of course he's had other affairs--perhaps lots of them! Thank Heaven for that! He's had some training in the arts of love. He understands women. He doesn't think they're merely business partners. Let me tell you, my dear Samuel, it would be better for you, and for me both, if you'd devoted a little of your valuable time to the despised art of rousing a woman to some degree of romantic passion-- if you'd given some of the attention you've lavished on carburetors to me--and possibly even to other women--I suppose you have been what is called 'faithful' to me since our marriage."

"I have!"

"Well, doubtless I ought to be highly gratified--"

"Fran! Do you want to marry this fellow Israel?"

"Heavens no! . . . Anyway, I don't think so."

"And yet you want to see him every day this fall."

"That's different. But not marry him. He's too much like plum cake--wonderful at a Christmas feast, but he'd bring indigestion. For a permanent diet I'd prefer good, honest, dependable bread-- which you are--please don't think that's insulting; it's really a great compliment. No! Besides, he doesn't want to! I doubt if he'd care for any one woman for more than six months. Oh, I believe him when he says that he's almost morbidly faithful to the one woman while it lasts, but--"

"Has he got a wife some place?"

"I don't think so. I don't know! Heavens! Does it matter?"

"It may!"

"Oh, don't try to be melodramatic! It doesn't suit your Strong Calm Manly type! Anyway, Arnold wouldn't marry me, because I'm not a Jew. He's just as proud of being a Jew as you are of being a Nordic. He ought to be! He's more or less related to the Mendelssohns and the Rothschilds and all kinds of really significant people. A cousin of his in Vienna--"

"Fran! Have you any idea how serious this business is?"

"Well, rather more than you have, perhaps!"

"I doubt it! Fran, you'll either marry him or cut him out, absolutely and completely."

"My dear Samuel, he might have something to say about that! He's not one of your meek Revelation secretaries. And I won't be bullied!"

"Yes, you will! For the first time! God knows you're getting off easy. Oh, I'm not the kind that would grab a shotgun and start off to get you and your lover--"

"Well, I should hope not!"

"Don't be so sure! I could turn that way, if you just went on long enough! No, I'm not that kind, especially. But, by God, I'm still less of the complaisant husband who's going to sit around and watch his wife entertain her lover, as you've planned to, this fall--"

"I haven't admitted that I plan to do any--"

"You've admitted it and more! Now you'll either come away and travel with me, and chuck this fellow and forget him, or I'll divorce you--for adultery!"

"Ridiculous!"

"Worse than that! Horrible! You can imagine how Brent and Emily will feel!"

Very slowly: "Sam, I never till this moment suspected that--I knew you were stupid and heavy and slow and fond of vulgar people, but I never knew you were simply a bullying rotten cad! No one has ever spoken so to me in all my life!"

"I know it. I've baby'd you. You regard yourself, young woman, as the modern American, with fancy European improvements. But I'm a lot more modern than you are. I'm a builder. I don't have to depend on any title or clothes or social class or anything else to be distinctive. And you've never seen it! You've just lambasted me because I

AM slow and clumsy, till you've stolen every bit of self-confidence I have. You've been the traitor to me in my own home. Criticizing! Not nagging, but just enjoying yourself by being so sweet and superior to me and humbling me. That was worse than your affair with this Israel."

"Oh, I haven't done that! Oh, I didn't mean to! I respect you so!"

"Do you respect me when you want me to sit around and be valet to your lover!"

"Oh no, no, no, I--Oh, I can't think clearly. I'm all confused. I--Yes, if you want, we'll leave for Spain tomorrow."

They did.

CHAPTER 21

Since the days of Alexander the Great there has been a fashionable belief that travel is agreeable and highly educative. Actually, it is one of the most arduous yet boring of all pastimes and, except in the case of a few experts who go globe-trotting for special purposes, it merely provides the victim with more topics about which to show ignorance. The great traveler of the novelists is tall and hawk-nosed, speaking nine languages, annoying all right- thinking persons by constantly showing drawing-room manners. He has "been everywhere and done everything." He has shot lions in Siberia and gophers in Minnesota, and played tennis with the King at Stockholm. He can give you a delightful evening discoursing on Tut's tomb and the ethnology of the Maoris.

Actually, the great traveler is usually a small mussy person in a faded green fuzzy hat, inconspicuous in a corner of the steamer bar. He speaks only one language, and that gloomily. He knows all the facts about nineteen countries, except the home-lives, wage- scales, exports, religions, politics, agriculture, history and languages of those countries. He is as valuable as Baedeker in regard to hotels and railroads, only not so accurate.

He who has seen one cathedral ten times has seen something; he who has seen ten cathedrals once has seen but little; and he who has spent half an hour in each of a hundred cathedrals has seen nothing at all. Four hundred pictures all on a wall are four hundred times less interesting than one picture; and no one knows a cafe till he has gone there often enough to know the names of the waiters.

These are the laws of travel.

If travel were so inspiring and informing a business as the new mode of round-the-world-tour advertisements eloquently sets forth, then the wisest men in the world would be deck hands on tramp steamers, Pullman porters, and Mormon missionaries.

It is the awful toil which is the most distressing phase of travel. If there is anything worse than the aching tedium of staring out of car windows, it is the irritation of getting tickets, packing, finding trains, lying in bouncing berths, washing without water, digging out passports, and fighting through customs. To live in Carlsbad is seemly and to loaf at San Remo healing to the soul, but to get from Carlsbad to San Remo is of the devil.

Actually, most of those afflicted with the habit of traveling merely lie about its pleasures and profits. They do not travel to see anything, but to get away from themselves, which they never do, and away from rowing with their relatives--only to find new relatives with whom to row. They travel to escape thinking, to have something to do, just as they might play solitaire, work cross-word puzzles, look at the cinema, or busy themselves with any other dreadful activity.

These things the Dodsworths discovered, though, like most of the world, they never admitted them.

More than cathedrals or castles, more even than waiters, Sam remembered the Americans he met along the way. Writers speak confidently, usually insultingly, of an animal called "the typical American traveling abroad." One might as well speak of "a typical human being." The Americans whom Sam encountered ranged from Bostonian Rhodes scholars to Arkansas farmers, from Riviera tennis players to fertilizer salesmen.

There were Mr. and Mrs. Meece from Ottumwa, Iowa, at a palm- smothered hotel in Italy. Mr. Meece had been a druggist for forty- six years, and his wife looked like two apples set one on top the other. They plodded at sight-seeing all day long; they took things exactly in the order in which the guide-book gave them; and they missed nothing--art galleries, aquariums, the King Ludwig monument in two shades of pink granite, or the site of the house in which Gladstone spent two weeks in 1887. If they enjoyed anything, they did not show it. But neither did they look bored. Their expressions showed precisely nothing. They returned to the hotel at five daily, and always dined in the grill at six, and Mr. Meece was allowed one glass of beer. He was never heard to say anything whatever to his wife except, "Well, getting late."

In the same hotel with them were the Noisy Pair: two New Yorkers who at all hours were heard, widely heard, observing that all Europeans were inefficient, that they could get no hot water after midnight, that hotel prices were atrocious, that no revue in Europe was as

good as Ziegfeld's Follies, that they couldn't buy Lucky Strike cigarettes or George Washington coffee in this doggone Wop town, and
that lil ole Broadway was good enough for THEM.

They were followed by other Americans: Professor and Mrs.
Whittle of Northern Wisconsin Baptist University--Professor Whittle
taught Greek and knew more about stained glass and the manufacture
of Benedictine than any American living, and Mrs. Whittle had taken
her doctorate at Bonn on the philosophy of Spinoza but really preferred fruit-ranching. The Whittles were followed by Percy West, the
explorer of Yucatan; by Mr. Roy Hoops, who sold motor tires; by
Judge and Mrs. Cady of Massachusetts--the Cadys had lived in the
same house for five generations; by Mr. Otto Kretch and Mr. Fred
Larabee of Kansas City, two oil men who were on a golfing tour of the
world, to take three years; by the brass-bound heel-clicking Colonel
Thorne; by Mr. Lawrence Simton, who dressed like a lily and spoke
like a lady; by Miss Addy T. Belcher, who was collecting material for
a new lecture trip on foreign politics and finance and who, off stage,
resembled a chorus girl; and by Miss Rose Love, the musical comedy
star, who off stage resembled a short-sighted school teacher.

Typical Americans!

Sam never lost the adventurousness of seeing on a railway car
a sign promising that the train was going from Paris to Milan, Venice,
Trieste, Zagreb, Vinkovci, Sofia and Stamboul. Though he became
weary of wandering, so that one museum was like another, so that
when he awoke in the morning it took a minute to remember in what
country he was, yet the names of foreign towns always beckoned him.

To Avignon, they wandered, to San Sebastian and Madrid and
Toledo and Seville. To Arles, Carcassonne, Marseilles, Monte Carlo.
To Genoa, Florence, Sienna, Venice, with two months divided be-
tween Naples and Rome and a jaunt to Sicily. To Vienna, Budapest,
Munich, Nuremberg. And so, late in April, they came to Berlin.

Sam might not tell of it when he went home, nor years later
remember it, but he found that to him the real characteristic of Making
a Foreign Tour had nothing to do with towers or native costumes, galleries or mountain scenery. It was the tedium of almost every hotel,
almost every evening, when they had completed their chore of sight-
seeing. There was "nothing to do in the evening" save occasional movies, or cafes if they were not too far from the hotel in the foreign and
menacing darkness.

Every evening the same. Back to the hotel, weary, a grateful cup of tea, and slow dressing. They never dared, after trying it once, to go down to dinner in tweeds and be stared at by the English tourists of the pay-in-guineas classes as though they were polluting the dining-room.

A melancholy cocktail in the bar. Dinner, always the same-- white and gold dining-room, suavely efficient black-haired captain of waiters pulling out their chairs, a clear soup of parenthetic flavor, a fish not merely white but blanched, chicken with gloomy little carrots, creme caramel, cheese and fruit. The same repressed and whispering fellow-diners: the decayed American mother in silver with the almost equally decayed daughter in gold, staring pitifully at the large lone Englishman; the young intellectual Prussian honeymoon couple, pre-tending to read and ignore each other, and the fat mature Bavarian couple, wanting to be cheery but not daring. The aged Britons--he with a spurt of eyebrows and positive opinions on artichokes and the rate of exchange; she always glaring over her glasses at you if you laughed or asked the head-waiter about trains to Grasse. The vicar of the local English church, moistly friendly, the one person who came and spoke to you but who, by his manner of inquiring after your health, made you feel guilty because you weren't going to his service next Sunday.

Then the real tedium.

Sitting till ten in the lounge, listening to an orchestra mildly celebrating the centenary of Verdi, reading an old Tauchnitz, peeping up uneasily as you felt more and more the tightening of personal ties with these too well-known, too closely studied strangers.

It was worse when the hotel was half empty and the desert of waiting chairs in the lounge looked so lonely.

Always the same, except in a few cities with casinos and caba-rets and famous restaurants--the same in Florence and Granada, in Hyeres and Dresden.

Every evening after such a siege of boredom Sam guiltily in-quired of himself why they hadn't gone out and looked at what was called the "Native Life" of the city--at the ways of that inconspicuous 99/100 of the population whom tourists ignored. But--Oh, they'd tried it. It wasn't a matter of dark-alley dangers; he would rather have liked a fight in a low bar. But foreign languages, the need of ordering a drink or asking a taxi fare in Italian or Spanish, was like crawling through a hedge of prickly thorns. And to go anywhere in dress clothes

211

save to tourist-ridden restaurants was to be tormented by stares, comments, laughter. The frankness with which these Italians stared at Fran--

No, easier to stay in the hotel.

Once in a fortnight Sam was able to let himself be picked up in the bar by some American or English blade, and then he glowed and talked beamingly of motors, of Ross Ireland. And Fran welcomed and was gracious with such rescuers . . . whatever she said in the bedroom afterward about manners and vulgarity.

But it thrust them together, this aching tedium of marooned evenings, and they were often tender.

And Fran was getting tired of the isolation of travel. He gloated that before long, now, she would be content to go home with him, to STAY, and at last, fed up on the syrupy marshmallows of what she had considered Romance, to become his wife.

Twilight in Naples, and from their room at Bertolini's they looked across the bay. The water and the mountains in the water were the color of smoke, and a few little boats, far out, were fleeing home before dark. In the garden below them the fronds of a palm tree waved slowly, and lemon trees exhaled an acrid sweetness. The lights at the foot of Vesuvius were flickering steel points. Her hand slipped into his and she whispered, "I hope the boats get safely home!" They stood there till palms and sea had vanished and they could see only the lights of Naples. Some one afar was singing "Sant Lucia." Sam Dodsworth did not know the song was hackneyed.

"Tee--ta--tah, tee de dee, tee--ta--tah, taaaa--da," he hummed. Italy and Fran! The Bay of Naples! And they would go on--to sun-bright isles, to the moon-hushed desert, pagoda bells, and home! "Tee--ta--tah, tee de dee--Santaaaaa Lucia!" He had won her back to be his wife!

"And they still sing that horrible grind-organ garbage! Let's go eat," she said.

He startled and sighed.

They were again companions, as they had been in their first days of Paris, and sometimes they had whole afternoons that were gay, trusting, filled with the vigor of laughter and long walks. They had again the sweetness of depending on each other. But Sam was conscious that their relationship had become self-conscious.

Much of the time Fran was straining to be friendly. Getting into a rut of it, they quarreled more often over tinier things.

He knew that he had bruised her, humiliated her, by his bullying in Paris, but he could not, in all his hours of agonizing about it, see what else he could have done. He tried to win her with little gifts of flowers, of odd carved boxes, and he fretted over her being chilly at night, hot at noon, tired in galleries, till she wailed, "Oh, don't FUSS so! I'm all RIGHT!"

"If I could only do things naturally and easily, the way that fellow Israel probably does," he sighed to himself . . . and fancied that she was sighing.

He caught himself being critical. For all his "trying to make it up to her," as he put it, he was testily aware of certain childishnesses in her which he had ignored.

In the matter of money she was a brat. She talked, always, of her thoughtfulness about economy; of jewing down a milliner from a thousand francs to seven hundred, of doing without a personal maid. But she took it for granted that they should have the best suite in the best hotel in every town, and she so used the floor maid and the hairdresser and so had to tip them that a personal maid would have been cheaper.

Sam would have liked to economize a little. He still brooded on the Sans Souci Gardens--though he never subjected his dream to her brisk ridicule, for he guessed what she would say about the idiocy of Italian palaces in Zenith. If he could ever coax her back, he would try the gamble of building (if she permitted him!), and in it he could use all the capital he had.

But he never spoke to her of money, and she never suggested that an ordinary room would do them as well as the royal suite, and if she made any comment at all it was only on the inferiority of that suite.

For hours at a time he assured himself of Fran's beauty, gracefulness, wit, and her knowledge of European languages and customs. He convinced himself--except in Venice, when they were with Mrs. Cortright.

Edith Cortright had been born in Michigan, daughter of a banker who became Secretary of the Treasury of the United States. In Washington she had married Cecil R. A. Cortright of the British Embassy, and gone with him to the Argentine, to Portugal, to Rome, to

213

Roumania, where he was minister, and on many vacations home to England. She was about the age of Fran, fortyish, and she had been a widow now for three years, wandering from England to Italy and back. A note from Jack Starling, Tub Pearson's nephew in London, sent her to call on the Dodsworths at the Danieli in Venice, and she invited them to tea at her flat, a floor of the Ascagni Palace; echoing rooms, stone floored, with tall windows on the Grand Canal, with the light from a marble fireplace on chests of smoky walnut and vast tables worn satiny with age.

Sam was at first not vastly taken with Edith Cortright. She was abrupt as she talked of diplomats, of villas on the Riviera, of Roman society, of painting. She was dressed in soft black, worn a little sloppily, and she was pale. But he saw how lovely her hands were, and realized that her quiet voice was soothing. He guessed that her intense eyes missed nothing.

Fran played up to Mrs. Cortright. She too talked of diplomats, she too had notions about villas and society and painting, and on their way home she informed Sam that her Italian accent was MUCH better than Mrs. Cortright's. Suddenly, though resenting his own criticism as though some one else were daring to make it, he felt that Fran knew considerably less than he--and she--had always assumed. Her Italian! She knew a hundred words! Villas! They'd never seen a Riviera villa from a more intimate position than the outside wall!

He reflected that Fran had an unsurpassed show-window display but not much on the shelves inside.

Then he was angry with himself; then he pitied her; then loved her for her childish shrillness of make-believe, her eagerness to be noticed and admired.

He wished they were going to see more of Mrs. Cortright. He felt that she really belonged to this puzzling, reticent thing called Europe and that she might make it clear to him.

Sam was surprised, felt rather guilty, to find that he was becoming more a master of the nervous art of travel than Fran. In Paris she had been supreme; had taken to language and manners and food hectically, while he stood outside. And she still insisted that he couldn't understand Italian waiters and shopping and lace shawls and cathedrals as she could. But while she was daily becoming more uncertain, he was daily developing more of a sure purpose in travel.

He was going back to make some such a "development" as the Sans Souci Gardens, and contemplating it he was becoming conscious that there was such a thing as architecture. Details that once he would never have noticed became alive: hand-wrought iron balconies, baroque altars, tiled roofs, window shutters, copper pans in kitchens seen from the street. He began, shyly keeping it from Fran, to sketch doorways. He began, in the evenings of hotel tedium, to read stray notes on architecture--guide-book introductions, articles in copies of Country Life found in the hotel--instead of news-stand detective stories.

It made him increasingly eager to be out each morning and to see new things, to collect knowledge; and somehow, increasingly, it was he who planned where they should go, he who was willing to confer with concierges and guides, and it was Fran who followed him.

The contrast between Fran and Mrs. Cortright kept annoying him. He was not very well pleased to see that after twenty four years of living with Fran he had not in the least come to know her.

Always, particularly when they had first come abroad, he had considered her clearly superior to other American women. Most of these others, he had grunted to himself, were machines. They sobbed about babies and dressmakers and nothing else. They were either hard-voiced and suspicious, or gushing. Their only emotion was a hatred of their men, with whom they joyously kept up a cat and mouse feud, trying to catch them at flirtation, at poker- playing. But Fran, he had gloated, had imagination and flair and knowledge. She talked of politics and music; she laughed; she told excited stories; she played absurd pleasant games--he was the big brown bear and she the white rabbit; he was the oak and she the west wind who ruffled his foliage--and she did it, too, until he begged mercy. She never entered a drawing-room-- she made an entrance. She paused at the door, dramatic, demanding, stately in simple black and white, where other women hesitated into a room, fussy and tawdry. And they glowered, those other women, when Fran gathered in the men and was to be heard talking with derisive gaiety about tennis, Egyptian excavations, Bolshevism--everything in the world.

He had been so proud of her!

And in Paris, at first--how different her devouring of French life from the flatness of the American women whom he heard in restaurants croaking, in tinny, Midwestern voices, "Mabel says she knows a place in Paris where she can buy Ivory Soap, but I've found one where I can get Palm Olive Soap for seven cents a cake!"

Ah, he had rejoiced, not of these was his Fran--swift silver huntress, gallant voyager, shrewd critic, jubilant companion!

And now, however he cursed himself for it, he could not down the wonder whether she really was any of these poetic things--whether she didn't merely play at them. He could never root out suspicion, planted when he had read her letter about Deauville and Arnold Israel, that she was in heart and mind and soul an irresponsible child. And the minute he was pleased with the bright child quality in her, the irresponsibility annoyed him. . . . Bobbing at cherries is not so pretty a sport at forty-three.

A child.

Now she was ecstatic--a little too demandingly ecstatic for his unwieldiness to follow her--over a moonlit sea, a tenor solo, or a masterpiece of artichoke cookery. Half an hour later she was in furious despair over a hard bed, a lukewarm bath, or a missing nail-file; and Sam was always to blame, and decidedly was to be told about it. He was to blame if it rained, or if they could not get a table by the window in a restaurant; it was not her tardy dressing but his clumsiness in ordering a taxi which made them late for the theater.

She was a child in her way of preening herself over every attractive man who looked interestedly at her along the journey--now that she had been converted to salvation by passion. And she was equally a child in laughing at, in forgetting, the older and less glittering men who were kind to them on trains and friendly at hotels. She forgot so easily!

Sam was certain that she had forgotten Arnold Israel. He identified certain Paris letters, with a thick, black, bold script, as Israel's. At first she was jumpy and secretive about them; then, in a month, she let them lie unopened. And once, apropos of a gesticulating operatic baritone, she began making fun of Israel's ardors. . . . He would almost have been gladder, Sam sighed, if she had enough loyalty to remember Arnold longer.

She was lovely quicksilver, but quicksilver is hard for a thick hand to hold.

A child!

He noted, too, her pretentiousness when she was with people like Mrs. Cortright. Fran let it be known that she herself was of importance. She rebuked people who--never having seen her before-- failed to know that she was an expert at tennis, French and good manners.

216

She didn't exactly say it, but she spoke as though ruddy old Herman Voelker, her respectable sire, had been at least a baron, and she was forever laughing at this fellow-traveler as being "common" and approving that other as being of "quite a good family--quite decent." She was like a child boasting to a playmate of her father's wealth.

But he felt it with a brooding pity that made him the fonder-- made it the harder for him to fight his way free from her capricious domination of his life.

So, after months given more to exploring themselves than to exploring Europe, they came in April to Berlin.

CHAPTER 22

The good Herr Rechtsanwalt Biedner was giving a dinner, at his flat just off the Tiergarten, to his second cousin, Fran Dodsworth, and to Fran's husband. Herr Dr. Biedner was very Prussian, with close-cropped head, small eyes, hard jaw, and sausage rolls at the back of his neck, and he was probably the kindest and pleasantest man the Dodsworths had ever met, and the most international-minded.

Now, in the spring of 1927, Berlin looked prosperous again; also Herr Biedner had an excellent law practise, and his home was as thick with comfort as a coffee cake with sugar. In the hallway was an armoire of carved oak, and the horns of a stag; in the living-room, about a monumental stove of green porcelain, was a perfect auction-room of old easy chairs, and what seemed like hundreds of portraits of the Kaiser, Bismarck, Von Moltke, Beethoven, and Bach clustered behind the grand piano.

Sam was edified to discover that a porcelain stove really could heat a room, and that the pianist of the family was not Frau Biedner or some unrevealed daughter but Herr Biedner himself, though he seemed to be a perfectly worthy and successful lawyer. He was also gratified by the sight of three wine glasses at each plate, and of slim green bottles of Deidesheimer Auslese, 1921.

But the conversation appalled him.

They were so kind, these half dozen German business men and their wives whom Herr Biedner had assembled to greet his American cousins, and they all spoke English. But they talked of things which meant nothing in the world to Sam--of the Berlin theater, of the opera, of a Kokoschka Austellung, of Stresemann's speech at the League of Nations Council, of the agrarian situation in Upper Silesia--

"Golly, this is going to be heavy going," sighed Sam. "I wish somebody would tell a funny story."

And with weighty politeness he answered the weightily polite queries of the woman next him: Was this his first trip to Germany? Was he going to stay long in Berlin? Was it really true that since Prohibition it was difficult to get wine in America?

The one light was the man beside Fran at dinner. With apparent gratification, Biedner had introduced him as Count Obersdorf, taking Sam aside to explain that Kurt von Obersdorf was the present head of one of the greatest Austrian families. His ancestors had owned castles, towns, thousands of acres, whole counties; they had had power of life and death; kings had bargained for their support. But the family had steadily grown poor the past two hundred years, and been finally ruined by the Great War, in which the Graf Kurt had served as major of Austrian artillery. Though his mother kept up a pretense of state, with two slew-footed peasant servants in a ruined old house in the Salzkammergut, Kurt was working in the Berlin bureau of the International Tourist Agency (the famous I.T.A.). He could not afford to marry. He had a reasonable salary; he was head of the I.T.A.'s banking department; but he had to "punch the time-clock," said Herr Dr. Biedner, obviously proud of this Americanism. "He is a fine sport about it. And he uses not much his title. His ancestors probably hanged my ancestors for shooting rabbits, but now he is like one of us here in my household, and he says that nowhere else in Berlin can he get a proper Suppe mit Leberknodel."

Being impressed by the title of count and by a vision of hardriding ancestors in armor, Sam assured himself that he wasn't in the least impressed by title or ancestors, and he studied the family hero attentively.

Kurt von Obersdorf was perhaps forty. He was a tall, loose, lively man, with thick black hair. He had dignity enough, but he was full of laughter, and you felt that by choice he would like to be a clown. He made love to every woman and made friends with every man. Fran blushed when he kissed her hand, and Sam felt less disconsolate, less swamped by foreigners, when Kurt shook his hand and babbled in an Oxford accent with occasional tumbles into comic- paper diction, "I know so much about your Revelation car. Herr Dr. Biedner tells me you were responsible for it. I am enchanted to see you here in Berlin. Since six years I have driven a Revelation, the same car, it belongs to a friend, it is very shabby but the other day I drove it to Wild Park at a hundred and fifty kilometers an hour. I was arrested!"

219

Kurt demanded to see the Biedner grand-child (rather a nasty child, Sam thought, but Kurt chittered at it boisterously); then he played the piano; then he mixed the cocktails which Herr Biedner regarded as suitable to Americans and which the good burgher guests tasted with polite and beaming anxiety.

"Lively fellow, that count. Shows off too much. Never sits still," Sam meditated, with a sound American disapproval of foreign monkey-tricks, and all the while he liked Kurt better than any one he had met since Paris.

All through dinner, Kurt concentrated on Fran.

Sam became restive as he overheard Kurt dashingly tell Fran just what her "type" was, and cheerfully insult her by announcing what he liked and what he detested about that type.

"Yes," Sam caught, "you regard yourself as very European, Mrs. Dodsworth, but you are altogedder American. You are brilliant. You are an automobile's head-light. You learn quick. But you hurry right out and use all you learn. You never have fun out of not letting anybody know you know something. You are very beautiful. I suppose, especial, you have the most beautiful hair I ever have seen. But you would be discontented if there came anybody who did not--wie sagt man?--who did not acknowledge it. You are a play--author and heroine and actor, every one together. A great play. But you could never just cook for some man."

"Why should I?" demanded Fran.

It came to Sam that he had heard this before.

Major Lockert, telling Fran about herself, delighting her by talking about her, stirring her to a desire for men who desired her.

Yes. Lockert had started this biological process which had set Fran alight, changed her into something altogether different from the Fran who had sailed with him--Or had he? Perhaps her first romance had uncovered the real, the essential Fran, whom neither he nor herself had known in the chill polite years of Zenith.

Damn Lockert!

And that aviator fellow, that Italian, Gioserro, had carried on the process. Damn Gioserro!

And Arnold Israel had really broken the delicate coating of ice over her. Damn Arnold Israel!

And now Kurt von Obersdorf, a man who could laugh, was going to lure her--Oh, damn Kurt!

Or should he damn Fran instead? Fran to whom life was a fashion- show.

Or damn the Sam Dodsworth who had thought carburetors more fascinating than the souls and bodies of women?

Anyway, he wouldn't have another Arnold Israel affair. Nipit-inthebud. Certainly would!

He worked up a good sound rage at Kurt von Obersdorf, and had it ruined the moment Kurt came to him, with Fran in tow, after dinner.

"Mr. Dodsworth," said Kurt, "I have behaved outrageously to your wife. She thinks I have insulted her because I say that she is only making believe when she thinks herself European--she is lovely, really, because she IS American! But I am so pro-American! I admire all things American so much--huge buildings and central heating and adding-machines and Fords. Can I please take you about Berlin? I would be very happy!"

"Oh, we mustn't trouble you."

"But it would be a pleasure! Your cousins, the Biedners, they were so very kind to me when I first came from Vienna, and I have had so little chance to repay. And the Herr Doctor is so busy with legal t'ings--aber fabelhaft! I have much more time. Let me have the pleas-ure of doing something for the Herr Doctor!"

But from the way in which Kurt looked at Fran, Sam won-dered if he might not have a livelier reason.

"Tomorrow--Sunday--are you free? May I take you out to a funny place for lunch?"

"That would be very kind of you," Sam said unenthusiasti-cally.

"Splendid! I call for you at twelve."

Their suite in the Hotel Adlon looked on the eighteenth-century Pariser Platz, smacking of royal coaches and be-wigged foot-men, and beyond the Branderburger Tor, at the end of Unter den Linden, they could see the thick woods and little paths of the Tiergar-ten. This Sunday morning, after the party at Herr Biedner's, was flooded with spring, such exultant and surprised reawakening as only Northern cities know. Sam bullied Fran out of bed at eight-thirty,

221

whistled while he shaved, devoured eggs in defiance of Fran's daily objection to American breakfasts in Europe (but she always managed to eat them if they were ordered for her), and lured her into the Tiergarten. The statues of portentous armored Hohenzollerns along the Sieges Allee they admired--neither of them had yet been properly told that the statues were vulgar and absurd--and they followed paths beside brooks, over little bridges, along a lake, to the Coney Island minarets which leered at them over the wall about the Zoo. Quite lost, they rounded the Zoo, stumbled on the Braustubl and had a second breakfast of Rostwurstchen and Munich beer thick as molasses. After the more languid airs of Italy, their northern blood was roused by the spring breeze, and they came back to the Adlon chattering, smiling, content, just in time to meet Graf Obersdorf in the Adlon lobby.

He bounced toward them as though he had known them a dozen years. "It is a good thing that I shall take you away today! It is such a beautiful weather and if you are not dragged off where you can only loaf, then conscientious tourists like you would go see museums and palaces and all kind of dreadful things!"

"I am NOT a conscientious tourist!" protested Fran.

Kurt shook his head. With his experience at the Internation Tourist Agency, he could not imagine an American who was not a collector of sights, who did not work at travel as though it were a tournament with the honors to the person who could last out the largest number of museums. He was as convinced that all Americans mark down credits for themselves in their Baedekers as are Americans that all Germans drink beer every evening.

He called a taxi. Sam was rather glad that Kurt had not wasted money on an apparently private limousine. If he were going to the country by himself, Sam fancied, Kurt would go quite gaily in a motor 'bus, and be friendly with the driver before they got there. Already he had seen Kurt plunge into lively conversations with the Adlon concierge, the news-stand man, two pages, and the taxi- driver; and most of the way out to the rustic haven disastrously named Pichelsberg, Kurt told riotously of how frightened he had been all through the war, of how he had been captured by a very small Italian with a very large rifle, and of how he had won a debate about the plays of Pirandello with the Italian major who had him in for questioning.

The driver stopped by the road to tighten the fan-belt, and Kurt skipped out to watch him.

"Kind of like an American, this fellow--this count," said Sam. "Got a sense of humor, and don't take himself too seriously."

"Oh no, it's a very different thing," Fran insisted. "He's completely European. Americans are humorous to cover up their worry about things. They think that what they do is immediately important and the world is waiting for it. The real European has a sense of a thousand years of ancestors like himself behind him; he knows that his love affairs or his politics or his tragedies aren't very different from a hundred that have gone before. And they aren't so violently ambitious for success--they want to fit into life as they find it rather than to move it about--and they'd rather retire to a little cottage hidden among trees than to build a big stucco house on a hill for strangers to admire. Count Obersdorf doesn't take himself seriously--but he takes Obersdorfs in general and Austrians in general and Europe in general seriously. And he IS rather a lamb, isn't he! I'll be glad, though, when he feels easier with us and becomes his own real thoughtful self--when he understands that we're not his 'conscientious tourists'--imagine!--but the sort that--"

"Yeah, nice fella," said Sam.

He was irritated by her self-election to superiority; he was bothered by her desire to have this new suitor consider her superior. When Kurt had scrambled back into the taxi she looked at him as fondly, as though he were a bright boy whom she wanted to amuse.

Sam sighed.

They left the taxicab at a path leading into thick scrub pines, and in the lazy warm day they ambled over pine needles to a shining river, the Havel, and along it to an immense waste of outdoor restaurant, the Erster Schildhorn, a block of tables set under trees by the river, attended by hysterically flying waiters. For all the haste of the waiters, it took a full hour and a half to lunch. And they liked it. In the spell of spring air, of rustling water, of good heavy stultifying food, they grew relaxed, content to sit and drink beer forever, to forget cities and hotel lobbies and motors and the social items in the New York Herald. Marinierte Herring and beer--noodle soup and beer--ham knuckle and butter- dripping mashed potatoes and beer--Apfel Strudel and whipped cream and coffee--the stolid Sam, the fiery Fran, the mercurial Kurt, they all gorged equally, and sat in the sun by the water, in a pleasant and anti-social coma, so deep a coma that Fran and Kurt did not talk and Sam was only mildly aroused by the fabulous spectacle of a man solemnly riding out on the Havel in a boat pro-

223

pelled like a bicycle, sausage legs revolving--a procedure as sacrilegious to Sam as rowing an automobile.

Without inquiring their desires--he was always a benevolent despot of a host--Kurt led them, when their eyes were cleared of the haze of food, on a walk of miles along the river and into Potsdam.

Here, Kurt explained, lived a small colony of the old Junkers, the court circle of before-the-war, ex-ministers and generals and their proud ladies, dispossessed by the republic. He was taking them to tea at the house of his aunt, the old Princess Drachenthal, whose husband, killed by the misery of the war which he had labored to prevent, had been an ambassador.

"The Crown Prince often comes in for tea. You will like my aunt. She is a dear old thing," said Kurt.

"Speak English?" Sam muttered uneasily.

Kurt looked at him curiously. "She was brought up in England. Her mother was the daughter of the Duke of Wessex."

Sam marched on tireless. Fran, in coat and skirt smart as a cavalry uniform, walked with the swift nervousness of a tennis player, while Kurt loped ahead and behind and to the side like an Airedale.

They passed country houses, square blocks of white, set in immense lawns; they passed beer gardens, festive and vocal; and came to the decorous gray flat-fronted houses of Potsdam, sedate as Gramercy Park or a crescent in Bath. It was a clean, homelike, secure kind of country, and Sam found himself liking its orderliness better than the romantic untidiness of Italy. And found himself not only liking but feeling at one with the Germans.

He still had a war psychosis. He had expected to find in Germany despotic and "sabre-clanking" officials and hateful policemen; had worked up an adequate rage in anticipation. He was nearly disappointed when he found the customs officials friendly, when he asked questions of a Berlin policeman and was answered with a salute and directions in English, and when their room waiter at the Adlon remembered having seen them at the Blackstone Hotel in Chicago! Now he admitted that in all of Europe, however interesting other nationals, however merry the Italians and keen the French, he found only the British and the Germans his own sort of people. With them alone could he understand what they thought, how they lived, and what they wanted of life.

He liked this Sunday stream of Berliners on excursion--vast families with babies and rye bread and pickles and cold ham; eager young men and girls, hatless, the cropped girls rather masculine as far down as the neck but thoroughly feminine below; and occasional strayed Bavarians faithful to green hats with feathers and deer- horn ornaments, green jackets, green leather shorts, and rucksacks-- the rucksacks not necessarily containing anything but a handkerchief, since to a true Bavarian a rucksack is worn not so much for portage as for elementary modesty; as some races conceal the face and some the chest so the Bavarians conceal the small of the back.

Fran protested against the infrequency of "native costumes"; she pointed out that despite the occasional Bavarians, most of these excursioners could not be told from a crowd in America. But that, after months of constantly eating the plum pudding of novelty, was precisely what Sam liked about them, and he was less homesick this afternoon than for weeks; he developed a liking for Count Obersdorf; he felt that the walk was "taking the kinks out of his legs"; he was glad that Fran had a lively companion in Kurt; and he came cheerfully up to the gloomy brown mansion of the Princess Drachenthal.

She was a fragile old lady, like a porcelain cup, and she seemed translucent as porcelain. She called Fran "my dear," and she welcomed Sam to Germany. Apparently Kurt had telephoned about the Dodsworths; she said that she was glad to have a "great American industrialist" see Germany first hand.

"My poor stricken country needs the co-operation of America. We look to you--and if you do not give back the glance we shall have to look to Russia."

She was apparently convinced that Sam had come in a limousine; she asked whether he had sent his chauffeur round back for his tea; and when she learned that Kurt and these visiting dignitaries had actually lunched at a low Volk Lokal and walked into Potsdam, she shook her head, as one not understanding. There were so many things the little old Princess did not understand in these machine- devoured days, she who as a girl had known the security of an old cow-smelling country house in Silesia and of a rose-red Tudor mansion in Wiltshire, in a day when counts did not work in tourist agencies, and America was a wilderness to which rebellious peasants ran off, quite unaccountably and naughtily. But there was the reality of breeding in her, and she tried to understand this bulky "great American industrialist" who was so silently pleasant, this vivacious American woman with the

225

marvelous ruffled blouse peeping from her little blue jacket, the age-less American girl whose gay poise reduced the Count Obersdorf to the position of rattle-headed boy.

Sam perceived the worn elegance of the Princess, took pride in Fran's deference, and found restfulness in the drawing-room, which had very bad gilt chairs, an over-ornamented porcelain stove with very bad plaques of bounding shepherdesses, very bad pictures of stag-hunting and moonlight, far too many glass cases with Prince Drachen-thal's decorations, far too many faded cabinet photographs of the '80's and '90's and yet, bad in all its details, was suggestive of aristocratic generations.

A retired German general came in for tea, with a refugee Rus-sian colonel-baron, a Frau von Something who was apparently so distinguished that no one thought of explaining her, and a handsome fervent boy, the Princess's grand-son, who was taking his examina-tions in law at the University of Bonn and who wanted, he said, to go to America. They were free of Renee de Penable's pretentiousness, as simple as a group at Tub Pearson's, decided Sam. No, they were sim-pler, for Tub would have to be humorous for the benefit of the ladies and gentlemen, no matter how it hurt. Kurt von Obersdorf had dropped all of the slight skittishness into which he fell when he pranced for Fran's benefit, and he was discussing Bolshevism with the Russian ex-colonel.

They somehow lured Sam into talking. He discovered himself being eloquent about chrome steel and General Motors stock, while Fran, in a corner, was deferentially lively with Princess Drachenthal.

"Sort of like coming home--no, it's more like coming home than coming home will be, because Fran is satisfied here. Oh, Lord, WILL she be satisfied in Zenith when--Oh, quit fussing! Course she will!" reflected the inner Sam, while the outer Mr. Dodsworth sagely informed them, "--and in my opinion the greatest fallacy in world-marketing today is a competition between American, German, French, English and Italian cars in South America, instead of all of us combin-ing to educate the South Americans to use more motors and especially to help them to build more through highways that would tap every square mile of the continent--"

He wondered why Fran had been uneasy, in Venice, with Edith Cortright, when she was suavely at ease with Princess Drachen-thal, far more of a personage.

"Because she was jealous? Because Mrs. Cortright, an American, has a position and a flat in a palace and everything? Or because she felt Mrs. Cortright could catch her easier when she was bluffing? No! That's unfair! Fran is no bluffer! Look how lovely she is to the old Princess, and how the Count and the General and everybody falls for her!"

They rode back to Berlin in the train, rather quietly. Sam hinted that Kurt must have an engagement for the evening, but Kurt protested, almost childishly, "Oh no! Are you bored with me? You must let me take you to dinner!"

"Of course, we'd be ENCHANTED," said Fran, and Sam, prodded with a look, achieved, "Mighty nice of you, Count."

"If you really like, I will show you a nice restaurant, and maybe later--if you are not too tired, Madame--we could go a little while to some place to dance. You dance, I know, like an angel."

"Next to Carry Nation and Susan B. Anthony," said Fran gravely, "I am probably the best dancer in America."

"They are famous dancers?" said Kurt.

"Yes, they're so good they're known in America as the Gold Dust twins," explained Sam.

"Really? And you dance like them, Madame? I shall have to be very good!" said Kurt.

While Fran dressed for dinner, Sam and Kurt had side-car cocktails in the Adlon Bar. Sam liked the scarlet Chinese Chippendale walls, with little Burmese figures; the somewhat obese Bacchanalians in the painting over the bar; the corners with settees comforting to a drinking man; and the fact that here was one place in Europe where no foreign language--i.e., any language save American, with traces of English--was ever heard.

At the bar were always half a dozen of the American business men stationed in Berlin--shipping-men, bankers, representatives of the movies, and for the American journalists it was a club, where they exchanged tips on Russia and Roumania, Breitscheid's coming speech and the Zentrum Party's capture of the schools.

"I like this; I see myself sneaking in here pretty often," Sam promised himself.

He forgot the bar in attention to Kurt's confidences. He had never known any one so frankly emotional about his friends as Kurt, nor one so eager to be liked.

"Shall I be rude if I talk about Mrs. Dodsworth?" urged Kurt. "She is so lovely! A kind of Arctic beauty, shining like ice. And yet so very warm-hearted and gracious and fun-ny. And such gallantry-- an explorer--but very elegant--like in a Roman, with many bearers and dressing for dinner in the jungle. One feels she could do anything she wanted to enough. Forever young. She is--perhaps thirty-five?--one would say she was twenty-eight. Our European women are very ge-mutlich, they are easy to be with, they wait on us, but not many among them have a sword-like quality like Mrs. Dodsworth and such high spirits--Oh, I hope I am not rude! She is lucky to be accompany with a great red Indian like you--a chief, sagt man?--who can guide and pro-tect her!"

Sam made the most awkward sound--something between "Thanks" and "Like hell!"

"As I said once, I admire America very much, and it is so kind of you two to come and bummel with me! And meet my friends."

"Kindness all yours, Count. Good Lord! Mighty nice of you to let us meet such nice people as the Princess and--"

"Oh, don't call me 'Count.' I am not a count--there aren't any more counts--the republic has come to stay--I am just a clerk for the I.T.A.! If I am only something with a title, then I would better be noth-ing! I shall be glad if you call me 'Kurt.' We Austrians are almost like you Americans in our fondness to call by the first name among people we like. Yes."

"Well, that's mighty nice of you--"

Sam wished that he could warm up. But he was conscious of waiting for Fran--of Kurt's waiting. He was annoyed at the prospect of again being admitted as Fran's patient escort, as he had been in Ma-dame de Penable's gang. Yet he felt that Kurt was honest in profess-ing admiration for both of them, and he forced himself to sound amiable:

"I guess one of the things we Americans fool ourselves about is claiming that we're the only really hospitable race in the world. Don't believe any stranger in America ever was received in a more friendly way than Mrs. Dodsworth and--than Fran and I have been here and in England. Mighty nice!"

Then Fran was upon them, in amethyst velvet, and with velvet she had put on a patronizing grandeur. The simple-hearted Kurt was confused; it took him ten minutes to understand that she was not showing displeasure in dropping her jollity, but merely playing a different role. Entreated to join them in a cocktail, she condescended. "It would be ever so amusing to have an aperitif in the bar, but do you really think one COULD?"

"Oh yess, it is quite proper . . . almost!" Kurt begged.

Sam said nothing. He had seen Fran enjoying too many drinks in too many bars, and not calling them "aperitifs," either.

She was full of high life amid the upholstery and expensive food of Horcher's, and she generously commended the Rheinlachs. But somehow she came out of it--somehow, sometime, Kurt began calling her "Fran," and she admitted him with "Kurt"; she laughed without admiring her own laughter, and, permitting them an entr'acte during her personal drama of The Sophisticated American Lady Abroad, she allowed them to be human and cheerful again. Kurt talked, less flamboyantly now, more naturally, and Sam realized that however Kurt might insist that he was no nobleman now but only a tourist- agency clerk, Kurt belonged to the once powerful of the earth and, but for the war, would be magnificence in a castle. His father had been gentleman in waiting and friend to the Emperor, his great- uncle, the field-marshal, had organized the war against Prussia, and he himself, as a boy, had played with the Archduke Michael.

Sam wondered whether, however genuine his family, Kurt was one of these fictitional adventurers who would be likely to borrow money, and to introduce swindlers to a rustic from the Middle West. He rejected it. No. If he knew anything about people, this man was honest, unselfishly fond of entertaining people. And the Biedners vouched for him, and to Fran's father, the canny old brewer, a Biedner had been almost as beautiful and dependable and generally Biblical as stock in a national bank.

Obviously Fran had no doubts whatever about Kurt von Obersdorf. In the glow of his stories about the frivolous days of old Vienna, she forgot her own charms. She consented when Kurt proposed that they go to the Konigin and dance; she consented when he proposed that they leave that decorative but packed haunt of the more sporting Junkers and venture to the vulgar Cabaret von Vetter Kaspar.

The wit there was devoted chiefly to the water-closet, and Sam was astonished to hear Fran shamelessly joining in Kurt's whooping laughter. Of course he laughed himself; but still--Well, this fellow Obersdorf, he enjoyed things himself so much that he made you feel like laughing at--well, at things that people didn't talk about in Zenith, anyway not in mixed company--But still--

They came out of the cabaret at one in the morning.

"Now just one more place!" Kurt demanded. "Such a place as I do not think you will see in America. Shrecklich! Such curious men hang out there and dance with one another. but you must see it once."

"Oh, it's pretty late, Kurt. I think we'd better be getting home," said Sam. An evening of stories, and a bottle of champagne, had warmed him to a point where it seemed natural to call Kurt by his first name, but not to a point where he forgot the joys of a good soft pillow.

"Yes, it IS late," said Fran, but vaguely.

"Oh no!" Kurt begged. "Life is so short! To waste it in sleep-ing! And you are here a so small time. Then you will wander on and perhaps I shall never see you again! Oh, you did enjoy today, did you not? We are good friends, nicht? Let us not be serious! Please! Life is so short!"

"Oh, of course we'll come!" rippled Fran; and, though Sam grumbled to himself, "Life'll be a damn' sight shorter if I don't get some sleep once in a while!" he looked agreeable as they heaved themselves into a taxicab.

Their new venture in restaurants was called "Die Neuste Ehe"--"The Latest Style in Marriage"--and after two minutes' view of it, Sam concluded that he preferred the old style. Here, in a city in which, according to the sentiment of the American comic weeklies, all males were thick as pancakes and stolid as plow-horses, was a mass of deli-cate young men with the voices of chorus girls, dancing together and whispering in corners, young men with scarves of violet and rose, wearing bracelets and heavy symbolic rings. And there was a girl in lavender chiffon--only from the set of her shoulders Sam was sure that she was a man.

As they entered, the bartender, and a very pretty and pink-cheeked bartender he was, waved his towel at them and said some-thing in a shrill playful German which Sam took to signify that Kurt was a charming person worthy of closer acquaintance, that he himself was a tower of steel and a glory upon the mountains.

It was new to Sam.

He stood gaping. His fists half clenched. The thick, reddish hair on the back of his hands bristled. But it was not belligerence he felt--it was fear of something unholy. He saw that Fran was equally aghast; proudly he saw that she drew nearer his stalwartness.

Kurt looked at the jocund bartender; quickly he looked at Fran and Sam; and he murmured, "This is a silly place. Come! Come! We go some place else!"

Already the manager was upon them, smirking, inviting them in two languages to give up their wraps. Kurt said something to him in a rapid, hissing German--something that made the manager sneer and back off--something so hateful and contemptuous that Sam reflected, "This Kurt is quite a fellow, after all. Wouldn't be such a bad guy to have with you in a scrap!"

As Kurt lifted the heavy brocade curtain before the street door to usher them out, the bartender, in a cat-call voice, shouted something final. Kurt's jaw tightened. It was a good jaw-line. But he did not turn and, out on the pavement, his face was full of an apology that was almost suffering as he begged of Fran:

"I am so sorry. I had never been there. I had just heard of it. I did not think they would be so dreadful. Oh, you will never forgive me!"

"But I didn't mind them!" Fran protested. "I think it would have been amusing to watch them, for a little while."

Kurt insisted, "Oh no, no, no! Of course you were shocked! Come! There is another place I do know, over the street. You will show me you forgive me by coming--"

They danced till three, at which hour every one in the cafe was sleepy except Kurt. The orchestra went home and, to the cheers of the grimly merry groups who were left slumbering over their champagne, Kurt trotted forward and played the piano like a vaudeville performer, and they all obediently awakened for the last dregs of joviality. A monocled officer-like German begged Fran to dance, and Sam was able to snatch three minutes of secret sleep.

He was gratified when, after he had grumbled, "Now we've GOT to go home," Fran and Kurt took him seriously enough to consent.

It was raining, and the street was like the inside of a polished steel cylinder. A late taxicab cruised up, but the doorman and his faithful big umbrella had gone home. Kurt whipped off his coat, wrapped it about Fran and, in shirtsleeves, stood waiting till Sam was inside the cab. . . . And he WOULD sit on the little folding seat and he wouldn't let them take him home, but escorted them to the Adlon, babbling, "It was fun, wasn't it! You do forgive me for the Neuste Ehe, don't you! It was a von-derful day, wasn't it! And you will come by me Wednesday evening for a little dinner to meet some friends? Oh, you must!"

Yes, they would, thank you very much--

In the extreme drowsiness of their room, Fran hinted, "You enjoyed it, didn't you, darling?"

"Yes, everything except the last hour or so. Got pretty sleepy."

"Kurt is a darling, don't you think?"

"Yes, he's a nice fellow. Mighty kind."

"But Heavens, what a bossy person he is! He simply demanded that I be shocked at that Den of Vice, and I had to do my best to please him--and you too, you pure-minded males! Well, he's a nice boy, and so are you, and I'm going to sleep till noon I LIKE Berlin!"

CHAPTER 23

Three days of museums, of art galleries, of palaces, of the Zoo. They went to Sans Souci, where Fran talked of Voltaire (she really had read "Candide") and Sam thought in a homesick way of the Sans Souci Gardens development in Zenith and snapped at himself that it was time to clinch with Fran, to make her come home and begin a new life of "making things."

They saw nothing of Kurt von Obersdorf--he merely telephoned to them eight or ten times and made them go out and see things. He so insisted that they see Molnar's "Spiel im Schloss" that they sulkily went, though by now Sam had convinced himself that he was right in thinking he didn't care greatly for plays in a language he didn't understand, and though Fran, exhausted by the florid endearments which had been poured upon her at a women's tea given by Frau Dr. Biedner, for once in her life wanted to go to bed.

She said that she understood every word of "Spiel im Schloss."

Sam said that he guessed it was pretty fine acting all right, and he thought he'd just slip down-stairs and have a nightcap in the bar.

He fell to talking with an American journalist who knew Ross Ireland; he had several nightcaps; and in general he enjoyed himself. When he slipped into their room, Fran was asleep. So, as he put it, he had got away with it, and he felt as exultant as a boy who has played hooky and discovers afterward that teacher has been sick all day.

In England Fran had learned to say Lift for Elevator, Zed for Zee, La-BOR-atory for LA-boratory, Schenario for Scenario, and Shi for Ski. And before she had ever left America she had been able to point her Europeanism by keeping her fork in her left hand. But now she added to her accomplishments the ability to make a European 7 by crossing it, and ardently she crossed every 7, particularly in letters to friends in Zenith, who were thus prevented from knowing what figure she was using.

The four great mysteries of life in post-war Berlin, not to be explained by the most diligent searching of history and economics and Lutheran theology, are all connected with apartment-houses, and thus are they: Why can no visitor get into an apartment-house after eight in the evening without protocols? Why are the automatic elevators kept locked, so that no visitor can use them? Why does no Berlin landlord provide modern locks, but always compel his tenants to carry a bunch of keys comparable in size to those used in the Middle Ages for closing cathedrals? Why does a landlord who has spent a hundred thousand marks on a marble staircase (with neat gilt edgings and mosaic inserts) refuse to spend a mark a night to provide lights in the hallways? They are dark. They are very dark. A light may be had by pressing a button, which provides illumination for a time, but in all the history of Berlin that time of illumination has never been known to last while a visitor climbed from the ground floor to the top.

On the top floor of an apartment house on the Brucken Allee lived Kurt von Obersdorf, and on the vertiginous way up to it Sam pointed out these four mysteries, and was pleased to have Fran agree with him.

They were received by Kurt's maid. She was an ancient thing, rusty and feeble and in some doubt as to what to do with Sam's hat and stick. While she puttered, Sam looked about. The apartment had a narrow corridor, the drab plaster rather flaked, and adorned with a yellow-stained engraving of St. Stefan's Dom in Vienna. Over a doorway were two crossed swords.

Suddenly Kurt bounced out on them, slimmer and looser than ever in dinner clothes, took Fran's wrap himself, spoke to the creeping servant with that mixture of scolding and family fondness which only a European can manage, and prattled:

"I am so glad! I was afraid you would be angry with me for my clumsiness about Die Neuste Ehe the other evening and punish me by not coming. Let me tell you who are the other guests. There are your cousins, Dr. and Frau Biedner, and the Baroness Volinsky--she is such a pretty girl, a Hungarian; her husband is a Pole, a terrible fellow; he is not coming, thank God!; and Theodor von Escher, the violinist--he is such a VON-DERFUL violinist!--and his wife, Minna--you will fall in love with her, and Professor and Frau Braut--he is professor of economics in Berlin University, such a brain, he knows more America than ANYBODY--he will prove to you that in two hundred years America will be a wilderness again, you will like him so much! They are a funny mix' lot, but all speak English, and I wanted you to meet different kinds. Fran, you look like a heaven's angel in ivory! Kom' mal"

He ushered them, as though they were royalty, into a small, shabby, friendly apartment in which three people seemed a crowd. The chairs of old brown leather were hollowed and listed; the couch was covered with what Sam viewed as "some kind of yellow silk," though Fran whispered later that it was "perfectly priceless old damask." The pictures were largely photographs of friends, officers in Austrian uniform. But there were shelves of wildly disarranged books, and Sam noted later that they were in German, English, Italian, and French. He observed a dozen ponderous and dismaying volumes on American law and banking and history, the sort of tomes which he had always admired in libraries and shunned in the home.

When the door to the right was opened for a moment, Sam saw a narrow bedroom with a mean camp bedstead, racks of gorgeous ties, a picture of a beautiful girl, a crucifix, and nothing much else. That, with the little dining-room and a mysterious kitchen somewhere and a bathroom old enough to be historic, seemed to make up the domain of the head of the house of Obersdorf.

There were cocktails, agitatedly mixed by Kurt in a glass pitcher, and there was dinner (not very good) and conversation (tremendous). Under Kurt's hectic captaincy, there was none of the timid burgher decorum of dinner at the Biedners'; also there was more to drink, including an Assmannshauser champagne which made Sam determined to explore the Rhine Valley. Any one who didn't shout from time to time received Kurt's worried attention. Kurt was convinced that a person who was silent in his house had either ceased to like him-- and probably for good reasons, for some hideous sin he had unconsciously committed against them--or else was suffering from a hidden malady which ought to be treated out of hand. But between the shouts, most of the conversation was carried on by Professor Braut.

When he first surveyed that learned man, who left with you the impression that he had whiskers even in his eyes, Sam had decided, "This bearded beauty may know something about economics in Germany, but I'll bet he doesn't know anything about the land of the safety- razor!"

Professor Braut turned to him. His accent was much thicker than Kurt's. "Please," he said, "I vonder if you coult tell me something I am trying to learn about agrarian movements in America."

"I don't know very much about them," said Sam. "Have you been in America?"

"Oh, a liddle--before the war. I was a professor in Harvard for a year, and in Leland Stanford a year, and I traveled maybe a year, but of course that is nothing to get any real knowledge of your great country."

Then, at Kurt's suggestion, Professor Braut gave a minute history of the Non-partisan League in North Dakota.

Through it he turned constantly to Sam for confirmation, and Sam-- who knew very little about North Dakota and precisely nothing about the Non-partisan League--nodded blandly. At the end, Sam addressed himself strongly:

"He knows more about your own country than you do! Sambo, you know nothing. Ignorant! I wish I hadn't given up thirty years to motor-cars. And I haven't really learned much here in Europe. A tiny bit about architecture and a little less about wine and cooking and a few names of hotels. And that's all!"

While Kurt chattered of the adventures of Archduke Michael as a chauffeur to a Hungarian Jew, Sam had a vision of learning and of learned men, of men who knew things with precision, without emotional prejudice, and who knew things which really affected the broad stream of human life; who considered the purposes of a thousand statesmen, the function of a thousand bacteria, the significance of a thousand Egyptian inscriptions, or perhaps the pathology of a thousand involved and diseased minds, as closely as he himself had considered the capacities of a hundred salesmen and engineers and clerks in the Revelation Company. He saw groups of such learned men, in Berlin, in Rome, in Basle, in both Cambridges, in Paris, in Chicago. They would not be chatterers. Oh, he pondered, probably some of them would be glib and merry enough over a glass of beer, but when it came to their own subjects, they would speak slowly, for to any given question there would be so many answers among which to select. They would not vastly please Fran; they would not all of them be dancers of elegance, and perhaps they would fail to choose quite the right waistcoats. They would look insignificant and fuzzy, like Professor Braut,

or dry and spindling. And he would be proud to have their recognition-
-beyond all recognitions of wealth or title.

How was it that he had not known more of them? In Yale,
teachers had been obstacles which a football-player had to get past in
order to carry out his duty of "doing something for old Yale." New
York was to him exclusively a city of bankers, motor dealers, waiters,
and theater employees. On this European venture which was to have
opened new lives to him, he had seen only more waiters, English spin-
sters marooned in hotels, and guides with gold teeth.

Scholars. Men who knew. Suddenly he felt that he might have
been such a man. What had kept him from it? Oh, he had been cursed
by being popular in college, and by having a pretty wife who had to be
surrounded with colored lights--

No, he rebuked himself. He couldn't get away with excuses
like that! In the first place, he was a dirty dog to be ungrateful for having been popular and for having had such a glorious girl as his Fran--
look at her now, laughing about the sanctity of the sausage in the
German social scheme--look at her, reducing the Count of Obersdorf,
kin of princesses and maybe kings, to bouncing admiration! No, he'd
been lucky.

Besides! A fellow did not become things--anyway not after
five or six or seven years of age. He simply was things! If he had had
the capacity to be a savant, nothing would have prevented.

Or--

Suddenly he felt better about it. Was it possible that in some
involved, unelucidated way, he himself was a savant in fields not admitted by the academicians as scholarship? He told himself that in the
American motor-world he was certainly not known merely as a pedler
and as a financial acrobat, but as the authority on automobile-
designing, as the first man to advocate four-wheel brakes. Hm. DID
that constitute him a scholar, or--

Or possibly an artist? He had created something! He had no
pictures in the academies, no books to be bound in levant, no arias nor
flimsy furniture named after him, but every one of the twenty million
motors on the roads of America had been influenced by his vision, a
quarter of a century ago, of long, clean streamlines!

Yes! And it didn't hurt a man to be a little proud of some honest thing he had done! It gave him courage to go on. Especially with a
wife like Fran, who was always criticizing--

Good God, had he really become confirmed, since the case of Arnold Israel, in this habit of seeing Fran not as his loyal companion but as a dreaded and admired enemy, to placate whom was his object in life? Was this the truth about his wanderings, all his future?

He hastily got out of that torturing wonder by sending his mind back to scholarship, while he looked intelligent and placidly ate Backhuhn and seemed to listen to Theodor von Escher on his own superiority to Kreisler.

Could he ever attain scholarship now? Was it too infantile a fancy to think of becoming the first great historian of motors, historian of something which was, after all, more important in social evolution than twenty Battles of Waterloo? Or could he learn something of architecture? For he really was a little tired of motors. They meant, just now, sitting at a desk in the Revelation offices. Could he really make better Sans Souci Gardens?

Anyway, he wasn't going on just being a Cook's tourist, rather less important to Fran than concierges and room-waiters. He'd do SOMETHING--

Or was this inner glow, so exciting and so rare--was it merely a reflection of drinking champagne and being warmed by Kurt's hospitality? Was his formless determination to "do something" and his belief that he still could "do something" only, in essence, like the vows of a drunkard?

"No, by God," swore Samuel Dodsworth.

"It isn't that. A drink or two, and a jolly bunch, do loosen me up. I'm slow at starting--Hm! Very slow! Here I am fifty-two years old, and just this last year or so I've wanted to be more than a money-coining machine. . . . To be SOMETHING. Though God knows what! . . . Eh?" (He answered furiously a chorus of accusers.) "I have been a good citizen! And I have brought up my children! And I have paid my debts! And I have done the job that was first at hand! And I have loved my friends! And now I'm not going to stand back the rest of my life and be satisfied and dead-- dead on my feet--dead!

"I wish I'd known Kurt before. I'd like to've gone off for a few weeks with him and Ross Ireland. Only I ought to've done it ten years ago, and now it's--But I won't LET it be too late!

"Hm! YOU let! It's what Fran will let her dear husband do--

"Why is it I always go back to that--as though it was she that cramped my style, instead of my own lack of brains?"

And, annoyed by the way in which thoughts scamper around in circles if you once let them loose, Sam came abruptly out of his meditation and was again the large and prosperous American husband of a lovely American wife, a worthy husband listening with meekness to the conversation of her European friends.

Sam had noted, and been rather surprised at it, that Kurt von Obersdorf did not condescend to a mere university professor, as any American of good family would have done. For all his love of gossiping, Kurt listened humbly when Professor Braut really got going, like a liner towed out through little ripples of talk, tugs yanking at its sulky ponderousness, but finally plunging into the long rollers of conversation.

Braut was lecturing Fran as though she were a rather small seminar. He did violence, while he talked, to the English W and V and T, yet in his earnestness, his was no comic dialect:

"Emotionally, as a Prussian, with the symbols of blood and iron, of Bismarck and Luther and der alte Fritz, I detest the prostituted elegance of Paris and the Italians, like children playing at Empire. Yet all the time I think of myself--most people like me think of themselves--more as Europeans than as German or French or Polish or Hungarian; we think of ourselves, whatever family differences we may have, as standing together against the Russians (who are certainly not European but Asiatic), against the British, the Americans--however we admire them--the Latin Americans, the Asiatics, the colonists. The European culture is aristocratic. I do not mean that boastfully; I do not speak of famous old families, like that of our friend Graf Obersdorf here. I mean that we are aristocratic, as against democratic, in that we believe that the nation is proudest and noblest and most exalted which has the greatest number of really great men--like Einstein and Freud and Thomas Mann--and that ordinary, undistinguished people (who may be, mind you, counts or kings, as well as servant maids) are happier in contributing to produce such great men than in having more automobiles and bath-tubs.

"And by the aristocratic tradition of the real Europe I do not mean any hauteur. I think perhaps I have seen more rudeness to servants--as well, of course, as more rudeness to masters--in America than anywhere in Europe. Servants here are not so well paid, but they have more security and more respect. An American thinks of a good cook as a low person; a European respects him as an artist.

239

"The European, the aristocrat, feels that he is responsible to past generations to carry on the culture they have formed. He feels that graciousness, agreeable manners, loyalty to his own people, are more important than wealth; and he feels that to carry on his tradition, he must have knowledge--much knowledge. Why, think of what the young European must learn, if he is not to be ashamed of himself!

"He must know at least two languages, and if he does not know them, his friends are sorry that he is so poor a linguist. He must have-- even though he may plan to be a stock-broker or an importer, or sell your automobiles, Mr. Dodsworth--he must have some understanding of music, painting, literature, so that he will really enjoy a concert or an exhibition of pictures, and not go there to make an impression. His manners must be so good that he can be careless. He must know the politics of all the great countries--I would bet you, Mrs. Dodsworth, that my four grandsons, though they have never been in America or England, know as much about President Coolidge and Secretary Hoover and Governor Smith as most Americans of their age.

"They must know cooking and wines. They themselves may prefer to live on bread and cheese, but they must be able to give their guests good dinners, and at not much cost--oh, so terribly little cost most of us can afford now since the war! And most of all, they must understand women, and the beginning of that--I t'ink Mrs. Dodsworth will agree--is really to like women, and to like them to BE women, and not imitation men!

"That is a small bit of the required training of the real European-- German or Swiss or Dutch or whatefer! And that training helps to keep us together, understanding each other, no matter how foolish we are and suicide with Great Wars! However we may oppose it, we are all at heart Pan-Europeans. We feel that the real Continental Europe is the last refuge of individuality, leisure, privacy, quiet happiness. We think that good talk between intelligent friends in a cafe in Vienna or Paris or Warsaw is more pleasant and important than having septic tanks or electric dish-washing machines.

"America wants to turn us into Good Fellows, all provided with the very best automobiles--and no private place to which we can go in them. When I think of America I always remember a man who made me go out to a golf club and undress in a locker room, where quite uninvited men came up and made little funny jokes about Germany and about my being a professor! And Russia wants to turn us into a machine for the shaving off of all the eccentricities which do not belong to the lowest common denominator. And Asia and Africa do not t'ink that human life and the sweetness of human life matter. But Europe, she believes that a Voltaire, a Beethoven, a Wagner, a Keats, a Leuwenhoeck, a Flaubert, give drama and meaning to life, and that they are worth preserving--they and the people who understand and admire them! Europe! The last refuge, in this Fordized world, of personal dignity. And we believe that is worth fighting for! We are menaced by the whole world. Yet perhaps we shall endure . . . perhaps!

"Some of us think that perhaps we shall prevail even against Americanization--which I may venture to define as a theological belief that it is more important to have your purchases tidily rung up on a cash-register than to purchase what you want. (And mind you--I am not so anti-American as I seem--I quite understand that the mystic process of 'Americanization' is being carried on as much by German industrialists and French exporters and English advertising-men as it is by born Yankees!) I think the echt Europe may be able to endure. For I remember always of Greece and Rome. Rome was the America of ancient history; Greece the perhaps over- cultured Continental Europe. Vi et armis, Rome conquered. Yet it was Greek architecture, Greek philosophy, and its gracefulness of body which revivified Europe in the Renaissance, more than Roman law.

"So! I deliver a lecture. Hasslich! Yet I must finish. To be clear, when I speak of the European you must understand that I speak of a very small, select, special class, which is far nearer to other members of that class in foreign nations than it is to most of its own countrymen. The beer-sodden peasant in a Gastzimmer at a country inn, or here in Berlin dancing in masses at Die Neue Welt, is not a European in that special sense. Neither is the bustling young business man on the Friedrichstrasse, or on the Rue de Rivoli, who is trying to sell vulgar porcelain or shoddy silk so fast as he can. Both of them would gladly emigrate to America and change leisure for automobiles. And also there are a few people born in America who DO belong to what I call 'Europeans'--your author Mrs. Edith Wharton, I imagine, must be so. But wherever they were born, there is this definite class, standing for a definite aristocratic culture--and most Americans who think they have 'seen Europe' go home without any idea at all of its existence and what it stands for, and they perceive of Europe just loud-tongued guides, and passengers in trains looking unfriendly and reading Uhu or Le Rire. They have missed only everything that makes Europe!"

Sam was surprised to find himself answering:

"Yes, that's about true. America thinks of the Europeans as a bunch of restaurant cashiers trying to do us on exchange--thinks of Europe as dead--nothing but pictures by men that lived three hundred years ago. We forget your Freud and Einstein--yes, and European aeroplane constructors, and this Youth movement in Germany, and the French tennis players that beat us. But you have just as untrue an idea of America. All over Berlin, in the book- stores, I see books about America; titles like 'The Dollar Land.' Well, I'll bet the French peasant that sticks the centimes away in the sock, and the German farmer, love the dollar ten times as much as the average American. We love to make money, but we love to spend it. We're all like sailors on a spree. We have to have every parrot that's on sale on the waterfront. And--

"Why do you suppose so many hundreds of thousands of Americans come to Europe? Not more than one out of a hundred Europeans who do go to America ever goes there to learn, to see what we have. And after all, a Woolworth Building or a Chicago Tribune Building or a Ford plant or a Grand Canyon or a Sharon, Connecticut-- and incidentally a mass of 110,000,000 people--might be worth study-ing. You of all people, Professor, know that most Europeans go to America just to make money. But why are the Americans here? Oh, a few of 'em to get social credit for it, back home, or to sell machinery, but most of 'em, bless 'em, come here as meekly as school-boys, to admire, to learn!

"What most Europeans think of America! Because we were a pioneer nation, mostly busy with farming and cod-fishing and chewing tobacco, a hundred years ago, Europe thinks we still are. The pictures of Americans in your comic papers indicate to me that Europe sees all Americans as either moneylenders who lie awake nights thinking of how they can cheat Europe, or farmers who want to spit tobacco on the Cathedral of St. Mark, or gunmen murdering Chicagoans in their beds. My guess is that it all comes from the tradition that Europeans started a hundred years ago. Here a few weeks back, when we were in Vi-enna, I picked up 'Martin Chuzzlewit' and waded through it. Funny, mind you, his picture of America a hundred years ago. But he shows a bunch of people along the Ohio River and in New York who were too lazy to scratch, who--"

"Sam!" warned Fran, but he strode on unregarding.

"--were ignorant as Hottentots and killed each other with re-
volvers whenever they felt like it, with no recourse. In fact, every
American that Dickens shows in the book is a homicidal idiot, except
one--and he wanted to live abroad! Well! You can't tell me that a degenerate bunch like that could have taken the very river- bottom
swamps that Dickens describes, and in three generations have turned
'em into the prosperous cement-paved powerful country that they are
today! Yet Europe goes on reading hack authors who still steal their
ideas from 'Martin Chuzzlewit' and saying, 'There, I told you so!' Say,
do you realize that at the time Dickens described the Middlewest--my
own part of the country--as entirely composed of human wet rags, a
fellow named Abe Lincoln and another named Grant were living there;
and not more than maybe ten years later, a boy called William Dean
Howells (I heard him lecture once at Yale, and I notice that they still
read his book about Venice IN Venice) had been born? Dickens
couldn't find or see people like that. Perhaps some European observers
today are missing a few Lincolns and Howellses!

"The kind of pride that you describe, Professor, as belonging
to the real aristocratic Europeans, is fine--I'm all for it. And I want to
see just that kind of pride in America. Maybe we've gone too fast to
get it. But as I wander around Europe, I find a whale of a lot of Americans who are going slow and quiet, and who are thinking--and not all
of 'em artists and professors, by a long shot, but retired business men.
We are getting a tradition that-- Good Lord! You said you'd been lecturing. I'm afraid I have, too!"

Kurt cried "To America!" and adumbrated "Yes, America is
THE hope of--And of course the paradise of women."

Fran exploded:

"Oh, that is the one most idiotic fallacy about America--and
it's just as much believed in America as in Europe--and it's just as
much mouthed by women as by men--and deep down they don't believe a word of it! It's my profound conviction that there's no woman
living, no real normal woman, who doesn't want a husband who can
beat her, if she deserves it--no matter though she may be president of a
college or an aviator. Mind you, I don't say she wants to be beaten, but
she wants a man who CAN beat her! He must be a man whom she respects! She must feel that his work, or his beautiful lack of work, is
more important than she is."

Sam looked at her in mild astonishment. If anything had been
certain about their controversies, it had been that Fran ought to be

more important to him than his work. He tried to remember just where she had got this admirable dissertation on feminism. Certain of the phrases he traced to Renee de Penable.

"And that's just what you do have in Europe, and what we don't have in America. Mind you, I'm not speaking of Sam and myself--he's awfully competent at beating me when I deserve it!"

Her jocular glance at Sam was admiringly observed by all assembled.

"I'm just speaking generally. Oh, the American wife of the prosperous classes--sometimes even among people who have no money visible to the naked eye--has privileges for which the European woman would envy her. She doesn't have to beg her husband for money. She has a joint bank-account. If she wants to study singing or advocate anti-vivisection or open a tea-room or dance with nasty young men at hotels, it never occurs to him to object. And so she's supposed to be free and happy. Happy! Do you know why the American husband gives his wife so much freedom? Because he doesn't CARE what she does--because he isn't sufficiently interested in her to care! To the American man--except darlings like Sam, here--a wife is only a convenience, like his motor, and if either one of them breaks down, he takes it to a garage and leaves it and goes off whistling!"

This time her glance at Sam told him what she need not have told him, but she went on with an admirable air of impersonality:

"Whereas the European husband, if I understand it, feels that his wife is a part of him--or at least of his family honor--and he would no more permit her this fake 'freedom' than he would permit one of his legs to go wandering off cheerfully without the other! He LIKES women! And another thing. Any real woman is quite willing, no matter how clever she is, to give up her own chances of fame for her husband, PROVIDING he is doing something she can admire. She can understand sacrificing herself for the kind of civilized aristocracy that Professor Braut speaks of; she can sacrifice for a great poet or soldier or scholar; but she isn't willing to give up all her own capabilities for the ideal of industrial America--which is to manufacture more vacuum-cleaners this year than we did last!"

Sam caught her eye. He said, very slowly, "Or more motor cars?"

She laughed. . . . What a jolly, pioneering, affectionate American couple they were!

She said affectionately:

"Yes, or more motors, darling!"

"And you're probably right, at that!" he said.

Every one laughed.

"When people talk about the American wife and the American husband," Fran went on, "they always make the mistake of trying to find out which sex is 'to blame.' One person will tell you with great impressiveness that the American husband is to blame, because he's so absorbed in his business and his men friends that he never pays any real attention to his wife. Then the next will explain that it's the wife's fault--'The trouble is that when the American husband comes home all tired out after the awful rush of our business competition, he naturally wants some attention, some love from his wife, but she expects him to hustle and change his clothes and take her out to the theater or a party, because she's been bored all day with not enough to do.' And they're both wrong. There's no BLAME--it isn't the fault of either. I am convinced that the fault belongs to our American industrial system, with its ideal of forced selling--which isn't a big enough ideal to satisfy any really sensitive woman. No! She prefers the European culture and tradition of which you spoke, Professor Braut."

"That's kind of hard on me, as one of the promoters of the American industrial system," said Sam.

"Oh, you, you old darling, you're not really an industrialist at heart--you're a researcher."

And again she looked at him so appreciatively that every one was edified at the sight of one happy American couple.

There was, at table and over coffee in the drawing-room, ever so much more conversation. Sam listened to it heartily, while within he was in a panic of realization that Fran, his one security in life now that work and children and friends were lost, had this evening definitely given the challenge that she was bored by him, that she desired a European husband, that the interlude with Arnold Israel, who was more European than Europe, had not been an accident but a symptom.

He watched her turning toward Kurt. He could not ignore her jealousy of Kurt's pretty little friend, the Baroness Volinsky.

The Baroness was a slim, slight girl with beautiful ankles and curly shingled hair. She had nothing much to say. Throughout dinner, Kurt had turned to her with a hundred intimate approaches-- "Do you remember Colonel Gurtz?" and "Vot a first night that was at 'The Patriot.'" Fran had concentrated on the Baroness Volinsky that chilling inquiring courtesy which is the perfection of hatred; had asked abrupt questions about Hungary--questions which somehow suggested that Hungary was an inferior land where the women wore wooden shoes-- and had not listened to the answers.

When they chattered their way into the drawing-room and Kurt sat on the arm of the Baroness's chair, Sam noted that within five minutes Fran was sitting on the other arm of the chair, and that she insisted on speaking French, which Kurt spoke admirably and the Baroness not at all. And shortly thereafter the Baroness went home, followed by the Biedners and the Brauts, then by the violinist, Von Escher, who said almost obsequiously to his wife, "Could you possibly find your way home in safety alone? I must go practise with my pianist--tonight is his only free time."

Minna von Escher, with a snippishness which surprised Sam, remarked to her husband that she had often found her way home alone!

During the agitated German adieux, Sam murmured to Fran, "We better go too, eh?" but she insisted, "Oh, let's stay a little while-- best part of the evening, don't you think?"

He didn't think. He merely looked passive.

Thus there were four together, Sam and Fran, Kurt and Minna von Escher, in that pleasant quiet after the gabble of conversation. In a corner of the room Kurt was showing Fran an enormous, very old-fashioned album of pictures of his boyhood home--apparently a castle in the Tyrol. Fran was in a leather chair; Kurt sat on the floor beside her, constantly bolting up to kneel and point out this old servant, that old schoolroom. They were locked in intimacy, forgetful of every one else.

Sam talked to Minna von Escher. She had a clown-like face, a Brownie-face, with a snub nose and too wide a mouth, but her eyes opened in such surprised roundness, there was such vitality in her speech, her hands and her ankles were so fine, that she was more attractive than most pretty women. She lay on the couch, full- length, rather petulant, and Sam sat by her, leaning over with his elbows on his legs, like an old man smoking on a fence rail.

"Your wife--she praises European husbands!" said Minna. "If she had one! Oh, they can be charming; they kuss d' Hand, they remember your birthday, they send flowers. But I get so very much tired of having my good Theodor make love to every woman he meets! Just now--of course he had to go practise with a man pianist, at midnight--well, he is by this time at the apartment of Elsa Emsberg, and if Elsa is a pianist or a man, she has changed much this past week--and she was MY friend in the first place! Oh, I am a European, but I wish once I had an American husband who would not sacrifice me to music and lof-affairs!"

She looked at him in a lively, appraising way, and suddenly Sam knew that she considered him an interesting big animal, that he could make love to her if he liked, and as much as he liked, and he was frightened by it.

He had always been monogamic. Now and then he had been attracted by some other woman, but he had been as shocked as though he were a priest. Perhaps the fact that his intimate life with Fran had not been very passionate had made him feel that the whole matter of sex stimulation was something rather shameful, to be avoided as far as possible. Certainly, when he tried to think about it, he escaped from thought with a gruff, "Oh, a fellow's got to be loyal to his wife, and not go getting mixed up in a lot of complications."

But just now he seemed insufficiently afraid of "getting mixed up." He caught himself noting that Minna had an exquisite body. He thought, "I ought to give Fran a dose of her own medicine." He looked away from Minna, and growled, "Oh, I guess most husbands in all countries are 'bout equally selfish; just take different ways of showing it." He looked away, but his look was drawn back to her, and he wanted to take her hand.

"Oh no, you would not be selfish!"

"Sure would!"

"No! I know you better! Big, terrifically strong men like you are always gentle and kind!"

"Hm! I wish you could have met some of the kind, gentle, big fellows from Harvard and Princeton that used to sit on my chest when I played football!"

"Oh, in sports it is different. But with women--You would be so gentle. But brave. Do you go hunting and camping much, and all those thrilling things, in your great American wilderness?"

"Well yes, I used to. I did quite a long canoe trip once, in Canada."

"Oh, TELL me about it!"

No one since he had left Zenith had shown so comforting an interest in him. He was not looking away from her now; he was swallowed by her expanding, flattering eyes as he labored:

"Well, it was nothing especial. Went with a friend of mine. We made about a thousand miles, with sixty-four portages, and the last five days we lived on tea, without sugar or condensed milk, and fish, and our tent got burnt up, and we slept under the canoe when it rained. Yes, that was good going. Hm! Like to do it again."

"Why don't you? Why don't you? I can imagine you wonderful in that wilderness."

"Oh, Fran--Mrs. Dodsworth--she doesn't care much for that kind of hiking."

"Hiking? Hiking?"

"Oh, you know." He made a vast circular gesture. "Going. Traveling."

"Oh yes. And she does not like it? Oh, I would!"

"Would you? I'll have to take you camping!"

"Oh, you must!" She seized his sleeve, excitedly shook it. "Don't make a joke! Do it!"

And he was certain that he could--and more certain that between Fran and Kurt, so innocently looking at pictures in their corner, was being woven a spider-web of affection. He felt helpless, he felt irritated, and that irritation submerged his rising fascination in Minna von Escher. No! He wasn't going to encourage Fran by giving her an example!

For a moment, while Minna was sputtering an account of her own courage and ingenuity on a North Sea voyage, Sam checked his suspicions. But he saw Fran blush at some remark of Kurt too low to overhear, saw her glance joined to his, and suddenly Sam was angry.

He grumbled at Minna, "Yes, must have been a mighty nice trip-- never done much yachting, myself--say, my Lord, it's getting late!"

He poured across the room: "Fran! Know what time it is? It's almost one!"

"Yes? What of it?"

"Well. . . . Pretty late. We were going out to see Brandenburg tomorrow."

"We don't HAVE to go tomorrow! Good Heavens! We're not on a Cook's tour!"

"Well . . . Kurt has to be on the job."

"Oh no-o!" begged Kurt. "It does not matter. I shall be so unhappy if you run away early!"

"Of course if you INSIST--" said Fran.

She sounded vicious. Kurt looked at them miserably, as though he was wondering what he could do to reconcile them.

"No, no! Just didn't want you to tire yourself out. And here's Mrs. Escher pretty near asleep," Sam crowed jovially. And everybody laughed, and everybody looked relieved, and everybody said that Yes, wasn't it much more fun to be together, just the Family, after the others had gone.

But Sam had poisoned their moment. They looked self-conscious, and talked about music. Minna von Escher, not at all pleased by Sam's coyness, made yawning signs of going home, and the party broke up in fifteen minutes, with effusive announcements of what a good time they had had.

And so, in the taxicab, when they had dropped Minna at a residence which was confoundedly out of their way, Sam and Fran again started the battle.

CHAPTER 24

After Fran had cried, "Good night--such a happy evening--auf Wiedersehen!" to Minna von Escher, she was silent for a minute, and it was a minute of sixty-thousand seconds, each weighted with fury, like the minute of suspense before a thunder-shower, in a meadow land where the grass turns poison-green with fear. Sam waited, trying to think of something to think.

She spoke in the manner of a school-teacher who has endured too much but who is still trying to keep her temper:

"Sam, Heaven knows I don't ask much of you in the way of social graces. But I do think I have a right to ask you not to be so selfish that you spoil not only all my pleasure but that of everybody else! I really don't see why you should always and unfailingly demand that everybody do what YOU want!"

"I didn't--"

"We were all perfectly happy, sitting there and talking so cheerfully. And I didn't notice that you were being so neglected-- certainly that dog-faced Von Escher woman was flattering you and your pioneer hardihood sickeningly enough, and you simply lapping it up! And it wasn't even very late--I don't suppose you'll ever learn that Berlin and Paris are not exactly like Zenith, and that sometimes people do manage to keep awake here after ten o'clock! Count Obersdorf was telling me all about his family, and it was frightfully interesting, and suddenly you feel sleepy and--bang! The great Samuel Dodsworth is sleepy! The great industrial leader wants to go home! Everything must break up immediately! Nobody else must be considered! The great I Am has spoken!"

"Fran! I'm not going to lose my temper and let you enjoy a row tonight. . . . At least I hope not!"

"Go on! Lose it! It wouldn't be such a novel and shocking sensation! I'm quite used to it!"

"You are like hell! You've never seen me lose it properly! The last fellow that did--Well, I paid the hospital bills!"

"Oh, the wonderful great hero that can knock people's heads off! That has all the charming virtues of a drunken lumberjack! That--"

"This is a little beside the point, Fran. I wasn't boasting--I was regretting. Listen, darling; now that you've blown off steam, can't you be reasonable a little while?"

Thus they reached the Adlon, bowed to the doorman as though they were in the best of humor, crossed the marble lobby, a fine, substantial, dignified couple, went serenely up in the elevator, and fell to it again:

"Fran, we've got to come down to cases. We've been drifting, without any plans, and I wanted to talk plans. . . . Maybe you were right about tonight. I didn't mean to sound grouchy when I suggested going home, and if I did, I'm sorry."

"It doesn't matter. As a matter of fact, it was probably a good thing. I have a slight headache, from too much cigarette smoke in that tiny place--I do wish you wouldn't always take your own cigars along and smoke them--it looks so pretentious. But let's not talk plans tonight. Heavens, if you were in such a mad passion to get away and get to bed, it's a little too much for you to want to stay up half the night talking about plans, when--"

"But I'm in a mood for it!"

"But I'm not! My dear man, is there any hurry?"

"But we'll put it off, the way we've BEEN putting it off, if we wait till tomorrow."

"Does it matter?"

"It certainly does! By God, I'm going to be a little stubborn myself, for once!"

"For once! Oh, Sam, as if you were ever anything else!"

"All right. Have it your way. If I'm always stubborn, you won't be surprised--"

"AND--PLEASE--DON'T--SHOUT!"

"I am not shouting! Fran, please quit playing the cat-and-mouse with me. Look here. It's getting to be time for us to go home, and I do like Von Obersdorf, but he's the kind of fellow that's always so surrounded with people that if we stay here we'll find ourselves mixed up with a whole lot of folks, and we won't get away for weeks."

251

"What of it? Isn't that what we want? Isn't it worth while really knowing ONE European city? Not that Kurt has anything to do with it. It's really my cousins, the Biedners."

"But it is Kurt that counts! He's a mighty nice kind chap, but he isn't satisfied unless everybody is having a party all the time, unless he sees you every day, and especially as he's sort of attracted to you--"

"Sam, are you hinting that he and I--Oh, this is too much! Just because I did like one man besides your high and mighty and sacred self, I can see that you're going to have the pleasure forever more of throwing it up to me, and of hinting the most outrageous things if I so much as have a polite talk with a man!"

"FRAN, FOR GOD'S SAKE STOP ACTING!"

"And for God's sake stop cursing! Oh, I don't know what's gotten into you! A few years ago, even a few months ago, you would never have dreamed of talking to me the way you do. And every day you're getting worse. You have no idea of the kind of language you use--"

"Stop acting! I know perfectly well that so far this Obersdorf fellow and you have been as innocent as babes. But I also know that you could get too fascinated by him--"

"Nonsense! All we have is the polite interest that any European gentleman and lady have in each other. It's just exactly what I was saying tonight! The American male is totally unable to think of any woman as an agreeable teatime companion--if I hadn't been too polite and wanted to protect you, I could have told them a lot more about American wives and husbands! You never think of any woman except as a potential mistress, or as too unattractive to interest you. Whereas Kurt--'Innocent as babes!' Why, of course we have been, and we'll go on being so!"

"You sure will! And if only for the reason that I'm not going to have another Arnold Israel affair!"

She did not flare back as he expected. She stood fixed, looking at him reproachfully, tears coming. She was suddenly young and helpless and pitiful, and she spoke slowly:

"Oh, Sam, that wasn't kind of you! I never remember things and throw them up at you, as you do with me. You never understood about Arnold. I didn't defend myself when you were angry about him. But he was Romance--probably my last--and certainly my first! You were always so good; I've admired you and respected you; but you've always been so sound, so cautious, whereas with Arnold there was danger and excitement and madness and--Just for once in a whole lifetime, I let myself risk danger! And I found I had a talent for it, too! And then, for you, I gave it up; I obediently settled down to plodding around from hotel to hotel, wherever you wanted to go. Arnold kept writing me, and I scarcely ever answered him, and now, of course, I've lost him for ever--for your sake! And then you insult me about him! Oh, Sam, that WASN'T generous!"

She cried a little, sitting twisted in a big chair, her cheek against the back of it.

Sam felt that there was something wrong, something self-dramatizing, about her version, but his sulkiness at being beguiled was less than his fondness of her. He stroked her hair; he said, more tenderly and intimately than for a long while:

"I was beastly. Forgive me. And besides, of course I know your friendship for Kurt is something quite different." He heard an inner, testy voice: "It isn't, and you know it, fool!" But he went on urgently, drawing a small gilt chair, ridiculous beneath his bulk, to her side, and holding her hand as he talked:

"Fran, I want to go home and get to work. I'm naturally an active sort of fellow. I can't stand this loafing any more. And I don't want to manufacture cars. Maybe I half agree with you in what you said about industrialized America, tonight. What I want to do--Oh, I suppose there'd be a lot of industrialization to it; certainly have to use modern methods in production and sales and advertising if we're going to meet competition. But there would be a kind of individual achievement, I'd hope, and a lasting--This is something I've been figuring on for nine-ten months now, but I haven't said anything about it because I wanted to be sure. And for once, it would be something you could take part in--"

She sat up with a bounce, tears dried, and demanded, "Oh, SAY it! Don't make a speech! Forgive me, darling, for being rude, but you DO take such a time--"

"Well, I want to have this clear, especially to myself. I never did pretend to be especially quick on the trigger!"

"As a matter of fact, you do think very quickly, once you have your facts, but you have a superstition--I fancy it started back in college, when you had to play up to Silent Hero role. You have some kind of a childish idea--oh, I know you so MUCH better than you do yourself!--you have an idea that it's somehow ridiculous for so big and solid a man as you are to speak quickly, and you've always suffered from it--"

"We're getting away from the point. Let me finish. As I say, this is a project that you could do as much with, and have as much fun with, as I could, and maybe more. Here's the idea:"

And, rather lumberingly, much interrupted, he outlined his notion of a better Sans Souci Gardens.

He had scarcely finished when she volleyed, "Oh, it's too utterly impossible!"

"Why?"

"You haven't the taste for that sort of thing--domestic architecture and decoration and so on. Why, Sam, I bet you can't tell me what the color of the last curtains we had in the drawing-room at home was!"

"They were--well, they were a kind--Now let's see. They were pale red."

"They were a sort of beige, with so little red in it that it didn't matter. Dear, I do see the fun of a new venture like that, but for YOU--
"

"Well, I personally attended to picking out the body colors and upholstery of the Revelation, the last five years, and I think it's generally admitted that they were the swellest--"

"You didn't, really. You depended on that awful lizzie, Willy Dutberry, that you had in the designing shop."

"Well, anyway, I picked out Willy, didn't I? And I had sense enough to follow his steer, didn't I?--even if he did wear side- whiskers and a pink tie! And for my development, I'll pick out-- Hell, Fran, I do know how to pick men! I don't pretend to know everything, even about autos. I don't need to. But I can--"

"And another thing, Sam. I do love you for wanting to produce something individual and lasting. But an American garden suburb-- Phooey! Nasty, jammed-together huddle of World's Fair exhibition buildings, with pretentious street names--"

"Then make one that isn't pretentious or jammed! People have to live somewhere! And I'd depend on you a lot for suggestions about good taste and all that--"

"It's awfully flattering of you, my dear, but I certainly do not intend--or certainly not till I'm a lot older--I don't intend to give all my days and nights to being sweet to a lot of horrible parvenus who want Touraine chateaux with Frigidaire furnishings and all at mail-order prices!"

They argued for an hour. Fran had recovered from her Duse role, and was alternately airy and pityingly maternal. Sam felt that he had somehow not made clear his plan, but she blocked his each new effort at being articulate, and they went to bed at three with nothing clear except that, while she might condescend to go home with him in a vague four or five or six months, she was not going to help him "build stone castles of cement, and brick manor houses of linoleum," and that she was refraining entirely on account of her artistic ethics.

Remumbling the whole talk again as he lay awake, Sam could not get quite straight how it had happened that he had again failed to lure her home.

"And she says I'm a bully. Well, as a bully, I class about 1/2 h.p., 2 m.p.h.," he sighed, as he fell asleep.

He dreamed that Fran had fallen from a cliff and lay dead below him, and that Minna von Escher had come to smirk temptingly at him. He awoke to revile himself, then to rejoice that it wasn't so. In the dawn, he sat up in bed to look at Fran, and she was so childish, even her little nose hidden under the sheets, that he could think of no slogan of deliverance from her power.

Dining with Kurt--at Hiller's, Borchardt's, Peltzer's, at the Bristol and Kaiserhof, at the simpler Siechen's and Pschorrbrau. Dining at the Winter Garten, on the terrace, watching the vaudeville performance. Dining at outdoor places round about the Tiergarten, as the weather grew warmer and the beer more refreshing. A motor flight to the country house of a friend of Kurt, where all one glorious Sunday afternoon they loafed in the garden or bathed in the Havel.

But the point was that they were always with Kurt.

And Kurt, though he liked Sam, admired him, yet had conceived that Sam and Fran, like so many other American couples he had seen squabbling into and out of the Internation Tourist Agency, were on the point of breaking. And to him, the Viennese, accustomed to tempestuous strays from the bitter mountains and gray plains to Eastward and the North, this cool eager American woman was more exotic, more stimulating, than any Russian or Croatian or Zingara. . . . And she had a useful income of her own. . . . And there was, in all honor, no reason why he should not be there when the break-up came, nor why Fran should not have the privilege of buttressing the ancient house of Obersdorf.

At least, so Sam guessed at Kurt's opinion, and he could not protest that the chart was altogether in error.

It was a slow task for Sam to admit that he, with the training of an executive and the body of a coal-heaver, could not bully or coax his slim wife into reasonableness when her romanticizing ran away with her and she disclosed a belief that she was so superior that he ought to accompany her wherever she cared to stroll, or to stand acquiescent while she beamed at Kurt.

It was impossible, but it was so.

Sam tried all the recognized methods of bullying her. Their naked and wretched squabble after Kurt's party was repeated. He insisted that she was "coming home to America and coming right now!" But what was he to do when she reminded him that she had an income, and when she asserted (she really believed it) that she could always earn her own living?

What, still less, could he do when, after a night when he had lain awake ribbing up righteous anger, they awakened to a sparkling, growing day, and they walked along the Canal, lunched well, drove to the Wannsee and back, and watched sunset over the Tiergarten; when she stopped, twitched his sleeve, and said gravely, "Oh, Sam darling, will you let me thank you for all the lovely places you've taken me? I'm so heedless and silly that often I don't speak of it, but all the while, inside of me, dear--"

Her eyes were wet.

"--I'm terribly grateful. Venice! Rome! Paris! And this quiet sunset. Thank you, dear. . . . And thank you for not being a Tartar husband--for understanding that I can be excited and friendly with nice little people like Kurt without being a hussy!"

Just what was he to do? Except perhaps to mutter, "Have I ever remembered to say I adore you?"

Nor could he turn on Kurt von Obersdorf, since Kurt was-- after much doubting Sam believed it--quite as fond of him as of Fran; since Kurt seemed eager to bring them together again, whatever it might cost himself in a chance at Fran's favors and fortune.

With the Dodsworths' isolation in Berlin, Kurt's ability to fall headlong in friendship, and Fran's liking for the glories of a Count, however dimmed, they three became a family, and as one of the family Kurt sought to soothe them. He was curiously impartial; with all his emotionalism he was a fair umpire. When Fran snapped at her husband for his inability to learn any German beyond "Zweimal dunkles," Kurt begged, "Oh, do not speak so crossly--that is not nize," and when Sam growled that he'd be damned if he'd sit till two A.M. watching her dance, Kurt would represent, "But you ought to be happy to see her so happy! Forgive me! But she is so lovely when she is happy! And she is fragile. She is easily broken by things and moods that we do not mind."

Kurt said--he really seemed to mean--that he too was lonely in Berlin, and though he very much did not want to intrude, he would be glad if he might play about with the Dodsworths every day that they remained. . . . And whatever his comparative poverty might be, he always paid his share of the bills.

"Be so much easier too if he weren't so damn' fair and square!" Sam sighed.

He had no proof, no proof whatever, that there was between Kurt and Fran anything more than this family affection.

Once or twice, as when the Berlin agent for the Revelation car looked Sam up and took him to a luncheon of the American Club, Kurt and Fran slipped away by themselves. He spent a conversational evening in the Adlon Bar while they went learnedly to the opera. After these outings, Fran looked rosy and content.

In London, thanks to the attentions of Mr. A. B. Hurd, Sam had retained something of a position as an industrialist. Since then, progressively, he had become merely the Husband of the Charming Mrs. Dodsworth. He saw it, though he could not see precisely how it had happened. In Berlin, he felt that no one considered him as anything save her attendant--even after the unfortunate incident of Herr Dr. Johann Josef Blumenbach.

Herr Blumenbach's card was brought up to Sam as he was about to change for dinner. "Don't know who he is. Still, name does sound kind of familiar. Probably some friend of HERS," Sam decided, and grumbled to the page, "Let him come up."

When he informed Fran, who was sewing a snap on an evening frock in her bedroom, she protested that she knew no

Blumenbachs. She followed him to their sitting-room, and sniffed. A square, bullet- headed, bristle-headed, swollen-nosed man was Herr Dr. Johann Josef Blumenbach, with ancient and absurd spats.

"Excuse me that I call on you, Herr Dodtswort'," he sputtered, "and please to excuse my English, it is I guess owful bad English that I speak. But I have some liddle interest in a motor factory and from the motor magazines, besides my cousin lives in America, in St. Louis, I know moch about your development of the streamline in owtomo-beelz. I vould be very pleast if Frau Dodtswort' and you would care to look over our factory."

Very suavely Fran eliminated Herr Blumenbach with, "That's very kind of you, Herr Uh, but we're leaving in just a couple of days, and I'm afraid we're going to be FRIGHTFULLY busy. You will excuse us, I'm sure."

He looked at her with a most active dislike; he snorted, "Oh, t'ank you very moch," and disappeared with quite ludicrous haste.

"His nerve! Probably hoped to get money out of you for some horrible gamble," she said placidly as Sam trailed her back to the significant business of sewing on the snap. "HORRID man! And YOU'D have taken an hour to get rid of him!"

When Kurt inevitably came in to pick them up for dinner, Sam inquired, "Ever hear of a man named Blumenback, Johann Blumenback or some such a name--something to do with motors?"

"But of course!" said Kurt.

"Horrid man," offered Fran.

"Oh no-o-o! He iss a very fine man. Very public spirited. And he is one of the two or three big men in the motor industry in Germany. He controls the Mars company--I suppose the Mars is the finest motor in Europe--"

"Of course! That's where I'd heard the name," muttered Sam.

"--and I wish you could meet him. He would give you everything inside on motor industry here. But I have not the honor to know him. I have just seen him in a Gesellschaft."

"We must hurry!" said Fran.

And Sam said nothing at all.

He thought, many times, that if he telephoned to Herr Dr. Blumenbach, he might be accepted and entertained in Berlin as the

Samuel Dodsworth he once had been--might thus again become that Samuel Dodsworth.

And he did nothing at all.

They had expeditions with the Baroness Volinsky and Minna von Escher, until Kurt, wounded to his little heart, as he could so often and so piteously be wounded, was convinced that no amount of advertising the merits of the pretty little baroness would make Fran like her. As to why Sam and Minna did not get along, he never understood, so he looked hurt and gave it up.

To Sam, Frau von Escher was a reminder that there were women who did not find him clumsy and cold, and he wanted to escape from that reminder. He could well enough picture falling into the entertaining distress of passion. He could even question whether it wasn't merely emotional indolence and fear of getting "mixed up," not morality, which had kept him "pure." Wasn't it because he did want to kiss Minna's wide derisive mouth that he was chilly to her, and contradicted everything she said . . . and gave Fran a chance to point out that he WAS rude and that it had been only her influence which had kept him amiable all these years?

"Hell!" said Sam Dodsworth wearily, and for all his searching he never found a more competent way of expressing it.

So he groped through the fog, and there was no path to be found. In the distance was the sound of menacing waters, and always he stumbled over unseen roots in a trance less real than any dream.

CHAPTER 25

It seemed a singularly undistinguished morning. Sam looked forward only to a vague dinner with Kurt and a friend from Vienna, and as Kurt had said nothing more ecstatic about his friend than that he was "soch a good fellow and he speaks seven languages and is so fonny," Sam knew that the fellow couldn't be up to much. For the afternoon they planned to see the exhibit of Kolbe's sculptures at Cassirer's and the French impressionists at the Gallerie Tannhauser, and Sam hoped (not very optimistically) to lure Fran out to Charlottenburg to inspect factories and tenements for laborers. . . . She liked to discuss what she called the Lower Classes with every one save members of the Lower Classes.

He lolled in the sitting-room of their suite, rather slovenly in dressing-gown and ancient slippers, which Fran was always going to replace by new elegance and never did. When he had finished reading the Paris American papers and had exclaimed over the fact that Mr. T. Q. Obelisk of Zenith had just landed in Europe and was going to squander an entire three weeks in Paris, he had nothing more to do. He thought of answering Henry Hazzard's last letter. But--oh, thunder, there was no news--He thought of having a drink, and answered that it was much too early in the day. He thought of going for a walk but--oh, he'd walked all over the inner city.

He mouched. He prowled through the sitting-room, turning over tourist agency folders about Java--the North Cape--Rio de Janeiro.

He peeped into the bedroom. Fran, in nightgown and fluffy pink knitted bed jacket, was still abed, but over her chocolate she was furiously trying to read the Vossische Zeitung and the Tageblatt with the aid of a dictionary, imagination, and discreet skipping. He looked admiringly at her display of scholarship, he said that it was going to be a swell day, and returned to the sitting-room to stare out at the Pariser Platz and wish he were home.

At a knock, he said "Come IN!" indifferently. It would be the room-waiter, to clear away.

It was a boy with a cable.

For a time Sam put off opening it. It pleased him to think that even in his insignificance here in Berlin, he was the sort of man who received cables. Then he read:

"congratulate us birth nine pound son stop emily splendid shape cheers stop your first grandchild harry mckee."

Sam stood glorying. He was not finished, after all--something of him had been carried on with this new life! And Emily would be so happy! How he loved her! And NOW, by golly, Fran would want to go home! They'd catch the next steamer and see the baby, Emily, Harry, Brent, Tub, Henry Hazzard--In maybe two weeks--

He paraded into the bedroom, trying to play-act, trying to sound unemotional as he remarked, "Um, uh, Fran--lil cable from Zenith."

"Yes?" sharply. "Anything wrong?"

"Well--Fran!" He went to kiss her; he ignored her slight impatience. "We're granddaddy and grandmammy! And the devils never let us know youngster was coming--prob'ly spare us worry. Emily has a son! Nine pounds!"

"And how--"

"She's fine, apparently. So Harry wires." In her quick, happy look he felt more secure and married and real than for weeks. "My God, I wish they had the transatlantic 'phone working from here, way they have from London now. We'd 'phone 'em, if it cost a hundred a minute. Wouldn't that be great, to hear Emily's voice! Tell you what I am going to do! I'll 'phone Kurt Obersdorf and tell him about our grandson. I've got to holler--"

Her face tightened. "Wait!"

"What's the idea?"

"I'm delighted. Of course. Dear Emily! She'll be so happy. But, Sam, don't you realize that Kurt--oh, I don't mean Kurt individually, of course; I mean all our friends in Europe--They think of me as young. Young! And I am, oh, I AM! And if they know I'm a grandmother--God! A grandmother! Oh, Sam, can't you SEE? It's horrible! It's the end, for me! Oh, please, please, please try to understand! Think! I was so young when I married. It isn't FAIR for me to be a

261

grandmother now, at under forty." With swiftness he calculated that Fran was now forty-three. "A grandmother! Lace caps and knitting and rheumatism! Oh, please try to understand! It isn't that I'm not utterly happy for Emily's sake, but--I have my own life, too! You mustn't tell Kurt! Ever!"

He knew then, well enough.

He was too hard hit to dare be angry. "Yes, I see how you mean. Yes, I--Well, I'll go cable to Emily and Harry."

It was that evening, before they went out to dinner with Kurt, that he noticed her new habit of perfuming the back of her right hand, and reflected, "I wonder if it has anything to do with his kissing her hand? Wonder? You don't wonder; you know!"

He saw further that she faintly perfumed the inside of her arm to the elbow, and he was a little sickened as he stalked out to the sitting-room and tried to divert himself by reading the list of Circular Tours in Great Britain and France in the "European Travel Guide" of the American Express Company, while waiting for her to finish dressing. It didn't altogether absorb him. He looked about the room. There were roses--sent by Kurt. There was Feuchtwanger's "Jud Suss"--sent by Kurt.

Then there was Kurt himself, knocking, coming in gaily, crying, "Is that wife of ours late again? Sam, I have brought you a box of real Havana cigars smuggled through without duty! Oh, my roses came! I am glad. Sam, haf you any idea how thankful a lonely poor man--and to a Wiener like me, Berlin is just as foreign as it is to you!-- so thankful to have Fran and you tolerate me while you are here! You are so good! . . . Fran! Are you not dressed? You are keeping your poor children waiting! If I were Sam, I would beat you! And my friend probably waiting in the lobby."

"Coming, Kurt!" she sang, lark-like.

And Kurt was kissing the back of her hand. And Sam Dodsworth said nothing at all.

But it was down in the bar, where they went to have cocktails and to wait for Kurt's friend, that the new and almost honestly analytic Sam Dodsworth caught himself in a situation more shameful and enfeebling than anything that had happened in their apartment. An American motor salesman, whom Sam had met at the American Club luncheon, stopped at their table to nod his greetings, and Sam caught himself saying, a little proudly, "Mr. Ashley, I don't think you've met my wife. And this is the Count Obersdorf."

"Mighty pleased to meet you, Count," said the motor man, after kissing Fran's hand in what he considered a European manner.

Sam sharply cross-examined himself. "Look here, Samba. Were you flattered to be able to introduce a Count? This tourist agency clerk! How long will it be before you become the kind of rotten soak that sits around boasting that his wife has a count for a lover? No! I'm not that bad, not yet. But I guess my mind is kind of sick, now. What the devil was it that hit me? I don't understand. Emily, my darling, with a son! Doesn't Fran want--"

Coolly, quite prosaically, he interrupted Kurt to demand of Fran, "Say, uh, remember I told you about that young lady--that cousin of mine--that's just had a baby? Wouldn't you like to skip back to America and see her?"

"Oh, I'd love to. But I don't suppose we'll see her till next autumn," said Fran placidly.

"Here comes my friend. SUCH a lovely fellow," said Kurt.

The second message from Zenith, from home, came in a letter which was handed to Sam at the desk, three evenings later, as they were going out to dinner with Kurt.

"From old Tub!" he chuckled, and tucked it into his pocket. When they were at table he suggested, "Mind if I glance at my letter?"

Tub wrote, in schoolboyish script:

How are you and how's all the lovely femmes in Europe? Well, you're not going to get away with hogging them much longer. Matey and I have finally decided about time we ran over and had a look at the old country and get a decent drink. She's a grand wife and likes her likker. We sail on May tenth, on the Olympic, arrive London probably 16th, and Paris the 21st--stay Savoy London and Continental Paris. In Paris about a week, then Holland, Belgium, Switzerland, Italy, south France, and sail from Cherbourg again on June 20th. Some fast trip, eh, but I bet we don't miss much, your last post card, and a hell of a tightwad you are about writing say you're going to Germany but don't see what you find there, can only get beer there and it's the bubbles that cure all your trouble that I want to taste again, you remember old song, champagne.

Now if you're too busy to remember old friends all right, but would be awfully glad if you could manage meet us London or Paris, or if along route afterwards send me schedule c/o Equitable Trust, 23 rue de la Paix.

Don't take any wooden money.

Sincerely, your friend,

THOS. J. PEARSON.

The letter had followed Sam from Paris to Rome to Berlin; Tub was already in London and would be in Paris in three days.

It was one of the few holograph letters Sam had received from Tub. Usually his laconic messages were dictated, typed on banking-house paper as stiff and luxuriously engraved as a bond. In it Sam felt an unfamiliar urgency; Tub was prepared to be angry, to consider himself deliberately slighted, if the Dodsworths did not appear in Paris to greet him and his jolly wife Matilde, otherwise Matey.

He interrupted Kurt--("Damn it! Seems at though, these days, I always have to interrupt that fellow in order to be able to speak to my own wife!") He crowed, "Say, who d'you think's in London and going to Paris? Tub and Matey!"

"Oh, really?" she said politely. She showed considerably more warmth in explaining to Kurt, "Tub is an old friend of Sam--quite a prosperous banker. If they come to Berlin, they'd be awfully happy to meet you. Oh! You said one day you wished you could get into a bank in America. Tub--Mr. Pearson his name is--might be able--"

"But we'll see him in Paris," Sam interrupted again. "Not coming to Berlin. And we ought to skip right down and be there to welcome 'em. Remember they've never been abroad before. I'll wire him in London tonight--might even see if I can get him on the 'phone--and we can probably get reservations for the Paris train for tomorrow evening."

Surely when Fran heard good old Matey gossip of their friends, when she scented Zenith again--The miracle had happened!

"But, Sam dear," Fran protested, "I don't see any reason under Heaven why we SHOULD go down! And you complaining of how tired you were of Paris when we left it! I know how fond you are of your friends, but I don't see why you should let them use you!"

"But don't you want to see Tub and Matey?"

"Don't be silly! Of course, I'd be very glad to see them. But to trot all the way to Paris--"

"But don't you WANT--I can't imagine your not wanting--"

"Well, if you must know, I think your good friend Mr. Tub Pearson is a little heavy in the hand. He always works so hard at being humorous. And you yourself have admitted that Matey is dreadfully uninteresting. And fat! Good Heavens, I've had them for twenty years! No, you can do what you'd like, but I'm not going."

"But I wouldn't be much good to 'em as a guide. I can't speak French."

"Exactly! Then why go? They can get along as every one else does."

"But you could make it so much pleasanter for them--"

"It's all very well to be friendly and that sort of thing, but I'm not going to travel fifteen hours in a dirty train for the pleasure of acting as an unpaid Cook's guide to Mr. and Mrs. Tub Pearson!"

"Well, all right. Then I'll go by myself."

"As you wish!"

She turned briskly to Kurt, and with excessive sweetness discoursed on the state of the theater in Central Europe. Kurt looked at Sam, troubled, wishing to say something soothing. Sam was very quiet all that evening.

It was she who opened the engagement when they were alone, at the hotel.

"I'm sorry about Tub, and I'll go down there--a beastly journey!-- if you absolutely insist--"

"I never insist on anything."

"--but I do think it's too ridiculous to be expected to be a guide-- and of course your beloved Tub will want to go to the most obvious and stupid and Americanized places in Paris--"

"No, I've decided you'd better not come. You're probably right. Tub will want to get drunk on Montmartre."

"For which charming occupation, my dear Samuel, you'll be a much better collaborator than I, I'm afraid!"

"Look here, Fran: I wonder if you have any idea how dangerous it might be for you, one of these days, if you go on being so airy and insulting with me? I'd stood--"

"'S the truth!"

"--a good deal. I can understand your not thinking Tub is any Endicott Everett Atkins, but how you can fail to enjoy giving a good time to a neighbor that we've known as long and as closely as we have Tub--Why you don't, just for once, forget what YOU'RE going to get out of it and think what you could GIVE--"

"Oh, put in the Beatitudes, too!"

"--is simply beyond me! I used to think you were loyal!"

"I am! The way I've refused to stand any one ever criticizing you--"

"Will you listen! Don't be so damned PERFECT, just for once! I used to think you were loyal, but between this business about Tub, and your lack of interest in Emily's boy--"

"Now I've had enough! You've quite sufficiently indicated that I'm an inhuman monster! Why, after I heard the news about Emily, I cried half the night, wanting to see her and the baby. But--Oh, if I could only make you understand!" She had thrown off her flippancy and was naked and defenseless in her seriousness. "I do rejoice that she has a child. I do love her. But--oh, I've tried to use my brains, such as they are, which I admit isn't very much, except that I do have common sense. I've tried not to be sentimental, and ruin myself, yes, and you, without doing Emily or anybody else any good! What good would it do if I were there? Could I help her? I could not! I'd just be in the way. Heavens, any trained nurse would be of more value than a dozen me's, and she's surrounded with only too much love and solicitude. I'd be just another burden, at a time when she has plenty. On the other hand, as it would affect me--

"When the world hears the word 'grandmother,' it pictures an old woman, a withered old woman, who's absolutely hors de combat. I'm not that and I'm not going to be, for another twenty years. And YET, most people are so conventional-minded that even if they know me, see me, dance with me, once they hear I'm a grandmother that label influences them more than their own senses, and they put me on the side-lines immediately. I won't be! And yet I love Emily and--

"Let me tell you, young man, when there WAS something I could do for her, and for Brent, I did it! I'm not for one second going to stand any hints from you that I'm not a good mother--and loyal! For twenty years, or anyway till Brent went off to college, there wasn't one thing those children wore that I didn't buy. There wasn't a thing they ate that I didn't order. You--oh yes, you came grandly home from the office and permitted Em to ride on your shoulders and thought what a wonderful parent you were, but who'd taken her to the dentist that day? I had! Who'd planned her party and written the invitations? I had! Who'd gotten down on her knees and scrubbed Em's floor when the maids had the 'flu and the nurse was away junketing? I did! I've done my work, I've earned the right to play, and I'm not going to be robbed of it just because you're so slow and unimaginative that you've lost the power of enjoyment and can't conceive any occupation beyond selling motors and playing golf!"

"Yes. I guess--I guess maybe there's a good deal to what you say," he sighed. "Well, it works out all right. I'll trot off and welcome Tub and then come back."

"Yes, and you'll probably enjoy it more if I'm not there. Men ought to get off by themselves now and then, away from the dratted women. Take my advice and get rid of Matey as much as you can--get her interested in buying a lot of clothes and you and Tub knock around together. You'll probably have a wonderful time. You do see now that I wasn't merely being beastly and unselfish, don't you?"

And she kissed him, fleetingly, and was cheerfully off to bed.

Even of such kisses there had not been over many, since the affair of Arnold Israel. The change in their intimacy was never admitted, but it was definite. It was not that Fran was less attractive to him; indeed more than ever he valued her sleek smoothness; but she had become to him a nun, taboo, and any passion toward her was forbidden. She seemed relieved by it; and they had drifted into a melancholy brother and sister relationship which left him irritable and hopeless.

They said nothing, neither then nor next day, of the tact that when Sam went to Paris, Fran and Kurt von Obersdorf would be left together. And these two, Fran and Kurt, very cheery and affectionate, saw him off on the evening train for Paris, and Kurt brought him as bon voyage presents a package of American cigarettes, a cactus plant, and a copy of the Nation, under the misconception that it was one of the most conservative of American magazines and especially suitable to the prejudices of a millionaire manufacturer.

Sam had to share his sleeping compartment with a small meek German who insisted, with apologetic gestures, on taking the undesirable upper berth, to which Sam was billeted. So when the German wanted to keep on the night-light, Sam could not object, and he lay in his berth staring up into a narrow vault made gloomier by that sepulchral blue glimmer which took away the oblivion of darkness and revealed the messy crowdedness of the compartment: the horribly lifelike trousers swaying against the wall, the valises wedged under the little folding table by the window, the litter of newspapers and cigarette butts. The train was loud with fury; it carried him on powerless; life carried him on powerless. Without Fran, he felt small, callow, defenseless. Why was he venturing to Paris, alone? He knew no French, really; he knew little of anything in Europe. He was marooned.

She had let him go off so casually. Was he going to lose her, to whom he had turned with every triumph and every worry these twenty- four years; whose hand had always been there, to let him warm and protect it, that he might himself be warmed and protected?

Or already lost her?

He brooded, a lumpy blanketed mound in the mean blue ghost-light.

What could he DO?

The train seemed to be running with such abnormal speed. Surely even the Twentieth Century had never raced like this. Anything wrong?

It would be nice if it were Fran in the upper berth; if her hand were drooping over the edge, so that he could see it, perhaps touch it by pretended accident--

Not that she'd be in the upper, though, if they were together!

When he awoke at three, his first loneliness for her had passed, and he worked up a good deal of angry protest.

This "adventurous new life" they'd been going to find--Rats! Might be for her, but he himself had never been so bored. All came of trying to suit himself to her whims. And then lose her, after all--

What would Kurt and she be doing while he was away?

And this business of her having been such a devoted mother! Ever been a time when the children hadn't had a nurse or a governess, with plenty of maids? If she ever did "get down on her knees and scrub a floor" it'd never happened more than once.

Oh, she'd meant it; she really did believe she'd been a sacrificing mother. Chief trouble with her. Never could see herself as she was. Never!

Yes, he'd have to rebel against her--or against his worship of her. Not been a go, his trying to be happy in her way. Make a life for HIMSELF. Be pretty darn' lonely for a while. Sure. But not impossible to make a new life--

There were women, to say nothing of men friends--

Suddenly he was taut with desire for Minna von Escher. He felt her lips; he saw her too clearly.

Well, there were gorgeous girls in Paris--Hang it, he was no washed-out Sir Galahad, like he'd read about in Tennyson! He'd been patient and sacrificing. Lot of good it'd done him! Why should Fran have all the love? He'd go out--

Then Fran's face, hovering in the wan blue dusk, a hurt, re-proving face, very pale, very pure. He could not wound her, even by thought. And so he tossed, helpless in the rushing train, turning from the desire to serve Fran to the desire for Minna's warm arms, and back ever to Fran . . . and back ever to Minna.

He breakfasted well in the restaurant carriage, and if he missed Fran, it was a relief to have a man's proper ration of bacon and eggs without having her chronic complaint that real Europeans don't take horrid heavy breakfasts. When he had lighted a cigar, Sam felt a faint exciting flavor in traveling alone, in going where he would.

He heard an American woman, at breakfast, say to her com-panion, "But the play I really liked was 'They Knew What They Wanted.'"

He heard no more. He pondered, "That's been the trouble with me, my entire life. It isn't simply that I've never got what I wanted. I've never known what I wanted. There are women who are better sports than Fran. Not so selfish. More peace. If I find them--

"Be funny if now I really were starting that 'adventure in new life' that we've talked so much rot about! Yes, I have known what I wanted--Fran! But probably as a kid wants the moon. (That's what she's like too--the moon on a still November night!) And if I can't have her--well, I hope I have the sense to find something else, and to take it. . . . But I won't!"

269

CHAPTER 26

He was going to surprise Tub and Matey at the station. He had gone to the Continental Hotel, at which Tub had reservations. From Berlin, he had merely wired Tub in London, "Be in Paris day or two after you arrive delighted see you"; from Paris he had telephoned to Mr. A. B. Hurd, of Revelation Motors in London, asking him to snoop about and find out from the Savoy porter what train Tub was taking.

Sam waited in the Gare du Nord, excited but pleasantly superior. HE was no American tourist, embarrassed by the voluble Parisians! He knew 'em! He could say to a porter, "Apportez le bagage de Monsieur a un taxicab" just as well as old Berlitz--almost as well as Fran. He swung his stick, strolled along the platform, and nodded to the gathering porters, feeling much as he had on the evening after the last game of the football season. When the lean swift French locomotive flashed in, hurling its smoke up to join the ghosts of smoke-palls that lurked under the vast roof of the train shed, he chuckled aloud.

"Old Tub! And Matey! First time in Paris!"

He looked over the heads of the crowd and saw Tub handing his bags out of the car window to a porter, saw him and the plump Matey hustle out of the car, saw him, with the blank worried nervousness of a man who doesn't expect to be met and who feels that the labors of travel are too much for him, wave his arms in the effort of explaining in Zenith French--dealcoholized French, French Hag-- where he wanted to go.

Swift, looming, Sam thrust through the crowd toward the Pearsons. He saw that Tub himself was carrying a small suitcase-- probably with Matey's famous and atrocious jewelry. He swooped on Tub, grasped his shoulder, and snarled (with one of the exceedingly few impersonations in his unhistrionic life), "Here, you, fella! Not allowed carry y' own baggage!"

Tub looked up with all the rage of an honest American who has been enfeebled by rough seas, doubted by customs officials, over-charged by waiters, overinformed by guides, misunderstood by French conductors; who has suddenly by thunder had enough and who is going to expose and explode the entire continent of Europe. He looked up, he looked bewildered, and then he said slowly, "Well, you damned old horse-thief! Well, you big stiff!"

They banged each other's shoulders, Sam kissed the suddenly beaming Matey, and they went down the platform together, Sam with one arm about Tub's shoulder and one about Matey's. He said sharply to the porter, "Un taxi, s'il vous plait"--just as the porter was waving to a taxi on his own--and Tub clamored, "Well, I'm a son of a gun! Say, you've certainly learned to parley-vous like a native, Sambo!"

They asked after Fran.

It hurt him that they seemed content to miss her, willing to believe that she "had a touch of 'flu and had to lie low a couple weeks, so she couldn't come down to welcome you." But he resented it only for a moment. There were so many exciting places to show Tub! It was delightful to have the Tub who had always been cleverer and more fashionable than he now regarding him as a sophisticated European and turning to him, admiring his dash and flavor.

And it was pleasant to be Tubbish and foolish and noisy without Fran's supercilious inspection.

Matey Pearson was a good soul. She was fat and pleasant. As a girl she had been the gayest and maddest of her set in Zenith; the fastest skater, the most ecstatic dancer, the most reckless flirt. Now she had three children--one was Brent's classmate in Yale--and she cultivated the Episcopal Church, a rare shrewd game of poker, and the choicest dahlias in Zenith. Fran said that she was vulgar. She said that Fran was lovely.

At the hotel she kissed Sam again, and cried, "Say, my heavens but it's nice to see a human being that's HUMAN again! Now you boys get to thunder out of here and let me unpack, and you go off and get decently drunk, but do try to be sober enough for dinner, which gives you two hours, if we dine at eight, and enough time too, sez I. Get out of here! I love you both. With reservations!"

To be alone with Tub Pearson, on Tub's first afternoon on the continent of Europe!

They had leapt over the barriers that had been erected between them since college--different vocations, rivalry as to the splendor of their several children, rivalry as to social honors, and this last flagrancy of Sam in living abroad while Tub stayed true at home. They were today the friends who had shared dress-shirts and speculations in Senior year.

From time to time they looked at each other and muttered, "Awful' good to be here with you, you old devil!"

Sam did not see that Tub was completely gray, that he was podgy, that round his eyes were the lines of a banker who day after day sharply refuses loans to desperate men. He saw the lively Tub whom he had protected in fights with muckers and whom he had admired for his wit; and while he held to his temporary superiority as the traveled man and tutored gourmet, he anxiously showed Tub all his little treasures.

He took Tub to the New York Bar, and impressed Tub as an habitue by casually asking whether anybody had heard from Ross Ireland. He took Tub to Luigi's, introduced him to Luigi, and recommended the scrambled eggs. He took Tub to the Chatham Bar; he was so fortunate as to find Colonel Kelly, the famous soldier of fortune; and he felt expansive and philanthropic; he felt, after this third highball, as though his European agonies really had been worth while, when he observed Tub's respectful attention to Colonel Kelly.

He felt that Tub was the finest and most lovable man living; that he was beyond belief lucky to have such a friend; and they returned to the Continental in a high state of philanthropy and Yalensianism.

Matey looked them over and sighed, "Well, you aren't much drunker than I thought you'd be, and now you better go in and wash your little faces in the bathroom and have a coupla Bromo Seltzers-- believe me, Sam, traveling with THAT man, I never fail to have some real genuine American Bromo along--and then if you can both still walk, we'll go out and have the handsomest dinner in Paree."

He took them to Voisin's, but when they were seated Tub looked disappointed.

"Not such a lively place," he said.

"No, I know it isn't, but it's a famous old restaurant, and perhaps the best food and wine in town. What kind of a place would you like? Find it for you tomorrow."

272

"Well, I don't know. I don't know exactly what I did think a Paris restaurant would be like but--Oh, I thought there'd be a lot of gilt, and marble pillars, and a good orchestra, and lots of dancing, and a million pretty girls, regular knock-outs, and not so slow either. I better watch meself, or I'll be getting Matey jealous."

"Hm," said Matey. "Tub has a good, conscientious, hardworking ambition to be a devil with the ladies--our fat little Don Juan!-- but the trouble is they don't fall for him."

"That's all right now! I'm not so bad! Say, can you dig us up a place like that, tomorrow?"

"I'll show you a good noisy dance place tonight," said Sam. "You'll see all the pretty chickens you want--and they'll come and tell you, in nine languages, that you're a regular Adonis."

"They don't need to tell me that in more than one language-- the extrabatorious language of clinging lips, yo ho!" yearned the class-wit.

"You're wrong, Sam," said Matey. "He DOESN'T make me sick--not very sick--not worse'n a Channel crossing. And you're wrong about thinking that I secretly wish he would go out with one of these wenches and get it out of his system. Not at all. I can get much more shopping money out of the brute while he's in this moon-June- spoon-loon mood. And when his foot does slip, how he'll come running back to his old Matey!"

"I don't know whether I will or not! Say, do we eat?"

The head waiter had been standing at attention the while. Sam was aching to show off his knowledge of restaurant French, and he held out his hand for the menu, but Tub seized it and prepared to put into the life of Voisin's all the liveliness and wit and heartiness he felt lacking.

"Do you sprechen Sie pretty good English?" he demanded of the head waiter.

"I think so, sir."

"Attaboy! Been in England, son?"

"Sixteen years, sir."

"Um, not so bad--not so bad for a Frog! Well now, look here, Gooseppy, we want Mrs. Voisin to shake us up something tasty, and you take the orders from me, Francois, and you bring me the check afterwards, too, see, and don't have anything to do with that big stiff

Lewis

there. He's a Scotch Jew. If you let him order, he'd stick us with stew, and then he'd make you take ten per cent. off the check. Now listen. Have you got any nice roast elephant ears?"

Tub winked at Sam, tremendously.

The head waiter said patiently, but not too patiently, "May I recommend the canard aux navets?"

But Tub was a conscientious Midwestern Humorist--he was a Great Little Kidder--he had read "Innocents Abroad" and had seen "The Man from Home," and he knew that one of the superbest occupations of an American on the grand tour was "kidding the life out of these poor old back numbers of Europeans." He tried again:

"Not got any elephants' ears, Alberto? Well, well! I thought this was a first-class hash-house--right up to the Childs class. And no elephants' ears?" The head waiter said nothing, with much eloquence. "How about a nice fricassee of birds' nests?"

"If the gentleman wishes, I can send to a Chinese restaurant for it."

"Tub," Matey observed, "the comedy isn't going over so big. You give Sam that menu now, and let him order, HEAR ME?"

"Well it was kind of a flop," Tub said morosely. "But I TOLD you this was a dead hole. I may not be the laddie buck that locks up the Bullyvards every evening, but I know a live joint from a dead one when it comes up and bites me. Well, shoot the works, Sam."

With a quiet superiority for which he would have deserved to be flogged, except that with Fran's monopolization of that pleasure he rarely had a chance at it, Sam swiftly ordered foie gras, consomme, frogs' legs, gigot of mutton, asparagus, and a salad, with a bottle of Chateauneuf-du-Pape, and though he ordered in French, so well trained were the head waiter and the sommelier that they understood him perfectly.

And again the luxurious inquiries about Home--WAS Emily really well?--how was Harry Hazzard's Lincoln sedan standing up?--what was this business about building a new thirty-story hotel?

They had dined at nine. It was eleven when Sam took them to Montmartre, to the celebrated "Caverne Russe des Quarante Vents," where Tub was satisfied in finding the Paris he had pictured. The Caverne was so large, so noisy, with such poisonously loud negro jazz-bands, such cover-charges, such incredible coat-room charges, such

274

abominable champagne at such atrocious prices, such a crowded dancing floor, such a stench of cigarette smoke and perfume and perspiration, such a sound of the voices of lingerie-buyers from Fort Worth and Milwaukee, such moist girls inviting themselves to one's table, such rude Hellenic waiters and ruder Hebraic managers, that it was almost as good as Broadway. A Frenchman had once entered the place, in 1926, but he had had to go as courier to a party from Birmingham, Alabama, and he resigned and utterly gave up the profession of courier the next day.

"Gee, this is some place!" exulted the Hon. Thomas J. Pearson (president of the Centaur State Bank, trustee of the Fernworth School for Girls, vice president of the Zenith Chamber of Commerce, vestryman of St. Asaph's P. E. Church), and straightway he was dancing with a red-headed girl like a little brass and ivory statue.

"Well--" philosophized Matey. "Eh? Heavens no, I don't want to dance in this stock exchange! Well, I might just as well PRETEND I don't mind Tub's chasing after all these little goldfish, because he'll do it anyway, and I might as well get the credit for being broadminded. Which I ain't! You old darling, Sambo, I was sorry Tub felt he had to uphold the banner of American Humor by making a goat of himself with that snooty waiter at that place--wh'd' they call it?--there tonight."

"Oh, good Lord, Matey, he's just like a--"

"You're going to say, 'He's just like a kid let out of school, and he's got to kick up his heels,' which if I remember the rhetoric that that old Miss Getz drummed into my mutton head in finishing school, is both a cliche and a mixed metaphor. Oh, I adore the fat little devil! He's awfully sweet when you can get him tied down at the domestic hearth, with no audience. But once that animal smells applause-- Honestly, I think that the sense of humor of the people that TALK about having a 'sense of humor' is a worse vice than drinking. Oh, well, it might have been worse. He might have turned out religious, or a vegetarian, or taken to dope. The little monkey! And he's drinking too much, tonight. I just hope he won't take enough so he'll wake up with a perfectly fierce head tomorrow, and feel so conscience-stricken that I'll have to give him the devil just to relieve him. Oh, I can do it-- and probably will!--but I want to enjoy myself, too, while I'm here, and I'm going to take home a great, big, expensive boule cabinet, if I have to forge a check for it!"

She consented, later to dance with Sam, though it was more like charging a mob than dancing. She was nimble, for all her plumpness; and as she did not, like Fran, point out his every clumsy step, his every failure to follow the music, he danced rather well with her, and enjoyed it, and recovered some of the high spirits with which he had met them at the train--spirits too high and romantic to last forever.

Tub dug out, somewhere, probably in the bar, a quite respectable fellow-banker from Indiana, and two Irish girls, whose art was commercialized but pretty, and everybody danced--everybody drank a good deal--everybody laughed.

Tub himself had so good a time that he showed the highest sign of pleasure known to an American: he wanted to "go on some place else."

They did--to another Caverne or Taverne or Palais or Cave or Rendezvous, with the same high standard of everything except wine and music and company and then, too brightly lit to waste any more time in dancing or flirtation or anything save sitting and really attending to drinking and humor, Tub insisted that they go back to the New York Bar, where, he assured Matey, they would "meet reg'lar fell's."

They did. In a corner table of the bar, under the sketches of Parisian celebrities, they were picked up by an American navy officer who had magnificent lies about the China coast, and somehow there was added to their party a free-lance journalist and a lone English corn-merchant, who talked a good deal, and very spiritedly, about the admitted fact that Englishmen never talk much and then shyly.

Tub, in one day, was a warmer habitue of the New York Bar than was Sam Dodsworth after a year. It was not merely that Sam was dogged by a sense of dignity, by a feeling that a Prominent Manufacturer ought not to be seen about barrooms, but also that he had a certain judicious timidity which suggested that there was no reason why the keen, hard-minded journalists who frequented the bar and exchanged gossip of kings and treaties should be interested in him. But Tub was a Professional Good Fellow--when he was away from the oak-panel and gold velvet vestry of St. Asaph's, the trustees' room at the Fernworth School, or the marble and walnut office at the Centaur State Bank, where he put on a pair of horn-rimmed spectacles which somehow prevented his eyes from twinkling or looking slyly humorous.

He hadn't forgotten one of the men he had met at the bar that afternoon. He called two of the journalists by their first names, and he was in general so full of prankishness that the lone naval officer broke into tears of relief and told them all about his most recent fight with his wife.

But there was one flaw in the joviality. Tub had drunk Burgundy at dinner, Napoleon brandy afterward, champagne all evening, and now he decided (in spite of the earnest counsel of Sam, Matey, the naval officer, the Englishman, the journalist, the waiter, and a few by-sitters) to show his loyalty to America and the Good Old Days by drinking real American rye whisky--and it was a very copious loyalty that he showed.

In the middle of the commander's story about his wife, Tub began to look listless, with fine lines of sweat-drops on his upper lip-- and it was only two in the morning and he had been drinking steadily for only twelve hours, which is not even par for a representative of Prohibition America on his first day in Paris.

Matey cried to Sam, "He's passing out! Can you take him off and kill him or something?"

In the seclusion of the wash-room, usefully close at hand, Sam washed Tub's face, fed him aspirin, scolded him, and they started home and--

All of Sam's romantic exultation was gone, the glow was gone, the childish belief that he had suddenly achieved freedom was gone, in a leaden light of reality. He was not angry with Tub. But he had felt warmth and assurance, he had felt--he admitted it--a protection against Fran in Tub's comradeship, and that was not enhanced in the unromantic service of holding up a man retching and swaying in a bar-room toilet.

They got Tub into a taxicab, while he protested that he was all right now and desired to return to his friends. Sam had to roar at him a good deal, and lift him in. During this knock-about scene, an open motor passed, and Sam saw that looking disgustedly out of it was Endicott Everett Atkins, with his high nose, his Roman imperial, and his Henry Jamesian baldness. Atkins turned to say something to the lady beside him.

Sam shivered. He fancied Atkins getting the information to Fran. He heard her saying, "Now was I right about your dear friend

277

Tub!" He felt cold and irritated. He was less gentle with Tub than he had meant to be.

Not till Matey and he had Tub in bed did it come fully to Sam that he might do well to forget himself and think of her.

"Hard luck!" he whispered. "But we all slip now and--"

"Oh, you can talk as loud as you want," she said placidly. "Gabriel with an augmented trumpet band wouldn't wake the little monkey now! But I do want to talk to you, and if he did wake up and want to go out again--Oh, well, there's no place to go but the bathroom. Heigh! Scandal in Zenith society! I guess this is that new American Jazzmania you read about!"

They sat absurdly in the bathroom, she on a white straight chair, he precariously on the cold edge of the tub, while she went on:

"No, I don't mind. Honestly! Tub doesn't get really potted more than once a year, and I never did think much of the females who lay for their menfolks and try to get an advantage over 'em when they have a chance like that. Life's too short!--too short to raise hell about anything except some real vice, like his being humorous and making speeches. Rather be friendly and--Sam! You old dear thing! When are you going to chuck Fran and let yourself be happy again?"

"Why, Matey, honestly, she and I are on the best terms--"

"Don't lie to me, Sam darling (you know how Tub and I DO love you!). Rather, don't lie to yourself! I know. Fran has written to me, now and then. Awful clever and jolly and uninterested. And you don't propose to sit there and tell me that if she wouldn't come home last summer and wouldn't come down from Berlin to see us, she isn't about ready to cut out Zenith entirely! And there's no reason why she shouldn't! She never was very much Zenith anyway . . . or she THOUGHT she wasn't! Only, Sam darling, ONLY, if she is going to cut out Zenith, she's going to cut out you, for even if you are kind of a Lord High Chancellor, still, same time, you ARE Zenith, and in the long run, after you've had your fling, you'd rather see the sunshine on a nice, ragged, old Middlewestern pasture than on the best formal Wop garden in the world!"

"Well--yes--I guess that's more or less true, Matey, but--"

He wanted to tell her of the Sans Souci Gardens dream; he dismissed the matter and struggled on:

"But that doesn't mean Fran doesn't appreciate Zenith and her friends and all that. Course she does! Why, she's always talking about Tub and you--"

"Yeah, I'll bet she is! 'My dear Samuel, IS it necessary for women like your dear Mrs. Pearson to use such vulgarisms as "I'll bet she is" all the time?'"

Though Matey's hearty and slightly brassy voice could never mimic Fran's cool melodies, there was enough accuracy in the impersonation to make Sam grin helplessly, and with that grin he was lost. Matey took advantage of it to pounce:

"Sam darling, I do know it's none of my business, and you can tell me so whenever you want to, but I figured that probably you've been so alone here, seeing nobody but the kind of folks that Fran wants, and--Sam, I've seen you change a lot, more than you know, this last ten years. You never were a chatterbox, but you did used to enjoy an argument or telling a nice clean smutty story, and you've been getting more silent, more sort of scared and unsure of yourself, while Fran has been preening herself and feeling more and more that it was only her social graces and her Lady Vere de Vere beauty that kept up your position, because you were so slow and clumsy and so fond of low company and so generally an undependable hick! And you have more brains in your little finger than--And you're kind! And humble--too damn' humble! And you want to know a fact twice before you say it once, and she--well, she wants to say it twice before she's learned it at all!

"Oh, golly, I guess I'm defying the thunderbolt. Shoot, Jupiter. . . . Now mind you, I LIKED Fran. I admire her. But when I think of how she's treated you, as though she were the silver-shod Diana of the outfit--and especially the way she shows it in public by being so pizen polite to you--well, I just want to wallop her! Now tell me to go to the dickens, darling. . . . Listen to that man Tub snoring in there! THERE'S an aristocratic, college-bred consort for you! The poor lamb! How sick and righteous he'll be tomorrow--up to about noon!"

Sam laboriously lighted a cigar, searched through a perfectly blank mind for something to say, and then, for the first time in months, he was talking candidly about something that really mattered to him.

"Yes, Matey, I'll admit there is something to what you say. I suppose I ought to be highty-tighty and bellow, 'How dare you talk about MY wife!' But--Hell, Matey, I am so sick and tired and confused! Fran is a lot kinder and more appreciative than you think. A lot of what you imagine is snootiness is just her manner. She's really shy, and tries to protect--"

"Oh, I am so tired, Sam, of hearing and reading about these modern folks--you get 'em in every novel--these sensitive plants that go around being rude and then stand back complacently and explain that it's because they're so SHY!"

"Shut up, now! Listen to me!"

"That sounds better!"

"Well, I mean--It IS true with Fran. Partly. And partly she enjoys it--gets a kick out of it--feels she's a heroine in a melodrama. . . . Damn this bathtub--coldest arm-chair I've found in Europe." Without a smile he laid the bath-mat on the edge of the tub, heavily sat down again, and went on:

"And she really thinks that having a social position is worth sacrificing for. And that it still matters to have a title. And I do know she makes me clumsy. But--Well, first place, I really am an old-fashioned believer in what we used to call the Home. I hate to see all the couples busting up the way they are. Think of the people we know that've separated or gotten divorced, right in our own bunch at home-- Dr. and Mrs. Daniels--think of it, married seventeen years, with those nice kids of theirs. And then, and I guess this is more important, Fran has got a kind of charm, fascination, whatever you want to call it, for me that nobody else has. And when she likes something--it may be meeting somebody she likes, or a good party, or a sunset, or music-- well, she's so wrought up about it that it seems as if she had a higher-powered motor in her, with better ground cylinders, than most of us.

"Even when she's snooty--oh, she's trying to have some FORM in life, some standards, not just get along anyhow, sloppily, the way most of us do; and then we resent her demanding that we measure up to what she feels is the highest standard. And her faults--oh, she's a child, some ways. To try to change her (even if a fellow could do it!) would be like calling in a child that was running and racing and having a lovely time in the sunshine, and making her wash dishes."

"And so she leaves you to wash the dishes! Oh, Sam, it's a thankless job to butt in and tell a man that in YOUR important opinion, his wife is a vampire bat. But it makes your friends sore to see you eternally apologetic to your wife, when she ought to thank her lucky stars she's got you! I swear she never, for one moment, with anybody, thinks what she can give, but only what she can get. She thinks that nobody on earth is important except as they serve her or flatter her. But--You've never been interested in any other woman, have you?"

"Not really."

"I wonder if you won't be? I'm making a private bet with myself that after another six months of carrying Fran's shawl, you'll begin to look around. And if you do, you'll be surprised at the number of nice women that'll fall for you! Tell me, Sam. Could you fall for them?"

"Well, I don't know. I don't believe in being deliberately unhappy for the sake of sticking to a bad bargain. If Fran and I did drift apart and I couldn't find some kind of security elsewhere, I wouldn't regard it as any virtue, but simply as an inability to face things as they are--"

"Ah hah! A year ago you wouldn't have admitted that! A year ago, if I'd dared even to thumb my nose at Fran, you'd've bitten me! Sam, you old darling, I never have criticized Fran before, have I?-- not in all these years. Now I feel that the bust-up has happened, and all that's needed is for you to see it, and then you'll be nice and heart-broken and sulky and unhappy, and after that you'll find some darling that'll be crazy about you and spoil you proper, and then all will be joyous tra-la--curse it, that sounds like Tub! And I'm going to bed. G'night, Sam dear. Like to ring us up about eleven?"

As he plowed down the vast corridors of the hotel to his room, too sleepy to think, Sam felt that this saint of unmorality had converted him, and opened a door upon a vista of tall woods and dappled lawns and kind faces.

CHAPTER 27

What Tub and Matey and Sam did during their week together may be deduced by studying a newspaper list of "Where to Lunch, Dine, and Dance in Paris," the advertisements of dressmakers, jewelers, perfumers, furniture-dealers, and of revues; and by reprinting for each evening the more serious features of Tub's first night in Paris.

It was a fatiguing week, but rather comforting to Sam.

Through it, the pious admonitions of Matey, along with the thought of Minna von Escher and his own original virtue, prepared him to yield to temptation--only he saw no one who was tempting.

The Pearsons begged him to go on to Holland with them, but he said that he had business in Paris; he spoke vaguely of conferences with motor agents. Actually, he wanted a day or two for the luxury of sitting by himself, of walking where he would, of meditating in long undisturbed luxurious hours on what it was all about.

He had two hasty, stammering notes from Fran, in which she said that she missed him, which was all very pleasant and gratifying, but in which she babbled of dancing with Kurt von Obersdorf till three A.M.--of a day with Kurt in the country--of an invitation from Kurt's friends, the Von Arminals, to spend the next week-end at their place in the Hartz Mountains. "And of course they'd be enchanted to have you also if you get back in time, asked me tell you how sorry they are you aren't here," her pen sputtered.

"Hm!" said Sam.

Suddenly he was testy. Oh, of course she had a "right" to be with Kurt as much as she liked. He wasn't a harem-keeper. And of course it would be puerile to rage, "If she has a right to be loose, then I have the same right." There was no question of "rights." It was a question of what he wanted, and whether he was willing to pay for it-- whether he wanted new, strange loves, whether he could find them, and whether he was willing to pay in dignity, in the respect that Fran had for him despite her nervous jabbings.

When he had seen the Pearsons off for Amsterdam, with mighty vows to meet them in Zenith within six months, when he had for an hour sat outside the Cafe des Deux Magots, brooding on the Franocentric universe which had cataclysmically replaced the universe of business and creating motors and playing golf, then sharply, gripping the marble top of the little table with his huge hand, he admitted with no more reservations that he was hungry as a barren woman, hungry for a sweetheart who should have Fran's fastidiousness, Minna von Escher's sooty warmth, and Matey Pearson's shrewd earthiness.

He dined alone in a little Montparnasse restaurant filled with eager young couples: a Swedish painter with an Italian girl student, an American globe-trotter with his Polish mistress, pairs of white Russians and Italian anti-fascists. They all twittered like love-birds and frankly held hands over the vin ordinaire and horse-meat. And here, as it was very cheap, there were actually French people, all in couples except when they belonged to enormous noisy family parties, and the couples stroked each other's hands, unabashedly nuzzled each other's cheeks, looked into each other's eyes, the world well lost.

It was spring--spring and Paris--scent of chestnut blossoms, freshness of newly watered pavements, and Sam Dodsworth was almost as lonely as though he were at the Adlon with Kurt and Fran.

When he thought of Fran's cool, neat politeness to him, he was angry. When he looked about him at youth in love, he was angrier. This passion, ungrudging and unabashed, Fran had never given him. He had been robbed--Or robbed her? All wrong, either way. Had ENOUGH--

Oh, he was lonely, this big friendly man, Sam Dodsworth, and he wanted a man to whom he could talk and boast and lie, he wanted a woman with whom he could be childish and hurt and comforted, and so successful and rich was he that he had neither, and he sought them, helpless, his raw nerves exposed. So searching, he strolled after dinner to the Select, which was rivaling the Cafe du Dome as the resort of the international yearners in Paris.

A man alone at a cafe table in the more intellectual portions of Paris, and not apparently expecting some one, is always a man suspect. At home he may be a prince, a successful pickpocket, or an explorer, but in this city of necessitous and over-friendly strollers, this city where any one above the rank of assassin or professional martyr can so easily find companions, the supposition is that he is alone because he ought to be alone.

But it is also a rule of this city of spiritual adventurers which lies enclosed within the simple and home-loving French city of Paris, this new Vanity Fair, of slimier secrets, gallanter Amelias and more friendly Captain Dobbinses than Thackeray ever conceived, that if such a solitary look prosperous, if he speak quietly to the waiters, not talk uninvited to the people at the next table, and drink his fine a l'eau slowly, he may be merely a well-heeled tourist, who would be gratified to be guided into the citadel of the arts by a really qualified, gently tourist-despising, altogether authentic initiate of the Parisian Hobohemia--a girl who has once had a book-review printed, or a North Dakota 'cellist who is convinced that every one believes him to be an Hungarian gipsy.

So it happened that when Samuel Dodsworth sat melancholy and detached at a table before the Select, four young people at another table commented upon him--psycho-analytically, biologically, economically; cleverly, penetratingly, devastatingly.

"See that big dumbbell there by himself?" remarked Clinton J. Gillespie, the Bangor miniaturist. "I'll bet he's an American lawyer. Been in politics. Fond of making speeches. He's out of office now, and sore about it."

"Oh, hell!" said the gentleman next. "In the first place he's obviously an Englishman, and look at his hands! I don't suppose you have room for mere hands in your rotten little miniatures! He's rich and of good family, and yet he has the hands of a man who works. Perfectly simple. He's the owner of a big country estate in England, crazy about farming, and prob'ly he's a baronet."

"Grand!" said the third, smaller, sharper-nosed man. "Perfect-- except for the fact that he is obviously a soldier and--I'm not quite sure about this, but I think he's German!"

"You all," said the fourth, a bobbed-haired girl of twenty with a cherubic face, rose-bud mouth, demure chin, magazine-cover nose, and the eyes of a bitter and grasping woman of forty, "make me very sick! You know so much that isn't so! I don't know what he is, but he looks good for a bottle of champagne, and I'm going over and grab it."

"What the devil good, Elsa," complained Clinton J. Gillespie, "is it for you to come to Paris if you always go talking to Babbitts like that fellow? You never WILL become a novelist!"

"Won't that be fierce--when I think over some of the novelists that hang around this joint!" rasped Elsa, and she tripped to Sam's table, she stood beside him, warbling, "I BEG your pardon, but aren't you Mr. Albert Jackson of Chicago?"

Sam looked up. She was so much like the edifying portrait of "Miss Innocence" on the calendar which the grocer sends you at New Year's that he was not irritated even by this most ancient of strategies. "No, but I wish I were. I am from Chicago, but my name is Pearson, Thomas J. Pearson. Loans and banking. Won't you sit down? I'm kind of lonely in Paris."

Elsa did not seat herself precipitately. It was impossible to say just when it was that she did sit down, so modestly did she slip into a chair, looking as though she had never had so unmaidenly an encounter, as though momently she would take fright and wing away. She murmured, "That was TOO silly of me! You must have thought I was a terribly bold little creature to speak to you, but you did look so much like Mr.--Mr. Jackson, who is a gentleman that I met once at my aunt's house in New Rochelle--my father is the Baptist minister there--and I guess I felt lonely, too, a wee bit--I don't know many people in Paris myself, though I've been here three months. I'm studying novel-writing here. But it was awfully kind of you not to mind."

"Mind? It was a privilege," Sam said gallantly . . . and within himself he was resolving, "Yes, you cute little bitch-kitty, you lovely little gold-digger, I'm going to let you work me as much as you want to, and I'm going to spend the night with you!"

And he was triumphant, after so much difficulty, at having been at last able to take the first step toward sin.

"And now, young lady, I hope you're going to let me buy you a little drink or something, just to show you think I'm as nice and respectable as if you'd met ME in your aunt's house, too. What would you like?"

"Oh, I--I--I've scarcely ever tasted alcohol." Sam had seen her flip off two brandies at the other table. "What DOES one drink? What would be safe for a young girl?"

"Well--Of course you wouldn't touch brandy?"

"Oh no!"

"No, of course not. Well, what would you most like?"

"Well--Oh, you won't think it's awfully silly of me, Mr. Uh--"

"Mr. Thomas--Pearson J. Thomas."

"Of course--how silly of me! You wouldn't think it was aw-fully silly of me, Mr. Thomas, if I said I've often heard people speaking about champagne, and always wanted to taste some?"

"No, I wouldn't think that was a bit silly. I'm told it's a very nice innocent drink for young girls." ("I will! And tonight! She picked on me first!") "Is there any particular brand of champagne you'd like to try?"

She looked at him suspiciously, but she was reassured by his large and unfanciful face, and she prattled more artlessly than ever:

"Oh, you must think I'm a TERRIBLE little silly--just a regu-lar little GREENHORN--but I don't know the name of one single brand of any kind of wine! But I did hear a boy that I know here--he's such a hardworking boy, a student--but he told me that Pol Roger, Quinze, I mean 1915, was one of the nicest vintages."

"Yes, I'm told it's quite a nice little wine," said Sam, and as he ordered it, his seemingly unobservant glance noted that one of Elsa's young men shrugged in admiration of something and handed another of the three a five-franc note, as though he were paying a bet.

"Am I going to have collaboration in my first seduction?" he wondered. "I may need it! I'll never go through with it! I'd like to kiss this little imp half to death but--Oh, God, I can't pick on a kid younger than my daughter!"

While he talked ardently to Elsa for the next half hour--about Berlin and Naples, about Charles Lindbergh, who had just this week flown from New York to Paris, and, inevitably, about Prohibition and the novels that she hadn't yet quite started to write--his whole effort was to get rid of scruples, to regain his first flaunting resolve to forget the respectable Samuel Dodsworth and be a bandit.

He was helped by jealousy and champagne.

After half an hour, Elsa started, ever so prettily, and cried, "Why! There's some boys I know at the second table over. As you are alone in Paris--Perhaps they might be willing to take you around a lit-tle, and I'm sure they'd be delighted to meet you. They're SUCH nice boys, and so talented! Do you mind if I call them over?"

"B' d'lighted--"

She summoned the three young men with whom she had been sitting and introduced them as Mr. Clinton Gillespie, late of Bangor, miniaturist, Mr. Charley Short, of South Bend, now in the advertising business but expecting shortly to start a radical weekly, and Mr. Jack Keipp, the illustrator--just what Mr. Keipp illustrated was forever vague. Unlike Elsa, they did not need to be coaxed to sit down. They sat quickly and tight, and looked thirsty, and exchanged droll sophisticated glances as Sam meekly ordered two more bottles of Pol Roger.

While taking his champagne, they took the conversation away from him. They discussed the most artistic of topics--the hatefulness of all other artists; and now and then condescendingly threw to that Philistine, Mr. Pearson J. Thomas, a bone of explanation about the people of whom they gossiped. After half a bottle each, they forgot that they thought of Elsa only as nice young men should think of a Baptist minister's daughter. They mauled her. They contradicted her. One of them--the sharp-nosed little man, Mr. Keipp--held her hand. And after an entire bottle, Elsa herself rather forgot. She laughed too loudly at a reference to a story which no Christmas-card cherub would ever have heard.

So jealousy and a very earnest dislike of these supercilious young men came to help kill Sam's reluctance.

"Hang it," he informed himself, "you can't tell me she hasn't been a little more than intimate with this Keipp rat! In any case, old Granddaddy Sambo would be better for her than this four-flusher. Give her a much better time. I WILL!"

His resolution held. Once he had accomplished the awful struggle of winning himself, once he turned from it to winning her, he began to see her (through a slightly champagne-colored haze) as wondrously desirable.

"Probably I'll kick myself tomorrow. I don't care! I'm glad I'm going to have her! Now to get rid of these young brats! Stop brooding, Sam, and speak your little piece! . . . I'll take her to the Continental, too, by thunder!"

Fran would have marveled to hear her taciturn Samuel chattering. Early he discovered a way of parrying these young geniuses--by admitting, before they hinted it, that he was a lowbrow, but that he ranked higher among the lowbrows than they among the highbrows.

This attack disorganized them, and enabled him to contradict them with cheerful casualness. He heard himself stating that Eddie

Guest was the best American poet, and a number of other things which he had heard from Tub Pearson and which he did not believe. His crassness was so complete that they were staggered, being accustomed to having gentlemen as large and as rich as Mr. Pearson J. Thomas deprecate their own richness and largeness, and admire the sophistication of Mr. Gillespie, Mr. Short, and Mr. Keipp.

Elsa agreed with him in everything; made him ardent by taking his side against them; encouraged him till (with a mild astonishment at his own triumphs of asininity) he heard himself asserting that vacuum cleaners were more important than Homer, and that Mr. Mutt, of the comic strips, was a fuller-blooded character than Soames Forsyte.

And meantime, he was buying.

Mr. Gillespie, Mr. Short, and Mr. Keipp never refused another drink. After the champagne, Elsa suggested brandies (she had forgotten that it was a beverage of which she had scarcely heard) and there were many brandies, and the pile of saucers, serving as memoranda of drinks for which he would have to pay, rose and rose in front of Sam, while the innocent pioneer part of the table in front of Mr. Gillespie, Mr. Short, and Mr. Keipp was free of anything save their current brandies.

But Sam was craftily delighted. Could anything better show Elsa that he was a worthier lover than the sharp-nosed Mr. Keipp?

He was talking, now, exclusively to Elsa, ignoring the young men. He was almost beginning to be honest with her, in his desire to have sympathy from this rosy child. He decided that her eyes weren't hard, really, but intelligent.

He finally dared to grope under the table, and her hand flew to his, so warm, so young, so living, and answered his touch with a pressure which stirred him intolerably. He became very gay, joyous with the thought of the secret they were sharing. But a slight check occurred to the flow of his confidences.

Elsa cooed, "Oh, excuse me just a moment, dear. There's Van Nuys Rodney over there. Something I have to ask him. 'Scuse me a moment."

She flitted to a table at which sat a particularly hairy and blue-shirted man and he saw her drop all her preening in an absorbed conversation.

He sat neglected by his guests at his own table.

288

In three minutes, Mr. Jack Keipp lounged to his feet, muttered, "Pardon me a moment" and Sam saw him join Elsa and Van Nuys Rodney and plunge into talk. Then Mr. Gillespie yawned, "Well, I think I'll turn in," Mr. Short suggested, "Glad met you, Mr. Oh," and they were gone. Sam watched them stroll down the boulevard. He wished that he had been pleasanter to them--even Shorts and Gillespies would be worth having in this city of gaiety and loneliness.

When he looked back, he saw that Elsa, Mr. Keipp, and Mr. Rodney had vanished, complete.

He waited for Elsa to come back. He waited an hour, with the monstrous pile of saucers before him as his only companion. She did not come. He paid the waiter, he rose slowly, unsmilingly beckoned to a taxicab, and sat in it cold and alone.

Some time in the night--and he was never quite sure whether he had been dreaming or half-awake--he heard Fran saying coldly, "My dear Samuel, don't you see at last--isn't it exactly what I told you?-- that you have less knowledge of women than a European like Kurt would have at eighteen? You American men! Fussing and fuming and fretting over the obvious question of whether or not you'll seduce that little harlot! And then unable to accomplish it! What a spectacle! But Kurt--in the first place, of course, Kurt would have taken Elsa away from there, away from her little parasite friends--"

It was Fran's very voice, and he had nothing to answer.

He awoke again to hear not Fran but himself jeering, "And the rottenest part of the whole thing was the cheap superiority you felt to those three little rats of would-be artists. Poor kids! Of COURSE they have to be conceited and supercilious, to keep their courage up, because they're failures."

And again, "Yes, that's all true, but I'll find Elsa again, and this time--"

CHAPTER 28

He slept badly; he rose at six and rang for breakfast. But at breakfast everything was gratefully clear to him.

He was so thankful that he had not gone astray with Elsa that he did not think of it for more than a second. All his thoughts blazed about Fran.

Why had he let the dissensions, the blame and impatience, all the nothings, grow into a barrier unreal but thwarting as a wall seen in a nightmare? All that was needed was a really frank talk with her! And this trip to Paris, confessing to Matey, being idiotic with Elsa, just being alone and away from Fran, had made it possible for him to be frank.

He'd been stupid. Fran was a child. Why not treat her as one, a lovely and much beloved child; be more patient, not be infuriated by her passing tantrums? A child. A lake mirroring sunny clouds and thunder squalls.

Just go back and say, "Look here, dear--"

He wasn't sure what he was to say after "Look here, dear," but he would be ever so affectionate and convincing. He did love her! Fran, with her eager eyes--

But what about Kurt von Obersdorf?

Well--belligerently--what ABOUT it! Either she was still innocent, and did not understand her danger, or she had fallen, and would regret it. In either case, when he had paternally explained the danger of free-lance lovers like Kurt, she would come to her senses and laugh with him at this make-believe enmity between them--yes! that was it--all a make-believe, an exciting game, like so many things in her secret and dramatic life! And they would go home together.

He would hasten to her. Now! If possible he would fly! He would see her late this very afternoon!

He had never been in an aeroplane, for all his professional interest in aviation engines. Like most sound people, he had always been slightly afraid of flying, but in his ardor now he despised his fear.

Then there rose such a hubbub of efficiency as he had not experienced since the most critical days of Revelation Motors. A demand that the porter find at what time the Berlin 'plane flew--it went at nine, two hours from now. Telephoning to demand a ticket. The room-waiter rushing down for Sam's bill. The valet de chambre packing. A motor ordered to take him to the flying-field.

Driving out, he felt a slight agitation. His much motoring had not hardened him to flying. But his apprehension was overcome by the prospect of seeing Fran in a few hours, and when he dismounted at the flying field, when he saw the great 'plane, its metal body and thick crimped metal wings as solid-looking as a steamer, when he saw how casually the pilot took his place in front and the attendants loaded luggage, all nervousness vanished in exultation. He climbed up a tiny stepladder, walked across the left-hand wing, and entered the little door like a child taken on a boat ride.

The cabin was like that of a very large limousine or a rather small omnibus. The seats were of leather, deep and easy as chairs in a club; the cabin walls were covered with stamped leather; the pilot was to be seen, with his intricacy of instruments before him, only through a tiny window forward. Save when he glanced out of the window beside him, Sam had no sense of being in anything so fantastic and fragile as an aeroplane. His half-dozen fellow passengers seemed casual about the whole thing. One of them, as soon as he was seated, opened a book and did not look up for an hour.

Sam was vastly ashamed that he had been diffident. He almost hoped for a little danger.

They started with no ceremonies--just at a gesture from the official in charge. They trundled along the ground for so long a time that Sam wondered whether they were overloaded, unable to rise. Suddenly a little qualm came--oh, it would be all right of course when they were high in air, going a steady course, but wouldn't it be rather nasty to leave the ground, to spin and toss as they climbed?

Actually, he never did know when they left the ground. They were bumping along the turf, very noisily, the propeller draft blowing the grass stalks backward; then, magically, they were ten feet up in the air, they were above the hangar roofs, they were as high up as the distant Eiffel Tower, and as for sensations, there were none save the lively inquiry as to why he didn't have any sensations.

He noted that the country below him was like a map; he told himself that he was thrilled when they passed over something like a fog bank--and rather more like a wash of soap suds--and he realized that it was a cloud and that they must be nearly a mile high in air. But he had read of the country looking like a map, of passing over clouds. In fact he experienced nothing of which he had not read many times-- until he noted, and this was something he had never read, that aero-plane travel, in calm weather, is the most monotonous and tedious form of journeying known to mankind, save possibly riding on a canal boat through flat country. How tired he got of looking at maps, hour on hour! He had less relationship to the country than in the swiftest motor, the most violent train.

It was so monotonous and safe-seeming that he laughed to re-member his nervousness; laughed the more when a French business man took out his portable typewriter, set it on a suitcase on his knees and, a mile up in the air, began placidly to type a letter.

He forgot, then, all about aviating and, just glancing out occa-sionally at distant green hills, he gave himself up to the thought of Fran. Oh, he would do anything for her . . . he would make her under-stand it . . . surely such devotion would bring her to his arms!

They had left Paris at nine; they were due to alight in Ger-many, at Dortmund, at twenty minutes to three. Before one they ran into a thunder-shower, and all the commonplace dullness of their flight was instantly snatched away.

Their little cabin seemed gruesomely insecure as the lightning glared past them, as they quivered in a blast of wind, as they ran into a dark cloud and for two minutes seemed lost in midnight, as they came out of the cloud into rain which crashed against the windows. Sam, who had cheerfully enough driven with motor racers at a hundred and ten miles an hour, was distinctly bothered. He was helpless! There was no ground to step out on, not even a sea to swim in, only the treacher-ous and darkened air.

The man across the little aisle from Sam--and Sam never did find out what was the snarly language he spoke--looked over, laughed deprecatingly, took out a bottle of cognac, drank long and gurglingly and, without a word, handed it over. Without hesitation Sam drank from the bottle and bowed his gratitude.

He tried to think of Fran again, and she remained a floating pale young face that outside his window kept pace in mid-air with the 'plane. But for a time she was only that.

They ran through the thunder-shower into rough air. They swooped upward, they fell a hundred feet--the sensation was precisely as in a dropping express elevator, which leaves one's stomach two floors above--they rocked and quivered like a dory in high seas.

The business man, who had uninterestedly kept up his typing all through the storm, quietly rose and was very sick in a little paper bag. At the sight, the agreeable philanthropist with the cognac was sicker, much sicker. And Sam Dodsworth wanted to be sick, and was distressed because he couldn't be.

For an hour and more they were shaken thus, helpless as dice in a box, and when with ineffable gratitude they circled down toward the flying field at Dortmund, Sam saw that there was another thunder-shower coming.

Had Fran or Tub Pearson been there to observe him, he might not have had the courage to admit that he hadn't the courage to go on to Berlin by 'plane, and it was hard enough in the presence of that rather demanding censor, Sam Dodsworth, but as they delicately touched the ground and taxied along--the aeroplane as innocent and demure as though it had never thought of such insane capering a mile in air--Sam determined, "Well, we'll call that enough for a starter, and go on by train!"

Though he reeled a little with land-sickness when he stepped out, he beamed with idiotic bliss on the recovered earth, the beautifully safe and solid earth.

There were taxicabs waiting at the flying-field, but it came to Sam that he did not know the German for even "station" or "train." In Berlin, he had depended on Fran. He looked disconsolately at the driver of the taxi in which a porter had set his bag, and grunted, "Berlin? Vagon? Berlin?"

"Surest t'ing you know, boss," said the taxi-driver. "Train for Berlin. Well, how's the folks back in the States?"

Sam said the inevitable.

"Was I THERE? Say, don't make me laugh! I was born in Prussia but I was twenty-six years in Philly and K.C., and then I come back here, like a boob, and I got caught by the army, and don't let nobody tell you that was any nice, well-behaved war, either! Jump in, boss."

On the Berlin train, Sam forgot Fran for three minutes, in anger at himself for having failed to go on by aeroplane. It betrayed him as irresolute and growing old. Was he soft? He determined that the coming autumn, with Fran or without, he would make another canoe trip in Canada; he would live sparsely, sleep on the ground, carry on the portage, paddle all day long, and make himself shoot the worst rapids. Yes! With Fran or without--

But it must be WITH! Surely Fran could not withstand the new passion he was bringing to her from his Paris venture.

His train reached Berlin just before midnight.

At the hotel he seized his suit-case without waiting for the doorman, and pounded into the lobby.

"My wife in?--Mr. Dodsworth, suite B7," he demanded, at the desk.

"I think the lady must be out, sir. The key is here," said the clerk.

Dismally, Sam followed the boy with his bag to the elevator.

He sent the key back to the desk. He told himself that he did so because he was tired and might be asleep before she returned.

She was not in the suite. It smelled of her, shouted of her. She had spilled a little pink powder on the glass cover of her toilet- table; on the turned-back bed was her nightgown with the Irish lace; a half-finished letter to Emily was on the desk in the sitting-room; and these shadows of her made her absence the more glaring. From midnight till half-past two he sat waiting for her, reading magazines, and all his furious and simple-minded excitement grew cold minute by minute.

At half-past two he heard laughter in the corridor. Hating himself for it, yet quite unable to resist, he sprang up, turned off the lights in the sitting-room, and stood in the dark bedroom, just beyond the door.

He heard the door opening; heard Fran bubbling, "Yes, you can come in for a moment. But not long. Poo' lil Fran, she is all in! What an orchestra that was! I could have danced till dawn!"

And Kurt: "Oh, you darling--DARLING!"

"Good evening," said Sam, from the bedroom door, and Fran sobbed, once, quickly.

"Just got back from Paris." Sam strode into the sitting-room, turned on the lights, stood there feeling clumsy and thick, wishing he had not been melodramatic.

"Oh, Sam, I am so glad you got back safe!" cried Kurt. "Fran and I have been dancing. Now I vill go home, and tomorrow I ring you up about luncheon."

He glanced at Fran, hesitated as though he wanted to say something, bowed, and was gone. Fran glared at Sam with lip-biting hatred. Sam begged:

"Dear, I came back so quickly--listen, dear, I flew--because I couldn't live without you! I'm not angry that Kurt and you were out so late--"

"Why should you be!" She tossed her gold and crimson evening wrap on the couch.

"Dear! Listen! This is serious! I've come back to you, willing to do everything I can to make you happy. I adore you. You know that. You're everything I have. Only we've got to cut out this nonsense of being homeless adventurers and go home--"

"And that's your idea of 'making me happy'! And now YOU listen--to repeat your favorite phrase! I love Kurt, and Kurt loves me, and I'm going to marry him! No matter what it costs me! We decided it tonight. And all I can say is I'm glad Kurt was too much of a gentleman to punch your head, as he probably wanted to, when you played that sweet, provincial trick of hiding in the bedroom to listen to us--"

"Fran, Fran!"

"Now don't play the injured and astonished small boy! You have no complaint. You've never known me. You've never known anything about me. You've never known what I wore, what flowers I put in your study, what sacrifices I made to cover up your awkwardnesses and help you keep your dull friends and your dull work and your dull reputation!"

"Fran!"

"Oh, I know! I'm being beastly. But I was so happy with Kurt-- till two minutes ago. And then I find you here, a prowling elephant-- oh yes, the great Mr. Dodsworth, the motor magnate, who has a right to commandeer my soul and my dreams and my body! I can't STAND it! Poor--yes, Kurt and I will be poor. Only, thank God, we'll have my twenty thousand a year! But that will be poverty among the sort of people he knows--"

She was altogether hysterical; she was tearing at her evening frock; and he was as appalled as a man witnessing a murder. He said timidly, "All right, dear. Just one thing. Does he want to marry you?"

"Yes!"

"Then I'll go away." He had a vision of such loneliness as he had known in Paris at the Select. "Can you get a divorce here in Germany?"

"Yes. I believe so. Kurt says so."

"You'll stay in Berlin?"

"I think so. A friend of the Biedners has a nice flat to let, over-looking the Tiergarten."

"All right. Then I'll go away. Tomorrow. 'Fraid it's too late to-night. I'll sleep on the couch here in the parlor, if you don't mind."

"Very well. . . . Oh, you WOULD play the role of the patient, suffering martyr at a time like this! You have just enough native in-stinct to guess that's the one way you can put me hopelessly in the wrong, and make me feel as if I'd been a dirty dog in not appreciating you--as if I must go back and be the dutiful dull consort. Well, I won't! Understand that!" He felt as though he were being driven into a corner. "Kurt has everything I've always wanted--real culture, learning, man-ners, even his dear, idiotic, babyish clownishness. Yes--I'll hurry and get it in before you graciously throw it up at me--yes and position. I ADMIT I'd like to be a countess. Though how unimportant that part is, a man like you could never understand. Yes, and physically Kurt has--oh, he hasn't your lumbering bull strength, but he rides, he fences, he dances, he swims, he plays tennis--oh, perfectly. And he has a sense of romance. But you'll go around telling all the dear dull people in Zenith that I didn't appreciate your sterling--"

"Stop it! I warn you!"

"--virtues, and that I'm a silly tuft-hunting American woman, and you'll enjoy sneering that for all his rank, the Count Obersdorf is only a clerk and probably a fortune-hunter, and that will make you feel so justified for all your dullness! Oh, I can see what a sweet time you'll have spreading scandal about me--"

"God!" Fran shrank at something in his face. He was standing by the center table. He had cooled his huge right hand by grasping a vase of roses. That hand slowly closed now, his shoulder strained, and the vase smashed, the water dripped through his fingers. He threw the mess, glass fragments and crushed flowers, into a corner, and wiped his bleeding fingers. The hysterical gesture relieved him.

She looked frightened, but she quavered gallantly, "Don't be mel--"

He broke in with a very hard, business-like: "We'll have no more melodrama on either side. I warned you that I'd fly off the handle. If you enjoy your little game of picking at me any more, it won't be a vase next time. Now there's just a couple of things to settle. That I go is decided. But--You're quite sure that Kurt wants to marry you?"

"Quite!"

"Been anything more than--"

"No, not yet--I'm sorry to say! There might have been if you hadn't come tonight. Oh, I'm sorry! Please! I don't mean to be quite as nasty as I sound! But I'm a little hysterical, too. Don't you suppose I know what people will think about me--what even Brent and Emily will think! Oh, I'll pay--"

"You will. Now will you promise me: see as much as you want to of Kurt, but promise me that you'll wait a month before you decide to sue for divorce. To be sure."

"Very well."

"I'll instruct my bank to send you ten thousand a year, on top of your own money. That seems to end everything."

"Oh, Sam, if I could only make you see that it was your ignorance, your impotence, and not my fault--"

Suddenly he had seized an astonished and ruffled Fran, thrust her into the bedroom, growled, "We've talked enough tonight," locked the door on her infuriated protests . . . berated himself for that ruffianism . . . sighed that he would lie awake all night . . . and, with no bedtime preparations save removing his coat and shoes, dropped on the couch and gone instantly and blindly asleep.

CHAPTER 29

In the morning he was cool, determined to clear off as soon as possible. She was no less cool. When he unlocked the bedroom door, at eight, she was already dressed, in crisp blue coat and skirt and plain blouse, and she looked at him as though he were a servant whom she had resolved to discharge for insolence. She said quietly:

"Good morning. You know, of course, that your mauling me and threatening me last evening made finally impossible any rapprochement between us."

"Eh? That's fine."

"Oh. Oh, I see. Very well, that makes everything so MUCH easier. At last we know where we are. Now I suppose you'll return to Paris, at least for a while."

"I suppose so. I'll take the evening train."

"Then you'll have a lot to do. I'm sorry to trouble you, but I'm afraid we'll have to make a number of agreements--about our house in Zenith, about finances, and so on--it's very generous of you to go on sending money, though I certainly should not take it unless I felt that, after all, running your house, entertaining your business acquaintances and all, perhaps I've earned it. And you'll have to pack--be something of a job to divide up the luggage, of course, now our things are all mixed up together in the trunks. So we must get busy. If you'll be so good as to order breakfast for us--and to shave!--which you decidedly need, if you'll permit me to say so!--I'll go down and have the concierge get your wagon lit and ticket. And I'll telephone to Kurt. I assume you will want to abuse him for a while--oh, he won't mind! And I think it might be good for my reputation here, so long as I'm in an anomalous position, which I can't expect you to understand or appreciate, if Kurt and I saw you off together on the train tonight."

"Fran, I'm not planning to get out any shotgun, but I most certainly will not see Von Obersdorf again, any time, under any considerations. For both my sake and his, I'm afraid you'll have to give up your idea of having your cake and eating it--of kicking me out and yet of having every one suppose you're a devoted and deserted wife. That's flat. UNDERSTAND?"

"Quite. Very well. And I should be glad if you'd find it possible not to yell at me any more, just this last day, so that I'll have a little pleasanter memory of you! Please order some orange juice for me. I'll be back by the time breakfast is here. You'll find your blue suit freshly pressed in the closet--I had it done while you were away."

At eleven, while Sam was packing and Fran was out buying another suit-case, into the sitting-room, into the bedroom, without knocking, came Kurt von Obersdorf, and Sam looked up to see him standing in the door, his fingers nervous on his palms.

"I know you did not want to see me. Fran telephoned me so. But you do not understand, Sam. I am not a gigolo or a Don Juan. I do love Fran; I would beg her to marry me if she were free. But if I told you how much I like and admire you, you would think I was a sentimental fool. I have kep' telling her she does not appreciate you. If I could bring you two together--oh, DON'T run off and desert her; she needs your steadiness! If I could bring you two together again, and keep you both for my ver' dear friends, _I_ would go away, instead-- yes, I would go today!"

Sam rose from the wardrobe trunk, dusted his hands, stood gravely in his shirt-sleeves:

"Suppose I just called your bluff, Von Obersdorf? Suppose I said, 'All right, you leave Berlin today, for good, and I'll stay.'"

"I would do it! I will! If in turn you promise me to be always more tender with Fran! Oh, I do not mean I can go forever, and hide myself. I am a poor man. I support partly my mother. But I can be called for business to Budapest, for three weeks. We organize now a new branch there. Shall I go?"

He looked the zealot, he said it like a crusader.

But Sam realized hastily, dismayingly, that he wanted to go; that he wanted to be free of Fran's play-acting; he realized that he was afraid to be left alone with her fury if Kurt should desert them.

"No," he said. "And I apologize. I believe you. Here's what we've got to do. Of course I have no way of knowing just how fond you are of Fran. But it certainly doesn't look as if Fran and I could ever get together again. Don't even know it would be a good thing, for either of us. What we have to do is to do nothing; let things take their course. I'm going. She stays. You stay. You see how you feel, and I'll see how I feel, and if you do love the girl--as I by God have and as I suppose I still do!--don't let any consideration for me stand in your way. I wouldn't, I guess, if the shoe was on the other foot. Not that I'm going to say any 'Bless you my children.' I feel more like saying, 'Damn you both!' But I can't see where you're to blame. No. Now I've got to finish packing. Good-bye, Obersdorf. Don't see me off tonight-- definitely don't want it. And I guess I ought to tell you that I'm afraid she's right. Guess you can make the girl happier than I can."

"But YOU--going alone--"

"Now hell's big bells on a mountain! Don't worry about me! I'm free, white, and twenty-one! Everybody's had too much consider- ateness for everybody else in this business! I figure that maybe it would have been a lot clearer-cut if one of us had been out-and-out hoggish and known what he wanted and just grabbed it. No. I'll be all right. Good-bye."

Kurt shook the proffered hand hesitatingly. Sam turned his back. When he looked up, Kurt was gone.

If Fran knew that Kurt had called, she gave no sign. All day she was courteous, brisk, and harder than enamel.

To pack for his journey--the journey to nowhere which might last forever--it was necessary to unpack the rather large number of trunks and bags which these spoiled children of new wealth had found necessary. Their baggage had for months been their only home. To divide it was like the division of property after a funeral.

But she was efficient about it, and horribly kind.

When she came to the shawl he had bought as a surprise for her that exciting day in Seville, she looked at it slowly, stroked it, started to speak, then firmly put it away in a drawer of the bureau. But it was harder when she came to the silly shell-box.

It brought back a day on the Roman Campagna, a windy radi- ant day of fast walking. They had found a tomb old as the Caesars, forgotten amid long grass, and had lunched in a palm-thatched outdoor booth at a peasant trattoria. A pedler came whining to their table with a tray of preposterous shell-boxes, and Fran seized one, crying, "Oh, DARLING, will you look at this adorably awful thing?" It was a mas- terpiece; a wooden box with cheap red velvet glued round the sides, and on top a scurf of tiny gilded sea-shells about a small streaky mirror. "Look! All my life--When I was a little girl, we had a maid (only I think we called her a hired girl!) that had a box EXACTLY like this, and I thought it was the most beautiful thing in the world. I used to sneak up to her little room, under the eaves, to worship, it. And I've always wanted one like it. And here it is! But of course one couldn't buy the horrible thing!"

"Why not?"

"Oh, could we? It would make me remember--Oh, of course not! Perfectly silly, with us traveling--"

But he rose to her fancy; he demanded of the old pedler, "How much liras? Eh?" and interrogatively held up five fingers.

After much conversation which neither Sam nor the pedler understood, and at which Fran giggled helplessly, Sam bought the object for seven lire, and that night Fran surrounded it with a pearl necklace and burned a candle in front of it. Then she had forgotten it-- but not quite thrown it away. It had made its way into one of those neglected drawers of a wardrobe trunk, one of those old attics of traveling, which contain bathing suits, walking shoes, solid histories intended to make journeying educational, and all the other useful staples which one surely will use, and never will.

Fran dove into this attic drawer busily; she drew out the shell-box, and stood holding it. Her eyes were deep, pitiful, regretful, and all their defense was gone. He looked back at her, helpless. And neither of them found anything to say, and suddenly she had snatched out of the attic drawer a never-used thermos bottle and their moment was gone.

A minute later when, after desperate groping for speech, he felt that it would be an ingratiating thing to say, "If I happen to go to Spain, would you like me to get you any lace or embroidery or anything?" she answered suavely, "Oh, thanks, thanks no. I fancy I may run down to the Balkans before long, and I believe there's some very decent embroidery there. I say, will you please notice that I'm putting these dress collars not with your day collars but with your evening shirts? Heavens, we must hurry!"

When a man straggles on the short death-walk from his cell through the little green door, into the room where stands the supreme throne, does he, along with his incredulous apprehension, along with trying to believe that this so-living and eternal-seeming center and purpose of the universe, himself--this solid body with its hard biceps, its curiously throbbing heart that ever since his mother's first worry has in its agonies been so absorbing, this red-brown skin that has glowed after the salt sea at Coney Island and has turned a sullen brick after wild drinking--the astonishment that this image of God and Eternity will in five minutes be still and stiff and muck--is he at that long slow moment nonetheless conscious of a mosquito bite, of a toothache, of the smugness of the messages from Almighty God which the chaplain gives him, of the dampness of the slimy stone corridor and the echo of their solemn march? Is he more conscious of these little abrasions than of the great mystery?

So busy were Sam and Fran at the station--buying magazines, looking over the new Tauchnitzes, seeing that his extra trunks were registered through to Paris--that they had no time to question whether this might be their last parting. They had dined in the crowded bar of the Adlon, too close to others to have the luxury of mourning; she had said nothing more emotional than "If you should decide to go to America, when you see Emily and the boy tell them that I'll come back and see them in a few months now. . . no matter what happens . . . unless they'd like to come over to Europe. Of course I'd like that . . . I put some new tooth-powder in the bottle in your fitted case."

She was as attentive as a courier at the station; it was she who with her quick inaccurate German persuaded the conductor to change Sam to a one-berth compartment, who prevented his giving the hotel porter, who met them with their band luggage and registered the trunks through, more than four marks as tip.

By general, it had been he, these months, who had borne the duties of tickets, luggage, reservations, while she sat back in cool elegance and was not shy about criticizing him for his errors. But tonight she led the expedition, she thought of everything, and he felt helpless as a maiden aunt. He had a new respect for her. . . . Perhaps, with Kurt, she wouldn't be a child any longer, but grasp reality. That made him the more disconsolate, the more hopeless of some future miraculous reconciliation. He saw her a woman reborn. It seemed to him that she was grasping the intricacies of daily life in Europe as deftly as she managed everything from the cook's salary to the women's club program in America. He could not imagine her, just now, going back to Zenith. Kurt von Obersdorf and the Princess Drachenthal and Europe had utterly defeated and put in their place Sam Dodsworth and Tub and Matey Pearson and Ross Ireland and the Midwest.

Thus his thoughts blundered and writhed while he ambled after her through the station--to the news-stand, to the cigar-stand, to the train-gate--feeling himself no closer to her polished and metallic briskness than he was to the bundle-lugging third-class passengers who plodded through the echoing immensity of the train-shed; and thus, with everything necessary and unnecessary accomplished and overaccomplished, they stood together beside his sleeper, his luggage stored, his ticket taken by the guard, and suddenly they tumbled like the falling Lucifer from the paradise of keeping busy to the inferno of feeling. She put it off a moment. She sighted the boy trundling his little platform wagon of wine and sandwiches and fruit; she cried, "Oh, you might want something to drink," and darted off to bring him back a flask of cognac.

There was nothing else.

The train took another diabolic three minutes to start. They walked up and down--a tail, well-tailored pair, obviously complacent and not much interested, not very emotional.

He took her arm, as he had so many times at so many railroad stations, but dropped it with hot guiltiness.

"No, PLEASE," she said, tucking her arm into his. "It is going to be a little hard to realize, isn't it, old thing! Oh, Sam darling, you and I can't get along together. And I do love Kurt. I stand by that! But we have been partners, good partners, in this funny business of life. . . . We've had so many happy times, just you and I together!" Her voice lost its confidence. "Shall I ever see you again? And--oh, my blessings, my dear--"

"Eeeeeein-steigen--bitte einsteigen!" cried the mourning voice of the guard.

"That means 'all aboard'?" croaked Sam.

"Yes. Quick!"

The train was starting as he climbed up to the vestibule. Fran stood alone. He saw her with a strange, impersonal pity. She seemed so slim and young and defenseless, so alone in the gray city. He realized that she was crying.

His heavy mature voice became young and shaky as he cried, "Dear, did I remember to tell you today that I adore you?"

The guard slammed the vestibule door, and as through an open window he craned to look back at her, he saw Kurt von Obersdorf running down the platform, he saw Fran droop into Kurt's arms, and he walked slowly into the roaring loneliness of his compartment.

CHAPTER 30

Kaleidoscope. Scarlet triangles and azure squares, crystalline zigzags and sullen black lines. Meaningless beauty and distortions that were the essence of pain. Such were the travels of Samuel Dodsworth, those summer months.

He longed to go home to Zenith, to have the solace of Tub and Matey, of Emily and Brent, of streets and corners and offices that respected him and did not sneer at him as an ignorant tourist. But to face the derision that would be his if he came back without Fran, to hear in every corner the delighted whispering which was the vicarious vengeance of men who wanted to be free of their own wives and took out their timorous hatred in snickering and twilight gossiping about the marital troubles of others--that he could not endure. And to face a gloating, damp, pawing pity, to face the morons who would suppose that he was so little that he would be gratified by their libeling Fran, his Fran, and by cumbersomely congratulating him on losing her, who was his very soul--that was not to be borne.

If he had had a job at home, he would probably have plunged back into it, and in a fury of papers and secretaries and telephone- calls have concealed himself from the scandal. But he hadn't. Just now the Sans Souci Gardens plan seemed to him as preposterous as his lifelong belief that he was man enough to hold his wife.

Yet twice, in Paris, he reserved passage to America, and twice he frugally went to the Cunard office and got back his passage money.

He crept over to London to hear the one language he knew, and fled from it because he did know the language, because some one might recognize him and pity him. He went on a German tour to the North Cape and the Baltic, got off at Riga, and fled from it because he did not know the language.

He returned to England, rented a motor, and toured along the old Roman road through Kent, stopping in villages of half-timbered houses and cottages covered with red tile shingles; into Sussex villages secret in still wooded valleys beneath the shining downs. He might have been seen, a very large man alone in a rather small car; a lone figure sitting on the sky-cut rim of a hill, hour on hour, clasping his knees, apparently brooding; a man alone in a public bar, listening to everything that was said--surprised and pleasant when some one spoke to him.

He felt the peace and security of the English valleys and farm-steads--and it made him the more restless because he was so definitely an outsider. He returned to Paris, and night after night he sat in American bars, and was put down as one of the beachcombers who have been something once but who have gone bankrupt--financially or nervously or alcoholically--and of whom one must pityingly beware.

He understood. So it came to pass that he spent most of his time alone, in his room in the Grand Universel. (It gave him a curious mean pleasure, now, to have a cheap single bedroom instead of a suite.) He drank a good deal. Sometimes he had a cognac instead of breakfast. But between blurred drowsinesses, he saw with clarity that he was utterly a man alone, that his work, his children, his friends, his habitual routine of life, and at last his wife, all the props and crutches with which he had been enabled to hobble through life as a Good Fellow, were gone, and that he had nothing upon which to depend except such solaces as he might find in his own brain. No one really needed him, and he was a man who had never been able to depend on any one to whom he could not give.

In childish, absurd ways he managed to kill time, day on day, in a fog which now and then mercifully concealed from him the needs of Samuel Dodsworth. Till noon he loafed in his room at the Grand Universel, frowsy in dressing-gown, taking an hour to read the Paris Tribune and Herald, taking half an hour to shave. He managed, once a fortnight, to spend an hour in having his hair cut, and though he tried to give the appearance of being a busy and important man, he was glad when he had to wait at the barber's; when he could, without looking ridiculous, spend that time in turning over Sketch and the Graphic. He took to having manicures-- he had despised the practise. He never admitted it to himself, but he neglected giving a hotel address to the Guaranty Trust, so that he might have a reason to plod to the bank for his mail every day.

He was grateful to the doormen and the mail clerks at the Guaranty Trust for treating him like some one who still mattered; and when he had a letter--they were few now, and most of them were from Fran, who seemed to desire to keep up a sisterly friendship with him-- he took it with fatuous dignity and retired to a table in front of a cafe on the Boulevard des Italiens to read it, to re- read it, though the most that he gathered was that she had found a charming new restaurant in Berlin.

Once a man who was asking for his mail at the Guaranty Trust said, "Aren't you Mr. Dodsworth of the Revelation Company? Met you, sir, at the motor show in New York."

Sam was so pleased that he asked the man to lunch, and telephoned to him often, to the end that the man, who had regarded Sam as one of his gods, saw that he was merely a solitary and common human being, and despised him and was uninterested.

And always Fran was with him, scolding at his weakness; always he saw her face. At twilight, and at three in the morning, when he could sleep no longer and rose to smoke a cigarette, he heard her saying, "Oh, Sam, I couldn't have BELIEVED that you could ever become a dirty drunk like this!" He nestled his head on her shoulder and weepingly confessed his failure as a human being and thereafter was racked with pity for her mad and gallant effort to be more than herself, so that he would gladly have done what he could to help Kurt to win her. . . . Samuel Dodsworth, so abnormally flushed that no friend of his hearty triumphant days would have recognized him, sitting on the edge of his bed, his hair wild and his pajamas wrinkled, smoking cigarettes, longing to telephone from Paris to Berlin and tell Fran that he hoped she would be the Countess Obersdorf, and kept from it chiefly by the thought that she wouldn't like it at all and would be very tart about it if he awoke her at three in the morning.

He had known unhappiness often enough, but never complete suffering like this--a suffering so vague and directionless and unreasonable that he raged at himself for his moody weakness--a suffering so confusing that he would have preferred any definite pain of the body. Fran was to him a madness. Now he cursed her for disloyalty and in long unmoving silences reviewed her superciliousnesses, but the result was no stout resolution to be free, but sudden pity for her--a fear that she would be slighted by Kurt's family--a picture of her alone and friendless, crying at twilight. He remembered in jagged reminiscences the most grotesquely assorted things--a white fur evening cape she had once had, and how she had prepared a lunch of coffee and salad and cold partridge on the roadside, when they had motored to

Detroit; her way of saying "I am a very sleepy young woman," and a
funny slatternly pair of pink wool bedroom slippers which she had
loved. He glowed in these relivings and came bolt out of them to ache
the more, till she was to him a spiritual virus from which he had to be
free.

He found Nande Azeredo; and he was rather completely untrue to Fran, and while he liked Nande, he could not persuade himself
to like being untrue.

He had gone back to the Cafe Select, hoping to see Elsa and
by some magic to take her away from the sharp-nosed Mr. Keipp.
There was no question now of willingness to be what he still called
"disloyal," there was only a question of keeping from going insane.
The moralities with which comfortably married clergymen concern
themselves did not exist for him now.

He did not see Elsa, and as he sat alone a tall, rather handsome
girl, with a face as broad between the cheek bones as a Tartar ambled
up, sat down uninvited, and demanded, in an English that sounded as
though it were played on a flute, "Vot's the trouble? You look down in
the mout'."

"I am. What would you like to drink?"

"Grand Marnier. . . . Did she die, or run away from you?"

"I'd rather not talk about it."

"So bad as that? Good. I talk about this place here. I will give
imitations of the people here."

And she did, merrily, not badly. She seemed to him quite the
brightest light he had found since Berlin. His guess was that she was
an artists' model; there were few professional prostitutes to be found at
the Dome or the Select, no matter how competent were some of the
amateurs.

She told him that she was Nande Azeredo, as though he ought
to know who she was.

Fernande Azeredo (he discovered presently) was half Portuguese, half Russian, and altogether French. She was twenty-five and
she had lived in nine countries, been married three times, and once
shot a Siberian wolf. She had been a chorus girl, a dress mannequin, a
masseuse, and now she scratched out a thin living by making wax
models for show-window dummies and called herself a sculptress. She
boasted that though she had had fifty-seven lovers ("And, my dear,

307

one was a real Prince--well, pretty real"), she had never let one of them give her anything save a few frocks.

And he believed her.

This alley-kitten--or alley-tigress--read him as such geniuses as Elsa and Keipp and Gillespie and Short had never done. She knew by divination that he was an American, a business man, graduate of a university; she knew that he had lost at love; she knew that essentially he was kindly and solid and not to be diverted by the obscenities with which she had amused other traveling Americans.

"You are a nize man. Maybe you buy me a dinner. Or I don't care a damn--you come to my little flat and I cook you a shop. I have not got no man, now. The last--oh, the dirty hound--I threw him out because he stole my fur coat and pawned it!"

And he believed her.

Her flushed vitality pleased him. Though she said nothing of importance, she uttered her little, profane, sage comments on the warfare between men and women with such vigor, she so assured him that he was large and powerful and real and that she preferred him to all of the limp poetasters about the place, that he was warmed by her companionship. And without mentioning Berlin or Kurt, without making it quite clear whether Fran had been sweetheart or wife, he forgot his "I'd rather not talk about it," and told her rather frankly of his illness.

Then he returned to his hotel, packed a bag, and spent three nights and days in the flat of Nande Azeredo.

She astonished him by the casual, happy, utterly proud way in which she served her Man. He had not known that any women save spinster secretaries could be happy in serving. She darned his socks and made him drink less cognac, she cooked snails for him so that he actually liked them, she taught him new ways of love, and when she found that he did not know them, she laughed at him, but affectionately. For the first time in his life he began to learn that he need not be ashamed of the body which God had presumably given him but which Fran had considered rather an error. He found in himself a power of intense passion such as, all his life, he had guiltily believed himself to lack; and sometimes Nande's flat seemed to him the Bower of Eden.

It was an insane little flat: three rooms, just under the roof, looking on a paved courtyard which smelled of slops and worse, and was all day clamorous with quarreling, children playing, delivery of charcoal, and the banging of garbage cans. Her dishes were cracked, her cups were chipped; the plaster walls were rain- streaked and Sam's roses she set out in a tin can; but on a couch covered with gold brocade lolled horribly a number of powdery-faced dolls, very elongated and expensive. Her clothes were in heaps and there was no concealment of sanitary appliances. And everywhere were instruments for the making of noise: a phonograph which by preference she turned on at three in the morning, rattles and horns left over from the last carnival, a very cheap radio--fortunately out of order--and seven canaries.

He could not, for a time, believe that Nande, whatever her virtues, was not calculating on what she would get out of him. When they were ambling the Rue de la Paix together (that street which Fran had seemed to know so well, but which Nande made living by telling the most scandalous tales about the shop-keepers and their favorites among the women clerks) he buzzed, "What'd you like me to buy you, Nan? Some pearls or--"

She stopped before him, planted her arms akimbo, and spoke furiously. "I am not vot you call a gold-digger! I am not lady enough! If when you get tired of me, you vant to give me a hundred dollars--or fifty--fine. But you must, by God, understand, when Nande Azeredo takes a man, it iss because she likes him! Pearls? What would I do with pearls? Can I eat pearls?"

She worked daily--though not for very many hours daily--at her atrocious modeling, and somehow she managed to bring him in precisely the sorts of English books he wanted: Shelley, for the vanity of remembering that he had been a University Man before he became a beachcomber, and detective stories, which he really read.

"Lord!" he reflected, "what a wife she'd make for a pioneer! She'd chuck this Parisian show like a shot, if she loved somebody. She'd hoe the corn, she'd shoot the Indians, she'd nurse the babies--and if she couldn't get Paris lingerie, she'd probably spin it."

But it was just her admirable vigor which after three days wearied him.

It was amusing, the first time, to see Nande, arms akimbo, in a shawl or a chemise, denouncing the grocer's boy for an overcharge of thirty centimes, denouncing him with so many applications of the epithet "Camel" that he blanched and fled. But it was much less amusing, the twentieth time she quarreled with tradesmen, waiters, taxi-drivers, and motorists--who, she believed, were in a conspiracy to run her down--and with Sam himself, for not eating more. She was so shrill:

her conversations started with a shriek and ended with a howl. He longed for a decent quiet. And always he saw Fran watching Nande and himself in mockery.

Whenever he stoutly convinced himself that Nande was beautiful as a young tigress and a miracle of loyal kindness, the cool wraith of Fran appeared, and Nande seemed then a blowsy gutter-looper. To his angry defense of Nande, Fran answered with the look she gave rude servants. She watched while Nande scrubbed the floor, bawling indecent lyrics; she slipped through the room just as Nande cheered Sam by slapping his rear; and he was turned into a schoolboy caught with the kitchen maid.

So he told Nande that business called him to Italy. She pretended to believe him; she begged him to be careful of cognac and women; she casually accepted a present of a hundred dollars; she saw him off.

As the train was starting, she slipped into his hand a little package.

He looked at it an hour or two afterward. It contained a gold cigarette case which must have cost her all of his hundred dollars.

Nande Azeredo!

He never wrote to Nande. He wanted to, but she was not one to whom you could say anything on paper.

She seemed to him a character in a play; a rather fantastic and overacted character; but she had definitely done something to him. She had, along with the glances of Minna von Escher, broken down all the celibacy which had plagued him, and however much he still fretted over Fran, imagined her loneliness in Berlin, let himself be wrung by pity for her self-dramatizing play at romance which was bound to turn into tragedy, he no longer felt himself her prisoner, and he began to see that this world might be a very green and pleasant place.

He was more conscious of the wagon lit than he had ever been, for he was wondering if he might not spend much of his life, now, in those homes for people who flee from life. . . . Blue upholstered seat, rather hard, with hard cylindrical cushions. Above the blue velvet, yellow and brown florid stamped leather, rough to a speculative touch. The Alarm Signal to stop the train, all labeled nicely in four languages for the linguistic instruction of tourists, which he always longed to pull, even if it cost him five hundred lire. The tricky little cabinet in the corner which turned into a wash-stand when one let down the folding shelf. And the detached loneliness of which he rid himself now and then by poking out into the corridor, to lean against the brass rail across the broad low windows, or to sit on the tiny folding seat. And outside, mountains; stations with vacant-faced staring loungers; plains which seemed to him altogether like the American Middlewest till suddenly the sun, revealing a high and distant castle on an abrupt cliff, restored to him the magic of foreignness.

Till now, Sam Dodsworth had never greatly heeded fellow passengers, except Americans who looked as though they might be good fellows with whom to gossip and have a drink. Of most of them, had you demanded a description from him after the journey, he would have said, "Oh, they looked about like anybody else, I guess--why?" He saw them not as trees walking but as clothes sitting.

But the incredible jar of being dismissed by Fran, the opening of his eyes to the possibilities of misery in the world, made him feel the universal pathos of things more sensitively than he had even on the exalted night when he had first beheld the lights of England. He felt-- no doubt sentimentally--akin to everything that was human; he saw-- no doubt often without reason--a drama, tragic or comic, behind all the face-masks of travelers, behind surly faces, stupid faces, mean faces, common faces. He a little forgot himself--and Fran and Kurt and Nande Azeredo--as he wondered whether that tight- mouthed woman had recently been burying her husband, whether that overdressed young salesman had a nagging wife at home, whether that petulant and snarling old man had lost his fortune. He studied the railroad workmen who stood back to let the train pass, and speculated as to which of them was about to be married, which was an ecstatically religious communist, which was longing to murder his wife.

Thus brooding, hour-long, not having to hasten back to the compartment and entertain Fran. Thus slowly and painfully perceiving a world vaster than he had known. Thus considering whether he was so badly beaten, so enfeebled by Fran's scorn, that he could never find the Not Impossible She and, with her, experience the not impossible self-confidence and peace.

He poked about Rome for a week, trying to persuade himself that he was studying architecture. It was hot, and he fled to Montreux, with a notion of swimming and cool mountains. Daily he examined schedules of sailings for New York and surmised that one of these days would find him fleeing aboard a steamer. He drifted to Geneva, solemnly viewed the League of Nations building, and in his hotel

311

wondered which of the not very exciting-looking gentlemen with top hats were famous ministers of state. Then, in a small restaurant, he heard, like an angelic trump, the voice of Ross Ireland, the correspondent: "Well, Sam, you old devil, where did you come from!"

They had many drinks.

With Ross he tramped for a week, rucksack on shoulders, through the Bernese Oberland. He felt rather foolish, at first, to be carrying a sack and walking dustily past large hotels, for he had been trained to feel that it was undignified for him to walk, except on a duck pass or a golf course. But he enjoyed seeing a view without the need, as a rich, busy, and motorized tourist, of having to hustle past it; he found himself breathing deeper, sleeping better, brooding less, and drinking beer instead of cognac. In fact he believed that he had discovered walking, and wrote enthusiastic recommendations of it on post cards to Fran, Tub, and Dr. Hazzard. He came to feel superior to large, plushy hotels. Ross and he ate dumplings and pig's knuckle; they rested at tiny tables in front of inns when they had panted into a village, sweaty and shoulders aching.

Ross insisted that whenever they "saw church-steeples and heard the bright prattle of children," those were the signs certain and indivisible of the proximity of beer, and however much they enjoyed the mountain-side lanes, they cheered up and hastened their step and began to listen for the bright prattle as soon as they saw a church steeple.

And Sam decided what he would do with the wreckage of his life.

He had not known that wandering could be so satisfying as it was with Ross Ireland, who never complained and became superior like Fran, or felt bound to be funny like Tub, or noisy like Nande; who was interested in everything from pig-pens to cloisters; and who enjoyed erecting theories of life more than anything save tearing them down.

Ross was going to the Orient again, after summer in Europe. He invited Sam to come along and Sam accepted, with more tingling anticipation than he had known since he had first sailed for England. . . . Turkestan, Borneo, Siam, Pekin, Penang and the sight of Java Head!

Ross was called to Paris, but that city meant for Sam, now, only too much loneliness and too much Nande, and he squatted in Gstaad, trying to be very healthy and full of fresh air. And before Ross had been gone forty-eight hours, Sam was thrown back into as much fidgety fretting as he had ever known.

He cursed himself for his weakness; he sought to sink himself in an enormous volume on English Gardens and Domestic Architecture of the Eighteenth Century; he sought to recapture a longing for the Orient; and it was in vain.

Bluntly, he could not go off to the Far East and leave Fran unprotected.

Oh, he told himself she did not need protection. His presence irritated her more than it soothed her, and he was a fool, and a puerile and whining fool, not to be able to cut loose from his mother's apron strings, now inconveniently worn by a wife. But--If anything went wrong there in Berlin--If Fran wanted to run to him for help, and he should be ten thousand miles away--

He couldn't do it.

He wondered, occasionally, if he wasn't confusing the need to serve Fran with the need of women in general, that basic need which he had just consciously discovered; he wondered whether, if it were a woman with some of Ross Ireland's sportsmanship and inquiring mind who had invited him to come along, he would not have found it possible to go, armored with a good, round, satisfying cliche like "Fran made her bed; let her lie in it."

No! He swore to himself that his care for Fran was authentic; was to him what prayer was to a hermit, and honor to a soldier; and always he wound up his fretful meditations with, "Oh, hell, I can't analyse it, but I'm not going to desert her! Only wish I could!"

He wrote Ross not to count on his company this coming autumn, and again fled from himself, but with himself, to Venice, because the current news photographs from the Lido, the pictures of gay companies on the beach, made it seem a place to divert a solitary man. And perhaps one of these exquisite gold and ivory Englishwomen--

No! He didn't want that sort. He wanted some one with Fran's fineness but with Nande's sturdiness, Ross Ireland's brains.

He was able to laugh at himself: "If there were such a woman anywhere, what would she want with you?"

But as, in the too-familiar blue-velvet and stamped leather wagon lit compartment, he clanked on toward Venice, he was not quite

313

Lewis

free of the pictures of lovely ladies on Lido beach; not quite sure that
he had in life any purpose beyond the quest of the Not Impossible She.

CHAPTER 31

Sam was not particularly enlivened by the Lido in season. The hotels seemed to him to smack of the Chicago World's Fair of 1893 with the added flavor of a Turkish bath; and the intimacy with which two-thirds of this basking, bathing, lunching, dancing society knew one another, whether they were Italian, English, American, or Austrian, made him feel utterly the outsider. He moved back into Venice, to the Bauer-Grunwald which, despite a German atmosphere which too readily reminded him of his Berlin debacle, was more welcoming than the Royal Danieli.

Venice is the friendliest city in the world. There are other cities in which friendlier people may be found, but in Venice it is the city itself, the spectacle of the Piazza San Marco, the cozy little streets, the open-fronted shops of the coppersmiths, the innumerable churches that are always open, the alternately effusive and quarrelsome gondoliers, the greedy but amiable pigeons, the soft sky, the rustling water of the Grand Canal, the cafes thrusting their tables halfway across the Piazza, the palaces so proud in their carved balconies and so cheerfully poverty-stricken in their present inhabitants, the crowd with nothing to do save stroll and wait for the band concerts, which are so amiable that here less than anywhere else in the world does the stranger miss the warm gossip of people whom he knows.

Sam found the waiting into which all his life had turned now more tolerable than it had been at any time save when he had been drugged with fatigue on his walking tour with Ross, or save when that rather soiled Salvationist, Nande Azeredo, had stooped to save him. He lay abed till nine, content with the sound of the Grand Canal outside his windows, the squabbles of gondoliers. He rose to lean placidly on the sill and look at the wonders of Santa Maria della Salute and San Giorgio Maggiore, seeming, on their tiny islands, to be floating out to sea; to watch the panorama of vegetable scows, brick scows, cement scows, wangling their way into side canals, while the bargees quarreled magnificently with the more aristocratic gondoliers and with the uniformed drivers of motor boats belonging to officials. He had a meager cup of coffee, and, buying the latest Paris Daily Mail, Chicago Tribune, and New York Herald on the way, ambled to the Piazza for his real breakfast.

In the afternoon, Florian's and the Aurora were the accepted haunts, shaded then from the biting sun, but in the morning it was the Quadri and Lavena's which were sheltered, and at one of these cafes he drank his coffee, nibbled at croissants smeared with clouded honey from Monte Rosa, and read the papers, excited at the news from Washington and New York, excited when he saw that some one he knew, Ross Ireland or Endicott Everett Atkins, had dined with a Celebrity at Ciro's. . . . And once, in the Berlin news, he saw that Mrs. Samuel Dodsworth had been the guest of honor at a dinner given by the Princess Drachenthal and that among those present had been the Count of Obersdorf, the Baroness de Jeune, Sir Thomas Jenkins of the Allied Commission, and the newly made Geheimrat, Dr. Biedner. He sat for a long time, looking vacantly across the Piazza, at the spate of tourists whose wives were kodaking them in the act of feeding the pigeons of St. Mark.

He worked at his new game of architecture. With Ruskin's "Stones of Venice" under his arm, he saw daily a new church, a new palace, and now and then he made sketches, not very bad, and was not displeased when loudly commenting tourists mistook him for an authentic artist. He lunched simply; he slept for an hour afterward, and betook himself then to the one real duty of a wise visitor in Venice--to spend most of the afternoon and evening sitting in the Piazza and doing nothing whatever save watch the spectacle.

It had been agreeable in Paris or on Unter den Linden to watch the parade, but there the motors, the horses, the brisk policemen had made it a hard and somewhat nervous spectacle. Here, where there was no traffic, where the marble-walled piazza was like a stage with the chorus of an incredibly elaborate comic opera, there was only a lazy and unharassed contentment. The crowd changed, every second. Now two Fascist officers paced by, trim in black shirts, olive-green uniforms, and gold-badged and tasseled service caps. Now it was two carbinieri with the cocked hats of Napoleon and the solemn manner of judges. Now a tourist steamer vomited a rush of excited novices-- inquiring Germans or stolid English, golden-haired Scandinavians, or Americans of whom the women were thrilled and the males cocked up their cigars and announced, very publicly, that if THIS was Venice, they didn't think it was so doggone much!

The guides, slightly less numerous but much more insistent than the cloud of pigeons, attacked every one who was not entirely engaged in the sacred act of being photographed, and yammered, "Me gide spik fine English, show you San Marco." The children fell under everybody's feet. The gatherers of cigarettes swooped on each butt as it fell. The English couples went by amiably contemptuous. And at last the sunset turned the dark leaded glass behind the horses of San Marco into gold.

He was content, by comparison with his active agonizing in Paris. But he was also lonely, despite the show of the Piazza. He had to have some one to talk to, and never did he meet any one whom he knew.

It was not easy for him to pick up acquaintances. Once he sat at a table next to a party of Americans. They did not seem very complex and difficult; they looked like small town merchants and professional men with their wives; and Sam took the chance. He leaned toward the nearest, a spectacled little man, and drawled, "On a tour?"

The little man looked scornfully cautious. HE'D read the papers! HE wasn't going to be taken in by any of your slick international crooks!

He sniffed "Yes," and he did not embroider it.

"Uh--enjoying Italy?"

"Yes, thanks!"

The little man turned his back, and Sam was flushed and shamed and much lonelier than before.

He was grateful when he was picked up by a large and lugubrious and green-hatted Bavarian who was apparently even more desolate than himself, and though they had in common only a hundred words of English, twenty of German, and ten of Italian, they were both strong men who could endure a lot of gesturing. They gave each other confidence in battling with gondoliers, and together they lumbered to the Colleoni and SS. Giovanni e Paolo, gaped at the glass-makers at Murano, and visited the Armenian monastery on the peaceful isle of San Lazzaro. Sam saw the Bavarian friend off at the station as regretfully as he had seen Ross Ireland off at Interlaken, and all that evening he clung to his favorite table at Florian's as though it was his only home.

He heard regularly from Fran, but where once her letters had been festal, now he hesitated to open them.

She complained a good deal. It had been rainy--it had been hot. She had gone to the Tyrol for a week (she did not say that Kurt had come along but he guessed it) and the hotels had been crowded. She had suffered unparalleled misfortune in having to stay at a small hotel where the food was heavy and the guests heavier. She had met a cousin of Kurt, an Austrian ambassador, and though she had showered blessings of wit and courtesy on the fellow, he had not appreciated her.

As to whether Sam himself was any happier, she never inquired.

Her letters left him always a little blue. And they did not suggest that she would like to see him.

He was in the Piazza, meditating on one of these letters, a little after four of a blazing afternoon. He saw a familiar-looking woman pass his table. She was perhaps forty; she was slim, rather pale. She wore black crepe, without ornament, and a wide black hat with a tiny brooch of brilliants. Her hands were as fine as lace.

He remembered. It was Mrs. Cecil R. A. Cortright, Edith Cortright, American-born widow of the British minister to Roumania (or was it Bulgaria?) who, on a hint from Tub's nephew, had asked them to tea at her flat in the Palace Ascagni in Venice, months ago. He darted up, to welcome the first recognizable face he had seen in weeks; he hesitated--Mrs. Cortright was not the sort of woman one greeted carelessly. He ventured again. He tossed a ten lira note on the table for the waiter, and, circling the square with his long stride, so arranged it that he met her as she was passing through the Piazzetta dei Leoni and entering the Calle di Canonica.

"Oh, how d'you do," he observed. "Do you remember having my wife and me to tea last spring--friends of Jack Starling--"

"Oh, but of course! Mr.--?"

"Samuel Dodsworth."

"You and Mrs. Dodsworth HAVE come back here soon."

"Oh, she's, uh, she had to stay in Berlin."

"Really? You're here alone? You must come to tea again."

318

"Be awfully glad to. You walking this way?" Quite fatuously, rather eagerly.

"Just a bit of shopping. There's a rabbit-warren of a pastry shop down here--Perhaps you'd like to come along, and come home for a cup of tea this afternoon, if you haven't friends waiting for you."

"I don't know a soul in town."

"In that case, you must come, surely."

He rolled beside her, bumbling, "Must be an awful lot of people you know at the Lido now, with the season on."

"Yes. Unfortunately!"

"Don't you like the rotogravure set?"

"Oh, that is a nice thing to call them!" she said. "I've been looking for a phrase. Some of them are extremely agreeable, of course; nice simple people who really like to dance and swim and don't go to the Lido just to be seen and photographed. But there's an international, Anglo-American-French set--smart women, just a little ambiguous, and men with titles and tailors and nothing much else, and sharp couples that play bridge too well, and three-necked millionaires that--well, they seem to me like a menagerie. There's a dreadful woman named Renee de Penable--"

"Oh, you know her?"

"How can any one help it! The woman contrives to be simultaneously in Paris, the Lido, Deauville, Cannes, New York, and on all known trains and steamers! You know her? Do you like her?"

"Hate her," remarked Sam. "Oh, I don't know's I ought to say that. She's always been awfully decent to us. But I feel she's a grafter."

"No, she's subtler than that. She is quite generous to ninety nine out of a hundred of her group--tramps in goldfoil!--so that she can get the dazzled hundredth to set her up in a gown shop or a charity society or something else that mysteriously collapses in two months. She's--oh, she's very amusing, of course."

"Neither do I!" roared Sam.

They smiled at each other, to the approval of seven youthful Venetians engaged in doing nothing and choosing the dimmest and smelliest Sottoportico to do it in.

Sam rejoiced that Edith Cortright might prove to be human, patient with large lost men. He was surer of it as he heard her bartering with the owner of the minute pastry shop for a dozen cakes. The proprietor demanded five lire, Mrs. Cortright offered two, and they compromised on three, which were their probable value.

Often enough Sam had seen Fran chaffering, but she was likely to lose her temper, more likely to make the shop-keeper lose his. With Mrs. Cortright, the baker shook his fingers, agonized over the insult to his masterpieces, asserted that his nine children and grandmother would starve, but she only laughed, and all the while he laughed back. He took the three lire with the greatest cheerfulness, and cried after them, "Addio!" as though it were a blessing.

"The good soul!" said Mrs. Cortright as they returned to the Piazza. "We do that every week. That's really the reason why I go to him myself, instead of sending a maid, who gets them for twenty centesimi less than I do, probably, and pockets ten. But this patissier is an artist, and like all artists, a conservative. He tries to keep up the good old days when buying and selling in Italy really was an adventure, because everybody made a game of bargaining--the days that Baedeker wrote of when he tells you to 'keep a calm and pleasant demeanor, when haggling.' But that's all passing, I'm afraid. Between the regulations of the Fascists, and the efficient business of impressing tourists, the shops are becoming as dependable as Swan and Edgar's or a Woolworth's, and about as appealing. I think I'll go back and end my few declining years on Mulberry Street, in New York. That's about the only part of Italy, now, that hasn't been toured and described and painted and guided to death; the only part that hasn't been made safe for the vicar's aunt."

In the presence of Fran and her aggressive smartness, Edith Cortright had been abrupt, hiding her heart behind dutiful courtesy as she hid her taut frailness of body beneath frocks of soft, non- committal black. But now, as they tramped to the Palazzo Ascagni, avoiding the sun in arcades and under vast walls above tiny streets, as they climbed the sepulchral marble stairs to her flat, and sighingly relaxed in the coolness of the vast rooms behind blinds streaked with poisonous sun, she was easy; in a subdued silvery manner, she was gay. It was as though she found everything in life amusing and liked to think about it aloud. And she seemed younger. He had thought her forty-five; now she seemed forty.

The stone floor of her drawing-room, laid in squares waxed to ivory smoothness, the old walnut of a Sixteenth Century armoire, suggested quietness, a feeling of civilization grown secure and placid through generations. The formal monastic chairs which had dignified the room when Sam had seen it in the spring--as well as the shameless over-stuffed Americanized arm-chairs with which Mrs. Cortright had eased the rigor of Venetian stateliness--had been replaced by wicker with chintz cushions.

Sam's spirit was refreshed here, his hot body was refreshed, and when Mrs. Cortright showed herself so superior to Expatriate Americanism that she dared to be American and to offer iced tea, he rejoiced in her more than in the mosaics of St. Mark's, which he had taught himself to admire with a quite surprising amount of sincerity. Mrs. Cortright and the room which illustrated her seemed to him quite as traditional as the faded splendors of the Princess Drachenthal at Potsdam; but he could reach Mrs. Cortright, understand her, not feel with her like an inanely smirking boy invited to tea by the schoolmaster's wife. He was a little afraid of her, a little afraid that behind her pallid restraint there might be comment on such a stumbling tourist as himself. But it was a fear that he could understand and answer, not a bewildering midnight strangeness.

He saw that in an age of universal bobbing, when no Fran would have dared be so eccentric, Mrs. Cortright kept her hair long, parted simply and not too neatly. And he saw again the lovely hands moving like white cats among the cups of taffy-colored majolica.

She did not talk, this time, of diplomats and Riviera villas and painting. She said:

"Tell me--Really, I'm not impertinent; I ask myself the same thing, and perhaps I'm looking for an answer for myself. What do you find in Europe? Why do you stay on?"

"Well, it's kind of hard to say." He sipped his iced tea, appreciative of the thin tart taste against his tongue. "Oh, I guess--Well, to be absolutely frank, it's because of my wife. I've enjoyed coming abroad. I've learned a lot of things--not only about pictures and all that, but in my own line--I'm a motor manufacturer, if you remember. For instance, I went to the Rolls- Royce works in England, and it was a perfect revelation to me, the way they were willing to lose money by going on having things like polishing done by hand instead of by machinery, as we'd do them, because they felt they were better done by hand. But--oh, I can understand how the artists that hang around places like Florence, and that don't care whether the government is monarchial or communist as long as the tea and the sunsets are good, can be perfectly content to stay there for years. But me--I'm getting restless at being so much of an outsider. I feel like the small boy that's never consulted about where the picnic will be held. I suppose I'm awfully low-brow not to care for any more galleries and ruins but--oh, I want to go home and MAKE something! Even if it's only a hen-coop!"

"But couldn't you make that here? In England, for example?"

"No. I'd feel the English chickens wouldn't understand my speaking American, and probably go and die on me."

"Then you don't want to stay? Why do you?"

"Oh, well, my wife still feels--"

Swiftly, as though she were covering a blunder, Mrs. Cortright murmured, "And of course she is lovely. I remember her with such pleasure. She must be an enchanting person to wander with. . . . And please don't feel that I'm one of those idiots who regard painting as superior to manufacturing--I neither regard it as inferior, as do your Chambers of Commerce who think that all artists are useless unless they're doing pictures for stocking advertisements, nor do I regard it as superior, as do all the supercilious lady yearners who suppose that a business man with clean nails invariably prefers golf to Beethoven."

It was not brilliant talk, nor did it dazzle Sam by novelty. In both Europe and America he had encountered all the theories about modern business men: that they were the kings and only creators in the industrial age: that they were dull and hideous despots. He had hacked out his own conclusion: that they were about like other people, as as-sorted as cobblers, labor leaders, Javanese dancers, throat specialists, whalers, minor canons, or asparagus-growers. Yet in the talk of Edith Cortright there was a sympathy, an apparent respect for him, a sugges-tion that she had seen many curious lands and known many curious people, which inspirited him. Incredulously, he found himself trying to outline his philosophy of life for her; more incredulously, found him-self willing to admit that he hadn't any. She nodded, as in like confession.

He urged: "I've enjoyed talking with you. Look here: Would I be rude if I asked you to go for a gondola ride, now it's getting cooler, and possibly dine with me on the Lido this evening, if you're free? I've been, uh--kind of lonely."

"I should be glad to, but I can't. You see my friends here are mostly the rather stuffy, frightfully proper, very sweet old Italian fam-ily sort who haven't yet got over being shocked by Colleoni. I'm afraid I couldn't go out in a gondola with you unless I were chaperoned--

bedragoned--which would be a frightful bore. But won't you come here to dinner tomorrow evening--eight- thirty, black tie?"

"Be pleased to. Eight-thirty. . . . But why do you stay in Europe?"

"Oh . . . I suppose America terrifies me. I feel insecure there. I feel everybody watching me, and criticizing me unless I'm buzzing about Doing Something Important--uplifting the cinema or studying Einstein or winning bridge championships or breeding Schnauzers or something. And there's no privacy, and I'm an extravagant woman when it comes to the luxury of privacy."

"But look here! In America you could certainly go gondoling--well, motoring--as you liked. Here you have to be chaperoned to avoid criticism!"

"Only with one class--the formal people that I've chosen (wisely or foolishly) to live with. My grocer and my dentist and my neighbor on the floor below (amiable-looking person--I rather fancy he's a gambler)--they don't feel privileged to help me conduct my af-fairs, or rather, they wouldn't if I were so adventurous as to be conducting any! At home, they would. It's only in Europe that you can have the joy of anonymity, of being lost in the crowd, of being your-self, of having the dignity of privacy!"

"You try New York! Get lost enough there!"

"Oh, but NEW YORK--Self-conscious playing at internation-alism! Russian Jews in London clothes going to Italian restaurants with Greek waiters and African music! One hundred per cent. mon-grels! No wonder Americans flee back home to Sussex or Somerset! And never, day or night or dawn, any escape from the sound of the Elevated! New York--no. But I am sure that there is still a sturdy, na-tive America--and not Puritanical, either, any more than Lincoln or Franklin were Puritanical--that you know. But tell me (to get away from my lost, expatriate, awfully unoriented and unimportant self), tell me frankly: what have you seen in Europe-- I mean that you'll remem-ber ten years from now?"

He slumped in his chair, he rubbed his chin, and sighed:

"Well, I guess about as much as I'd get out of reading the steamship and hotel ads in a New York Sunday paper! I know a little less than when I started. Then, I knew that all Englishmen were icicles, all Frenchmen chattered, and all Italians sat around in the sun singing. Now I don't even know that much. I suspect that most Englishmen are friendly, most Frenchmen are silent, and most Italians work like the devil--pardon me!"

"Exactly!"

"I've learned to doubt everything. I've learned that even a fairly successful executive--and I WAS that, no matter how much of a loafer I seem now--"

"Oh, I know!"

"I've learned that even a fairly good garage boss like myself isn't much good at deciding between Poiret and Lanvin, or between Early English and Decorated. No American business man ought to go abroad, ever, except to a Rotary convention, or on a conducted tour where he's well insulated from furriners. Upsets him. Spoils his pleasure in his own greatness and knowledge! . . . What have I learned? Let's see: The names of maybe fifty hotels, of which I'll remember five, in a few years. The schedules of half a dozen de luxe trains. The names of a few brands of Burgundy. How to tell a Norman doorway from Gothic. How to order from a French menu--providing there's nothing unusual on the bill. And I can say 'How much' and 'TOO much' in English, French, German, Italian, and Spanish. And I think that's about all I've learned here. I guess they caught me too late!"

CHAPTER 32

With his second drink, at Florian's, after dinner, he recaptured a rare exhilarating glow at the thought of travel, alone and fast. He could go as he would: North, South--the very names had magic: NORTH and snow-drifts among silent pines; SOUTH and bamboo huts in the jungle; EAST and a cranky steamer jogging up a purple strait; WEST and a bench by a log cabin in the Rockies, with a lake two thousand feet below, and himself, strong and deep-breathing as he had been at thirty, smelling the new-cut chips, the frosty air. Yes! He would see them all! He wouldn't go back to an office!

He had twenty, perhaps thirty years more. He would have a second life; having been Samuel Dodsworth he would go on and miraculously be some one else, more ruthless, less bound, less sentimental. He could be a poet, a governor, an explorer. He'd learned his faults of commercial-mindedness, of timidity before women. Correct 'em! He'd seen the gaps in his knowledge. Fill 'em!

Twenty years more!

Start right now. Tomorrow he would take up Italian. Tomorrow he would write to Ross Ireland about that jaunt to the Orient. Yes!

After the comfort of tea with Edith Cortright, he had been lonelier than ever. For five minutes he had planned to flee to Fran. But fried scampi and a drink solaced him; a second drink set his imagination dancing. Then he wanted another drink--and didn't want it.

No! He shook himself. He hated this flabby, easy escape through alcohol into a belief in his own power and freedom. He wasn't (proudly) one of the weaklings who took refuge from problems in the beautiful peace of the gutter, where the slime covered one's ears from the nasal voices of the censors who were always demanding of a tired man a little more than he could do.

But was that true? Was anything he had thought true--even this easy disgust at easy escape? Was it possible that he was unable to fall permanently into drunkenness, to disintegrate, to scorn all decent scorn and be content with a Nande Azeredo in a stinking garret, not because he was too strong but because he was too weak-- too weakly afraid of what Fran, Tub, Matey, strangers like Mrs. Cortright, would say? Was it possible that it took more courage to be a hobo, deliberate, out and out, than to go on living like a respectable manufacturer while he ached like a Verlaine? Was dry rot really braver than a moist and dripping rage of defiance?

He gave it up.

He was so tired of dragging out his little soul and worrying over it! If he could only be laughing, unthinking, with Tub Pearson. Or if Mrs. Cortright had been willing to dine with him--

Mrs. Cortright. Now there was a woman! As proper as Fran and as worldly, yet as indifferent to titles and luxury as Nande.

"Mighty sweet woman!"

He thought again about that third drink, then vehemently didn't want it, vehemently retired into the respectability from which for a moment he had thought he might escape. For at the next table was an American party, full of merriment and keeping their brother from falling by setting an edifyingly bad example.

There were three men, three women. Apparently some of them were married to some of the others, but they seemed confused as to who was married to whom.

They noted Sam, and one of the men staggered over to shout, "American, ain't you? Well, say, why the lone fiesta? Come over and join a live bunch!"

Rather pleased, Sam went over and joined.

"Just arrived?" he asked, as was proper.

"You bet. Landed at Naples, yesterday," said his host. "Came over on a Wop ship--elegant boat too--and say, boy, that was some trip, too, I'll tell the cock-eyed world! Say, I've heard about wet voyages, but this trip--say, I bet I never went to bed before three G.M. once, the whole way over! And the girls--say, they were just as good as the men. Dorine here, she drank two bols champagne in two hours, and the whole bunch were so crazy about the Italian officers--say, the officers had to brush 'em off the bridge every time they wanted to do any fancy navigating! And that gave us boys a chance to get in a little petting ourselves! Some trip! Say, if you could have seen the nightshirt parade the last night out! Boy! Some trip!"

326

One of the women--and save for her damp eyes a most spinsterish and unaphrodisiac lady she appeared--cried, "Some trip is right! And I've got a date to meet the second officer in Paris. He's going to lay off one trip. And maybe I'll just keep him laid off. Maybe I'll decide to buy me a nice little boy friend. Some baby! Oh, those Or-iental eyes! Say, Pete, for the love o' Gawd, ain't you going to buy our little friend here"--she pointed at Sam with a thin, chaste, overmanicured, and rather wobbly forefinger--"a lil drink?"

But Sam declined. His vision of the beauties of the gutter had vanished with haste and a ludicrous squawking. He was grimly again the Sam Dodsworth who was proud of keeping in shape. He accepted, with irritating signs of pleasure, a lemonade (it was the first he had tasted in months) and sat wondering about these fellow- countrymen.

He could not place them. In age they seemed to run from thirty to forty. They were not so vulgar nor so vicious as at first they seemed. Once in a while they were betrayed by alcohol into revealing that they did have vocabularies and had perhaps read a book. He suspected that two out of the three men were university graduates; that all six of these loud-mouthed libertines were, at home, worthy deacons and pallbearers. He had known in Zenith of "young married couples," theoretically responsible young doctors and lawyers and salesmen, who turned dances at country clubs into a combination of brothel and frontier bar. But he had not gone to such dances. These people were none of his! Then, shocked, he realized that perhaps they were. Were these oafs anything but younger and gayer and slightly more amorous Tub Pearsons?

They were not altogether to blame. They were the products of Prohibition, mass production, and an education dominated by the beliefs that one goes to college to become acquainted with people who will later be useful in business, and that the greatness of a university is in ratio to the number of its students and the number of its athletic victories.

Or so Sam brooded.

He had heard much of the "sexually cold American woman." Heaven knows, he raged, he had felt it in Fran! Yet with these riotous women, it was the lack of chill which he resented. The amiable lady who was going to "buy her" a second officer had, during Sam's stay at the table, kissed one of the men, held the hand of another, and was now turning her withered excitement on himself: "Say, you're some husk! Gee, I bet you hurt the lil ole golf ball's feelings when you slam it one!"

He smiled bleakly.

He thought of seeing Mrs. Cortright next evening. He had recalled her only as a pleasant, unexciting, worthy person, but now he saw her as a Grecian vase, he saw her as a bowl of alabaster within which a fire could be lighted.

"A finish to her--like a European," he reflected. "Yet she's American, thank God! I couldn't fall for a real European. Has to be somebody that could look at an old gray New England barn with the frost on it, in October, and get a kick out of it, without my having to explain."

His long, ambling thoughts were interrupted by his original host's inquiring:

"You been here in Venice some time?"

"Yes. Several times."

"Well, maybe you can explain--Hope I'm not stepping all over anybody's feet, but me--Well, this is the first time I've ever been abroad, and I'd always thought Venice would be kinda like a musical comedy. But of all the darn' slow places--Why, there isn't a first-class cabaret in town! Nothing but a lot of run-down tenements with a lot of carvin's on 'em and a bunch of Chicago Drainage Ditches in between!"

"Well, I like it!"

"But what do you like about it?"

"Oh, lots of things. Especially the architecture."

But what his mind saw, as he blurted out something about being tired and took his leave, was no vision of arching bridges, of secret alleys and the quivering reflection of airy towers; it was the memory of Edith Cortright serene in her Venetian palace.

"She couldn't possibly go out and grab things, like Fran," he reflected, as he clumped toward the Bauer-Grunwald. "She's definitely a 'great lady.' Yet I'll bet that at heart she's lonely. She wouldn't mind cooking for her man any more than Nande would. Oh, damn it, Sam, why are you so simple? Why do you insist on thinking everybody else is lonely, merely because you are?"

It was a small and placid dinner at Edith Cortright's, on Thursday evening. The only guests besides Sam were an English couple who were vaguely and politely something important--very politely but very vaguely. If Sam did not find them cheery, he was amused by the pleasant carelessness of Mrs. Cortright's household.

The Fran who liked to quote poems about Gipsies and Villon and the Brave Days When We Were Twenty-one was, in private life, a sergeant major. Theoretically, she was the mother confessor and breezy confidante of all her servants and of the plumber, the postman, and the bootlegger. Practically she was always furious at their incompetence. She was chummy with them only when they assured her of her beauty and power; when the seamstress gurgled that Fran had the most exquisite figure in Zenith, or when the corner druggist asked her if his new hat was really correct English style.

Or so Sam brooded.

Edith Cortright seemed to have no discipline, no notion as to her servants' duties. They argued with her. They contradicted her. The butler said that she HAD ordered broccoli; and the maid came in with clacking slippers. They were always chattering. They seemed to be sharing some secret joke with her; and when she smiled at Sam, in her tired way, after a voluble colloquy with the butler, he wished he could be admitted to their tribal companionship.

A stone floor the dining-room had, and walls of hard plaster, with strips of Syrian embroidery. About the walls were chairs, stately, uncomfortable, inhuman. The windows, giving on the Grand Canal, were immensely tall. It was an apartment for giants to live in. Sam felt that into this room had strode men in armor who with gigantic obscene laughter had discussed the torture of pale protestants against the Doge, and that they; not so unlike Edith Cortright for all her gentleness, had guffawed here with servants purple-uniformed, slatternly, and truculent.

The English couple crept away early. After their flutter of good- bye's, Sam lumbered to his feet and sighed, "I guess I'd--"

"No. Stay half an hour."

"If you'd really--And how I have come to hate hotels!"

"You really liked having a home."

"I certainly did!"

"Why do you stay away from it? Isn't it--"

Then she laughed, lighted a cigarette, held it with arching fingers. "I suppose it's rather ludicrous, my trying to give advice--and my own life such a mess that I endure it only by getting rid of all ambition, all purpose, and just floating, trying to get along with as little complication as possible."

They talked slowly, and mostly they talked in silence. It was tranquil in that vast cool room above the Grand Canal. Out on the harbor, bands of singers in gondolas chanted old Italian ballads. They were, actually, rather commercialized, these singers; not for romance and the love of moonlight were they warbling, and between bursts of ecstasy they passed the hat from listening gondola to gondola, and were much rewarded by sentimentalists from Essen, Pittsburgh, and Manchester. The songs were conscientiously banal-- "Donna e Mobile" and "Santa Lucia" for choice. Yet the whole theatric setting and the music across the water lured Sam into a still excitement.

"I can't imagine you in any complications," he wondered.

"I shouldn't use that word, perhaps. All the complications are inside myself. It's just that certain conditions of life have rather taken my confidence in myself away from me, and I'm so afraid of doing the wrong thing that it's easier to do nothing."

"That's how I feel myself! Though with you, I can't imagine it-- you're sure of yourself."

"Not really. I'm like a man learning a new language--he can do it beautifully as long as he can introduce the subjects of conversation and use the words he knows--he can talk splendidly about Waiter, bring two more coffees, or What is the next train for Turin, but he's lost if somebody else asks the questions and insists on talking about anything beyond page sixty in the Hugo Method! Here, in my own flat, with my own people, I'm safely on this side of Page Sixty, but I'd be horribly fluttered if I stepped out on Page Sixty- one! . . . By the way, I shall be very happy if you're bored by your hotel here and care to come in for tea now and then."

"Awfully good of--"

Without much consciousness of rising, he had strolled to the open window. "I do appreciate it. . . . Feel rather at loose ends."

"Why don't you tell me about it? If you care to. I'm a good confidante!"

"Well--"

He flung out with a suicidal defiance.

"I don't like to whine--I don't think I do, much--and I don't like admitting I'm licked. But I am. And I'm getting a little sick of not being able to sleep nights, brooding about it. Too damn much brooding probably!" He tramped out to the narrow balcony, above the canal and the sound of splashing water. On this balcony once (though Sam did not know it) Lord Byron had stood, snarling to a jet-bright lady a more pitiful and angry tale.

Edith Cortright was beside him, murmuring--oh, her words were a commonplace "Would you like to tell me about it?" but her voice was kind, and curiously honest, curiously free of the barriers between a strange man and a strange woman. And with her Venice murmured, and the songs of love.

"Oh, I suppose it's a very ordinary story. My wife is younger than I am, and livelier, and she's found a man in Berlin, and I guess I've lost her. For keeps. . . . Oh, I know I oughtn't to undress in public like this. But I swear I haven't before! Am I rotten to--"

She said quickly, "Don't! Of course you're not. I'd be glad if I could tell my own story."

"Please!"

"And I haven't told people, either, not even my friends, though I suppose they guess--Perhaps you and I can be franker with each other because we are strangers. I do understand how you feel, Mr. Dodsworth. I suppose the people I know here and in England and at home believe that I lead such a nun-like existence because I had an idolatrous worship of the late Honorable Cecil R. A. Cortright. Such a charming man! Perfect manners, and too perfect a game of bridge! Wonderful war record--M.C., D.S.O. Actually my husband was--He was a dreadful liar; one of these hand-kissing, smiling, convincing liars. He was a secret drunkard. He humiliated me constantly as a backwoods American; used to apologize to people, oh, so prettily, when I said 'I guess' instead of the equally silly 'I fancy.' And his dear mother used to congratulate me on my luck in having won her darling. Oh, I'm sorry! Beastly of me! Fatal Venetian night!"

Her quick breath was not a sob but a sound of anger. Her hand gripped the thin fluted railing of the balcony. He patted it shyly and said, as he would to his daughter Emily, "Maybe it's good for both of us to tell our troubles a little. But--I wish I could HATE my girl. I can't. And I imagine you can't hate Cortright. Might be good for us!"

"Yes," dryly. "It would. But I'm beautifully beginning to be able to. I--Have you ever seen Malapert's etchings? Let me show you a book of them I received today."

331

He dutifully looked at etchings for fifteen minutes, and said farewell rather pompously.

Trudging home, along dark pavements which hung like shelves above swarthily glittering rios, through perilous-looking unlighted archways, he was by turns guilty over having talked of Fran, impatient with himself for having too touchy a conscience, raging at the late Cecil Cortright as a scoundrel, and joyous that behind her fastidious reticence Edith Cortright could be blunt.

It was the guiltiness which persisted when he awoke. Edith would be hating him for having blatted about Fran, for having led her to talk. When for half an hour he had been trying to compose a note of apology, a note came from her:

No, you did not say anything you should not have, and I don't believe I did. I write this because I think I know how remorseful all Americans are after we have said something we really think. Put it down to Santa Lucia who, though I don't really know my hagiology, is probably the patroness of sentimentalists like you and me. Would you like to come in for tea at five today?

EDITH CORTRIGHT.

CHAPTER 33

Daily, for a fortnight, he saw Edith Cortright--at tea, at dinner, at lunch on the Lido. She apparently forgot her discomfort at being unchaperoned, and went architecture-coursing with him, went with him to the summer opera, sailed with him to Torcello and Malamocco--sailing gondola with orange lateen sail, from which they looked back to Venice floating on the dove-colored water.

He talked, of Zenith and Emily, of motors and the virtues of the Revelation car, of mechanics and finance. He had never known another woman who was not bored when he tried to make clear his very definite, not unimportant notions on the use of chromium metal. And she, she talked of many things. She was a reader of thick books, with a curiosity regarding life which drifted all round its circumference. She talked of Bertrand Russell and of insulin; of Stefan Zweig, American skyscrapers, and the Catholic Church. But she was neither priggish nor dogmatic. What interested her in facts and diagrams was the impetus they gave to her own imagination. Essentially she was indifferent whether the world was laboring toward Fascism or Bolshevism, toward Methodism or atheism.

He followed her through all her mazed reflections. He was not rebuffed by her ideas as so often he had been by Fran's pert little learnings. (For Fran wore her knowledge as showily as she wore her furs.)

Of themselves they talked rarely, and they believed that they talked but little of Fran and Cecil Cortright. Yet, lone sentence by sentence, they told their married lives so completely that Sam began to speak of "Cecil" and Edith of "Fran," as though they four had always been together. When she realized it, Edith laughed.

"We ought to make an agreement that I shall be allowed to speak of Cecil for just as many minutes as you do of Fran. Or we might compose a sort of litany--

'Oh, Lord, Cecil was irritable before breakfast, 'And Lord, Thou knowest Fran did not appreciate streamline bodies'!"

And once she got below the surface and told him that subconsciously he had WANTED to lose Fran to Kurt, or to any other available suitor.

Yet there was always between them a formality, even when they used each other's first names as well as those of their eternally problematic mates. They did not discuss their souls. They did not discuss why it was that they seemed to like each other. The nearest they came to intimacy was in planning, almost childishly, their "futures."

He said abruptly, at coffee after dinner in Edith's flat, "What shall I do? Shall I go back to America, without Fran? And shall I do the job I've been trained to, or play with some experiments? Let me tell you of a couple of silly ideas I have."

He outlined his plans for caravan building, and for venturing on Sans Souci Gardens villages.

"Why not do both?" suggested Edith. She seemed to take his desired experiments more seriously than had Fran. "I like your idea of trying to make a suburb that would be neither stuffy nor too dreadfully arty--no grocery clerks coaxed to dance on the green. And the caravans would be fun. Cecil and I had one for two months in England."

"Do you mean to say you did the cooking?"

"Of course I did! I'm an excellent cook! I babble of Freud and Einstein, but I know nothing about psycho-analysis, nothing about mathematics. But I do know garlic and taragon vinegar! I really love housekeeping. I should have stayed in Michigan and married a small-town lawyer."

"Could you like a town like Zenith? After Venice?"

"Yes if I had a place of my own there. Here, everything decays-- lovely decay, but I'm tired of being autumnal. I'd like hot summer growing and spring budding for a change--even if the corn-stalks were ugly!"

Then, first, did it occur to him that it was not quite ludicrous to think that Edith and he might some day return together to Zenith, to work and to life. He said little to himself, nothing at all to her, of what seemed dimly to be growing as a secure and healing love, yet a day or two after he seized the impulse and showed Edith the letter from Fran.

Fran's letter revealed more of herself and of her relation to Kurt than anything she had written:

I haven't heard from you for a week, old man, I admit I haven't been much on correspondence either but I haven't been feeling any too merry and bright, I think too much city I really MUST get out into the country and Kurt and I--you really are an old DARLING and awfully generous I realize it to let me talk so frankly about him and still be friends with me--we're going to try to go to the Harz Mountains for a week.

It's been a funny thing--you always think I have no meekness but honestly I have shown quite biblical humility in trying to fit myself to his so-different life. He's let me fuss over his funny PATHETIC little flat--oh, Sam, it just breaks my heart the way that flat reveals how POOR the poor man is, that ought to be a great nobleman like his ancestors and I suppose would have been if it hadn't been for the war which after all was not his fault. At first I was irritated by the complete sloppiness etc. etc. of his dear funny old servant then I thought maybe it was because she has such an ELEMENTARY kitchen equipment, honestly it was about what you would expect in Kurt's native wilds a FRIGHTFUL old coal stove that she has to stoke up all the time and the flues do not draw. I wanted to give him a jolly new electric range and he finally consented, though not readily, honestly--please, pretty please, I hope this won't hurt your feelings and as I say I know how GENEROUS you are, but you can't have any idea how proud he is! But it was the cook who balked. No! She wouldn't have a nice new electric range or an electric dish-washing machine! She PREFERRED their own familiar things! She's truly feudal--isn't that almost as hard as "truly rural" that we used to say in school!--and so is Kurt. I think perhaps I realized that with a chauffeur, of course Kurt can't afford his own chauffeur or even car yet though I do believe with his real genius for finance he will be a very rich man on his own inside another ten years but he can't afford one now but whenever he can get him he uses an Austrian chauffeur at a hire garage near here that was a private in Kurt's own regiment during the war and that really is almost practically like Kurt's own chauffeur.

Well, at first do you know I was shocked by their chumminess. The chauffeur would tell the Herr Graf that the Herr Graf was wearing lovely new gloves today, and Kurt would ask him about his sweetheart and they would joke about it and Kurt would tell him he

335

Lewis

ought to make his sweetheart an honest woman and the chauffeur would waggle his finger in a knowing way that made me angry, and so one day I jumped on Kurt about it and my dear! the way he turned on me!

He said, "You are a bourgeoise! I am feudal! We who are feudal can be familiar with our servants because we know they cannot ever be impertinent!"

Sam laid down the letter, and it was of Edith and her way with servants that he was thinking.

I find myself settling, dear old man, no matter if we have apparently busted up for keeps and it IS rather tragic if one suffers one's self to think about it after the many, many happy years we DID have together, DIDN'T we, but if we did break up, I do know you will go on being my FRIEND and be glad to know that I DO find myself settling down to my job of being a European. It hasn't been easy and I can't expect you to understand the pains, the almost agony I have given to it. Sometimes I am frankly lonely-- for whatever you may say about me to Tub and your DEAR Matey, oh, Sam, I suspect you talked about me to her in Paris far more than you ever admitted--but I mean, whatever you may say about me, perhaps with a lot of justice, at least you must admit that one of my probably few virtues has been a rather rare FRANKNESS and HONESTY, and frankly at times I have been very lonely, have wished you were here so I could tousle your funny old thick hair. And sometimes I have been frightened by the spectacle of one lone femme Americaine facing all of censorious Europe. And sometimes--you know his dear childish enthusiasm without very much discrimination-- I have been a little bored by some of Kurt's Dear Old Friends. Yet I love and I think I am coming to really understand the THICKNESS of European life. Our American life is so thin, so without tradition.

Sam laid down the letter and thought of the tradition of pioneers pushing to the westward, across the Alleghenies, through the forests of Kentucky and Tennessee, on to the bleeding plains of Kansas, on to Oregon and California, a religious procession, sleeping always in danger, never resting, and opening a new home for a hundred million people. But with no comment he read on:

I have learned, and I must say with some surprise which has probably been good for my little ego that Kurt thinks much more of a violinist or a chemist than of the nicest prince with the most quarteri- est quarterings living. And--for whatever you may think about me you must admit that I DO understand the Europeans and I really am Euro- pean!--and do grasp it--I haven't had too much difficulty following him. Oh, my dear, do forgive me if this hurts you, but he is what the romantic novelists call MY MAN! I have some stunning plans for him. I think I see the way, I can't of course give away any details even to you, but I think I see a way of getting a certain great American bank to establish a branch in Berlin, and making Kurt the head of it.

You would probably be amused you certainly wouldn't know your wild Fran how meek she is if you saw her letting Kurt boss her in all sorts of little things yes and I suppose big ones too but still he IS so dear--he always notices what I wear, honestly he bullies me really dreadfully about my clothes but at the same time is always willing to go shopping with me which you must admit, for all your gorgeous big- ness you never were. Oh my dear I suppose it is unpardonable to write to YOU about HIM this way and if I stop to think about it and re-read this letter probably I never shall mail this letter that I'm writing in my ducky little coloraturo (or is it coloratura) flat on an evening that if I must confess is a little lonely and makes me feel like a lost lorn tourist AMERICAN but we are friends aren't we--phone ringing must answer bless you,

    F.

He had the letter at ten in the morning. At twelve he was ring- ing at Edith's flat. He thrust Fran's letter at her without a word. When Edith had read it she sighed, and suggested:

"It's so hot here. I've been thinking of going down to Naples-- to Posilipo, out on the point, where it's cool--and taking a little house on the estate of the Ercoles. Baron Ercole has a big place, but he's frightfully poor. He's an ex-diplomat; he teaches law in the University of Naples; and the poor darlings live mostly by renting villas on their place. Why don't you come down with me? I don't think there's much more to be said about your Fran, after this letter. It might be good for you to swim and sail at Naples, instead of sitting here brooding. Would you like to come?"

"Decidedly! But what about your friends who are so eager to be scandalized--"

"Oh, not the Ercoles. They'll believe I'm having an affair with you, and be delighted--they've lived in too many countries, in the diplomatic corps, to have many morals. They'll like you. Edmondo Ercole and you will have such a good time being silent together! Oh, that sounds like Fran, I imagine! I'm sorry!"

In the sunset an Italian hilltown, battlements and a shaggy tower on a rock abrupt amid the sloping plain. The windows of the town took the low sunlight and blazed one after another as the train passed. "As though the houses were full of gay people," said Edith. He looked at it with still pleasure. He felt that her presence had unlocked his heart; had enabled him, for the first time, to see Italy.

He had, theoretically, been in Naples before, but as they drove from the station to the Villa Ercole he realized that all he had seen--all he had seen anywhere in Europe--had not been the place itself but Fran's hectic and demanding attitudes; her hysteria of delight over a moonlight, or her hysteria of annoyance over bad service. In Edith's quiet presence he perceived that Naples was not, as he had remembered it, a rather grim, very modern barricade of tall apartment houses, but a series of connected villages extending for miles along the bay, between blue water and hills into which human beings had burrowed like gophers.

The driver of their taxi, being Neapolitan, was in a rage so long as any vehicle was on the road ahead of him, and as that was always, their journey was a series of escapes from death. Yet even in this chariot race, Sam expanded and nestled into contentment, as in the old days of overwork and brief vacations he had relaxed into delight on his holidays in a canoe.

He patted Edith's hand in an effort to express his happiness, as he saw Vesuvius roll up, with its trail of smoke--toward Naples, now, promising good weather; saw Capri with the dots of white houses on the lofty plateau between the ruin-dotted mountains; saw sun-washed Sorrento at the foot of its giant promontory; saw the villas of Posilipo below the cliff up which their taxi was racing.

The taxi passed a yellow plaster gatehouse, with a bobbing concierge--a smiling, life-loving, plump Italian woman, with innumerous children about her--and instantly they were free of the roaring thoroughfare, free of banging traffic, ejaculatory drivers, shouldering trains, suicidal children, and cluttered little shops for the sale of charcoal and wine. The park of the Villa Ercole dropped from that high-lying thoroughfare down to the bay, with a roadway twisting and redoubling on itself like a mountain trail. They sped among enormous pines, between whose framing trunks he saw, across the suave bay, the bulk of Vesuvius, as absolute in its loneliness as Fujiyama. They passed half a dozen plaster villas, yellow as old gold, very still, remembering glories not quite past. In a modern stone wall, supporting a stretch of the corkscrew road, was a patch of thin ancient Roman brick set in a herring-bone pattern and above it the fragment of a marble bust, the head of a warrior whose villa may have stood here two thousand years ago.

There was no sound, even of birds, no sound from the street above-- a minute away yet inconceivably far.

"Lord, how quiet it is here!" said Sam.

"That's why I wanted to come here--that and the Ercoles."

On the last sweeping curve of the driveway, just before it came to an end before the tall chateau in which the Ercoles themselves still dwelt, Edith bade the driver halt at a tiny wooden bridge which led across to what seemed to be the top story of a yellow plaster tower whose lower stages were hidden beneath the cliff beside them.

"There's our house!" she said. "It's the funniest house in the world! It's on three levels. The garden is so steep that you can enter it from any floor. And there are really only about two rooms to a floor."

She led him, across the bridge and along a toy-house hallway, to the simplest of bedrooms. The floor was of shining stone; on the walls there were no pictures, but only a majolica Virgin and Child. The high narrow bed, with neither headboard nor footboard, had four slender posts at the corners. It was covered with a gold encrusted brocade, rather worn. There was a naked-looking white steel washstand, a fine oval mirror, two heavy brocade chairs, a heavy oak table set out with pens and stationery, a brazier for charcoal, and nothing else whatever--yet there was everything, for outside the French windows was a terrace, apparently the roof of a room below, which gave on the bay, so that the room was filled with the sparkle of southern sun on southern waters and with the image of Mount Vesuvius and its distant indolence of smoke.

"This is your room, I suppose," said Edith. "But, good heavens, there's no wardrobe, no place even for your brushes and razor!

Bianca--Baroness Ercole--probably hasn't been able to afford them yet--wrote me she was just refurnishing this house, hoping to rent it."

"I don't mind. Keep my stuff in wardrobe trunk," said Sam. He was glad of the simplicity, glad that the room was free of the stuffiness of much furniture. He could see himself rejuvenated here, in this cool shrine, with the sweet air and the beaming sea outside, and with Edith's unsentimental friendship to make him believe in himself.

They went on the balcony-terrace and Sam cried out. The shore-line from Posilipo to Naples, which had been below them and hidden from them on their drive to the villa, was romantic enough for a Christmas calendar--and no amount of Fran's scolding had kept Samuel Dodsworth from liking chromo art. The bay was edged with cliffs, eaten into vast caves. Mysterious stairways climbed from the rocks at the edge of the water, disappearing into holes in the cliffs. Sam reflected how excited he would have been as a boy to find these vanishing stairways, after reading in Stevenson and Walter Scott of secret passageways, of smugglers and underground chambers.

To a tiny beach at the foot of a cliff a fisher-boy, barefoot and singing, was drawing up his unwieldy boat. His skin was golden in the sunlight.

It is true that just then shot into sight a four-oar shell, rowed by members of a club fostered by the Fascists, but this spectacle, contemporary as though it were on the Thames, Sam ignored. It did not suit his romantic private vision of the Bay of Naples.

The villas along the bay were white and imposing upon the cliff- tops, at the head of sloping canyons filled with vines and mulberries, or, set lower, mediaeval palaces of arcaded and yellowed marble with their foundations in the water. It was late in the afternoon, and the mellowed glow lay on distant Naples, vast tawny pyramid rising to the abrupt bastions of Castel Sant' Elmo, a city enchanted, asleep these hundreds of years in the lazy light.

He muttered, "This place--this place--"

"Yes. Isn't it!" she said.

For hours they seemed to have been absorbed in the kindly radiance but it was probably three minutes since they had entered the house. No servant had answered her knock on entering, none had disturbed them since. They continued exploring; went down the rough stone staircase of the tower-cottage, found her bedroom, as primitive as his; and down to the ground floor. They came into a drawing-room, floored with waxed and polished tiles of old dark red, a room large enough to tolerate fifteen-foot windows hung with damask, full-blooming camellia trees in tall stone wine-jars, and a long table of rosewood decorated with bronze, a table over-decorated yet curiously elegant. Sam scarcely noticed two women, in calico and dust-caps, who were on their knees finishing the polishing of the floor. He gaped when the younger and more slender sprang up, fled to Edith Cortright, and kissed her.

Edith said, smiling, brisker than he had ever known her, "Bianca, this is my friend Mr. Dodsworth--Sam, your hostess, Baroness Ercole."

And, altogether unabashed at being caught in the crimes of poverty and work, the Baroness Ercole made him welcome with her smile, gave him her wax-crusted hand to kiss, and invited them to dinner.

CHAPTER 34

He found a new Edith Cortright, a surprisingly vigorous and outdoor Edith, once she was away from Venetian proprieties. She gave up soft black for a linen sailor-blouse and a shocking skirt; she showed a talent for swimming, sailing, tennis, and managing the house. The Ercole estate, with its half a dozen villas, was like a private village, and a hectic village life it was into which Sam had come. The smiling Italian servants walked without warning into any room, at any time-- embarrassed him by bouncing into his bedroom when he was shaving, cheerfully conducted the fish-pedler into the drawing-room at tea-time, and at all hours, under all windows, squabbled and laughed and gab-bled and made love and sang. And there were so many of them belonging to the various villas. Sam was always discovering some new cottage--half-dug in the cliffs, or atop a coach house, or mysteriously under it with its door opening on another level--filled with gardeners or gatekeepers or maids, with their children, their goats, their puppies, their rabbits, and long-faced Italian cats.

The Baron and Baroness Ercole and their friends--officers who came out from the barracks, navy officers, young professors from the university--were as gay and welcoming as any American country club set priding itself on hospitality. They played tennis, they organ-ized dances, they motored (at appalling speed) to festivals in distant mountain villages, and in everything they made Edith and Sam a part of their own. Half of them did not speak English, but their smiles rec-ognized him as an old friend.

Alone, Edith and Sam explored Capri and Sorrento and Pom-peii; were drawn up to the terror and fumes of Vesuvius; crept through the back alleys of old Naples, where one street is given up to fish, one to vegetables, one to the most cheerfully lugubrious artificial funeral wreaths and to votive pictures depicting the escape of pious persons from shipwreck, runaway horses, and falling bricks through the inter-vention of the saints.

Fran, who insisted that she "despised sight-seeing," had yet been so ejaculatory, so insistent that he should realize to the full whatever most struck her, that he had had to work hard at travel, and had been conscious only of collecting unrelated impressions. Edith was lazily indifferent to his liking things. With her, he let his mind loaf, and slowly some sense of the real Italy came to him, some feeling that it was not a picturesque show but a normal and eager life.

They came home, dusty from Naples, for tea in the dim huge room looking on the bay. The late-afternoon glow over the piled hill of Naples faded to misty blue. The last high light in the scene was the smoke of Vesuvius, a fabulous flamingo hue in the vanishing sunlight. As the bay turned to a blue fabric woven with silver threads, the lights of braziers came out cheerfully in the little fishing boats. And in the twilight hush, Edith's voice was quiet, not pricking him with demands for admiration of her cleverness, her singular charms, but assuring him (though actually she talked only of the Ercoles, perhaps, or politics, or antipasto) that she was happy to be with him, that she took strength from him by giving him strength.

He assumed that he was strong and primitive as the west wind, that she was sophisticated and fragile, utterly a creature of indoors, and he was the more startled on the day when they rested on the stone wall by the orange grove. It was an ancient, crumbly, slatternly stone wall, lizards darting from the crevices, moss and tiny weeds like a velvet cushion along the top. Below, in the hollow, was a tile and plaster house of three irregular flat-roofed and terraced stories, apparently not connected, entered by doorways above crazy stone flights of steps, all curiously like a New Mexican pueblo. The grove climbed from the hollow to the highway above--orange trees, lemons, a palmetto or two, with vines stretched upon the elongated branches of mulberry trees. Where a group of boulders intruded on the slope, the earth between rocks had been painfully turned into tiny vineyards, a yard or two square, protected by little stone walls. The grove suggested centuries of minute and patient labor, yet it was disorderly, the ground rough and littered, the trees a tangle, with no straight lines.

"You wondered," said Edith, perched on the wall, "whether I could stand a canoe trip, sleeping on the ground. What do you think of this orchard?"

"Don't quite see the connection."

"What do you think of it? How does it strike you--as an efficient person?"

"Well, the fruit looks all right, but it seems kind of higgledy-piggledy. And it's darned hot, here on this wall!"

"Exactly! Well, the Italian peasant loves the heat, and he loves just the bare ridged ground--the earth, earthy earth! He loves earth and sun and wind and rain. He's a mystic, in the highest sense of that badly escorted word. The European is the same everywhere, in that. The Tyrolese love the sharp smell of the glaciers, the ragged mountain-slopes that almost frighten me, so that they die of homesickness abroad. The Prussian loves that thick sandy waste and the bleak little pines. The French villager doesn't mind the reality of manure piles and mud puddles in front of his house. The English farmer loves his bare downs with their sharp little furze bushes. They love earth and wind and rain and sun. And I've learned it from them. You wonder if I could 'stand' sleeping on the ground! I'd love it so much more than you! I'm so much more elementary. Here, we may have ruins and painting, but behind them we're so much closer to the eternal elements than you Americans. You don't love earth, you don't love the wind--"

"Oh, look here now! What about our millions of acres of plowed fields? Nothing LIKE it, outside of maybe Russia! What about our most important men, that get out in the fresh air and motor and golf--"

"No. Your farmers want to get away from their wash of acres to the city. Your business men drive out to the golf club in closed se-dans, and they don't want just bare earth--they want the earth of the golf course all neatly concealed by lawn. And I--you think of me as sitting in drawing-rooms, but here you've seen me reveling in sea wa-ter and running on the beach. And often and often when you think I'm napping in my room, I sneak out to that little bit of walled-off garden just above the house and lie there in the hot sun, in the wind, smelling of the reeking earth, finding life! That's the strength of Europe--not its so-called 'culture,' its galleries and neat voices and knowledge of lan-guages, but its nearness to earth. And that's the weakness of America-- not its noisiness and its cruelty and its cinema vulgarity but the way in which it erects steel-and-glass skyscrapers and miraculous cement-and-glass factories and tiled kitchens and wireless antennae and popu-lar magazines to insulate it from the good vulgarity of earth!"

He wondered about it. He admitted that he had seen only an indoor Europe. With hotel lounges, restaurants, bedrooms, train coupes, even galleries and cathedrals and a few authentic homes, he was familiar enough. But he realized that he had but little sense of the smell of earth in the changing countries. He could remember St. Stefan's Kirche in Vienna, but he could not remember the colors of the Austrian Alps, the sound of mountain streams, the changing smell of the crowded and musty pines at dawn, at noon, and in the dusk. He had talked with Spanish waiters but he had not been silent with Spanish peasants.

Perhaps, as she said, it was he who was the decadent and ephemeral flower of an imperiled civilization and she who was the root, not to be killed; he saw that she had more essential lustiness than he, more endurance than the lively but glass-encased Fran, vigorous enough in joy but wilting and whimpering under trials. The Ercoles, Kurt von Obersdorf, Lord Herndon, they were not to be crushed. In humility he turned to the eternal earth, and in the earth he found contentment. He had daily less need to "buzz out and look at things," as Fran put it. He sat for hours with Edith, or alone by the bay, staring at the miraculously involved branches of a cypress, discovering the myriad minute skyscrapers in a patch of moss. And he began to desire to have--with Edith--a farm at home, and not a gentleman's showplace, to increase social credit, but an authentic farm, smelling of horses and cattle and chickens, with cornfields baking at noon, mysterious in their jungle-like alleys. This simple-hearted ambition stirred him more, gave him more feeling that he had something secret and exciting to live for, than any of the business plans which were rousing him again to self-respect. . . . But it must be with Edith. . . . He smiled a little to think of himself, this bucolic lump, drawn back to earth by her thin unearthen hands. Edith! He understood better the slim starry Virgins before whom sun-black peasants bowed in Italian chapels.

He asked himself, then, "Am I in love with Edith--whatever this 'being in love' means?"

He had never so much as kissed her; only three or four times had he even patted her hand. He felt, sometimes, that behind her reticence there could be an honest passion, uncramped by the desire to make an impression, but he drifted on in a curious contented languor, willing to wait for exaltation. He found that when she was away, he missed her--had every moment some idea or observation he desired to share with her. But that was to him a lesser hint of what Edith Cortright had done to him than his increase in self- confidence.

It took him a time to perceive that perhaps he really was accepted by Edith, by the Ercoles and the various Captain Counts and Professores Dottores whom the Ercoles knew, as something more than the provincial, insensitive, Midwestern manufacturer whom Fran had pitied. Baron Ercole did not explain with bored patience when Sam asked elementary questions about Fascismo. Edith was not tart with him when he grumbled that he did not like the Narcissus in the Naples Museum.

They did not expect him to be an authority on sculpture, Chianti, Roman history, or the ranks of Italian nobility. Apparently they not only expected him to be precisely what he was, but admired him for it. He was at first embarrassed, made rather suspicious, by the Baroness Ercole's admiration of him as a strong oarsman, a kindly companion, a frank talker, a sound financier, but day by day he saw that she meant it. In this most Italian Italy he might without apology still be a most American American. Light seemed to be woven into the very texture of his face that these months past had been heavy and lifeless and unhealthily flushed; and his eyes flickered as of old they had in talk with his daughter Emily.

"You are real," they all said, in one way or another, and "I AM real!" he began to gloat.

He slept tranquilly, conscious in his sleep of the security of Edith's presence on the floor below, shielding him against terror. He did not awake now at three, for a cigarette and brooding about Fran.

But once, late at night, he thought that he heard Fran calling, a sharp, beseeching "Sam--oh, SAM!" and he sprang up, stood swaying, bewildered as he realized that she was not with him, probably never would be again.

And the time, which he forgot as soon as possible, when Edith came into the room when he was writing and he raised his head, smiling, with "my Fran!"

Edith's only effort to correct his provincial ways was in a gentle urging, "Let yourself enjoy life, Sam! You're typically American in being burdened with a sense of guilt, no matter what you do or you don't do."

This may conceivably have had some connection with the fact that when he appeared with Edith, when they went to dinner with one of the Ercoles' friends or to the Excelsior for tea, more people looked interestedly at him, standing casually beside her, than in the days when he had been anxious to make an impression for Fran's sake. He no longer minded meeting strangers or having to listen to their foreign accents. He took them as they came.

He awoke one morning to lie looking at the bay and to realize that he was definitely and positively happy.

He had written to Fran a good deal about Edith. Fran was polite in her comments; she sent her greetings to "Mrs. Cortright"; and she was still politer, almost effusively jolly, when she wrote to him from Berlin that she was at last suing for divorce. With the term of residence she already had, the process would take three months. She was very pleasant about the fact that the grounds would be desertion, and the affair free of scandal.

He remembered how excited they had been when they had gone to Chicago together and he had bought her first little string of pearls; how proud she had been of them, and how grateful. . . . Then he felt curiously free.

When he reluctantly brought this decisive letter to Edith, she read it slowly, and ventured, "Do you mind awfully?"

"Oh yes, a little."

"But it does clear things up, doesn't it! And--I hope it won't break your beautiful new calm!"

"I won't let it!"

"But I've seen you so badgered by her letters!"

"Yes, but--I say! Could you ever possibly consider going to a place like Zenith to live?"

"Of course. Do places differ so much?"

"Would it amuse you to work on a plan like these garden suburbs?"

"I don't know. It might."

It was an hour afterward, when they had pretended to keep placidly busy with books and writing letters, that Edith burst out:

"Sam! About your suburbs. Something could be done--not just Italian villas and Swiss chalets--for a town with a tradition of Vermont Yankees and Virginians in buckskin. Why shouldn't one help to create an authentic and unique American domestic architecture? Our skyscrapers are the first really new thing in architecture since the Gothic cathedral, and perhaps just as beautiful! Create something native--and not be afraid to keep in all the plumbing and vacuum-cleaners and electric dish-washers! Dismiss the imitation chateaux. The trouble with the rich American is that he feels uncouth and untraditional, and so he meekly trots to Europe to buy sun-dials and Fifteenth Century mantelpieces and refectory tables-- to try to buy aristocracy by buying the aristocrats' worn-out coats. I like my Europe in Europe; at home I'd like to watch people make something new. For example, your motor cars."

"Then you would like a place like Zenith, that's growing?"

"How can I tell? I'd certainly like the adventure of trying it."

He felt that her hesitation was more promising than the enthusiasms of Fran. Suddenly a horde of Ercoles were trouping in, planning a swim, and no more that day, nor the next, did they speak of Fran, of Zenith, of themselves. But when they said good night, he kissed her hands, and her eyes dwelt upon him.

They were dining at Bertolini's, high above Naples, looking out toward Capri, and he was talking of possible schemes: a two-story caravan with a canvas-sided collapsible upper floor, so that the caravan could pass under arches en route; a caravan that could turn into a house boat, carrying its own hull along, collapsed; a summer resort entirely for children whose parents were going abroad; a dozen fantastic, probably practical plans. She was amused by them, suggested improvements, and Sam was lustily content.

But after his second cognac the orchestra played selections from the Viennese operettas which Fran loved, and he remembered how happy he had been with Fran in Berlin, at first. It came to him that if Kurt failed to marry her, she would be a bewildered and lonely exile; and through the music, through the darkness beyond the music, he saw her fleeing, a desolate wraith; and while Edith gossiped most amiably, Sam's heart was heavy with pity for the frightened and bewildered child Fran, who once had laughed so eagerly with him.

But, back at the Villa Ercole, he stood with Edith on the terrace and across the whispering darkness of the bay, he saw the cone of Vesuvius with a thin line of fire.

"Don't worry it too much!" said Edith suddenly, and he was grateful that she understood his cloudy thoughts without making him wrap them in cloudier words.

CHAPTER 35

For days they drifted in perfect calm, and he was proud that the enervating thought of Fran was gone from him.

All one morning they explored the ridge above Posilipo, found fragments of a Roman emperor's villa and the carp-pond in which he used to drown his slaves as the best fish-food, and discovered the mausoleum which, history asserts, was the tomb of Vergil, or of some one else. They straggled home, up the long street which was a wilderness of children and carts, and sank down sighing in the cool drawing-room.

"Collatzione, Teresa," he ordered, then: "Curious, Edith, but this house that you've rented, and that belongs to an Italian I never saw till the other day, is the first that I ever felt was really mine. I actually dare give an order!"

"But I'm sure your Fran never MEANT to be a domestic dictator. . . ."

The gardener had left the mail on the table, but Sam did not pick it up till after lunch, and then but carelessly. On top was a letter from Fran. He pretended, not very skillfully, that he had to go to his room, and he read Fran's letter alone:

I haven't much excuse, probably I've been a fool and not appreciated you but anyway, maybe with no right to, I am turning to you rather desperately. Kurt's mother finally came up from Austria. She was pretty rude to me. She indicated, oh quite clearly that for the Catholic and Highly Noble Kurtrl to marry a female who was (or soon would be) heinously divorced, who was an American, and who was too old to bear him heirs, would be disastrous. And she didn't spare me very much in putting it that way, either. Not a pretty scene--me sitting there smoking in Kurt's flat and trying to look agreeable while she wailed at Kurt and ignored me. And Kurt stood by her. Oh, his nice little sentimental heart bled for me, and since then he's such a good time being devastated and trying to take both sides at once. But he "thought ve had better put off the marriage for maybe a couple of years till ve von her over." God! Is he a man or a son? There ain't going to be no vinning over, and no marriage! I'm sick of his coward-ice, when I risked so much, but why go into that.

If you still care to bend your Olympian head and forgive the probably wicked and unforgivable Magdalene or however it's spelled, I should be glad to join you again, anyway I've stopped divorce pro-ceedings. Of course I realize that in saying this so honestly, without efforts to protect myself as most women would, I risk another humilia-tion at your hands such as I had from Kurt. Of course I don't know how far you have committed yourself in the rather strange relations with this Mrs. Cortwright in which you have apparently had so much pleasure and relief from my aggravating self, though how you could be willing to take snubs from the highly proper Italians by thus living with her openly instead of concealing things is beyond--

Oh forgive me, forgive me, dear Sambo darling, forgive me, your bad child Fran! I sound so beastly and snotty when in my heart I'm desolated and scared and lost and I turn to you as the Rock of Ages! I wrote so abominably and unjustly because I'm so wretched, so desperate, and I won't even tear it up--I want you to know that if you do let your bad Fran come back, she probably hasn't learned as much as she should in her mediocre little tragedy, she'll probably be just as snobbish and demanding as ever, though God knows I don't want to be, I am so tired of thread-bare grandeurs now and want so much to be simple and honest.

I think you will credit me with not trying to come back just be-cause you are rich and strong, and Kurt poor and honest. It's just--Oh, you know what it is! I venture to turn to you because I do know that once, anyway, you loved me a great deal. And if we could manage to stick together, it will be so much better for Brent and Emily--oh, I know, probably it's shameless of me to speak of that so late, but it is true.

I find there is a boat leaving Hamburg September 19, Cher-bourg the next day, the Deutschland and if you CARE to join me on it, or meet me in Paris, I should be--Oh Sam, if you still do love me, you mustn't be proud, you mustn't take this chance to punish me, but come, because otherwise--Oh, I don't know what I WILL do! I've been so proud! Now I feel the world is jeering at me! I don't dare leave my flat, don't dare answer the phone and hear their pitying laughter, I have my maid answer it for me, and usually it is still Kurt, but I'll never see him again, never, he talks of killing himself but he won't--his Mamma wouldn't let him!

As soon as you get this, won't you please telephone me here, from Naples.

If you feel like coming, I hope this will not inconvenience your hostess, Mrs. Cortright, whom I remember so agreeably in Venice, kindly give her my regards. But I hope that my appeal may be somewhat more important to you than even your social duty to that doubtless most charming lady who is I am sure much less irritating than I.

Her whole handwriting changed then; he felt that the rest of the letter had been written hours later:

Oh, Sam, I do need you so, did I ever tell you that I adore you?

Your shamed and wretched little Fran.

He blundered down to the drawing-room, snorting, "Got to run into Naples. May be late for tea. Don't wait."

"What is it?"

"Oh, it's nothing."

He fled from her.

All the way down, on the tram, he asked himself whether he wanted to have Fran again, and whether he was really going to join her, and to both he answered with perfect blankness. But when he asked whether he wanted to leave Edith, he denied it, sharply, with fury, reflecting wretchedly how good she had been, how honest, how understanding, and perceiving there was rising in him a passion for her greater than the mystic vexation with which Fran had fascinated him.

And he was going to desert Edith, going to be weak enough to betray her?

"Oh, probably," he sighed, when for an hour, at the American Express Company, he had been waiting for the telephone call to Berlin.

351

He seemed to wait forever.

He was as conscious of the scene in the express office as though he had sat there for years. A picture of a big New York Central locomotive. Racks of pamphlets about spicy places--Burma and Bangkok and Sao Paulo--he would never see them now, because Fran would find them crude and unfashionable. A tourist lady writing letters and between sentences boasting to her mother of the WON-DERFUL corals she had found on the Piazza dei Martiri--

Then startlingly, "Your Berlin call!"

He heard Fran's voice, quicksilver voice, eagerness of the wildly playing child in its lifting mutations:

"Oh, Sam, it really is you? You really are coming, dearest? You do forgive poor Fran?"

"Sure. Be on the boat. ON THE BOAT. Yes, the nineteenth, yes, sure, we'll talk over everything, good-bye, honey, you better get the tickets as you're there in Germany. GET THE STEAMER TICKETS, good-bye, honey, I'll wire you a confirmation."

He walked back most of the way, looking old and slow and sweaty, laboring over the coming scene with Edith. She would be very polite but surprised, contemptuous of him for returning to the servitude of Fran's witchery.

He slunk in a few minutes after six.

She was reading by the great window in the drawing-room. She glanced up, then, wondering, "What is it? What's happened?"

"Well--"

He stood by the window, making much of clipping and lighting a cigar, and he did not look at her as he grumbled, "Fran's lover, this Count Obersdorf, has turned her down. His mother thought she was kind of declasse--divorce and all that. Poor kid, that must've been hard on her. She's given up the idea of divorce, and she's sailing for home. She'll be kind of--Oh, people'hl talk a lot, I guess. I'm afraid I'll have to go with her. Fact, I'll have to catch the midnight for Rome, tonight. . . . I wish there were some way of telling you all that you've--"

"Sam!"

She had sprung up. He was astonished by the fury in her quiet eyes.

"I won't let you go back to that woman! And I won't see you killed--yes, killed!--by her sweet, gay, well-mannered, utter damned selfishness! Her only thought about anybody is what they give her! The world offers you sun and wind, and Fran offers you death, fear and death! Oh, I'd seen how you've aged five years in five minutes, after one of her complaining letters! And you won't be helping her-- you'll just make her feel all the more that she can do any selfish, cruel thing she wants to and come out of it unscathed! Think of Peking and Cairo! No! Think of the farm you could have in Michigan, among the pines! Think of how natural and contented you'd be--yes, WE'D be-- back there--"

"I know, Edith; I know every bit of it. I just can't help it. She's my child. I've got to take care of her."

"Yes. Well." The passion did not fade from her eyes, but snapped out, as though one should turn off a light, and she said dully, "Sorry. I was impertinent. At least let me help you pack."

Throughout the packing, dinner, and the rather dreadful waiting afterward, when he could not find two civil words to put together, she was a little abrupt of speech, very courteous. She asked questions about Zenith. She politely hoped that she might see him "and Mrs. Dodsworth" some distant day. Only once was she near to intimacy, when, after a torturing pause, she blurted, "There really isn't much to say, is there! But I do want you to know that because you've seemed to like me, you've given me a new assurance."

When he tried to counter with florid compliments, she bustled out to the kitchen.

The sound of the coming taxicab released him from the eternity of sitting dead in a tomb. While the servants straggled out with his luggage, he held her hand, patting it.

"It is all ready, Signore," said the maid. She received the highly expected tip, and with a "Com' beck soon!" which sounded sincere, she vanished.

In the twilight outside the tree-shadowed door, he awkwardly shook hands with Edith, but while he was trying to say something agreeable, she cried:

"It's too late now. But I thought that some day--I thought it would be easy for me to talk, and I would tell you all sorts of things about how I feel and think. That it's been pleasant to be with you. That you're bigger than you know, not smaller, like celebrities. That you've made me willing to stop being afraid of the world, and to attack it again. I've felt--" She seized his rough sleeve. "That curious feeling, always a surprise every time I was with you, of 'Why, it's you!' That feeling that you were different from any other living person--not necessarily one bit finer but--oh, different! I shouldn't say any of this, but before it's quite too late--too late!--I want to try to be reckless. But I can't say any of the things I thought. Bless you, my dear! And God keep you through the wickedness of this Happy Ending!"

He kissed her, a terrible clinging kiss, and lumbered over to the roadway and his taxicab. He looked back. She seemed to start toward him, then closed the door quickly. Through a window he heard her voice, weary and spiritless: "Only one for breakfast, Teresa."

He was alone with a yawning taxi-driver, as a breeze came up from the bay in the Southern darkness.

CHAPTER 36

Fran was lovely, very young, in a gray-squirrel mantle.

"I got it for almost NOTHING, at the summer sales in Berlin," she said. "Why is it most women never can seem to economize? I'll bet your wonderful flame, Mrs. Cost--Cortright? funny, I never CAN seem to remember her name--she's frightfully clever, I'm sure, but I'll bet she'd have paid twice as much for it."

The late September was cold even for mid-Atlantic. Fran smoothed the fur, draped it closer in her steamer-chair. She seemed to him like a leopard with its taut limbs hidden by a robe.

Now, after tea hour on the S.S. Deutschland, a raging sunset smeared the waves with a frightening crimson. They smelled a storm. The ship ducked before the attacking waves. But Fran was full of live- liness and well-being. As she talked, she nodded every instant to people they had met aboard, the men who were always in a knot about her at the dances, the matrons who talked of "that charming Mrs. Dodsworth--she told me she was much younger than her husband--he's a little slow, don't you think--but she's so fond of him--looks after him like a daughter."

Fran cuddled down in her richness of fur.

"Oh, it's nice to be GOING somewhere!" she said. "I bet we'll both be crazy to start off somewhere, maybe back to Paris, when we've been home a few months. (What an ATROCIOUS hat that woman has on and my DEAR, will you regard her shoes! Why they ALLOW peo- ple like that in the first cabin?) And you can't know how tired I got of sticking around Berlin forever 'n' ever! Oh, you were so right about Kurt, Sam dear. I don't know how you guessed it! You'd be the first to admit you aren't usually so AWFULLY good at judging character, ex- cept in the case of business men, but you were right with--Oh, he was so BOSSY! He was furious if I so much as suggested I'd like to run down to Baden-Baden by myself. And where he got the idea that he was so important--Oh, his family may be as old as the Coliseum--the Coliseo--but when I saw his mother, my DEAR, the most awful old country frump--"

"Don't!" said Sam. "Don't know why, but I kind of hate to hear you riding Kurt and his mother that way. They were probably hurt, too."

Most graciously, quite forgivingly, "Yes, you're right. Sorry, M'sieu! I'll be a good girl. And of course everything is all right now. After all, it's such a wonderful Happy Ending to our wild little escapades! We've both learned lots, don't you think? and now I won't be so flighty and you won't be so irritable, I'm sure you won't."

There was dancing in the verandah cafe. Young Tom Allen, the polo player--young Tom, all black and ivory and grin--came to ask her to dance. She smiled up at him, airily patted Sam's arm, and scampered away, while Tom seemed to be holding her hand under shelter of her squirrel robe.

The sunset was angry now, the color of port wine.

Sam staggered around and around the slanting deck, alone, and alone he stood aft, looking back in the direction of Europe. But there was only foggy gray.

He awoke, bewildered, at two in the morning. The storm had come; the steamer was pitching abominably. In his half sleep he heard Edith whimpering in her sleep in the twin bed beside him. Smiling, glad to comfort her who had been all comfort to him here in sunbright Naples, he stretched out his arm, sleepily stroked her thin wrist.

He startled, he sat up and gasped, at the astonishment of hearing the voice of Fran.

"Oh, thank you! Nice of you to wake me up. Having a kind of nightmare. My, it's rough!"

In his agitation he tightened his fingers on her wrist.

"Oh, Sam, DON'T--Oh, don't be ARDENT! Not yet. I must get used-- And I'm so sleepy!" Very brightly: "You don't mind, do you? Nighty-night!"

He lay awake. In the watery light from the transom he saw the sheen of her silver toilet things on the dresser. He thought of this tremendous steamer, pounding the waves. He thought of the modern miracle of the radio, up above, of the automatic electric steering apparatus. Yet on the bridge were sailors, unautomatic, human, eternal. The ship, too, was eternal, as a vehicle of man's old voyaging. Its creaking seemed to him like the creaking of an ancient Greek trireme.

But while his thoughts reached out thus for things heroic, he heard her placid breathing and he smelled not the sea gale but perfume that came from little crystal vials among her silver toilet-things that were vaster than the hull of the steamer, stronger than the storm.

He felt that he would never sleep again.

He closed his great fist, tight. Then it relaxed, and he was asleep.

He roused to hear her bubbling, in a stormy dawn:

"Are you awake? Don't let me disturb you. Horrid morning! Let's get up some bridge. We'll get Mr. Ballard and Tom Allen. He's a dear boy, isn't he! Though I feel like a mother toward him. Oh, Sam, if you aren't too sleepy--Oh. While we're in New York, I think I'll see if I can't pick up a really nice Chinese evening wrap. Tom told me about a shop. Of course I have those others, but they're getting so shabby, and after all, you don't expect me to look a fright, like Matey Pearson, do you! I'll make her eyes start out of her head with the Marcel Rochas frock I got in Paris, and think, I only had two days to get it in! Zenith will simply foam at the mouth! Oh, after all, it IS kind of nice to be going home--for a while--after all we've gone through--and Sam, I wonder if you understand that _I_ understand probably you were just as brave and honest as I was, even with the hideous suffering I had to face in Berlin! And--Oh, I don't know what reminded me of it, but you must be careful with the Ballards. I'm afraid you bored them last evening, talking about Italian motors. You must remember that they have a villa in Florence, and they're used to the real Italy, and artists and the nobility and so on. But of course it doesn't matter. And--Do you mind ringing for coffee? That's an old dear!"

The scent of her perfumes seemed stronger than by night, in the sleep-thickened air of the stateroom.

He slowly raised himself to ring for the steward. He had said nothing whatever.

She blissfully dropped off to sleep again, and he bathed, dressed, swayed out on deck. The open portion of the promenade dock was protected by canvas against which the water crashed, sending streams between the lashings to trickle along the deck. He labored forward, stood solemnly at a window looking ahead at the bow plunging into the waves, at the foam hurled over the forepeak, at a desolate immigrant in a tattered old raincoat trying to keep a footing on the forward deck.

It was black ahead. To a landsman it was menacing. Yet there was strength in the stormy air and, after a long breath, stretching out his great arms, Sam began to plow around the deck.

His eyes seemed turned inward; his lips moved a little in his meditation.

After half an hour, breakfastless, he suddenly climbed the stairs from A Deck to the Boat Deck and, down a narrow corridor, past the tiny florist-shop, came to the wireless bureau--a narrow desk across a small room, like a telegraph office in a minor hotel.

Emotionlessly, he wrote and handed in a message to Edith Cortright: "Will you be Naples three weeks from now?"

He went down to breakfast. All morning and half the afternoon he played bridge, watching Fran flirt with the ebullient Tom Allen.

The answer to his radio came just before tea-time: "No but shall be venice for couple months bless you edith."

For an hour, while Fran made much of tea with half a dozen men, Sam sat alone in the smoking-room, pretending to read whenever any lone and necessitous drinker came in to look for a drinking companion.

At the dressing-hour, he said mildly to Fran, "I wonder if we mightn't have dinner here in our stateroom tonight? I want to talk about things. We've sort of avoided it."

"Good Heavens, Sambo, what's come over you? Do you regard it as particularly cheerful to dine in this beastly little hole of a room on a rough night like this? Besides! I promised the Ballards we'd join them in the grill for dinner--such a common, stupid commercial crowd in the salon."

"But we must talk."

"My dear man, I think we'll manage it, with four full days ahead of us on this steamer! I'm really not going off to the Riviera or any place, you know!"

It was not till late in the evening that he had his chance. As they came down to the stateroom at bedtime, Fran very lively after a session in the smoking-room, he said, without prelude:

"Not much use trying to do it tactfully. Wanted to, but Fran, we can't make a go of it, and I'm going back and join Edith Cortright."

"I don't quite understand. What have I done now? Oh, my God, if you haven't learned--You haven't learned anything, not one single thing, out of all our sorrows! Still criticizing me, and such a kind sweet way of springing something beastly cruel on me just when I've been happy, as I have tonight!" She faced him, hands clenched. "Will you KINDLY, Mr. Dodsworth, be a little less mysterious and tell me just what it is I've done to hurt your tender little feelings THIS time?"

"Nothing. We just can't make a go of it. You don't get me. I'm not making a scene. I'm not trying to bully you. I meant just what I said. I'm going back to Italy, from New York, on the first ship. I'm not blaming or criticizing--"

She sat abruptly on the chair before her dressing-table. She said quietly, with fear edging her voice, "And what is to become of me?"

"I don't know. If I did, I wouldn't have met you on the ship."

She moaned. "Oh! You do manage to hurt! I congratulate you! You see, I've been flattering myself you really wanted to come back to me!"

He started to say something comforting, then held it back in panic, as if in danger. "I'm not going to be polite, Fran. You know how awfully I've loved you, a good many years. You tampered with it. . . . What's going to become of you? I don't know. But I guess it'll be just the same thing that's been becoming of you this past couple of years. You haven't needed me. You've found people to play with, and plenty of beaux. I suppose you'll go on finding them--"

"And this is the man that 'loved me awfully'--"

"Wait! For the first time in all our arguments, I'm going to think of what would become of ME! I can't help you. I'm just your attendant. But me--you can kill me. I didn't used to mind your embarrassing me and continually putting me in my place. Didn't even know you were doing it. But I do now, and I won't stand it!"

"Was it your dear Mrs. Cortright who taught you that lovely theory? about embarrassing you? After the years when I've never allowed one single soul to criticize you--"

"Understand? I'm FINISHED!"

He did not, unfortunately, leave her in any heroic and dignified way. He flounced out of the stateroom like a child in a tantrum. And that was because he knew that only by childish violence could he escape from her logic, and because he knew that he must escape, even over the side of the lurching ship. For she was indeed perfectly logical and sound. She knew what she wanted!

It was misery for him to look out at her from the taxicab which he was taking to the Italian Line dock, after three days in New York; to see her standing in front of the hotel, alone, deserted, her eyes pitiful, and to realize that he might never see her again. The look in her eyes had been the meaning of life for him, and he was deserting it.

They were dining at the Ritz in Paris, Edith and Sam, feeling superior to its pretentiousness, because that evening they had determined to return to America, when his divorce should be complete, and to experiment with caravans. They were gay, well dined and well content.

But after his second cognac the orchestra played selections from Viennese operettas, and he remembered how happy Fran and he had been in Berlin. He remembered the wretchedness of the letter he had received from her that day. She was staying with Emily in Zenith; she said that she was seeing no one; that his "DEAR friends Tub and Matey" were a little too polite; and that she was thinking of going, in a few days, to Italy--

Through the darkness beyond the music, he saw her fleeing, a desolate wraith, and his heart was heavy with pity for the frightened and bewildered child who once had laughed so eagerly with him.

He came out of his silence with a consciousness that Edith was watching him. She said lightly, "You enjoy being sad about her! But hereafter, every time there is a music, I shall also think of Cecil Cortright. How handsome he was! He spoke five languages! How impatient I was with him! How I failed him! How virtuous it makes me feel to flay myself! What a splendid, uncommon grief I have! Dear Sam! . . . What a job it is to give up the superiority of being miserable and self-sacrificing!"

He stared, he pondered, he suddenly laughed, and in that laughter found a youthfulness he had never known in his solemn youth.

He was, indeed, so confidently happy that he completely forgot Fran and he did not again yearn over her, for almost two days.

Also from Benediction Books ...
Wandering Between Two Worlds: Essays on Faith and Art
Anita Mathias
Benediction Books, 2007
152 pages
ISBN: 0955373700

Available from www.amazon.com, www.amazon.co.uk

In these wide-ranging lyrical essays, Anita Mathias writes, in lush, lovely prose, of her naughty Catholic childhood in Jamshedpur, India; her large, eccentric family in Mangalore, a sea-coast town converted by the Portuguese in the sixteenth century; her rebellion and atheism as a teenager in her Himalayan boarding school, run by German missionary nuns, St. Mary's Convent, Nainital; and her abrupt religious conversion after which she entered Mother Teresa's convent in Calcutta as a novice. Later rich, elegant essays explore the dualities of her life as a writer, mother, and Christian in the United States-- Domesticity and Art, Writing and Prayer, and the experience of being "an alien and stranger" as an immigrant in America, sensing the need for roots.

About the Author

Anita Mathias is the author of *Wandering Between Two Worlds: Essays on Faith and Art.* She has a B.A. and M.A. in English from Somerville College, Oxford University, and an M.A. in Creative Writing from the Ohio State University, USA. Anita won a National Endowment of the Arts fellowship in Creative Nonfiction in 1997. She lives in Oxford, England with her husband, Roy, and her daughters, Zoe and Irene.

Visit Anita at http://www.anitamathias.com, and on
http://theoxfordchristian.blogspot.com, her Christian blog;
http://wanderingbetweentwoworlds.blogspot.com/, her personal blog, and
http://thegoodbooksblog.blogspot.com, her literary and writing blog.

The Church Thad Had Too Much
Anita Mathias
Benediction Books, 2010
52 pages
ISBN: 9781849026567

Available from www.amazon.com, www.amazon.co.uk

The Church That Had Too Much was very well-intentioned. She wanted to love God, she wanted to love people, but she was both hampered by her muchness and the abundance of her possessions, and beset by ambition, power struggles and snobbery. Read about the surprising way The Church That Had Too Much began to resolve her problems in this deceptively simple and enchanting fable.

About the Author

Anita Mathias is the author of *Wandering Between Two Worlds: Essays on Faith and Art*. She has a B.A. and M.A. in English from Somerville College, Oxford University, and an M.A. in Creative Writing from the Ohio State University, USA. Anita won a National Endowment of the Arts fellowship in Creative Nonfiction in 1997. She lives in Oxford, England with her husband, Roy, and her daughters, Zoe and Irene.

Visit Anita at http://www.anitamathias.com, and on
http://theoxfordchristian.blogspot.com, her Christian blog;
http://wanderingbetweentwoworlds.blogspot.com/, her personal blog, and
http://thegoodbooksblog.blogspot.com, her literary and writing blog.

CPSIA information can be obtained at www.ICGtesting.com
Printed in the USA
LVOW061204251112

308662LV00002B/421/P